The Bodyguard

ALSO BY KATHERINE CENTER

The

Bodyguard

KATHERINE CENTER

ST. MARTIN'S PRESS
NEW YORK

First published in the United States by St. Martin's Press, an imprint of St. Martin's Publishing Group

THE BODYGUARD. Copyright © 2022 by Katherine Center. All rights reserved. Printed in the United States of America. For information, address St. Martin's Publishing Group, 120 Broadway, New York, NY 10271.

www.stmartins.com

Designed by Devan Norman

Library of Congress Cataloging-in-Publication Data

Names: Center, Katherine, author.
Title: Bodyguard / Katherine Center.
Description: First Edition: | New York : St. Martin's Press, 2022.
Identifiers: LCCN 2022005286 | ISBN 9781250219398 (hardcover) |
    ISBN 9781250219404 (ebook)
Subjects: LCGFT: Novels.
Classification: LCC PS3603.E67 B63 2022 | DDC 813/.6—dc23
LC record available at https://lccn.loc.gov/2022005286

Our books may be purchased in bulk for promotional, educational, or business use. Please contact your local bookseller or the Macmillan Corporate and Premium Sales Department at 1-800-221-7945, extension 5442, or by email at MacmillanSpecialMarkets@macmillan.com.

First Edition: 2022

10 9 8 7 6 5 4 3 2 1

For my grandparents, Herman and Inez Detering

You left us many gifts to carry forward, and I am thankful for all of them—most especially, these days: your hugs, your warmth and kindness, and all my memories of a childhood spent scampering around your Texas ranch.

I miss you both—but in the best, most grateful way.

The Bodyguard

One

MY MOTHER'S DYING wish was for me to take a vacation.

"Just do it, okay?" she'd said, tucking a lock of hair behind my ear. "Just book a trip and go. Like normal people do."

I hadn't taken a vacation in eight years.

But I'd said, "Okay," the way you do when your sick mom asks for something. Then I'd added, as if we were negotiating, "I'll take *one* vacation."

Of course, I hadn't realized it was her dying wish at the time. I thought we were just making middle-of-the-night hospital conversation.

But then, suddenly, it was the night after her funeral. I couldn't sleep, and I kept thrashing around in my bed, and that moment kept coming back to me. The way she'd held my gaze and squeezed my hand to seal the deal—as if taking a vacation could be something that mattered.

Now it was three in the morning. My funeral clothes were draped over a chair. I'd been waiting to fall asleep since midnight.

"Fine. Fine," I said, out loud in bed, to no one.

Then I belly-crawled across the covers to find my laptop on the floor, and, in the blue light of the screen, eyes half-closed, I did a quick search for "cheapest plane ticket to anywhere," found a site that had a list of nonstop destinations for seventy-six dollars, scrolled like I was playing roulette, landed randomly on Toledo, Ohio—and clicked "purchase."

Two tickets to Toledo. Nonrefundable, it would turn out. Some kind of Valentine's Day lovebirds package.

Done.

Promise fulfilled.

The whole process took less than a minute.

Now all I had to do was force myself to go.

BUT I STILL couldn't sleep.

At five in the morning, just as the sky was starting to lighten, I gave up, dragged all my sheets and blankets off the bed, shuffled to the walk-in closet, curled up on my side in a makeshift nest on the floor, and conked out, at last, in the windowless darkness.

When I woke, it was four in the afternoon.

I jumped up in a panic and stumbled around my room—buttoning my shirt wrong and kicking my shin on the footboard—as if I were late for work.

I wasn't late for work, though.

My boss, Glenn, had told me not to come in. Had *forbidden* me to come in, actually. For a week.

"Don't even think about coming to work," he'd said. "Just stay home and grieve."

Stay home? And grieve?

No way was I doing that.

Especially since—now that I'd bought these tickets to Toledo—I needed to find my boyfriend, Robby, and force him to come with me.

Right?

Nobody goes to Toledo alone. Especially not for Valentine's Day.

It all seemed very urgent in the moment.

In another state of mind, I could have simply texted Robby to stop by after work and just pleasantly invited him to come with me. Over dinner and drinks. Like a sane person.

Maybe that would have been a better plan.

Or led to a better result.

But I wasn't a sane person at the moment. I was a person who'd *slept in her closet.*

By the time I made it to the office that afternoon—just as the work day was ending—my hair was half-brushed, my shirt was half tucked in, and my funeral pantsuit still had a program with my mom's high school graduation photo on the cover folded up in the jacket pocket.

I guess it's weird to head in to work the day after your mom's funeral.

I'd researched it, and the most common bereavement leave from work was three days—though Glenn was making me take five. Other things I'd researched as my sleepless night wore on: "how to sell your parents' house," "fun things to do in Toledo" (a surprisingly long list), and "how to beat insomnia."

All to say: I wasn't supposed to be here.

That's why I hesitated at Glenn's office door. And that's how I wound up accidentally eavesdropping—and overhearing Robby and Glenn talking about me.

"Hannah's going to shit an actual brick when you tell her" was the first thing I heard. Robby's voice.

"Maybe I'll make you tell her." That was Glenn.

"Maybe you want to rethink it entirely."

"There's nothing to rethink."

And that was enough. I pushed open the door. "What are you re-thinking entirely? Who's going to tell me what? Why exactly am I going to shit a brick?"

Later, I'd glimpse myself in the mirror and get a specific visual for what the two of them saw in that moment as they turned toward my voice—and let's just say it involved bloodshot eyes, half my shirt collar crumpled under my jacket lapel, and a significant amount of tear-smeared eye makeup left over from the day before.

Alarming. But Glenn wasn't easily alarmed. "What are you doing here?" he said. "Get out."

He also wasn't a coddler.

I staked my territory in the doorway with a power stance. "I need to talk to Robby."

"You can do that outside of work."

He wasn't wrong. We were practically living together. When we weren't working, that is. Which was most of the time.

But what was I supposed to do? Go stand in the parking lot?

"Five minutes," I bargained.

"Nope," Glenn said. "Go home."

"I need to get out of my house," I said. "I need something to do."

But Glenn didn't care. "Your mother just died," he said. "Go be with your family."

"She *was* my family," I said, careful to keep my voice steady.

"Exactly," Glenn said, like I'd made his point for him. "You need to grieve."

"I don't know how to do that," I said.

"Nobody does," Glenn said. "You want a manual?"

I gave him a look. "If you've got one."

"Your manual is: *Get out of here.*"

But I shook my head. "I know you think I need to"—I hesitated for a second, not exactly sure what he thought I needed to do—"sit around and think about my mom, or whatever. . . . But, honestly, I'm fine." Then I added, and this wasn't untrue: "We weren't even that close."

"You were close enough," Glenn said. "Scram."

"Just let me . . . file things. Or something."

"No."

I wish I could say that Glenn—built like a tank with a bald head freckled like somebody had sprinkled them from a shaker—was one of those bosses who seemed gruff but really had your best interest at heart.

But Glenn mostly had Glenn's best interest at heart.

And Glenn had clearly decided I wasn't fit for work right now.

I got it.

It had been a strange time. I'd barely made it home from an assignment in Dubai when I got a call from the ER that my mother had collapsed in a crosswalk.

Suddenly, I was arriving at the hospital to find that she couldn't stop throwing up, and she didn't know what year it was or who was president. Then getting a diagnosis from a doctor with lipstick on her teeth that my mom had end-stage cirrhosis—and trying to argue with the doctor, saying, "She doesn't drink anymore! She *does not* drink anymore!"

Then, that evening, going to her place to get her fuzzy socks and favorite throw blanket and finding her hidden stash of vodka. Frantically pouring every last bottle down the kitchen sink and running the faucet to wash away the smell, thinking all the while that my biggest challenge was going to be getting her to turn her life around.

Again.

Assuming there would be more time.

Like we all just always do.

But she was gone before I even fully realized that losing her was possible.

It was a lot. Even Glenn, who had the emotional intelligence of a jackhammer, understood that.

But the last thing I wanted to do was *stay home and think about it*.

I was going to talk him into letting me come back to work if it killed us both.

And then I was going to talk Robby into coming to Toledo.

And then maybe, just maybe, I could get some sleep.

In a power move that kind of dared either of them to stop me, I walked farther into the office and sat down in the empty chair across from Glenn's desk. "What are you talking about?" I asked, shifting the subject a little. "Are you having a meeting?"

"We're having a conversation," Glenn said, like he knew I'd eavesdropped.

"You don't have conversations, boss," I said. "You only have meetings."

Robby, handsome as ever with black lashes edging his blue eyes, met my gaze like I'd made a good point.

I took a second to appreciate him. My mom had been so impressed the first time I introduced her. "He looks like an astronaut," she'd said—and that was exactly right. He also had a buzz cut, drove a vintage Porsche, and was wildly overconfident. In the best, sexiest, most astronautish way. My mom was impressed with me for dating him. I was impressed with myself, to be honest.

Robby was not just the coolest person I'd ever dated—he was the coolest person I'd ever *met*.

But that wasn't the point. I turned back to Glenn. "What is it, exactly, that you're going to make Robby tell me?"

Glenn sighed, like *I guess we're doing this*. Then he said, "I was going to wait until you had"—he looked me over—"at least taken a shower . . . but we're opening a branch in London."

I frowned.

"A branch in London?" I asked. "How is that bad news?"

But Glenn kept going. "And we're going to need somebody to—"

My hand flew up. "I'll take it! I've got it! I'm in!"

"—set up the office there and get it established," Glenn finished. "For two years."

Hello? London? Going to London with a huge project that would require so much workaholism that nothing else would even matter for two whole years?

Screw the vacation. Sign me up.

Just the thought sent relief breaking over me like waves: *A life-obliterating work project like that could potentially distract me from all my problems forever.*

Yes, please.

But that's when I noticed Robby and Glenn looking at me funny.

"What?" I asked, glancing between them.

"It's going to be one of the two of you . . ." Glenn said then, gesturing between Robby and me.

Of course it was. I was the protégée Glenn had been grooming for years, and Robby was the sexy hotshot he'd stolen away from the competition. Who else would even be in the running?

I still didn't see the problem.

"And that means," Glenn went on, "that whoever doesn't go will need to stay here."

But that's how much I loved my job: Even the prospect of a two-year separation from my boyfriend didn't faze me. Like, at all.

That's also how desperate I was to get back to work.

"I'll announce the London decision after New Year's," Glenn said. "And until then, consider yourselves in competition for the spot."

There was no competition. I was getting that spot.

"It's fine," I said with a shrug, like *What?* "We've competed before." I nodded at Robby. "We like competing. And two years is not that long, no matter who wins. We can make that work, right?"

If I'd been paying better attention, I might have noticed that Robby was less eager about everything than I was. But I was a little too desperate in that moment to think about anyone but myself.

I was afraid to feel the full impact of losing my mother. I was terrified to get stuck at home with nothing to distract me. I was tunnel-visioned on escaping—preferably to a distant country—as soon as possible.

Next week, Robby and I were scheduled for a three-week assignment in Madrid together, but I wasn't even sure how I'd make it that long.

First, I had to survive my remaining bereavement days.

"From what I just eavesdropped," I said, gesturing back at the doorway, "I was expecting bad news."

"That wasn't the bad news," Robby said, glancing at Glenn.

I looked over at Glenn, too. "What's the bad news?"

Glenn refused to hesitate. "The bad news is I'm taking you off Madrid."

Looking back, me showing up at the office like that—all wild-eyed and bed-heady and desperate—probably wasn't helping. Maybe I should've seen it coming.

But I didn't.

"Off Madrid?" I asked, thinking I must have heard wrong.

Robby fixed his gaze at the window.

"Off Madrid," Glenn confirmed. Then he added, "You're not in the right headspace."

"But . . ." I didn't even know how to protest. How could I say, *That's the only thing I have to look forward to?*

Glenn shoved his hands into his pockets. Robby stared out the window.

Finally, I asked, "Who are you sending in my place?"

Glenn glanced at Robby. Then he said, "I'm sending Taylor."

"You're sending . . . Taylor?"

Glenn nodded. "She's our next best thing," he said, like that should settle it.

It didn't.

"You're sending my best friend and my boyfriend away and leaving me alone for three weeks? Just *days* after my mother died?"

"I thought you said you weren't that close."

"I thought *you* said we were close enough."

"Look," Glenn said. "This is what they call a business decision."

But I shook my head. This wasn't going to work. "You can't just ground me and dismantle my entire support system. That's my trip. Those are my clients."

Glenn sighed. "You'll go next time."

"I want to go this time."

Glenn shrugged. "I want to win the lottery. But it's not going to happen."

Glenn was the kind of guy who believed adversity only made you stronger.

I took a minute to breathe. Then I said, "If Taylor's going on my trip, where am I going?"

"Nowhere," Glenn said.

"*Nowhere?*"

He nodded. "You need to rest. Plus, everywhere's full." He scrolled through his laptop. "Jakarta's taken. Colombia's taken. Bahrain. Those oil execs in the Philippines. All taken."

"But . . . what am I supposed to do?"

Glenn shrugged. "Help out around the office?"

"I'm serious."

But Glenn kept going. "Take up knitting? Start a succulent garden? Double down on personal growth?"

Nope, nope, nope.

But Glenn held fast. "You need some time off."

"I hate time off. I don't want time off."

"It's not about what you want. It's about what you need."

What was he—my therapist? "I need to work," I said. "I do better when I'm working."

"You can work here."

But I also needed to escape.

Now I felt a flutter of panic in my throat. "Hey. You know me. You know I need to move. I can't just sit here and—and . . . and *marinate* in all my misery. I need to be in motion. I need to go somewhere. I'm like a shark, you know? I just always have to be moving. I need to get water through my gills." My hands gestured at my ribcage, as if to show him where my gills were located. "If I stay here," I finally said, "I'll die."

"Bullshit," Glenn said. "Dying's a lot harder than you think."

Glenn hated it when people begged.

I begged anyway.

"Send me somewhere. Anywhere. I need to get out."

"You can't spend your entire life running away," Glenn said.

"Yes, I can. I absolutely can."

I could tell from his face we'd hit the wall. But I still had some fight left in me.

"What about the thing in Burkina Faso?" I asked.

"I'm sending Doghouse."

"I've got three years on Doghouse!"

"But he speaks French."

"What about the wedding in Nigeria?"

"I'm sending Amadi."

"He hasn't even been here six months!"

"But his family's from Nigeria. And he speaks—"

"Fine. Forget it."

"—Yoruba and a little bit of Igbo."

That was the crux of it. Glenn had a rep to protect. "I'll send you," he said like we were done here, "when it's a good fit. I'll send you when it's best for the agency. I'll never send you over somebody more qualified."

I narrowed my eyes at Glenn in a way that just dared him to fight me. "There's nobody more qualified than me," I said.

Glenn looked me over, using his well-honed powers of observation like a weapon.

"Maybe, maybe not," he said at last. "But you buried your mother yesterday."

I met his eyes.

He went on. "Your pulse is elevated, your eyes are bloodshot, and your makeup is smeared. Your speech is rapid, and your voice is hoarse. You haven't brushed your hair, your hands are shaking, and you're out of breath. You're a mess. So go home, take a shower, eat some comfort food, grieve the death of your mom, and then figure out some god-damned hobbies—because I guarantee you this: You're sure as hell not going anywhere until you get your shit together."

I knew that tone in his voice.

I didn't argue.

But how, exactly, was I supposed to get back to work if he wouldn't let me get back to work?

Two

HAVE I EXPLAINED what I do for a living?

I usually try to put that off as long as possible. Because once you know—once I actually name the profession—you'll make a long list of assumptions about me . . . and all of them will be wrong.

But I guess there's no more avoiding it.

My life doesn't make much sense if you don't know what my job is. So here goes: I am an Executive Protection Agent.

But nobody ever knows what that is.

Let's just say I'm a bodyguard.

Lots of people get it wrong and call me a "security guard," but to be clear: That's not even remotely what I do.

I don't sit in a golf cart in a supermarket parking lot.

What I do is elite. It takes years of training. It demands highly specialized skills. It's tough to break into. And it's a strange combination of glamorous (first-class travel, luxury hotels, off-the-charts wealthy people) and utterly mundane (spreadsheets, checklists, counting carpet squares in hotel hallways).

Mostly, we protect the very rich (and occasionally famous) from all the people who want to harm them. And we get paid really well to do it.

I know what you're thinking.

You're thinking I'm five-foot-five, and female, and nothing even close to brawny. You're conjuring a stereotype of a bodyguard—maybe a club bouncer with skintight shirtsleeves squeezing his biceps—and you're noting that I'm pretty much the opposite of that. You're wondering how I could possibly be any good.

Let's clear that up.

Steroid-inflated bruisers *are* one type of bodyguard: a bodyguard for people who want the whole world to know they have a bodyguard.

But the thing is, most people don't.

Most clients who need executive protection don't want anyone to know about it.

I'm not saying that the big guys don't have value. They can have a deterrent effect. But they can also do the opposite.

It all depends on the type of threat, to be honest.

Most of the time, you're safer if your protection goes unnoticed. And I am fantastic at going unnoticed. All women EP agents are, which is why we're in high demand. No one ever suspects us.

Everyone always thinks we're the nanny.

I do the kind of protection most people never even know is happening—even the client. And I'm the least lethal-looking person in the world. You'd think I was a kindergarten teacher before you'd ever suspect that I could kill you with a corkscrew.

I *could* kill you with a corkscrew, by the way.

Or a ballpoint pen. Or a dinner napkin.

But I'm not going to.

Because if things ever get to the point where I have to kill you, or anybody else, I haven't done my job. My job is to anticipate harm before it ever materializes—and avoid it.

If I have to stab you in the eye with a dinner fork, I've already failed.

And I don't fail.

Not in my professional life, at least.

All to say, my job is not about violence, it's about avoiding violence. It's much more about brains than brawn. It's about preparation, observation, and constant vigilance.

It's about predictions, and patterns, and reading the room before you're even in it.

It's not just something you do, it's something you are—and my destiny was most likely set in fourth grade, when I was first recruited as a carpool monitor and got a Day-Glo sash and a badge. (I still have that badge on my nightstand.) Or maybe it was set in seventh grade when we moved into an apartment that was around the corner from a jujitsu studio, and I convinced my mom to let me take classes. Or maybe it was set by all those terrible boyfriends my mother could never stop bringing home.

Whatever it was, when I saw a recruiting booth near the campus jobs kiosk during my freshman year of college with a navy and white sign that read ESCAPE TO THE FBI, it was pretty much a done deal. Escape was my favorite thing. When I tested off the charts on conscientiousness, pattern recognition, observational skills, listening retention, and altruism, they recruited me right up.

That is, until Glenn Schultz came along and poached me away.

And the rest became history. He taught me everything he knew, I started traveling the world, this job became my entire life, and I never looked back.

The point is, I loved it.

You have to love it. You have to give it everything. You have to be willing to step in front of a bullet—and that's no small choice, because some of these people are not exactly lovable—and getting shot hurts. It's high stakes and high stress, and if you're going to do it right, it has to be about something bigger than you.

That's really why people who love this job love this job: It's about who you choose—over and over every day—to be.

The luxury travel is pretty great, too.

Mostly, it's a lot of work. A lot of paperwork, a lot of advance site visits, a lot of procedural notes. You have to write everything down. You're constantly on guard. It's not exactly relaxing.

But you get addicted.

This life makes regular life seem pretty dull.

Even the boredom in this job is exciting somehow.

You're on the move. You're never still. And you're too busy to be lonely.

Which always suited me just fine.

That is, until Glenn grounded me in Houston—at the very moment when I needed an escape the most.

THAT SAME DAY Glenn took me off the Madrid gig, my car wouldn't start—and so Robby wound up driving me home in his vintage Porsche in the pouring rain.

Which was fine. Better, actually. Because I still hadn't invited him to Toledo.

Maybe it was the rain—coming down so hard that the wipers, even on the highest setting, could barely clear it—but it wasn't until we made it to my house that I noticed Robby had been weirdly quiet on the drive home.

It was too wet for me to get out right then, so Robby turned off the car entirely and we just watched the water coat the windows like we were at a car wash.

That's when I turned to him and said, "Let's go on a trip."

Robby frowned. "What?"

"That's why I came to the office today. To invite you on vacation."

"On vacation where?"

Now I was regretting the randomness of the choice. How, exactly, do you sell Toledo?

"With me," I answered, like he'd asked a different question.

"I don't understand," Robby said.

"I've decided to take a vacation," I said, like *This isn't hard.* "And I'd like you come with me."

"You never take vacations," Robby said.

"Well, now I do."

"I've invited you on three different trips, and you've weaseled out of all of them."

"That was before."

"Before what?"

Before my mother died. Before I got grounded. Before I got taken off Madrid. "Before I bought nonrefundable tickets to Toledo."

Robby looked me over. "Toledo?" If he'd been confused before, now he shifted to full-on befuddled. "People don't go on vacation to Toledo."

"Actually, they have world-renowned botanical gardens."

But Robby sighed. "There's no way we're going there."

"Why not?"

"Because you'll cancel."

"What part of 'nonrefundable' don't you understand?"

"You really don't know yourself very well, do you?"

"I don't see the problem," I said. "You wanted to do this, and now we're doing it. Can't you just say *Awesome* and accept?"

"I actually can't."

His voice had a strange intensity to it. And in the wake of those words, he leaned forward and ran his fingers over the grooves of the steering wheel in a way that got my attention.

Did I mention that I read body language the way other people read books? I can speak body language better than English. For real. I could list it on my résumé as my native tongue.

Growing up as my mother's child had forced me to learn the opposite of language: all the things we say without words. I had turned it into a pretty great career, to be honest. But if you asked me if it was a blessing or a curse, I wouldn't know what to say.

Things I read about Robby in that one second: He wasn't happy. He dreaded what he was about to do. He was doing it anyway.

Yep. Got all that from his fingers on the steering wheel.

And the tightness in his posture. And the force of the next breath he took. And the tilt of his head. And the way his eyes seemed to be using his lashes like a shield.

"Why?" I asked next. "Why can't you accept?"

Robby looked down. Then a half-breath, a quick clench of the jaw, a steeling of the shoulders. "Because," he said, "I think we should break up."

Impossible, but true: He shocked me.

I turned to look at the dashboard. It was textured to look like leather.

I really hadn't seen that coming.

And I always saw everything coming.

Robby kept going. "We both know this isn't working."

Did we both know that? Does anybody ever *know* a relationship isn't working? Is that something you *can* know? Or do all relationships require a certain amount of unreasonable optimism just to survive?

I said the only thing I could think of. "You're breaking up with me? On the night after my mother's funeral?"

He acted like I was catching him on a technicality. "Is my timing the most important thing here?"

"Your *appalling* timing?" I asked, stalling for my brain to catch up. "I don't know. Maybe."

"Or maybe not," Robby said. "Because don't forget. You weren't even all that close."

Just because it was true didn't make it right. "That's not relevant," I said.

I guess timing really does matter. I'd been sleeping on a hospital sofa for days, up five times a night while my mother retched into a plastic bucket. I'd watched her shrink to a skeleton in that flimsy hospital gown.

I'd watched the life that had given me life drain away before my eyes.

After that, I'd arranged the funeral. All the details. The music, the food. I'd played host all day to high school friends, coworkers, ex-boyfriends, AA friends, and drinking buddies. I'd ordered the flowers, and zipped the back zipper on my black dress all by myself, and even put together a slideshow.

Robby had it wrong.

Because, despite everything, I loved her.

I didn't *like* her, but I loved her.

And he'd underestimated me, as well. Because it's so much harder to love someone who's difficult than to love someone who's easy.

I was stronger than even I knew. Probably.

But I guess I was about to find out.

Because as the rain started to ease up, and as I pressed the pads of my fingers to the window glass, I heard myself say, in a soft, uncertain voice that even I barely recognized, "I don't want to break up. I love you."

"You only say that," Robby said then, his voice tinged with a certainty I'll never forget, "because you don't know what love is."

GLENN HAD WARNED us about this a year ago—back when it all started.

As soon as he'd heard the gossip, he called us into the conference room, and shut the door, and lowered the mini blinds.

"Is this really happening?" he demanded.

"Is what really happening?" Robby asked.

But this was the legendary Glenn Schultz. He wasn't falling for that. "You tell me."

Robby held his best poker face, so Glenn turned to me.

But mine was even better.

"I'm not going to stop you," Glenn said. "But we need a plan in place."

"For what?" Robby asked, and that was his first mistake.

"For when you break up," Glenn said.

"Maybe we won't break up," Robby said, but Glenn refused to insult us all by responding.

Instead, like a man who'd seen it all and then some, he just looked back and forth between the two of us and sighed. "It was the rescue assignment, wasn't it?"

Robby and I met each other's eyes. Had we fallen for each other

in the wake of an assignment to rescue a custody kidnap in Iraq? Had
we survived gunfire, a car chase, and a death-defying midnight border
crossing only to fall into bed together at the end—if for no other reason
than to celebrate the fact that we were, against all odds, still alive? And
was the adrenaline of that assignment still powering our semisecret office romance all these months later?

Obviously.

But we admitted nothing.

Glenn had been in this business too long to need something as pedestrian as verbal confirmation. "I know better than to interfere," he
said. "So I'm just going to ask you one question. It's the easiest thing in
the world for agents to get together—and it's the hardest thing for them
to *stay* together. What are you going to do when it ends?"

I should have held eye contact. That's Negotiations 101. *Never look
down.*

But I looked down.

"Really?" Glenn said to me, leaning a little closer. "You think it's
going to *last*? You think you're going to buy a house with a picket fence
and go to the farmers market on weekends? Get a dog? Buy sweaters at
the mall?"

"You don't know the future," Robby said.

"No, but I know the two of you."

Glenn was pretty pissed, and that was not unreasonable. We were
his investment, his kids, his favorites, and his retirement portfolio all
rolled into one.

Glenn rubbed his eyes and when he looked up, he was breathing in
that noisy way that had earned him the nickname "The Warthog."

He stared us down. "I can't stop you," he said, "and I'm not going to
try. But I'll tell you this right now. There'll be no 'leaving the company'
when this crashes and burns. You'll get no pity from me, and you won't
get a letter of recommendation, either. If you apply somewhere else,
I'll torpedo you with the worst reference in the history of time. You're
mine. I made you, I own you, and goddammit nobody in this room gets
to quit. Not even me. Understood?"

"Understood," we both said, in unison.

"Now get out of my sight," Glenn said, "or I'll send you both to Afghanistan."

THAT WAS A year ago.

It's funny to think how much I'd pitied Glenn's pessimism back then. His third wife had just left him—not uncommon in this job, since you're gone more than you're home. I remember mentally shaking my head at him as I walked away from the conversation. I remember thinking that Robby and I were going to prove him wrong.

Smash cut to a year later: Robby dumping me in the rain, like he was doing us both a favor.

"It's for the best," he said. "You need to grieve, anyway."

"You don't deserve my grief," I said.

"I meant your mother."

Oh. Her. "Don't tell me what I need."

Robby had the nerve to look wounded. "Be civil about this."

"Why should I?"

"Because we're both adults. Because we know what's at stake. Because we never really liked each other all that much, anyway."

That stung like a slap. I met his eyes for the first time and tried not to sound surprised: "We didn't, huh?"

"That's fair to say, right?"

Um, no. That wasn't fair to say. It was incredibly crass. And wrong. And probably a lie, too—a way for Robby to absolve himself. Sure, he'd dumped me the day after my mother's funeral, but what did that matter if "we never really liked each other all that much, anyway"?

But fine. Whatever.

Though I could think of a hotel room in Costa Rica that might claim otherwise.

In the humiliation of that moment—*Had I really just told a man I loved him while he was breaking up with me?*—it was as if Robby wasn't just taking his love away . . . but all love.

That's what it felt like.

What can I say? It's hard to think straight in a crisis, and the conclusion I landed on was that my only way to keep going was to get back to work. I didn't need hobbies. I didn't need to learn crochet. I needed to get back to the office, and get a new assignment, and win that position running the branch in London. It was as clear as needing air. I needed to do something. Go somewhere. Flee. Now more than ever.

But before I could step out of the car into the rain and forget him entirely, there was one question I still had to ask.

I looked straight into Robby's eyes. And then, in a tone like I was just calmly curious, I said, "You said things between us aren't working. Why is that again?"

He nodded, like that was a fair enough question. "I've given some thought to that over the past few months—"

"*Months*?"

"—and I've decided, ultimately, it comes down to one thing."

"Which is?"

"You."

My head gave an involuntary shake. "Me?"

Robby nodded, like saying it out loud had confirmed it. "It's you." And then, in a tone like he might even be giving me helpful advice, he said, "You have three deal-breaker flaws."

The words echoed in my head as I braced for them. *Three deal-breaker flaws.*

"One," Robby said, "you work all the time."

Okay. He *also* worked all the time. But fine.

"Two," Robby went on, "you're not fun, you know? You're so serious every minute."

Um. Holy shit. How do you argue with that?

"And three," Robby said with anticipation, like we were really getting to the clincher, "you're a bad kisser."

Three

A MONTH LATER, I was still enraged about it.

A bad kisser? A *bad kisser*?

I mean, "workaholic"? Fine. There's no shame in being fantastic at your job.

"Not fun"? Whatever. Fun was overrated.

But a "bad kisser"?

That was the kind of insult that would haunt me to my grave.

Unacceptable.

Just like the state of my entire life.

My mother died. Then I got grounded from my job. Then the longest relationship of my life ended with the most insulting insult in the world. And there was nothing I could do about any of it. My mother stayed dead, my ex-boyfriend and my best friend left for three weeks on my assignment to Madrid, and I stayed home. In Houston. With nothing to do and no one to do it with.

It's a blur how I even survived.

Mostly, I did anything at all to keep busy. I reorganized the file room at the office. I did local mini assignments. I repainted my bathroom tangerine orange without asking my landlord. I cleaned out my mother's place and listed it for sale. I took six-mile runs after work in hopes of tuckering myself out. I counted the purgatory-like seconds until I could get the hell out of town.

Oh, and I slept every night on the floor of my closet.

Those four weeks took a thousand years. And in all that time, I can only remember one truly good thing that happened.

Going through my mother's jewelry box, I found something I thought was lost—something that would have seemed like junk to anybody else. Buried under a tangled necklace, I found a little silver beaded safety pin that I'd made at school on my eighth birthday.

The colors were just like I remembered: red, orange, yellow, pale green, baby blue, violet, white.

Beaded friendship pins had been big at school that year—we all made them and pinned them to our shoelaces—and so on the day our teacher brought in pins and beads, we were ecstatic. She let us spend recess making them, and I'd saved my favorite to give to my mom. I loved the idea of surprising her on a day she'd be giving me presents with a present of my own for her. But I never got to give it to her in the end.

Somehow, before the next morning, it was gone.

In the wake of that day, I'd looked for it for weeks. Checking and double-checking the floor of my closet, the pockets of my backpack, under the hallway rug. It had been one of those long, unsolved mysteries in my life—a question I'd carried for so long: How had I lost something so important?

But fast-forward twenty years and there it was, safely stashed in my mom's jewelry box, waiting for me like a long-hidden answer. Like she'd been keeping it safe for me the whole time.

Like maybe I'd underestimated her a little bit.

And myself, too.

Right then and there, I'd looked through her necklaces to find a sturdy gold chain, then I'd clipped the beaded pin to it like a pendant.

And then I wore it. Every day after that. Like a talisman. I even slept in it.

I found myself touching it all the time, spinning the smooth beads under my fingertips to feel their cheery little rattle. Something about it
was comforting. It made me feel like maybe things were never quite as
lost as they seemed.

On the morning when Robby and Taylor were coming back from
Madrid—a morning when we were having a meeting in the conference room where Glenn had promised to give me a new assignment,
at last—I touched that pin so much I wondered if I might wear it out.

The point was: I was about to get an assignment. I was about to escape. It didn't matter where I was going. Even just the idea of leaving
turned my heart into a rippling field of relief.

Now I would disappear from here.

And then, for the first time in so long, I would feel okay.

All I had to do was survive seeing Robby again.

We're very dismissive, as a culture, about heartbreak. We talk about
it like it's funny, or silly, or cute. As if it can be cured by a pint of Häagen-
Dazs and a set of flannel pajamas.

But of course, a breakup is a type of grief. It's the death of not just
any relationship—but the most important one in your life.

There's nothing cute about it.

"Dumped" is also a word that falls short of its true meaning. It
sounds so quick—like a moment in time. But getting dumped lasts forever. Because *a person who loved you decided not to love you anymore.*

Does that ever really go away?

As I waited at the table in the conference room, the first person
there by a mile, that's what hit me: Robby leaving had felt like a confirmation of my worst, deepest, most unacknowledged fear.

Maybe I just wasn't lovable.

I mean, yes—I was a good person. I had many fine qualities. I was
competent, and I had a strong moral compass . . . and let's add: I was a
pretty great cook. But how does anybody just ever assume they'd be somebody else's first choice? Was I better than all the other great people in the
world? Was I special enough to be *the one* somebody picked over everybody else?

Not for Robby, I guess.

I didn't want to see him again. Or think about it. Or have a self-esteem crisis.

I just wanted to get the hell out of Texas.

THE FIRST PERSON to arrive in the conference room was Taylor. My best friend. Freshly back from Madrid with my ex. Though that wasn't her fault.

Her hair was shorter—a little European bob—and tucked behind her ears, and she was wearing mascara, which was new, and made her green eyes pop. I squealed at the sight of her and took off running, catapulting myself into her arms.

"You're back!" I said, hugging tight around her neck.

She hugged me back.

"I killed all your houseplants," I said, "but that's the price you pay for leaving."

"You killed my plants?"

"Didn't you see the corpses?"

"On purpose?"

"By accident," I said. "A combination of neglect and overattention."

"That does sound lethal."

Taylor gave me that big smile she's famous for.

We'd talked on the phone much more this time than we usually would on assignment. Mostly because I kept crying and calling her.

She was good about it, she really was. She let me process and vent and agonize to my heart's content—even when I kept waking her up.

Seeing her now, I realized how long it had been since I'd asked her about *her*.

"How was the trip?" I asked.

"Fine," she said.

Not much of an answer.

As we sat down, I could not rein in the impulse to lower my voice and say, "And how is he?"

"How is who?" Taylor asked.

"A person who rhymes with 'Blobby.'"

"Ah," Taylor said, her face tightening a little in a way that made me feel rooted-for. "I think he's fine."

"'Fine' is a thing for you today."

"It means he's not , . . not okay."

"That's a shame."

"More importantly," she asked. "How are *you*?"

"I've been stuck here for a month," I said. "I'm dying."

Taylor nodded. "Because you need water in your gills."

"Thank you!" I said, like *At last*. "Thank you for believing in my gills."

Just then, Glenn walked in. "Stop talking about your gills," he said.

"She's a shark," Taylor said, in my defense.

"Don't encourage her."

Other folks followed him in, and the conference room filled up. Amadi—so ever-likable with his round nose and wide smile—was back from Nigeria. Doghouse, back from Burkina Faso, had grown a beard to cover the burn scar on his jaw. Kelly was just back from Dubai with some gold hoop earrings that exactly matched her blond curls.

I tried not to watch the door for Robby.

I maintained good posture. I arranged my face into a pleasant, fine-thanks-and-how-are-you expression so precisely that my cheek muscles started quivering. I ignored the white noise *shh*-ing in my ears.

Finally, just as Glenn was clearing his throat to begin, Robby strolled in.

His buzz cut was longer. He wore a new, slim-cut suit, a tie I'd never seen, and his famous Vuarnets—even though we were inside. Though he whipped them off just as he entered the room.

Dammit. He made it work.

He'd always been better at style than at substance.

Did it ache to see him? Did it suck all the air out of my chest? Incapacitate me with emotion? Feel like I'd just swigged down a whole bottle of heartbreak?

No, actually.

This is good, I thought.

Wait. Was this good?

This meant I was over him, right? My endless time in Houston-slash-purgatory had done the trick. They say time heals all wounds. Was that it? Was I done?

Or had the past month just destroyed my ability to feel anything at all?

As Glenn revved up the meeting, I held my breath.

Please, please, please, I found myself thinking. *For once, just let me get off easy.*

Sometimes I wonder if I jinxed myself in that moment.

Because when Glenn started the meeting—leading with my new assignment—it hit me pretty fast that it was not going to be the escape I'd been holding my breath for.

"First things first," Glenn said, as the room quieted, pointing at me. "Let's talk about the new assignment for Brooks." Glenn always called me 'Brooks.' I couldn't guarantee he even knew my first name. "It's a juicy one," Glenn went on. "Outside our normal wheelhouse. Should be pretty absorbing. It's actually a new assignment for everybody in here. Kind of an all-hands-on-deck situation. But Brooks will be the primary."

Glenn gave me a little nod. "She's earned it."

"Where is it?" I asked.

"I think what you want to know is 'Who is it?'"

"Nope," I said. "I definitely want to know *where*."

"Because this client," Glenn went on, his voice reminding me of how people talk to their dogs before they give them treats, "is really, really famous."

We didn't protect a lot of famous people at Glenn Schultz Executive Protection. If we'd been based in LA, that would have been different. But we were based in Houston—so we got mostly oil executives and business people. The occasional entertainer coming through town. I once did some remote location assessments for Dolly Parton, and she sent me a lovely thank-you note.

But that was about it.

I looked at Glenn's face. He was suppressing a smile.

He was actually excited. And Glenn never got excited about anything.

He went on. "This particular assignment happens to take place in the great state of Texas—"

"Texas?!" I demanded.

Glenn ignored me. "Just right here in our friendly hometown of Houston, so—"

"Houston?!" I scooted my chair back.

In eight years of receiving assignments, I had never once protested a location. That's just not how this job works. You don't care where you go. You go where they send you. It's fine.

But.

It had been a rough month.

Let's just say I was right on the verge of doing something unprofessional.

But then Glenn told us who the principal was.

Pulling his lips back into a very pleased-with-himself smile, as if this good news would cancel out any bad news that might ever happen again, Glenn did his big reveal. "The principal for this one," he said, clicking the remote for the whiteboard and flashing a movie poster up for us all to see, "is Jack Stapleton."

The whole room gasped.

Robby launched into a coughing fit.

Kelly let out a shriek like she was at a Beatles concert.

And that's when, despite everything I had just decided about how getting myself to London would be the answer to all my problems, I said, "You know what? I quit."

Four

I DON'T HAVE to tell you who Jack Stapleton is, of course.

You probably gasped, too.

My attempt to quit got totally lost in the chaos.

I'm not sure anybody even heard me—except for Glenn, who brushed that declaration off with a glance, like I was an annoying insect. "You're never quitting. Like I already said."

I'd been waiting to get out of Texas like a drowning person waiting for a rope. The disappointment of being *still stuck here* made me feel short of breath.

But I'll tell you something. Hearing the name Jack Stapleton didn't *not* get my attention.

Was protecting a two-time, back-to-back Sexiest Man Alive here in Texas better than protecting some gray-toothed, watery-eyed, pear-shaped oil executive somewhere else?

Fine. Maybe.

Glenn certainly thought so.

"This one's a doozy folks," Glenn said, getting his groove back. "It's a good thing Brooks had time to rest up, because this one's gonna keep her busy."

I hadn't said yes yet, of course.

But, then again, I never said no.

Glenn clicked the remote for the digital whiteboard and flashed a red-carpet photo of Jack Stapleton, in all his six-foot-three dreaminess, up on the conference room screen. "I take it from the collective gasp that we all know who this man is."

He started clicking through photos. We did this for every new client, but let's just say that it wasn't normally quite this . . . engaging. The first few were professional shots: Jack Stapleton in a T-shirt so snug, it looked airbrushed. Jack Stapleton in ripped jeans. Jack Stapleton in a tux with the bow tie undone, staring into the camera like we were all about to follow him to his hotel room.

"This really is the client?" Doghouse asked, double-checking.

Obviously, yes. But we all waited to hear it again anyway. Because it was just so unbelievable.

"Affirmative," Glenn said. Then he looked over at Kelly. "Don't you have a thing for him?"

"What am I?" Kelly said. "A teenager?"

"I feel like I've heard his name come up."

"Functioning adults do not have 'things' for actors," Kelly declared to the room.

That's when Doghouse, right next to her, put a boot up on the conference table and gave Kelly a sly smile. "Pretty sure she's got socks with Stapleton's face on them."

"Those were a *gift*," Kelly said.

"But you wear them," Doghouse pointed out.

"It's weird that you know that."

But that just made Doghouse grin bigger. "Isn't his picture the home screen on your phone?"

"That's classified. And it's weirder that you know *that*."

"The point is," Glenn said, pointing at Kelly as a cautionary tale. "Be professional. Anything you own with the client's face on it—"

Doghouse started counting off examples: "T-shirts, tattoos, string bikinis . . ."

"Get rid of it now," Glenn finished.

Kelly flared her nostrils at Doghouse, but he just gave her a wink.

But Glenn wasn't here to play. This was a big-deal client and a high-profile gig. He clicked ahead to some paparazzi shots, and we saw Jack Stapleton in a plaid shirt shopping at a farmers market. Jack Stapleton in a baseball cap crossing a parking lot. Jack Stapleton wearing—*holy Mary, sweet mother of God*—clingy board shorts at the beach, rising up out of the waves, and glistening like a Roman deity.

Taylor spoke for all the women in the room when she let out a long, low whistle.

I felt Robby glance over at the sound, but I didn't look. Kept my eyes on the prize, as it were.

"Ladies," Glenn said. "Let's not objectify the principal."

The men around the table murmured in agreement.

And just on the heels of that, Glenn clicked to a slide that got the other half of the room whistling. "And this," Glenn said, "is his girlfriend."

It was Kennedy Monroe, of course—running Baywatch-style along a perfect beach, not even one dimple of visible cellulite, as if she had the ability to live-photoshop herself in real time. Everybody knew they were dating, and gazing up in awe at the whiteboard, it was no mystery why.

She had a kind of weaponized beauty that made all its own rules.

A couple—ever since costarring in *The Destroyers*. They'd just been on the cover of *People* together.

That said, I'd always found it an odd pairing. She was, after all, most famous for the scandal where she falsely claimed to be Marilyn Monroe's granddaughter and got sued by Monroe's estate. And then Jack Stapleton had been quoted in an *Esquire* interview saying, "She's like a conspiracy theorist—about herself."

Wow. How did I know this much about them without even trying?

Kelly seemed to be having the same visceral reaction to her that I was. "Will she be here?" she asked, nostrils flaring.

"Nah," Glenn said. "Just threw that one in for fun." He clicked up another slide—this one of a guy who looked so much like Jack Stapleton that it made you want to rub your eyes.

"Is that the principal?" Amadi asked, like we were being tricked.

"It's his older brother, Hank," Glenn explained. Then he brought up a picture of Jack, and we studied the two side by side like a find-the-differences picture game.

That's where Glenn paused the slideshow. "I can't imagine there's a person in this room who hasn't seen *The Destroyers*," he said. "And you probably all know the basics of how, right after opening weekend, Jack Stapleton's younger brother Drew was killed in an accident. That was two years ago. Jack stepped out of the public eye, moved to the remote mountains of North Dakota, and hasn't made a movie since."

Yes, we all knew that. Everybody in America knew that. Babies knew it. Dogs knew it. Maybe even earthworms.

"The accident got covered up. I mean," Glenn shook his head with admiration, "they did a fantastic job. There are no details anywhere, and I've had Kelly on this all day."

We nodded at Kelly. She was the best dirt-digger we had.

"If I'd known why you had me on this," Kelly said, "I'd have worked harder."

Glenn stayed focused. "All you can find anywhere," he went on, "are the basics: car accident. Jack and his younger brother were together. Only Jack survived."

Glenn flashed a photo of Jack and his brother Drew at some premiere, in suits, smiling for the cameras with their arms around each other. We gave it a moment of silence.

Then Glenn went on. "But there are rumors. Rumors that Jack was driving—and there might have been alcohol involved. Kelly's working to see if she can confirm."

Kelly wrinkled her nose and shook her head like it wasn't going well.

So Glenn went on. "What we do know is that, in the wake of that accident, the family has been estranged. In particular, there seems to be bad blood between Jack and the older brother. There's no reporting we can find that explains the rift."

Glenn flashed a photo of the family from before the accident—two sweet looking parents and three grown boys—a paparazzi photo taken in the stands of a stadium.

"Also, despite Stapleton's stated intention of retiring from acting, he is still under contract to make the sequel to *The Destroyers*. He's been fighting in court to break it, and it's unclear at this point who'll prevail, but he hasn't left North Dakota for any voluntary reason since. Until now. He arrives in Houston today." Glenn checked his watch. "Landed twenty-three minutes ago."

"He finally comes out of hiding, and he picks *Houston*?" Robby said.

"Hey," Kelly said, like she was offended. "We're not so bad."

Robby shook his head. "Nobody comes here on purpose."

Glenn seized the meeting back. "Jack Stapleton's not coming here on purpose, either."

"He's *from* here," Doghouse volunteered, proud to know some trivia.

"Correct," Glenn said. "He's from here. And his parents live on a ranch out past Katy on the Brazos River. And his mother was just diagnosed with breast cancer, and so he's coming home to stay for a while."

"That's why it's happening so fast," Doghouse said.

It was fast. We'd normally take weeks, at least, to get prepped for something like this.

"Yes," Glenn said. "She got her diagnosis on Monday, and her surgery is scheduled for Friday morning."

"Aggressive protocol," Amadi said. His father was an oncologist.

Glenn nodded. "From what I understand, it wouldn't be your first choice of cancer. But it's not unbeatable."

We all noted the double negative.

"What's the duration of the assignment?" I asked then.

"Unclear. But it's my understanding that Stapleton intends to stay for the run of her treatment."

"Weeks?" I asked.

"At least. We'll know more when the family does."

It was so strange to think of Jack Stapleton as having a family—or as having any kind of life outside of his primary role of giving us all something to ogle about humanity.

And yet, there it was. Jack Stapleton was a real person. With a mom. Who was sick. And a hometown. And now he was coming to Houston.

Glenn changed the slide show to a series of photos of a modern, three-story house. "He's rented a place in town near the medical center. We couldn't get access until today, but here are some photos from the rental listing."

What normal people would have seen in those photos was a brand-new, high-end, luxurious modern house, with high ceilings and huge windows and lush landscaping. It had a pale-blue front door with a potted fiddle-leaf fig plant next to it. It looked like something out of *Architectural Digest*.

But we all looked at those images through a different lens.

The fiddle-leaf fig made for a pretty picture, but it wasn't relevant to anyone in this room. Unless we could hide a security camera in it. The high wall around the yard meant it would be hard for a stalker to scale it. The circular driveway out front was a little too close to the structure. That giant oleander bush would need to be trimmed. The rooftop patio would be easy for a sniper to access. In night shots, the lighting out front was much more about mood than visibility.

Glenn walked us through the security features. "Security cameras galore—even one interior, motion-activated, in the front hall. Top-of-the-line alarm system and high-tech locks with remote access. Though the client's representative says he forgets to use it."

Red flag. Uncooperative client.

I raised my hand. "Did he hire us? Or was it, like, his manager or something?"

Glenn paused. And with that pause, we all knew the answer. "A little bit of both," he said. "His manager technically hired us. But it's at the strenuous urging of his team. And the studio that's about to make the *Destroyers* sequel."

It was not uncommon for our clients to have "teams."

"Why is the team 'strenuously urging' him to hire security?" I asked.

"He's had some stalkers in the past," Glenn said, "and one of them lives here in town."

The table gave a collective nod.

"So the first strategy, of course, is to conceal the fact that he's here at all for as long as possible. But that's a wild card. He is widely recognizable—"

Kelly let out a "Ha!"

"But," Glenn went on, "he's been off the grid for a while, so he might not be in the forefront of people's minds. And he does seem to avoid the spotlight pretty well these days."

That was good. The less spotlight, the better.

"He has indicated that he'll accompany his mother to her surgery and appointments. Other than that, he plans to lie pretty low."

I was trying to remain uncommitted, but my brain was already starting to churn and work out the strategy. We'd need to get the hospital architectural plans. Do a site visit in advance. Find the best ingress and egress options. Secure a private waiting area.

"What's the situation on the former stalker?" Doghouse asked.

Glenn nodded and pulled up a photo. A mugshot of a middle-aged woman with no-nonsense hair, pale-pink lipstick outside the lines, and, most notably, wearing earring bobs with Jack's face on them.

"Don't you have those earrings?" Doghouse said to Kelly.

She flung her ballpoint pen at him, next to her. When it clattered down to the table, she took it back.

We all relaxed. A female stalker was a good thing. Women didn't tend to kill people.

"A lot of activity in the two years before *The Destroyers* came out," Glenn said, "but less since the brother died and Stapleton went off the grid." Glenn put up a list on the screen and gestured at it. "In five years, she's sent hundreds of letters, some of them threatening. Lots of online harassment, too—most of it trying to frighten him into dating her."

"Oldest trick in the book," I said.

I heard Robby laugh at that.

Glenn went on. "She took trips to LA and found his house. He woke up one morning and discovered her asleep in his bathtub, clutching a doll with a photo of his face taped onto it."

"So, standard lady stalker stuff," Taylor said.

"Correct," Glenn nodded. "She's done everything from knitting him sweaters to threatening suicide if he didn't impregnate her."

"Isn't she kind of . . . past childbearing age?"

"Not according to her."

"Any death threats?" Amadi asked.

"Not that we know of. Not from her, anyway. There was a recent series of unhinged insults on a fan site from a username"—Glenn checked his notes—"WilburHatesYou321. We're keeping an eye on it."

"Guess we know how Wilbur feels," Kelly said.

"Why does the name Wilbur just not seem threatening?" Taylor asked.

"Because," I answered, "Wilbur's the pig in *Charlotte's Web*."

"Aww," Kelly said.

"Ladies," Glenn said. "Focus, please."

"If you wanted us to focus," Kelly said, "you shouldn't have kicked things off with that beefcake slide show."

"They're drunk on hormones," Doghouse said.

Kelly elbowed him. "You wish."

The briefing was far more . . . brief . . . than usual because we'd only just gotten the case. Catching up and doing all our normal due diligence would be a scramble. Glenn broke us into teams to get to work.

Glenn assigned Robby to analyze Jack's media coverage, including his Instagram, to find out how much of his personal information was out there. He assigned Doghouse to do a physical assessment on the rental house in town—including architectural plans and features, crime info on the neighborhood, and a deep dive into the security system. He told Amadi to gather everything he could on the parents' ranch. He assigned Kelly to compile a dossier on the recently hired housekeeper, and Taylor to create a comprehensive portfolio on all past stalker activity.

And me?

Glenn tried to send me to the beauty parlor.

"What the hell?" I said, right there in the meeting.

"You're the primary on this one, Brooks. You need to look the part."

"First of all," I said, "I haven't agreed to be the primary."

Glenn flared his nostrils. "You will."

I looked down at my suit. I looked fine. Didn't I?

Glenn went on. "If you needed a burka, we'd get you a burka, and if you needed a sari, we'd get you a sari—so since you are headed to the fancy rent-a-mansion of a Hollywood A-lister, we're getting you a makeover."

"I don't need a makeover," I said—but then I regretted it right away.

The whole room burst out laughing.

"You're going to shadow Jack Stapleton like *that*?" Robby said.

I touched my plain brown hair, which was already falling out of its low bun, and then glanced down at my outlet-mall Ann Taylor pantsuit. "Maybe," I said.

On assignment, I wore whatever blending in required. I'd worn everything from little black dresses, to leather jackets, to tennis outfits. I'd dressed like a teenager, like a punk rocker, and like a frumpy schoolmarm. I was happy to be incognito. I'd do anything to play the part right.

But no matter what I wore on assignment, I always returned to my set point of the Ann Taylor pantsuit—with flats, not heels, because you always have to be able to run.

Footwear really is crucial.

I was still reacting to the makeover idea when Robby said to Glenn, "You should give this gig to Kelly."

Kelly shrieked with delight at the idea—even though Robby had zero authority to make that call.

Glenn was not a fan of being challenged. He turned to Robby. "What was that?"

Robby flicked a glance in my direction, so we all knew exactly who he was talking about. "She's not right for it."

"That's not up to you."

Robby gave a half-shrug and said, "Just saying." And before I had time to even consider if he maybe had a good point, he kept going. "Just look at her," he said. "She can't pass in that world."

Jesus, Robby.

Was this how he was going to compete for the London thing? By sabotaging me?

But I shifted my attention from Robby's petulant face—which suddenly seemed so much more punchable than I'd ever noticed before—and panned to the right until I landed on Glenn.

"You're saying I'm the primary on this whether I like it or not?"

"That's exactly what I'm saying."

"Why?"

"Because if you want to have a chance at the London job, you need to do it, and do it right. If you don't knock this assignment out of the park . . . then Robby's going to London, and you're staying right here in Texas on office duty forever."

He held my gaze in a little mini standoff.

Then he added, "You should be thanking me."

"I'll pass on that."

"You're doing this," Glenn said. "And you don't get to complain, or dial it in, or feel victimized, or pout because life is unfair. Life *is* unfair. That's not news. I know exactly what Robby did to you, and I know this isn't exactly the escape you were looking for—"

"It's not an escape at all," I interrupted.

"—but this is the best opportunity you've got. So you're making the most of it. And that starts with a new goddamned wardrobe so you're not standing next to the Sexiest Man Alive looking like a sad temp who needs a shower."

Did he think I'd be cowed by insults? I ate insults for breakfast. I squared my shoulders. "Why are you making me prove myself when you already know what I'm capable of?"

"I know what the old you was capable of. This you? I'm still not sure."

Fine. I thought. I wasn't entirely sure, either.

Was it everything I wanted? No.

But was it something?

And was I desperate enough to do anything?

"Fine," I said.

"'Fine' what?"

"Fine, I'll make the most of it."

Glenn looked at me over his reading glasses. "Damn right, you will."

"But," I added, lifting both my eyebrows and pausing so he'd know exactly where I drew the line. "There's no way I'm doing a frigging makeover."

I WANT TO tell you that I was a very cool person who was not flustered by fame. Taylor had once run into Tom Holland at a bar in LA, and she'd lit a cigarette for his friend with a Zippo lighter like a badass. No big deal.

I would not have been so chill.

Reviewing Jack Stapleton's file, I had to admit, to myself if no one else, I was the opposite of chill.

On paper, he was no different than any other client. He had a bank, and credit cards, just like everybody else. He had two cars back in North Dakota—a vintage Wagoneer and a pickup truck—but he'd leased a Range Rover for his time in Houston. He'd had asthma as a child, and he had a current prescription for sleeping pills. Under "Known Enemies" he had several pages of crazed fans who'd appeared and disappeared over the years, but that was about it. Under "Known Associates/Lovers," it listed Kennedy Monroe—and somebody, probably Doghouse, had written in "hubba hubba" by her name.

No surprise there.

A normal file. A normal file, dammit.

Fine. Okay. I was not unaware of Jack Stapleton's charm.

I mean, I wasn't a fangirl like Kelly. I didn't have the man's face on my *socks*.

But I'd seen most of his movies—except for *Fear of the Dark*, which was a slasher film and not my thing. I'd also skipped *Train to Providence* because I heard he sacrificed himself to the zombies in the end, and why would I want to see that?

But I'd seen all the others, including *The Unhoneymooners* so many times I'd accidentally memorized the scene where he confesses, "It's so exhausting pretending to hate you." His dramatic work in *A Spark of Light* was tragically underrated. And even though *You Wish* was widely panned for including every single rom-com trope in history—including, of all things, a mad dash to the airport—they still did those tropes really well, and so it was one of my perennial go-tos when I was feeling down.

Also, the way he kissed Katie Palmer in *Can't Win for Losing*? Oscar worthy. Why wasn't there an Oscar category for Best Kiss? He should go down in history for that one kiss alone. The first time I saw it, it just about killed me.

Like, I almost died from delight.

So it was not *not* a big deal that I'd just been assigned to protect him.

Note the double negative.

He was not *not* on my radar. I was not *not* affected by the thought of him.

I'd never have admitted it—least of all to myself—but I did have what you could describe as a perfectly normal, nonpathetic, comfortingly mild, not-at-all creepy little crush on him.

You know, in the way you might have a crush on the captain of the football team in high school. You're not going to *date* the captain of the football team. You know your place—and your place is: A scribe for student government. A student liaison for community service. Vice president of the spreadsheet club.

It's just a little sunny place for your fantasies to wander. Sometimes. Occasionally. In between your many other more important things to do.

No harm in that, right?

Wasn't that ultimately what movie stars were *for*? To be fantasies for the rest of us? To add imaginary sprinkles to the metaphorical cupcake of life?

But now the reality was going to collide with the fantasy.

It was the reason I wanted to say no.

I *liked* the fantasy. I didn't want Jack Stapleton to become real.

Plus, how could you protect a person who made you nervous? How could you stay focused with an actual god-living-among-humans just feet away from you? Glenn had a professional rep to protect, but so did I. I was supposed to impress the hell out of Glenn if I wanted the London job, but what was I going to do if Jack Stapleton showed up one day in that same navy and cornflower-blue baseball Tee he'd worn in *The Optimist*?

Good God. I might as well just quit now.

I'd seen Jack Stapleton kiss fictional people, bury a fictional father, beg for fictional forgiveness, and sob fictional tears. I'd seen him take a shower, brush his teeth, curl up under the covers at bedtime. I'd seen him rappel down a cliff face. I'd seen him hug his lost-then-found child. I'd seen him scared, and nervous, and angry, and even naked in bed with the love of his life.

None of it was real—of course. I knew that. I mean, I wasn't *crazy*.

It wasn't real, but it seemed real. It *felt* real.

I already cared about him, is what I'm saying. That distance you always maintain with your clients? He had already breached it—even though I'd never even met him.

Plus, there was just something about Jack Stapleton that I liked. The shape of his eyes—kind of sweet and smiley. The deadpan way he delivered his lines. The way he gazed at the women he loved.

Oh, it was going to be a long assignment.

But—and here came the pep talk—not impossible.

The guy on screen wouldn't be the same person in real life. Couldn't be. The guy on screen said funny things because funny writers wrote his lines. The guy on the screen looked picture perfect because the production department styled his hair and put his makeup on and chose his clothes. And the washboard stomach? You don't get those for free. He probably spent hours and hours maintaining that thing. Hours that would've been far better spent, say, fighting poverty, or rescuing homeless pets, or, I don't know, reading a book.

Maybe, if there was mercy in the universe, he'd be nothing like I always imagined.

Maybe he'd be as unlikable as most of my clients were.

Unlikable might help.

But I'd also take dumb. Rude. Slug-like. Pompous. Narcissistic. Anything that could demote him to an ordinary, real, mildly irritating person like everybody else . . . and let me get my work done.

I mean, sure. I'd have preferred to keep the fantasy.

But reality had its uses, too.

Five

CUT TO: ME ringing Jack Stapleton's fancy doorbell in the Museum District.

In my standard pantsuit. Without the makeover I had so valiantly refused.

Kind of regretting that victory now.

This was an intake meeting, and I'd done dozens of them. Usually, the whole team went—primaries and secondaries—to meet in person and gather information. But the team was scrambling too hard right now to take the time.

So, today: just me.

Alone, and talking myself through the moment. *You got this.*

Once you learn to look at the world from a perspective of personal security, you can't look at it any other way. I couldn't walk into a restaurant, for example, without assessing the threat level in the room—even when I was off duty. I couldn't not notice suspicious people, or vehicles that circled the block more than once, or empty vans in parking lots, or "repair crews" that may or may not've been doing surveillance. Honestly, I couldn't get into my car without a three-step process: checking for signs of entry, checking the tailpipe for blockages, and checking under the chassis for explosives.

In eight years, I'd never once just walked out to my car and gotten in.

I must've seemed like the craziest person ever.

But once you know how terrible the world is, you can't *unk*now.

No matter how much you might want to.

I wasn't sure exactly how much Jack Stapleton knew about the world, but part of my job today, and going forward, was to educate him. You absolutely have to get buy-in from the principal, because you really can't do it alone. Making it clear that protection is necessary without freaking anyone out is a crucial task at the beginning.

You have to calibrate exactly how much clients can handle.

Arriving at Jack Stapleton's door, I clutched a checklist of things to cover so that he could hold up his end of the safety bargain. I also had some basic in-person tasks that his assistant in LA couldn't do for him: fingerprints, a blood draw, a handwriting sample. Plus, a list of questions that Glenn called the VPQ—Very Personal Questionnaire—that gathered info on tattoos, moles, fears, weird habits, and phobias. Normally, we'd do a video recording, too, but, obviously, for this guy: no need.

Anyway, that was all I had to do. Stick to the script.

But wow, did I feel nervous.

And that was before he shocked the hell out of me by opening the door.

Shirtless.

Just opened up the front door. To a total stranger. Utterly naked from the waist up. What kind of a power move was that?

"Jesus Christ!" I said, spinning around and covering my eyes. "Put some clothes on!"

But the image of him was already burned into my retinas: Bare feet. Frayed Levi's. A corded leather necklace encircling the base of his neck, just above his collarbones. And I don't even have words for what was happening in the midsection.

I squeezed my eyes tighter.

How the hell was I supposed to work with that?

"Sorry!" he said, behind me in the doorway. "Timed that wrong." Then, "It's safe now."

I made myself drop my hand and turn back around . . .

Where I beheld Jack Stapleton halfway through the process of wriggling into a T-shirt—six-pack muscles undulating like they wanted to put me in a trance.

Let me just stop the clock right here for a second, because it's not every day you stand in Jack Stapleton's doorway, squinting directly into his magnificence, while he does a completely normal yet utterly astonishing thing, like put on a T-shirt.

What was it like, you must be wondering, for me to live through that moment?

Maybe this will help: *My brain shut down.*

Like, I lost the power of speech.

I know he asked me a question somewhere in there.

But I cannot tell you what it was.

Nor could I answer him.

I just stood there, gaping, like a widemouth bass.

He's just a person, you're thinking. *Just a person who happens to be famous.*

Sure. Fine.

But *you* try stepping into that moment and not just falling *mute with awe.*

I dare you.

Can I also just add that I really hadn't expected him to answer the door at all? I assumed it would be an assistant, or a secretary, or a posh British butler in a morning coat and tails—anyone but the man himself.

Add to that, he was bigger than he looked.

And he looked pretty big to start with.

I felt really tiny, in comparison. Which was not my favorite power dynamic.

And I'll add—and maybe this goes without saying—he was . . . *alive.*

As opposed to a celluloid representation of himself.

He was a living, breathing, three-dimensional creature.

Which was new.

I was getting a good look now, and he wasn't nearly as buff as he had been in *The Destroyers*—and of course not—*right?*—because who can keep a five-hour-a-day workout regimen going indefinitely? So instead of witnessing a jacked-up, bemuscled he-beast, I got a slightly less defined, more subtle yet somehow more sophisticated, ordinary, everyday washboard stomach.

A washboard stomach that didn't have to try too hard.

Which made him seem more human. Which should have been a good thing.

But more human made him more real.

And he wasn't supposed to be real.

The real Jack Stapleton was less tan than his movie posters. The real him had irises that were more gray than blue. The real him had a little nick where he'd cut himself shaving. His lips looked a bit dry, like they needed some ChapStick. His hair was shaggier than I'd ever seen— *How long since he'd had a haircut?*—and flopping over his forehead in a way that just begged somebody to brush it off to the side. He had a Band-Aid on the back of his hand, and he wore a beat-up drugstore sports watch, and he had glasses on, of all things. Not cool-guy Prada glasses—just the kind of slightly bent glasses that regular people actually wear for seeing.

That's how I knew I wasn't dreaming, by the way. Because it never would have occurred to me to put a bent pair of ordinary glasses on Jack Stapleton.

And they somehow made him look both better and worse.

Exhausting.

OKAY, LET'S START the moment back up.

Where were we? Oh, yeah:

Holy shit.

Friends and neighbors, I just met Jack Stapleton.

Barefoot. In Levi's. Wearing a leather necklace that made me rede-fine all my opinions about leather necklaces.

"You're early," he said then, interrupting my ogle. "I was just getting dressed."

I was still mute. I opened my mouth, but nothing came out. I could hear myself wanting to say, "I am exactly on time," in a professional, even imperceptibly irritated voice—but I couldn't actually orchestrate the required squeezing of the diaphragm to make it happen.

Using every ounce of willpower I had, I ratcheted my open mouth closed.

That was something, at least.

He frowned at this for a second, and then he said, "Wait. *Are* you early? Or am I late?" He checked his watch. "You know what? I'm still on mountain time."

All I could do was not gape.

"Are you thinking that North Dakota is central time?"

No response, but I did maintain eye contact.

He went on. "Because I get that a lot. North Dakota *is* central time, mostly. Except for the southwest corner. Where I happen to live."

He was unfazed by one-sided conversations.

This must happen to him a lot.

But now he turned and waved for me to follow. "Come on in," he said, heading farther back into the house.

I closed the door behind me and trailed him to the kitchen. *Get a grip*, I scolded myself. *He's just a person! He cut himself shaving! He's not even all that tan anymore!*

"Cool pin necklace, by the way," he called back as he walked.

Like a reflex, I touched my beaded safety pin. Huh. Observant.

And the pin must have been even more of a talisman than I'd real-ized, because only then did I magically remember how to talk. "Thank you," I said—though it came out more like a question than a reply.

In the kitchen, Jack Stapleton bent down and started rummaging through the cabinet under the sink, like regular people sometimes do.

Imagine that. They're just like us.

"I'm new here," he was saying, as I watched, "so I don't really know what we have, but just let me know anything you need, and I'll get it for you."

He turned and stood up then with a caddy full of cleaning bottles, scrub brushes, sponges, and trash bags, which he set decisively on the counter in front of me.

I frowned at him.

"For cleaning," he said.

I shook my head.

He frowned again. "Aren't you the . . ."

And then—so newly grateful for the power of speech—I answered with, "Executive Protection Agent."

Just as he said, "Cleaning lady?"

Really? Here I am in my best pantsuit, and he's thinking "cleaning lady"?

Maybe Robby was right. Maybe I couldn't pass.

"I am not the cleaning lady," I said.

He frowned. "Oh." And then he waited, like *Who are you, then?*

"I'm the primary Executive Protection Agent on your personal security team."

He really looked baffled. "You're the what on my what?"

I sighed. "I'm in charge of your security detail."

"I don't have a security detail."

Well, this was new. "Pretty sure you do."

At that, he clamped his hand around my arm just above the elbow— not so hard that it hurt, but hard enough that I couldn't mistake the strength of the grip—and he led me back out the front door. In truth, it's a grip I knew how to get out of, but I was so befuddled by what was happening, I just followed like a lamb.

Outside, he closed the door behind us and locked it.

Then, he got back to business. "You're telling me you're not the housekeeper?"

"Do I look like the housekeeper?"

Jack Stapleton shrugged, like *Why not?*

I should've let it go. "How many housekeepers show up for work in a silk blouse?"

"Maybe you were planning to change?"

Okay. Done with that. I gave a sharp sigh. "I am not the housekeeper."

That's when he held up his finger, like *Just a sec*, turned, and walked down the driveway digging his cell phone out of his pocket.

After a few steps, I heard him say, "Hey. A person just showed up here claiming to be personal security."

Wait. Was he suspicious of me?

I couldn't hear the response.

But I could hear Jack Stapleton loud and clear. "We decided against that already. Twice."

He was kicking the crushed gravel on the driveway.

"But that was years ago."

A pause.

"It won't work. It'll be a disaster. There has to be another way."

Another pause.

Jack Stapleton and whoever he was talking to—His manager? His agent? His guru?—went round and round. I don't know if he didn't realize that I could hear him, or if he didn't care . . . but he vociferously protested my presence in his life, right within earshot.

It stung a little. To be honest.

He argued for so long that I finally sat down on the little bench near the potted fiddle-leaf fig, noting that it could be used to smash the window behind it and should be moved, or sold, or thrown away. With nothing else to do, I half-heartedly assessed the property—distance from the street: *adequate*; lack of driveway gate: *suboptimal*; potential skull damage from one of those landscaping rocks: *lethal*—more out of habit than anything else.

Had I ever shown up for an intake meeting with a client who didn't even know he'd hired me?

No. This was a first.

It was unsettling to think that he didn't even want me there.

Most people were at least somewhat grateful for your help.

By the time he was finished arguing, fifteen minutes had gone by. He walked back, looking angry—a facial expression that, weirdly, I already recognized. I'd seen that face in *Something for Nothing*, right after the drug dealers confronted him. I'd also seen it in *The Optimist*, after he got cheated out of winning the cooking contest. I'd just met this man, but I already knew the funny little dimple that inevitably appeared on his chin when he was really pissed off.

And there it was.

As I stood up, I was not un–pissed off myself. We could've been done by now. I could've been home and already punched out for the day.

"Did you not know they were hiring us?" I asked, as he got close.

"I just thought we'd decided against it," he said.

"Guess not," I said.

"I mean," Jack said, "I did decide against it. But the studio decided for it."

"I thought you wanted out of that contract."

"I do," he said. "But what you want and what you get aren't really the same thing."

Not untrue.

"Anyway, their lawyers want them to protect their assets."

"Is that what you are?"

Jack nodded. "Absolutely. They don't want trouble. And they do want me to stay alive."

"I'm sure everybody wants that," I said.

"Not everybody," he said. "Isn't that why you're here?"

True enough.

As I nodded, Jack Stapleton really looked at me for the first time since I'd arrived: his new housekeeper-slash-bodyguard. I felt his gaze like a physical sensation—like sun rays on my skin. I'd looked at him so many times. It was unbelievably weird for him to actually look back.

He let out a long, defeated sigh. "Let's talk inside."

INSIDE, AS HIS anger-dimple will testify, he stayed pissed for a while.

Though I hoped it was more at the studio than at me.

We sat at his dining table, and I unclutched the accordion folder I'd been holding to my chest since I got there. It felt strangely naked to release it.

Jack Stapleton was now slumped in defeat on a dining chair. "Just do what you normally do," he said.

I took a breath. "Okay."

What I normally do. This was better. We were back in my wheelhouse.

"I'm Hannah Brooks," I began. "I've protected dozens of people in every type of situation imaginable."

This was an introductory paragraph I'd memorized. I used it the same way, every time, when I met new clients. It was comforting to recite it, like singing an old favorite song.

"Executive protection is a partnership," I went on. "We're here to help you, and you're here to help us. What you need from us is competence and experienced guidance, and what we need from you is honesty and compliance."

Jack Stapleton wasn't looking at me. He was checking his texts.

"Are you texting right now?" I paused to ask.

"I can do both," he said, not looking up.

"Um. Not really. But okay."

Nothing to do but keep talking. As I remembered who I was, I gained momentum. I pushed the handout I'd brought for him across the table. Printed on the cover page was our guiding principle. I recited it out loud. "The object of personal security is to reduce the risk of criminal acts, kidnapping, and assassination against a principal through the application of targeted procedures to normal daily life."

Jack Stapleton looked up. "Assassination? Really? I've got a fifty-year-old stalker who breeds show corgis."

But he couldn't derail me now. "Constant awareness is the cornerstone of good personal security," I went on. "In addition, security measures must always match the threat. Based on our level of knowledge at current, your threat level is relatively low. Of the four levels—white, yellow, orange, and red—we presently list you at 'yellow.' But we expect the news of your visit to Houston to break at some point, and when it does, we'll up your classification to 'orange.' The strategy is to have systems in place to make that transition quickly."

Jack Stapleton frowned. This was a lot of high-level jargon coming from the cleaning lady.

I went on. "All security is a compromise between the demands of the threat level and the reasonable hopes of the client to live a somewhat normal life."

"I gave up on normal life years ago."

"We'd like you to read this guidance carefully and familiarize yourself with your responsibilities toward your own safety. Anything you can do to prevent yourself from being successfully targeted helps us all keep you safe."

"Again," Jack said, "this lady mostly knits Christmas sweaters with my face on them. They're actually kind of impressive."

I stood up a little taller. "All successful kidnappings and assassinations happen because of one final factor and one final factor only: the element of surprise."

"I'm really not worried about being assassinated."

"And so the number one thing we need from any protected figure is awareness. Most people sleepwalk through their lives, barely cognizant of the dangers everywhere. But people under threat don't have that luxury. You must train yourself to notice the people and objects around you—and to question them."

"You're kind of like a talking textbook, did you know that?"

"I've worked for Glenn Schultz for eight years and made my way to the highest rungs of his organization. I have a PPO certificate, as well as advanced training in countersurveillance, evasive driving, emergency medicine, advanced firearms, and close combat. But if I do my job right, we'll never need any of that. You and I and the team, working together, will anticipate threats and diffuse them long before any crisis occurs."

"I think I liked you better as the maid."

I met his eyes. "You won't say that at threat level orange."

He looked away.

I took a breath. "I can sense from your body language that you're not too interested in reading the handout, so I'll summarize the most important guidelines for VIPs." I ticked off the list on my fingers, going faster than necessary, just to show off:

- Don't meet with strangers at unknown locations.
- Don't book restaurants in your own name.
- Don't travel at night.
- Don't frequent the same clubs and restaurants.
- Walk in groups whenever possible.
- Don't drive a distinctive vehicle.
- Alert the police to any new threats.
- Keep your gas tank at least half-full at all times.
- Always keep your car doors locked.
- Avoid stopping at traffic lights by pacing your speed.
- Establish special code words to indicate all is okay.

There was more, but he was smiling at something on his Instagram.

I stopped talking and waited for him to notice.

After a long pause, he looked up. "What was that last one?"

I quoted myself: "'Establish a code word to indicate all is okay.'"

"What's the code word?"

I decided on the spot. "The code word is 'ladybug.'"

Jack dropped his shoulders. "Could we do something a little more badass? Maybe 'cobra'? Or 'beast mode'?"

"The client doesn't get to choose the code word."

Clients chose the code words all the time.

But that's what you get for texting while I'm talking.

Jack frowned. "How am I supposed to remember all those rules?" he asked next.

"Read the handbook," I said. "Many times. With a highlighter."

It's possible my tone was a little sanctimonious.

Jack set down his phone with a sigh. "Look," he said. "I won't be going to clubs or restaurants—or meeting with strangers at unknown locations. I'll just be staying home—or going with my mother to her doctor's appointments." He sighed. "I will also . . . under duress . . . make a few trips out to my parents' ranch, but God willing, those visits will be short and rare. And that's it. I'm not here to have fun, or make trouble, or *get assassinated*. I'm just here to be a good son and help out my mom."

"Great," I said. "That makes our job easier."

He started to pick his phone back up.

I added, "I just need to collect fingerprints, a handwriting sample, and a vial of blood, and we can call it a day." I was forgetting the Very Personal Questionnaire. But I was doing pretty well, all things considered.

"A vial of blood?" he asked.

I nodded. "I'm trained in phlebotomy." Then I glanced down at his forearms. "And you've got veins like firehoses, anyway."

He put his arms behind his back. "What do you need blood for?"

"Basic bloodwork. And to confirm your type."

Now he was blinking in disbelief. I enjoyed shocking him a little.

This was way better than being the maid.

"Your assistant filled in your blood type on the form as AB negative," I said, "and, if that's confirmed, you're lucky, because that's my blood type, too."

"Why does that make me lucky?"

"We always like to keep at least one person on the team who can act as a donor for our principal," I said, pulling out the rubber tourniquet and snapping it. "So you might've just met your own personal blood bank."

Six

TEN MINUTES LATER, I had everything I needed, and I was packing up my stuff, more than ready to get out of there.

There was something so exhausting about all that handsomeness.

Seriously. It was unabated. It was relentless. It was *grueling*.

And I wasn't even looking at him! *He* was looking at *me*.

Finally, I paused to look back. "What?"

"You're nothing like I thought you'd be," he said.

I gave him a look. "Right back atcha."

"I expected you to be bigger, for one," he said.

"You didn't even know I was coming."

"*Today*, I didn't know. We were planning to hire you before, though. Then I changed my mind."

"And then the studio changed it back."

"Something like that."

Jack was still assessing me, and I can't begin to describe how strange it was to be the watchee rather than the watcher.

He went on, "I guess I thought you'd be more of a tough guy."

I was not a tough guy. I was the opposite of a tough guy. But I wasn't telling him that. "Nothing about this job requires you to be a tough guy."

"What does it require?"

"Focus. Training. Awareness." I tapped my head like I was pointing to my brain. "It's not about being tough. It's about being prepared."

"But *a bodyguard*, you know? I just feel like you should be larger. You're, like, tiny."

"I am hardly tiny," I said. "You just happen to be enormous."

"What are you? Five-four?"

"I am five-six, thank you." I was five-five.

"So what would you do if some massive guy tried to beat me up?"

"That would never happen," I said. "We'd anticipate the threat and remove you from the scene before it ever came to that."

"But what if it did?"

"It wouldn't."

"But just—hypothetically?"

I sighed. "Fine. Hypothetically, if it did—which it wouldn't—I would just . . . take him down."

"But how?"

"I've done jujitsu since I was six, and I'm a second-degree black belt."

"But what if he was really big?" Jack lifted up his arms like a bear.

I squinted at him. "I don't think you understand how jujitsu works."

He squinted back.

"You don't believe me?" I asked. "Do you realize how sexist that is?"

"It's not sexist . . ." he protested. "It's just . . . physics. How does somebody your size take down somebody my size?"

"That's not physics," I said. "That's ignorance."

"Show me," he said.

"What?"

"Jujitsu me."

"No."

"Yes."

I sighed. "You want me to take you down? Right now?"

"I mean, not really. But I do think I'd sleep easier if I knew for a fact that you could."

"You're saying you want me to hurt you? For real? Because if I do what you're suggesting, I'll definitely knock the wind out of you—and possibly dislocate your shoulder, too."

This was a genuinely bad idea.

But I guess Jack did want me to hurt him, because he grabbed my hand and dragged me out his back door, across the patio, to a patch of grass by the pool. "Bad idea, bad idea, bad idea," I said, as he tugged me behind him.

"See how easy it is for me to manhandle you, though?" he called back.

And I guess that's when I gave in. I was never a big fan of being underestimated. Especially by a guy who thought I was the cleaning lady.

He wanted me to hurt him?

Fine. I'd hurt him.

When we reached the grass, he let go of my hand and jogged off a little further. Then he U-turned and came back at me, launching into a run.

I guess we were doing this.

Sigh.

By this point, there was no decision to make. Once a six-foot-three guy starts running straight for you—there are no decisions left. You just do what you're trained to do.

As soon as he reached me, I grabbed his left wrist with both hands, yanked it down, and rammed my hips into his. The trick here is to get a rolling motion. You're pulling his arm and shoulders down while you're shoving his lower half up—and then forcing a roll over the pommel of your butt.

It sounds more complex than it is.

To sum up: You tuck your head, and over he goes.

That's physics.

In less than a second, he was flat on his back.

Moaning.

"You asked for it, buddy," I said.

As I stared down at him, his eyes found mine. And then, for the first time since I'd been there, he smiled. A big admiration-saturated smile. "Oh God, that hurts," he said.

"I told you," I said.

He cradled an arm around his midsection, panting. Or wait—was he laughing? "You're such a tough guy!"

"I'm really not."

"You're awesome," he said.

"That was never in question."

Next, he flattened out and spread his arms wide, staring up at the sky. "Thank you, Hannah Brooks! Thank you!"

Why on earth was he thanking me?

Then he shouted at the clouds. "You're hired!"

But I refused to be amazed with him about something I'd done a thousand times. It wasn't amazing. It was just training. "I was already hired," I said.

"You're hired again! You're double hired! You're hired with great fanfare!"

I shook my head and walked back inside to get him some ice.

WHEN HE MADE it to the kitchen minutes later, still panting, still aglow with appreciation, he looked, shall we say, like he'd just learned a vital life lesson.

I secured an ice pack to his shoulder with tied-together dish towels, refusing to be flustered, now, in a slower moment, by the proximity of his body to mine.

"Your shoulder's really going to hurt for a few days," I said.

"Worth it," he said.

"Take some ibuprofen before bed."

"Okay, doc."

"And next time I tell you I'm good at something," I said, "don't make me hurt you to prove it."

"Roger that."

I gathered up my stuff and then turned to say goodbye, clutching my folder of paperwork to my chest like I had before—but feeling like a whole new version of the girl who'd walked in here.

Nothing like flipping a man on his back to bolster your self-esteem. *Recommend.*

"So it looks like we start in earnest tomorrow," I said, checking the tentative schedule Glenn had given me. "You want to drive out to your parents' place in the morning, right?"

Jack nodded.

"We've got a team assessing the route right now," I said. "This is much more rushed than our normal prep time, but we're just going to fake it till we make it."

Jack was looking down. He didn't answer.

"We can bring a remote team with us tomorrow, and they can assess the ranch property while we're out there—get some cameras installed, evaluate the layout." That felt like a good plan.

But then Jack said, "Actually, that can't happen."

I shook my head. "What can't happen?"

"We can't take a security team out to my parents' place."

"Why not?" I asked.

He took a deep breath. "Because my parents can't know anything about this."

"Anything about what?"

He gestured around, like *All of it*. "Threats, stalkers, personal security."

"How is that supposed to work?"

He shook his head. "My mom's sick, you know? She's sick. And if she knows about this, she'll worry. Even though there's really nothing to worry about. I've had stalkers for years—I'm totally immune to all that by now. But I've never told her about anything scary—and I'm sure as hell not starting the week she has surgery for cancer."

"But . . ." I said. Then I wasn't sure what to say.

"She's a worrier," Jack said. "Like, a world-champion worrier. And she's facing some test results that are . . . not great. And ever since my brother died . . ." Jack stared at his hands like he didn't know how to finish that sentence. "For me, I admit—a bodyguard is a good thing. I get it. But for my mom? Not good. I was reading up on treatments online, and stress can really impact people's outcomes. I can't make things harder than they already are on her. The only way to do this is to make sure my parents never know who you are."

"But . . . how?"

"Your website says 'Outside-the-box solutions for every scenario.'" He turned his phone toward me to show me the website for proof.

"*That's* what you've been doing on your phone?" I demanded.

Jack shrugged. "It's one of the things I've been doing on my phone."

I gave him a look. "The web designer wrote that."

"Your boss—what's his name? Frank Johnson?"

"Not even close. Glenn Schultz."

"He says much of the surveillance can be done remotely."

Did Glenn already know about this and not tell me?

Jack went on. "He says you can stay close to me and a second group can monitor from afar."

"But if you're toting an agent along everywhere you go, won't that kind of tip your family off?"

"Not at all."

I put my hands on my hips. "Why not?"

"First," Jack said, "my parents are sweet and impossibly gullible. And my big brother barely speaks to me. Second, you don't look anything like a bodyguard." He tilted his head a little and gave me his most heart-melting smile. "And last but not least?" he said. "We're going to tell them you're my girlfriend."

BACK AT THE office, Glenn was still in the conference room, and half the team was there with him. It was all-hands-on-deck to get this Jack Stapleton project going.

I didn't care.

"Nope," I said to Glenn, charging right up to the head of the conference table. "That's a hundred percent nope."

Glenn didn't even look up. "Are we talking about the 'girlfriend' thing?"

"Is there anything else to talk about?"

"It's not a dealbreaker. We've done weirder things for clients."

"*You've* done weirder things for clients," I said.

"You've seen the man. Would it really be so awful?"

"I can't believe you knew, and you didn't tell me."

"I thought it might be better coming from his own famously handsome mouth."

"Well, it wasn't better. It was worse. I was totally unprepared. I have never walked out of a client's house like that."

"That's on you."

"No, it's on you. You didn't warn me."

He kept his voice reasonable. "I didn't warn you because it's not nearly as big a deal as you're acting like it is. His threat level is mild. He's been off the radar. The press doesn't know he's here. The money's good. This is the definition of easy."

"You be his girlfriend then!" I said.

Glenn flared his nostrils.

"Or anybody else here."

Kelly's hand shot up. "I volunteer as tribute."

"Perfect. Send Kelly!" I said. "Or send Taylor."

"You're the best I've got," Glenn said. "And it's gonna be a tricky one."

"You just said it was 'the definition of easy.'"

"It's both! It's easy and tricky! And I need a top person. And that's you."

"Don't flatter me," I said.

Glenn leaned in closer. "Look," he said. "He's estranged from his family. He'll barely see them. So what if you have to do a little bit of covering when they're nearby. From the looks of things, that shouldn't be too often."

"Glenn. His family's the whole reason he's here."

But Glenn shook his head. "From what we've gathered, his relationship with his older brother is completely nonexistent."

"What about the parents?"

"That's less clear. Either way, he doesn't spend much time with any of them."

I didn't know how else to protest. "Everything about this feels wrong."

Glenn kept his eyes on me. "You've been incognito before."

"To the *outside world*. Not to the client."

"The family's not the client. Jack Stapleton's the client."

"Same thing," I said.

"You won't be bored anymore, that's for sure," Glenn said.

"Hello?" Kelly said, waving to the room. "I said I'll do it. I'm volunteering. You don't even have to pay me. I'll pay *you*."

"It's unethical," I said, turning to her.

But Kelly flung her arm toward the photo of Jack Stapleton still lingering on the whiteboard. "Who cares?"

Was it unethical? Ethics were a little hard to gauge in this business. The thing about private security was, it had exploded in recent years—partly because the world was more dangerous for rich people and partly because those same people were more paranoid. Agents came from all backgrounds with different kinds of training—ex-military, ex-police, even ex-firefighters, like Doghouse. Most agents freelanced. Nothing was standardized. It was like the Wild West, really—with people doing anything they thought they could get away with. It meant more freedom, but also more risk—and a lot more shenanigans.

Ultimately, we were only accountable to the clients. We had to keep them happy, and for the most part, we did whatever they asked. I once had a client ask me to cover his $7,000 bar bill. I once went skydiving with a Belgian princess. I once spent a night keeping an eye on a client's panther.

Was this Jack Stapleton thing that much weirder?

You served at the pleasure of the client, is what I'm saying. At least, if you wanted to get paid.

It's likely everybody in that conference room saw the situation clearly except for me. If Jack Stapleton wanted a pretend girlfriend, he got a pretend girlfriend. And if I wanted to work for Jack Stapleton, then that's what I had to be.

"The point is," Glenn went on, "it's such a great opportunity for you."

"And it's money for you."

"It's money for all of us."

I was still shaking my head. "We can't do a proper job under these parameters."

"It'll be harder, yes." Glenn conceded. "But keep in mind: His threat level is almost white."

I gave him a look. "It's yellow."

Kelly jumped in. "But a very light yellow. Almost like a lemon sorbet."

Glenn pointed at Kelly. "Stop naming cutesy shades of threat levels."

Glenn wasn't taking me seriously. So I said, "I think you've got dollar signs in your eyes."

It was a test. To see how he'd react.

I told you I could read faces, right? By the way his jaw tightened, I could read that Glenn was insulted. That's when I started to cave.

He genuinely thought we could handle this.

"Do you think I'm just going to throw us all into the fire?" Glenn said. "Everybody's reputation's riding on this—especially mine. I'm saying it's doable. I'm saying there are strategies for making it work."

I sighed. "Like what, exactly?"

"A remote backup team, for one. Cutting-edge surveillance tech. Placing you as the eyes and ears on the inside with full twenty-four-hour backup teams on the outside."

I guess I could kind of see his point.

Then Glenn upped the ante.

"The point is," he said, "if you want any chance of getting the London position, you're going to get on board."

"So I'm doing this whether I like it or not."

"Pretty much. But it would be nicer if you'd like it."

I looked around the room. Everyone was watching me. Why *was* I making such a fuss?

"How about this," Glenn said next, both of us aware that he had all the power. "Do this without complaining, and I'll send you wherever you want for your next assignment. You can take your pick. The Korea thing's back on. You want it? It's yours."

I'd been waiting for another Korea assignment ever since the last one got canceled. "I do want Korea," I said.

"Done," Glenn said. "Six weeks in Seoul. Endless bowls of black bean noodles."

I tried that idea on for size.

"Is that a yes?" Glenn asked. "Are we settled? No more whining and foot-dragging?"

I was just about to say yes, and we were just about to have a deal . . . when I heard Robby's voice behind me.

"Are you serious?" Robby said. "This is never going to work."

Everybody turned to stare at him. Timing had never been Robby's thing.

Robby was looking around the group like the whole room was crazy. "Is everyone kidding? This has to be a joke."

Was he worried about my safety? Was he protesting the way that Glenn was strong-arming me? Was he—maybe—jealous?

I studied the layers of outrage on his face.

And that's when Robby cleared everything up. He held his hands out toward me in a *Behold!* gesture and said, "Just look! Nobody in a million years will ever possibly believe that this person, right here, bested the legendary Kennedy Monroe to become Jack Stapleton's girlfriend."

FIRST THINGS FIRST. We could settle the Jack Stapleton thing later.

I flew the ten steps to where Robby was standing, grabbed him by the knot of his necktie so tight that it choked all the pompous, judgmental asshattery off his face, and I dragged him by the neck out to the reception area.

Hoping to yell at him alone.

But of course everybody followed us.

I was too mad to care.

"What is your problem, man?" I demanded, letting go as he coughed and sputtered. "The last time I saw you, you were dumping me. It's been radio silence from you for a full month, and now you show back up here and act like you're the one who was wronged? Is this how you compete for London? With insults and name-calling like a grade-school bully? What is happening"—and here I pressed my pointer finger to his forehead—"in that testosterone-soaked, raisin-sized brain of yours that you cannot stop pelting insults at me? In front of everybody! What! Is! Wrong with you?!"

Our entire audience, semihidden behind the ficus plants, waited for Robby's answer.

But before Robby could say anything, the elevator dinged, and the doors slid open.

And out stepped Jack Stapleton.

You really can't overstate the drama of the collective indrawn breath at the sight of The Destroyer himself, in the flesh, stepping into our office. Of all places.

I, of course, had already met The Destroyer. I'd rolled his fingers around on an ink pad. I'd forced him to copy the lyrics of the Aretha Franklin song "Respect" for his handwriting sample. I'd stuck him with a needle. And I may or may not have dislocated his shoulder.

So I wasn't quite as shocked to see him as everybody else.

But even I was shocked.

Same T-shirt, same jeans—but now wearing a baseball cap and sneakers, too. He looked just ordinary enough to put ordinary people to shame. I looked around at my coworkers, staring: Amadi, the valedictorian of his high school and now a kindhearted dad of three; Kelly, the stress-knitter who had made scarves for every person in the office; Doghouse, the ex-firefighter who'd gotten his nickname not because he was *in everyone's doghouse*—but because he compulsively fostered homeless puppies.

Jack Stapleton's presence in our office made them all seem more real. And they made him seem . . . unreal.

We waited for him to do something.

So he took in the sight of my finger on Robby's forehead and said, "Are you bullying that poor coworker?"

I dropped my hand. "What are you doing here?"

He aimed his gaze right at mine, lit up those legendary gray-blue eyes, and said, "Hannah Brooks. I really need you."

Back by the copy machine, Kelly released a burble of vicarious delight.

Jack took a couple of steps closer to me. "I need to apologize for not giving you the whole picture sooner. And I need to say that I understand your hesitations. And"—here, he dropped to his knees on the industrial carpet—"I need to ask you to be my girlfriend."

Every single person in the room was frozen still.

"Get up," I said, trying to grab Jack by the shoulders and—*What?* Somehow hoist all two-hundred-plus pounds of his solid muscle back up? "You don't have to do this."

But he was unbudgeable. *Duh.*

"I really need your help," he went on. "I have to be here for my mom, and I can't show up here and bring danger, or risk, or—you know—*assassinations* with me. And I can't make this moment any harder on her than it has to be. Please, please take the assignment. And please help me protect her by concealing who you really are."

"What are you doing?" was all I could think of to say.

He pulled my hands into his. "I'm begging," Jack answered. "I'm begging you."

His expression was so earnest, so plaintive, so intense . . . for a second, I thought he might cry.

And I was dumbfounded. Again. For the second time that day. Because nobody cries like Jack Stapleton.

Do you remember how he cried in *The Destroyers*? Most people remember the moment when he blows up the mineshaft. And of course the scene where he gives himself surgery with no anesthesia. And the catchphrase, "Never say goodbye." But what actually made that movie great was the sight of an action hero, at his darkest moment, thinking he'd lost everyone he loved and failed them beyond recognition, weeping tears of grief. You never see that, ever. That's what made that movie a classic. That's what made it better than all the hundreds of others just like it—that raw, human moment of vulnerability coming from the last guy you'd ever expect. It made us all want to be better people. It made us all love him—and humanity—just a little bit more.

Anyway. This scene in the reception area was a little like that.

But with ficus plants.

He didn't wind up crying, in the end. But just the suggestion of it was enough.

Jack Stapleton—*the* Jack Stapleton—was on his knees.

Begging.

And here's the truth. This should have been the epiphany when I realized that Jack Stapleton deserved all his fame and more. Everything he did right then held me, and everyone else, spellbound.

The man could *act*.

He leaned his kneeling body forward and looked up at me with his hands clasped. "I'm begging you to help my sick mom," he said.

I mean, come on.

I'm not made of stone.

"Fine," I said, summoning a rather Oscar-worthy fake nonchalance. "Stop begging. I'll be your girlfriend."

And then I went ahead and snuck one peek at the slack-jawed expression on my terrible ex-boyfriend's lousy, ratty, deplorable face.

Which, to be honest, felt like a win for the good guys.

And for humanity.

And especially, at last, for me.

Seven

THE NEXT MORNING, I drove west out Interstate 10 with Jack Stapleton in his shiny black Range Rover to meet his parents—fully in character as his pretend girlfriend.

Glenn had sent over a pretend wardrobe for the pretend girlfriend, courtesy of a personal-shopper lady friend of his. No pantsuits allowed.

Fair enough.

That's how I wound up wearing an embroidered sundress with sandals, my hair wrapped in a messy bun.

I guess it's hard to feel professional in a sundress with puffy cap sleeves. It was late October, I should mention, but that can mean anything in Texas, weather-wise—and it was a solid eighty degrees outside. Even so, I felt underprepared, a little bit chilly, weirdly naked, and uncharacteristically vulnerable.

I missed my pantsuit, is what I'm saying.

And yet.

I could see why Jack would want to do it this way. When my mom was sick, I'd been all about bolstering her spirits, and keeping her hopes alive, and protecting her from despair. I got it. The idea that Jack might be in danger could be very stressful. It's hard enough being sick.

I'd thought about it last night as I'd driven the freeway—doing a quick route assessment out to the ranch and back—and I decided I was fine with it.

In theory, at least.

Now, today, as it was actually happening, I was less fine.

I sat primly in the passenger seat with my knees pressed together, feeling *not myself.*

Jack Stapleton, in contrast, positively lounged in the driver's seat, steering with one hand and manspreading like a champion. Hair unbrushed defiantly. Chewing gum. Wearing aviator sunglasses like he'd been born in them.

We were going to a ranch, so I guess I'd expected a cowboy look from him. But he seemed more like we were heading for a weekend at the Cape—a snug blue polo and stone-colored khakis with loafers and no socks.

True, I grew up in Houston. You might guess I'd been to a ranch before. But, honestly, no. I'd been to the Eiffel Tower, the Acropolis, the Taj Mahal, and the Forbidden City in Beijing, but I'd never been to a Texas ranch.

I guess I was always too busy escaping.

Until now.

I touched the skin of my knees and worried about how naked they were. Should I have worn jeans? Did I need to worry about rattlesnakes? Fire ants? Cacti?

I had a pair of stop-sign-red cowboy boots that my mom had given me for my eighteenth birthday, saying every Texas girl should own a pair of boots. I'd never had a good reason to wear them until now. They weren't part of my official girlfriend wardrobe, but I'd packed them on principle. Right? If I wouldn't wear them on a ranch, I'd never wear them anywhere.

Maybe I should put them on. For tarantula protection, if not for style.

Behind his shades, I saw Jack glance over at my hands. "Are you nervous?" he asked.

Yes. "No."

"Good. This won't last long. My parents will be glad to see us, but my brother hates me, so he'll get rid of us pretty fast."

"We're probably going to need to talk about that."

"My brother?"

"Yep."

"Nope."

"I'm just saying, the more I know, the better I can help you."

"So therapy is included?"

"Sometimes."

"You signed the nondisclosure agreement, right?"

"Of course."

Jack thought about it. "Yeah. I'm still not talking about it."

"Your call," I said. I'd been so flustered the first time we met that I'd forgotten to run through the Very Personal Questionnaire, and now seemed like as good a time as any. I pulled my "J.S." file out of my bag. "Let's do some other questions, though." We still had thirty minutes on the freeway.

Jack didn't agree to answer, but he didn't refuse, either.

I pulled out a ballpoint pen. "Are you on any drugs that we need to be aware of?"

"Nope."

"Any vices? Gambling? Hookers? Shoplifting?"

"Nope."

"Obsessions? Secret lovers?"

"Not at the moment."

"You sound awfully monkish for a world-famous actor."

"I'm taking a break."

Noted. I went on. "Anger management problems? Deep dark secrets?"

"No more than anybody else."

Mental note: a tad evasive there.

I turned back to the list. "Medical concerns?"

"Picture of health."

"Markings?"

He frowned. "Markings?"

"On your body," I clarified. "Tattoos. Birthmarks. Moles—remarkable or otherwise."

"I have a freckle shaped like Australia," he said, pulling to untuck his shirt.

"Stop!" I said. "I know what Australia looks like." I wrote down "Australia freckle" and then went on. "Scars?"

"A few. Nothing to write home about."

"At some point, I'll need to get pictures of everything."

"Why?"

I refused to hesitate. "In case we need to identify your body."

"My *dead* body?"

"Your *live* body. Like in a ransom photo. Not that it would ever come to that."

"That's disturbing."

I kept going. "Other physical abnormalities?"

"Like?"

Most people just answered the questions. "I don't know. Crooked toes? Extra tooth? Vestigial tail? Get creative."

"Nothing's coming to mind."

Okay. Next. "Sleeping difficulties?"

I waited for him to demand examples, but instead, after a pause, he just said, "Nightmares."

I nodded, like *Got it*. "Frequency?"

"A couple of times a month."

A couple of times a month? "Recurrent?"

"What?"

"Is it the same nightmare every time?"

"Yep."

"Can you tell me what it's about?"

"Do you need to know?"

"I mean, kind of."

He worked the steering wheel like he was considering his options. Finally, he said, "Drowning."

"Okay," I said. It was only one word, but it felt like a lot. Next question. "Any phobias?"

A pause.

Then a curt nod. "Also drowning."

I noted that in the file and was about to move on when he added: "And bridges."

"You have a phobia of bridges?"

He kept his voice tight and matter-of-fact. "I do."

"The idea of bridges or actual bridges?"

"Actual bridges."

Huh. Okay. "How does that manifest?"

He chewed on the inside of his lip as he weighed his options, deciding how much to share. "Well, in about twenty minutes, we're going to come to part of the highway that goes over the Brazos River. And when that happens, I'm going to pull over, stop the car, get out, and walk across the bridge on foot."

"What about the car?"

"You're going to drive it over the bridge and wait for me on the other side."

"Is that how you always cross bridges?"

"It's how I prefer to cross them."

"But what if you're by yourself?"

"I try not to be by myself."

"But if you are?"

"If I am, I hold my breath and keep going. But then I have to pull off the road for a while."

"Why do you pull off the road?"

"To throw up."

I took that in. Then I asked, "Why are you afraid of bridges?"

"Do I have to tell you?"

"No."

"Then let's just say that America's infrastructure isn't nearly as sturdy as we'd all like to think. And leave it at that."

WE NEVER DID finish the questions.

When we got close to the Brazos bridge, Jack really did pull over on the shoulder just before the bridge, get out of the Range Rover, and walk across on foot.

I did my part and drove to meet him on the other side.

I waited for him, leaning against the bumper of his car, rocking from the blasts of 18-wheelers zooming by, watching the tension in his face and the focus of his eyes as he made a straight line from one shore to the other.

Wow. How many people have driven past a random pedestrian walking across a highway bridge, never realizing it was megastar Jack Stapleton?

When he reached me, his face was pale and there was sweat on his forehead. "You weren't joking," I said.

"I never joke about bridges."

He got back in the driver's seat and rolled down the windows, and, with that, he shifted back into character as a relaxed, carefree guy who had it all.

"You've asked me a lot of questions today," Jack said then. "I haven't asked you even one."

"And we should keep it that way."

"I can't ask you questions?"

"You can *ask* . . ." I said with a little I-don't-make-the-rules shrug.

But the question he asked wasn't what I was expecting.

He turned and looked me up and down. "Have you done any acting?"

Given where we were headed at that very moment and the collaboration I'd just signed up for, this was one I probably needed to answer.

A first.

I thought about it. "I've portrayed a few barnyard animals in a few Christmas pageants."

"So that's a full no."

I tried to give him something. "There are elements of acting to my job. Sometimes I have to play a kind of role in a situation. But it's mostly about blending into the background, or vaguely seeming like a personal assistant."

Jack nodded, thinking.

"Never anything so . . . *detailed*, though."

"Okay," he said, still thinking. "I'm going to tell them that you're my girlfriend, and that should do a lot of the heavy lifting. Once that's established, I'll do most of the work. I mean, who lies about having a girlfriend? All you really have to do is just be pleasant."

"Be pleasant," I said, like I was writing it down.

"Yeah, like, you don't have to memorize lines, or deliver a soliloquy. This isn't Shakespeare. Just be normal, and the context should do the rest."

"So I don't have to act like I'm madly in love with you?"

He gave a little sideways glance. "Not unless you want to."

"What if they don't believe you? That I'm your girlfriend?" I hadn't re-alized how vulnerable it would feel to ask this question until I was doing it.

But Jack gave a confident nod. "They'll believe me."

"Why?"

"You're totally my type."

I couldn't resist. "Cleaning ladies are your type?"

He pointed at me. "That was an honest mistake."

I actually had no idea how I was going to pass for Jack Stapleton's girlfriend. I did not buy for a second that I was his type. I'd done a thorough Google search on him and I'd seen enough Barbie dolls to last me a lifetime. One of them had clearly had so much cosmetic surgery, I couldn't help but wonder if her mother missed her face.

Not to mention Kennedy Monroe.

"Hey—" I said then. "What about your real girlfriend?"

"What do you mean—'real girlfriend'?"

I gave a sharp sigh. "I think your parents might notice that I am not Kennedy Monroe."

Jack puffed out a laugh. Then he said, "My parents don't pay attention to that stuff."

"Are you saying your parents don't know you're dating Kennedy Monroe? You were on the cover of *People*! In matching sweaters!"

"It's possible."

"It's really not. Nobody doesn't know that."

Jack thought about it. Then he shrugged. "If they ask, I'll just tell them we broke up. But they won't ask. They know nothing in Hollywood is real."

Was Kennedy Monroe not real? Suddenly, I felt too shy to ask.

I tried to imagine anyone believing that Jack would downshift from Kennedy Monroe to me. Just how gullible were these parents? Were they in comas?

The sound of Robby saying there was no way I could pass echoed through my mind, and I so hated that I agreed with him.

But here we were.

Jack was still noodling on it. "I think our best option is just for you to smile a lot."

That didn't sound too hard.

"Just smile. At them. At me. Just smile until your cheeks hurt."

"Got it."

"How do you feel about me touching you?"

How did I feel about Jack Stapleton touching me? "What kind of touching are we talking about?"

"Well, the way I am around girlfriends . . . I'd say that I tend to touch them a lot. You know. If you're into someone, you just want to be touching them."

"Sure," I said.

"So, that could add some authenticity."

"Agreed."

"Would it be okay for me to hold your hand?"

Not a hard question. "Yes."

"Can I . . . drape my arm over your shoulders?"

Another nod. "That sounds acceptable."

"Can I whisper things in your ear?"

"That might depend on what you're whispering."

"Maybe it's better to ask: Is there anything you *don't* want me to do?"

"Well, I prefer you to keep your clothes on."

"That's a given," he said, "while hanging out with my parents."

"But just broadly," I said. "In general. No surprise nakedness."

"Agreed. And right back at ya."

"And I can't imagine that you'd need to kiss me . . ."

"I've already thought about that."

He'd already thought about that?

"We can use stage kissing," he said. "If we get in a pinch."

"What is stage kissing?"

"It's what you do in a play. It looks like a kiss, but your mouths don't actually touch. Like I could cup your face and then kiss my thumb." He lifted his hand off the steering wheel and kissed his thumb for demonstration.

Ah. "Okay."

"Probably shouldn't try that today."

"No."

"Those take some practice."

Practicing fake kissing with Jack Stapleton . . . "Got it." Then I added, "And obviously, of course, if you need to do a real kiss for some reason—that's fine. I mean, I'm fine with it, if it's necessary. I mean, I won't be mad."

Good God. I sounded like a loony bird.

"Noted," Jack said, moving right along as if he encountered this particular brand of looniness all the time. Which he probably did. He went on: "I guess what I'm trying to say is that I appreciate what you're doing for me—and my mom—and I don't want to make you uncomfortable."

"Thank you."

"I'll try not to make any wrong moves, but if I mess up, just tell me."

"Same," I said.

And with that, he cranked up the radio, rolled back the sunroof, and found himself a fresh piece of cinnamon gum.

Eight

THE STAPLETONS' RANCH was many long, labyrinth-like roads from the highway—deep in farm country. You had to pass fields of corn and cotton and pastures full of cows. There was even a field with real live longhorns.

When we arrived, Jack turned onto a half-mile, gravel entry road that started at a cattleguard, crossed a wide-open field, and seemed to go on forever.

"How big is this ranch, anyway?" I asked, starting to suspect that it was not small.

"Five hundred acres," he said.

The sheer size made it more real for some reason. This was an actual place. Those were genuine barbed-wire fences. Bona fide humans lived here. This was really happening.

But it didn't really happen, in the end.

We never made it to the ranch house.

I saw the house up ahead in the distance—white stucco with a red Spanish-tile roof—but halfway up the gravel entrance road, we spotted a guy out in the field who could only be Jack's brother. I don't want to call him a poor man's Jack Stapleton, but that's about right. Same jawline. Same posture. He had on brown ropers and a plaid shirt and a blue gimme cap.

"Is that your brother?" I asked.

Jack nodded. "Yep. Meet my folks' ranch manager and my own personal nemesis, Hank Stapleton."

Jack stopped the car and shifted to Park right there in the one-lane road. We watched as Hank pulled a hay bale off the back of a pickup bed and dropped it by his feet. Then he looked up and saw us.

He went still and stared. He didn't wave. He didn't walk toward us. Just pulled off his work gloves and watched us, all wary, like he'd seen a coyote or something.

And I'll tell you this: The minute those guys locked eyes, every muscle on Jack's body tightened. It was downright animalistic.

Estranged? Yeah, that about captured it.

I thought about those rumors that Kelly had never been able to confirm. The car accident. The possibility that Jack had been driving after drinking. Did Hank Stapleton seem like he might be looking at a drunk-driving manslaughterer who had covered it all up to save his career?

Sure. Why not?

He certainly wasn't looking at someone he was glad to see.

"Stay here," Jack said. And as he got out and walked into the field toward his brother, it definitely had a Shootout-at-the-O.K.-Corral vibe. I could almost hear the spaghetti-western theme music.

Were they going to have a fight out there, with Jack all sockless in a pair of Italian loafers like a city slicker?

I put my fingers on the door handle, ready to spring out if Jack needed me.

Then I waited, watching.

Was I going to eavesdrop on them?

Most definitely.

I rolled down the windows and cut the motor—and, at first, I thought I couldn't hear them. Until I realized they weren't actually talking. Unless you could call hostile silence a type of conversation.

Finally, Hank said. "I see you brought an entourage."

"Just my girlfriend."

Hank glanced my way. "That doesn't look much like Kennedy Monroe."

I cringed. No shit.

Jack shook his head. "Stop reading *People*. We broke up."

"You haven't been here in two years, and you bring some random brand-new girlfriend?"

"Trying to even up the teams."

"For the record, I don't want you here."

"For the record, I already knew that."

"Mom insisted. And Dad wants what Mom wants."

"I knew that, too."

"I don't need you making this any harder for her than it has to be."

"Agreed."

A long silence. What were they doing?

Then Hank said, "Anyway, you can head back to the city. She's not up for a visit today."

Jack looked over toward the house. Then back at Hank. "Is that her assessment or yours?"

"She's in bed with the curtains drawn, so I expect we're in agreement."

"Where's Dad?"

"He's with her."

When Jack spoke again, his voice was tight. "You could have let me know before I drove all the way out here."

A pause. "I don't have your number. Anymore."

They may have said other things after that, but I confess—I missed them.

Because right then, out of nowhere, like something out of a horror film, a giant face appeared at my open car window.

A giant, white cow face.

It was close enough that I could feel its humid, otherworldly breath washing over my skin. I don't want to say the cow snuck up on me, but let's just say the field had been empty up to that point and then suddenly—*Boom*.

What were the cow's intentions? We'll never know.

But in one second, there it was.

And one second later, the face came through the open window and licked my forearm.

With its rough, green tongue.

Maybe I screamed.

Or maybe not.

It's a blur.

I definitely made a noise of some kind, though—loud enough to get that cow, and apparently the whole herd that was right behind it, to gallop away a few steps, before seeming to run out of energy, slow to a stop, and turn to stare at me.

At this point, I, in the Range Rover, was surrounded by a whole herd of white, floppy-necked, sad-faced cows.

And I'm not going to pretend it wasn't scary.

Of course, cows aren't generally regarded as terrifying creatures. But here's what you never realize when you see them on milk cartons, or on TV, or even in some distant field: They. Are. Enormous.

They make even Jack Stapleton look small.

So even though I was safely encased in a luxury SUV, I could still feel my heart going double-time in my chest. I was surrounded by them. A hundred? A thousand? A whole hell of a lot. All with limpid black eyes, and surprisingly feminine lashes, staring point-blank into my soul.

Whatever noise I'd just made, it startled Jack, too.

At the sound, he turned and started running back toward the car—and the genuine concern I saw on his face right then only amplified my anxiety.

In my defense, here are the facts as I experienced them:

1. I was attacked by a cow.
2. Fine. I screamed.
3. Jack Stapleton came running.

Doesn't that feel like cause for concern?

At the edge of the herd, Jack slowed, adjusting into a calm saunter, but he kept his eyes on me. He entered the crowd of beasts and walked calmly among them until he'd reached the driver's door.

He climbed in.

"What happened?" he said then, looking me over, all intense.

I blinked, like *Duh*.

"Are you hurt? What was it?"

"*What was it?*" I said. "Look around!"

Jack looked around—but didn't seem to see anything. "What am I looking for?"

"What are you looking for?" I asked, and then I launched my arm in a panoramic, as if to say, *Behold. Terror in all directions.*

Now his expression was shifting. "Do you mean . . ." And then he gave the tiniest headshake, like he was rejecting the guess even as he was making it: "The cows?"

Keeping my eyes on his, I nodded.

"The *cows*?" he confirmed. "We're talking about the cows? That's why you just screamed?"

I tried to recalibrate. "In case you haven't noticed, we're fully surrounded."

"Yeah," he said. "By cows."

I could feel his tone shifting, but I wasn't sure what it was shifting to. "There are millions of them," I said.

"There are thirty," he said, "to be exact. A herd."

"Are they . . ." I didn't quite know how to put it. "Angry?"

Jack squinted a little. "Do they look angry?"

I double-checked my read on them, just baldly standing there, staring. "It feels a little aggressive."

Jack turned to me then, in fascination. "Are you afraid of these cows?"

"I'm not going to comment on that."

"You, who flipped me on my ass without even trying?"

"These cows make you look like a dollhouse person."

"But you know that cows are gentle creatures, right?"

"I've heard of people getting trampled by cows. That happens."

"Well, sure. If you trip and fall right in front of one that's already running, maybe. But on the aggression scale . . ." He tilted his head and thought about it. "Nope. They're not even on the scale."

Now I felt like I had to stand up for myself. "I wasn't the only person scared just now. You came running like a shot."

"Yeah. Because you screamed."

"Why did you think I did that?"

"I didn't know. Copperhead snake? Fire ant attack? Murder hornets? Something *scarier than cows*?"

But whose side was I going to take besides my own? I doubled down and declared: "One of them attacked me."

"Define 'attacked.'"

"It licked me. With intention."

Now he was suppressing a smile. "You mean, as if it might—what? Eat you?"

"Who knows what its endgame was?"

"'Trampled by a cow' might be a thing. '*Eaten* by a cow' is definitely not—in any way, ever—a thing."

"The point is, I was licked. By its green tongue. I didn't even know cows had green tongues."

Jack's expression got totally hijacked by amusement now. He closed his eyes, then opened them. "Cows don't have green tongues. It's the cud."

I stared at him.

"It's grass," he said. "It's regurgitated grass."

"What!" I thrashed around, trying to wipe off my already-dry arm again on my sundress.

Watching this made Jack actually laugh. He leaned forward and rested his forehead on the steering wheel, and I watched his shoulders shake.

"What?" I said. "It's legitimately disgusting."

This just made his shoulders shake harder.

"What is so funny?"

Now he leaned back against the headrest, still laughing. "You're afraid of cows."

"Um, hello? We are outnumbered." I looked around. "We are totally surrounded. I mean, what happens now? Do we just have to live here?"

But Jack just kept laughing. "I thought it would be a banana spider, at least."

"You think I'd be scared of a spider?"

"You've clearly never seen a banana spider."

"Can you just get us out of here, please?"

"Now I kind of want to stay. This could be a reality show." Then his face just relaxed into a big grin. "My money's on the cows."

I glared at him until he put the car in drive and slowly eased forward into the herd. I put my hand over my eyes, but after a second, I had to look. The herd was moving for us, stepping away, like *Whatever.*

As he turned off the gravel road and into the field, steering a bumpy and wide U-turn over ant beds and thistle bushes, Jack just kept laughing, wiping at tears with one hand and steering with the other.

"Oh God," he said finally, as we pulled back up onto the gravel, now driving away from the house, back toward town. "Thank you so much."

"What are you thanking me for?" I asked.

But Jack just shook his head in amazement. "I did *not* expect to laugh today."

Nine

BY THE TIME we made it back to Jack's house in the city, I was ready for some relief.

Everything about that trip to the country was destabilizing—from the dress I was wearing to the cow attack.

I was not going to love being undercover.

But the team had taken the day to finish outfitting the city house, and so the garage was now set up as an onsite security headquarters. More surveillance cameras were up and operational—mostly outside, around the perimeter, in spots where stalkers were most likely to lurk, supplementing the ones at his back door, the patio, and inside his front hallway.

We wouldn't be here all the time. He was only threat level yellow, after all. I'd put in a regular, twelve-hour shift and then Jack would be on his own for the night. We'd instruct him, again, to read the handbook and make good choices on his own—and we'd monitor the security cameras for significant movement. Different members of the team would be on call.

All this was standard.

Once we got back to the house, I could fall into my normal role. I changed out of the dress, which somehow felt too fluttery to allow me to do my job right, and back into a pantsuit, and then I stood just outside Jack's door in the at-ease position. Me and the fiddle-leaf fig.

The plan was this: On normal days in the city with Jack, I would be the primary agent, staying with him wherever he went during my shift. Doghouse was the secondary agent, as backup. And then there was a remote team of Taylor and Amadi doing light remote surveillance—mostly monitoring the cameras.

Kelly wasn't involved. Glenn had decided the socks with Jack's face were a dealbreaker.

Robby wasn't on the team, either. I wouldn't have expected Glenn to pass up an opportunity to force us to work together. Glenn was a big fan of punishment. Especially if he could mete it out himself.

But it wasn't my job to question him. No Robby was fine with me.

On the days that Jack and I had to visit his parents, the teams would flip: Taylor and Amadi would be primary agents, doing heavy surveillance remotely with Doghouse, and I would be secondary, a set of eyes and ears on the inside, but mostly just there to not blow my cover.

It goes without saying that I preferred being primary.

I also preferred being able to do my job right.

How exactly was I supposed to compete for London, if all I could do was stand around in a cotton dress?

Being back in town felt good. Standing guard at a front door is not always the most thrilling use of time, but compared to feeling useless while being menaced by cattle, it was surprisingly comforting.

At one point, Jack popped his head out to see if I'd like a cappuccino.

I didn't meet his eyes. "No, thank you."

"You sure?"

"Don't break my concentration."

Toward the end of my shift, Taylor and Robby showed up at the property to make a few notes on the garden layout.

"What are you doing here?" I said to Robby. "You're not on this assignment."

"*Everybody's* on this assignment," Robby said. "This is a team effort. We're a team."

"That's not how it usually works."

"We don't usually have clients this famous."

IT WAS ALMOST time for me to punch out, and Taylor and Robby had been gone a while, when I decided to give the surveillance cameras one more check. We had the monitor set up at a makeshift desk, but I didn't even sit in the rolling chair. I just leaned in to scroll through the camera views—just for a quick all-clear before heading home—when I noticed something on the monitor.

Down in the corner of "Pool 1" camera view I saw what looked like a pants leg and part of a shoe.

All my hackles went up. I enhanced the image to get a better look, and then I adjusted the camera angle to the right.

And that's when I saw something I never, ever would've expected to see.

In Jack Stapleton's garden, out by the pool house, partially hidden behind a Palmetto tree . . . Robby, my ex, and Taylor, my friend . . .

Were kissing.

Each other.

Robby . . . who had dumped me a month ago on the night after my mother's funeral . . . and Taylor . . . who had come over right afterward to console me while I cried . . .

Were kissing.

And worse than that: *on the job.*

There's no way to describe how it felt to live through that moment. My eyes tried to look away but could only stare, *Clockwork Orange*–style, as the two of them went on and on, all tangled and pressed together, sucking face like hateful teenagers.

Remember when I couldn't feel any feelings about Robby?

Well, that cured that.

The closest word I have for it is panic. Just an agonizing, urgent feeling that I needed to turn it off, or make it stop, or find some way for it to *not be happening*. Then add some rage. And some humiliation. And disbelief, too—as I tried, and failed, to understand what I was seeing.

It was a physical feeling—burning and searing, like my heart was pumping acid instead of blood.

Up until that moment, I didn't even know that feeling existed.

At some point—*Five minutes later? Five hours?*—I heard a voice over my shoulder. "They should get fired for that, huh?"

I turned. It was Jack Stapleton, his eyes on the monitor.

As I looked at him, he looked at me, and his expression shifted from amusement to concern. "Hey," he said. "Are you okay?"

But I didn't know what to do with my face. It was like the muscles didn't work right. My eyes stayed wide and bewildered, and my mouth couldn't seem to close itself.

Jack certainly didn't know how universe-shattering this moment was for me, and the last thing I wanted was for him to find out. I wanted to cover. To smile and shake my head and say, "idiots," like they were just dumb coworkers who I was judging for fooling around on the job.

But I couldn't smile. Or shake my head. Or speak.

What was Jack even doing here, anyway? Shouldn't he be inside doing movie star stuff?

And then I realized something else, as Jack pulled the cuff of his shirtsleeve over the heel of his hand, lifted it to my face, and started dabbing at my cheeks.

I was crying.

My eyes were, at least. Without my permission.

After a few dabs, Jack pulled his hand away to show me how the wetness had darkened his cuff, and, with a tender voice I remembered from the grand finale of *You Wish*, he said, "What's going on here?"

At last, I shook my head. A historic achievement, all things considered.

Activating the neck muscles seemed to release the jaw muscles as well, and I was able to close my gaping mouth. With that, I became functional enough to look away.

"Are you crying?" Jack asked, trying to step around.

Of course I was. Obviously I was. But I shook my head.

"I thought you were a tough guy."

"I already told you: I'm not."

"I believe you now," Jack said.

"It's allergies," I insisted.

But I didn't even sound convincing to myself.

"What are you allergic to? Your coworkers kissing by my infinity pool?"

I should have gone with "pollen." Right? A classic.

But instead, as my brain short-circuited, I felt that acid bleeding out from my heart and saturating me from the inside. What was I allergic to? I was allergic to disappointment. I was allergic to betrayal. I was allergic to friendship. To hope. To optimism. To life, to work, to humanity in general.

And so just I answered with, "I'm allergic to everything," and I walked out of the garage.

Jack let me leave, which was a relief.

I didn't want to talk, or process, or explore my feelings, for God's sake—and even if I had wanted to do any of those things, I would never in a million years have done them with him.

You don't talk about your life with clients.

You just don't.

You wind up knowing everything about your principals—but they never know anything about you. And that's how it has to be.

But here's the thing: The clients never understand that. It feels so much like a real relationship, it's hard to keep it clear. You're traveling together, going to bars together, skiing together, hanging out at the beach together. You're there for their ups and downs, their fights, and their secrets. Your purpose in their lives is to create security so they can feel normal.

If you're doing a good job, they do feel normal.

But *you* never do.

You never lose sight of your purpose. And part of keeping that focus is knowing—backward, forward, inside out, and upside down—that they are not your friends.

Friends might wipe the tears off your face with their shirtsleeves, but clients never should.

Which is why I had never once in eight years cried in front of a client. Until today.

You have to maintain professional distance, or you can't do your job. And the only way to do that while spending every minute of every shift together is to never, ever share anything personal. Clients ask personal questions all the time. You just don't answer. You pretend you didn't hear, or you change the subject, or—most effective of all—you turn the question back on itself.

The answer to "Are you scared?" should be "Are *you* scared?"

The answer to "Do you have a boyfriend?" should be "Do *you* have a boyfriend?"

See how easy that is? Works every time.

And what's more? They never even notice.

Because mostly, when people ask you about you, what they really want to talk about is them.

Right?

It's hard to describe the maelstrom of emotions churning around inside me as I made my way out to the driveway with the singular goal of getting to my car and heading home. Shock, agony, humiliation—all there, sure. But add to that: a sense of deep disappointment at letting myself get caught by a client in a real moment of emotion.

Was there a way to recover?

He'd seen the tears, yes. But he couldn't know for sure exactly what they meant.

I'd go home, regroup, and then—only then—if there was time and I was so inclined, would I let myself think about what I'd just witnessed.

Or maybe not.

Because if I just witnessed what I thought I did, it meant that in one short month, I'd lost every single one of the three most important people in my life.

Mother. Boyfriend. Best friend.

And now I was truly alone.

The realization threatened to bring me to my knees.

I had to get out of there. I had to make it to my car.

But that's when Robby—not even on the team—showed up again a few feet away.

He stopped walking when he saw me, and I did the same back to him.

"Oh, hey," he said.

Could he see my face? Could he tell that I knew?

"Shift's over," I said, maxing out the syllables I could access. "Heading home."

"Great. Yeah. I think we're good here."

I put my head back down to keep walking.

"Hey—" Robby said then, taking a few steps fast, like he was going to intercept me. "Can I talk to you about something?"

"Nope," I said.

"Just for a minute," he said, surprised at my answer.

"You're not even supposed to be here, Robby. Don't make me report you to Glenn."

"Thirty seconds." Was he *bargaining*?

"I'm tired," I said, shaking my head.

But now Robby jumped around to fully block me. "It's kind of important."

Was I going to have to fight him? For God's sake, I just wanted to go home. "Not today," I said, starting to gird my strength for whatever I needed to do to *not have this conversation*.

But that's when Robby looked up right behind me, and then I felt a weight settling on my shoulder.

It was Jack Stapleton. Draping his arm around me, as I'd already given him permission to do.

"She's pretty tired, Bobby," Jack said, pulling me sideways against him in a squeeze.

"It's Robby," Robby said.

"I'm getting a vibe like she really just wants to go home right now," Jack went on. "Maybe it's from the *words she's saying.*"

Robby, of course, couldn't go against the client.

He looked at me, but I looked away.

"You're not going to make her report you to Glenn, are you?" Jack turned to me. "Or if you're too busy, I could do it."

I felt more than saw Robby's shoulders drop in defeat.

Jack gave it another second, as if to say "Are we done here?" And then, decisively, he steered me down the driveway toward my car, leaving Robby staring after us.

Later, in an effort to get Robby in trouble, I'd report everything but the kissing to Glenn.

And it would backfire.

I'd say, "Robby just showed up here for no reason and inserted himself into the assignment."

And Glenn would say, "That's a great idea."

I'd frown. "What is?"

"Putting Robby on this assignment."

"No, I—"

"I'm still deciding between the two of you for London, you know," Glenn would say.

Of course I knew.

"Anyway, he's the best we've got for video surveillance. And you know I never want to miss a chance to torture anyone."

"Haven't you tortured me enough?"

A wink from Glenn. "I meant him."

Was Glenn clueless? A sadist?

Little bit of both, maybe.

Either way, he added Robby to the team—and gave me the credit.

But that night, as Jack fished around in my purse for my keys and then hit the unlock button, I didn't see any of that coming yet. I didn't see much, really—other than what was right in front of me: Jack guiding me to the passenger side, opening the door, sitting me down, and leaning across me to buckle me in.

He smelled like cinnamon.

Again: not something I'd normally let a client do.

But so little about this assignment was normal.

When Jack walked around to the driver's side, got in, and started the car, I didn't stop him.

As we pulled away from his house, I mustered a weak, "What are you doing?"

"I'm taking you home."

"But how will you get back?"

"I'll borrow your car," he said, "and come back to get you in the morning."

Jack Stapleton was offering to pick me up in the morning? "That seems like a lot of work."

"What else do I have to do these days?"

"Your profile says you are a late sleeper. Like noon-to-afternoon late."

"I can set an alarm." Then a pause. "Was that guy your boyfriend?"

"Was that guy *your* boyfriend?"

Ugh. I was too haywire to do it right.

Jack frowned and tried again. "You weren't dating that guy, were you?"

"I'm not going to talk about this with you."

"Why not?"

I leaned my head back against the seat and closed my eyes. "Because I don't talk about my life with clients."

Even just telling a client that I didn't talk about my life with clients was more than I'd ever told a client.

Another tactical error, for sure—but I was too numb to care.

"Just tell me that guy is not your boyfriend."

"That guy is not my boyfriend," I repeated mechanically. And then I don't know if it was just some meaningless sparking in my short-circuiting brain, or a new comprehension that following the rules didn't seem to get you anywhere, or a hunch that maybe nothing really mattered, after all . . . but two seconds later, I added, "Anymore."

Ten

I MADE MY acting debut with Jack's family the next day at the hospital.

By accident.

But first, we had to sneak him in.

His mother had a VIP room where Jack could wait during her surgery, so the day should have been easy.

The plan was to get him to the room unnoticed—early, by six that morning—so he could see his mom before they wheeled her out. Then he'd wait there until the surgery was over, while Doghouse and I monitored the hospital halls and the rest of the team snuck out to the Stapletons' ranch to install a few secret security cameras. Things on our end were simple. All Jack had to do was stay in that room.

"You can't leave the room," I explained on the drive over.

"At all?"

"Just stay in the room. It's not hard."

"Isn't that a little much?" Jack asked.

"If you'd read the handout—" I started.

"I'm not a handouts guy."

"This is a high-threat situation," I went on. "There are multiple opportunities for you to be seen, recognized, photographed—"

"I get it."

"Once you're seen here, everything gets harder. So just do what you're told."

"Got it," Jack said. Then he added, "You should know I'm already good at this, though."

I looked over.

He said, "I bet the oil guys you usually protect aren't used to hiding. But I've been making myself invisible for years."

"That can't be easy," I said. "Being you."

"There are tricks. Baseball caps are surprisingly effective. Glasses seem to break up people's pattern-matching. Not making eye contact helps, too. If you don't look at people, they tend not to look at you. Though the big thing is to just keep moving. Just keep going. As soon as you break stride, they see you."

"You do know more than my average oil executive," I said, letting my voice sound impressed.

"See? And I didn't even read the handout."

I glanced over at him. He was doing it all: the baseball cap, and the glasses, plus a gray button-down. But even trying to look as unremarkable as possible, he still just . . . glowed.

"Those execs have a big advantage over you, though," I said.

"What's that?"

"Nobody cares about them except me and the bad guys."

Then Jack narrowed his eyes and studied me. "Do you care about them?"

"I mean, sort of," I said.

"That sounds like a no."

"I care about doing my job right."

"But you don't care about the people you're protecting."

I shouldn't be saying any of this. Where was my head? "Not in the traditional sense, no."

Jack nodded and thought about it.

Did he *want* me to care about him? What a strange expectation. "Caring about people actually makes it harder to do a good job," I said then, in my own defense.

"I get it," Jack said.

Anyway, he wasn't wrong about himself. He *was* good at this. He knew exactly how to move through a space without being spotted. We brought him in through a delivery entrance and up the service elevator. The hallway was deserted, and Doghouse and I saw him make it to the door and disappear through it without a hitch.

That was one huge hurdle cleared. The doctors and nurses on his mom's team had signed nondisclosure agreements. Now all Jack had to do was stay there.

But he didn't stay there.

Just before lunch, after I'd stood at the end of the hallway long enough to know there were 207 floor tiles from edge to edge, I saw Jack walk out of the room and start meandering off down the hallway, like he was headed to the nurses' station.

"Hey!" I shout-whispered. "What are you doing?"

But Jack didn't turn.

What was he thinking? Hadn't we just talked about this? He couldn't just wander loose.

I trotted after him. "Hey! Hey! What are you doing? Hey! We talked about this! You're not supposed to leave the—"

Right then, I caught up, and I grabbed his forearm, and he turned to look at me . . .

And it wasn't Jack.

It was his brother. Hank.

"Oh!" I said, the second I saw his face—dropping his arm and stepping back.

Shit.

Now that I saw him, Hank was clearly not Jack. Hank was an inch or so shorter. And a little bit broader. And his hair was a shade or two darker. His sideburns were shorter. And none of those details should have escaped me.

If I'm honest, the smell of the hospital, and the lighting, too, reminded me of when my own mother was sick—which wasn't all that long ago—and it had me slightly off my game.

Hank Stapleton was staring at me. "Did you just tell me I can't leave the room?"

"I'm sorry," I said. "I thought you were Jack."

Hank tilted his head. "Can *Jack* not leave the room?"

What to say? "He wasn't planning on it," I said. "No."

Hank tilted his head. "And who are you?"

"I'm Hannah," I said, hoping we could leave it at that.

Apparently not. He shook his head and frowned, like *Is that supposed to mean something?*

And then I did what I had to do. I said, "I'm Jack's girlfriend." But I swear it felt like the biggest, fakest, most unconvincing lie in the world.

But here's the surprise miracle: He bought it.

"Oh, sure," Hank said, looking me over, remembering. "The one who's afraid of cows."

How did he know that? Did my scream give it away?

He went on. "Did you come to see my mom?"

My head started nodding as my stomach turned cold. I wasn't ready. I hadn't prepared to meet the family. I wasn't even wearing my girlfriend clothes. But there wasn't another answer. "Yes."

"She just woke up," Hank said. "I'm going for ice chips."

"I'll get them," I offered, wanting to get him back into the room. He wasn't Jack, but he was close enough to make trouble.

Plus, I needed a minute to regroup.

"You go on back," I said. "I brought flowers, but I forgot them in the car. So—ice chips. Next best thing."

Flimsy. But he shrugged and said, "Okay."

On the way to the nurses' station, I explained it all to Doghouse's earpiece. "I'm going in," I said. Then, ice chips in hand, I started toward

Connie Stapleton's room—but I paused when I caught my reflection in the chrome elevator doors.

Did I look like a girlfriend? *Anybody's*, even?

It was hopeless, but I tried *zhuzh*-ing myself a little bit, anyway. I took off my jacket and hid it behind a potted plant. I rolled my sleeves and unbuttoned the top button of my blouse. I unwrapped my hair from its bun and shook it out to fluff it. I popped my collar for a second before deciding I was too nervous to pull that off.

I'd just have to make it work.

I mentally reviewed what I knew about Jack's parents from the file. Dad: William Gentry Stapleton, a veterinarian, now retired. Went by Doc. Widely beloved by all who knew him. Once rescued a newborn calf from a flooded oxbow lake. Married to Connie Jane Stapleton, retired school principal, for over thirty years. High school sweethearts. They'd spent five years in the Peace Corps, rescued homeless horses, belonged to a recreational swing-dancing club, and were, by all accounts, good people.

I knocked on the door, and then I opened it as I said, redundantly, "Knock, knock."

The three Stapleton men were seated around Connie Stapleton's bed in chairs they'd pulled close. She was sitting up a little, wearing a dab of lipstick with her feathery white hair neatly brushed—and looking somehow more put-together than a postsurgery patient in a hospital gown had any right to.

She could have pulled off a popped collar. If she'd had a collar to pop.

At the sight of them—live, actual people—I started overthinking it. What kind of expression would Jack's girlfriend have on her face? *Warmhearted? Concerned?* What did those expressions even look like? How did you arrange your features? How did actors even do this?

I settled on a half smile, half frown and hoped it was convincing.

Jack must have read my panic because he popped up and strode right toward me. "Hey, babe," he said in a pitch-perfectly affectionate voice. "I didn't know you were coming."

"I brought some ice," I said.

Jack was looking at me, like *I thought you were staying in the hallway.*

I just blinked at him, like *Change in plan.*

He could tell I was nervous.

That must've been why he kissed me.

A stage kiss, but still.

He walked right up to me without breaking stride, cupped both hands on either side of my jaw, leaned in, and planted a not-insignificant kiss on his own thumb.

And then he . . . lingered there.

His hands were warm. He smelled like cinnamon. I could feel his breath feathering the peach fuzz on my cheek.

I was so shocked, I didn't breathe. I was so shocked, I didn't even close my eyes. I can still see the whole thing in slo-mo. That epic face coming closer and closer, and that legendary mouth aiming right for mine and then docking itself on that legendary thumb, stationed right at the corner.

Technically, it was not a real kiss.

But it was pretty damn close.

For me, anyway.

As he pulled back, my knees wavered a little. Did he know I was going to swoon? It was like he sensed it coming. Maybe that's what happened to every woman he kissed—real or fake. He latched his arm around my waist, and by the time he said, "I'd like you all to meet my girlfriend, Hannah," he was basically holding me up.

They took in the sight of us.

"Hello," I said weakly, sagging against him, but lifting my free hand in a little wave.

Did I expect them not to believe it?

I mean, maybe. It was so patently obvious that we were two totally different categories of people. If they'd thrown their newspapers and reading glasses at me and shouted, "Get outta here!" I wouldn't have been surprised.

But that's when Jack said, "Isn't she cute?" and gave me a noogie on the head.

Next, Hank swooped over to take the ice chips. "She brought your ice chips, Mom."

On the heels of that, Doc Stapleton—looking gentlemanly, pressed, and neat in a blue oxford and khakis—took my hand, patted it, and said, "Hello, sweetheart. Come take my chair."

I shook my head. "I can stand."

"She's adorable," Connie Stapleton said, and her voice just pulled me toward her with its warmth. Then she reached for my hand, and when I took hers, it was soft like powder. She squeezed, and I squeezed back. "Finally. Someone real," she said then.

And suddenly, I knew what to do with my face. I smiled.

"Yes," Connie said, looking over at Jack. "I like this one already."

Just the way she said it—with such full, unearned affection—made me feel a little bashful.

Connie met my eyes. "Is Jack sweet to you?"

What could I say? "Very sweet," I answered.

"He's good-hearted," she said. "Just don't let him cook."

I nodded. "Got it."

Next, she asked the boys to help her sit up better. She was a little nauseated and a little dizzy, so they took it slow. But she was determined. When she was ready, she looked at all the faces around her bed. "Listen—" she said, like she was about to start an important topic.

But that's when her oncologist walked in.

We all stood to greet him—and he definitely did a double take when he saw Jack, like he'd been told to expect a famous actor in that room, but he hadn't really believed it.

"Hey, Destroyer," the doctor said with a little sideways grin. "Thanks for saving humanity."

"Thanks for saving my mom," Jack said, graciously nudging us back toward reality.

The doctor nodded and checked his clipboard. "The margins around the edges of the tumor were negative," she said. "Which means it was very self-contained."

"That's great, Mom," Jack said.

"That means no chemo," the doctor went on. "We'll still have to do radiation, but that's not for eight weeks, after the surgery's all healed. Right now, it's about just resting, and staying hydrated, and following the discharge instructions." He turned to Connie. "We'll get you on the radiation schedule, and then everybody can take a breath until it's time to start that up."

What everybody wanted him to say was that she was fine—that she'd be fine.

Finally, Jack did it. "Is the prognosis . . . ?"

The doctor nodded. "The prognosis is pretty good, though no guarantees. If the site heals well, after her course of radiation she's got a good chance of being okay."

Jack and Hank, standing right next to each other, let out matching sighs.

You'd never know they were mortal enemies.

The doctor gave some more details, pulled a privacy curtain while he examined the site, then reemerged, saying, "I almost forgot the most important thing."

We all stood at attention. "What's that?"

The doctor pointed right at Jack. "Can I get a selfie?"

ONCE HE WAS gone, Connie Stapleton got down to business.

"I'm not going to ask you to stay for the radiation, Jack," she said.

"Mom. I can stay."

"It doesn't start for eight weeks. You need to get back to your life."

"Mom, I don't—"

She shook her head, cutting him off. "But I am going to ask you for something else."

Now Jack narrowed his eyes like he should've seen that coming. "What's that?"

She paused.

We waited.

"It's been a hard few years for us. For all of us. And I'd like some good time with you before you go."

Jack nodded. "I'd like that, too."

"So here it is," she went on. "I don't know how much more time I have left on this earth. Getting cancer really clears a few things up in your head, and after much soul-searching, I've decided there is one thing, only one thing, that I truly want right now, and I need you all to make it happen."

"This sounds like a big ask," Hank said.

"What is it, sweetheart?" Dr. Stapleton asked, leaning in.

That's when Connie gave us the most irresistible, *there's literally no way you can possibly refuse me* smile and said, "I want Jack—and his cute new girlfriend—to come stay with us out at the ranch until Thanksgiving."

Eleven

"FOUR WEEKS!" WAS all I could say on the drive back to Jack's house. "There are *four weeks* until Thanksgiving!"

"Technically," Jack pointed out, "it's three and a half."

I ignored him. "I can't spend four weeks doing things I *like* to do, much less pretending to be your girlfriend."

"Thanks for that."

"You know what I mean."

"It's her dying wish," Jack pointed out.

"She's not dying," I said.

"She's *probably* not dying."

"We're *all* probably not dying. You could get hit by a bus tomorrow."

"I'm not thrilled about this, either. But it kind of simplifies things. It gives us a clear end point. Four weeks, and we're done. I go back to North Dakota, you go . . . wherever it is you go."

"Korea, thank you." Even just at the idea of it, I felt a flash of relief. The timing was good, actually. The Seoul assignment started up in early December.

"This could have lingered on and on. This is objectively better. It's like ripping off the bandage."

"Ripping off the bandage," I corrected, "for *four weeks*."

"Three and a half. Let's talk to your boss."

"I already know what Glenn's going to say. He's going to say I can't deny her this request. That it's not that big of a deal. That the remote teams can handle everything—especially if we're in an isolated location like the ranch. He's going to call it 'practically a paid vacation' and demand to know why, exactly, it's unacceptable to have to lounge around at the country residence of a world-famous movie star. He'll say there are worse fates than being trapped in a remote location with a beautiful man."

If Jack noticed me calling him "beautiful," he played it cool. "And what will you say?"

I closed my eyes. "I don't know."

"He's not wrong, you know. The ranch is great. There's an orchard, and a hammock, and a wilderness area near the oxbow lake. We can hunt fossils on the banks of the Brazos, and ride the retired circus horse, and go fishing. It *would* be like a paid vacation."

"I don't like vacations," I said.

"It really wouldn't be like work, is what I mean."

"I like work. I prefer work."

"You could relax."

"I never relax."

"I just mean there are worse things than being trapped there with me."

"I'm sure you're delightful, it's just—"

"That sounded sarcastic."

"Look—"

"I know it's a strange ask."

"It's not strange, it's impossible."

"You saw her back there. That's my *mom*, Hannah."

It was so strange to hear my name come out of Jack Stapleton's mouth, it threw me off for a second. I tried to regroup. He clearly thought if he asked sweetly enough, I'd just do this for him. Or maybe if he paid me enough money. This was a guy who probably got everything he wanted. If he didn't understand why this couldn't happen, I didn't know how to explain it. I finally settled on, "I don't know you."

"I'm not so bad."

"I just can't."

"Are you saying no?"

Did anyone ever say no to Jack Stapleton? "Yes. I'm saying no."

Jack frowned at that, like it was a really novel concept.

He looked so bewildered, in fact, that as I studied his profile, I questioned myself.

I *was* saying no, wasn't I?

I mean, *four weeks*! That was a long time to never come up for air. There would be no way to do any of my usual work stuff in that scenario. I'd just have to wear girlfriend clothes and do girlfriend things and be . . . trapped behind that facade. I couldn't be that passive. I'd been stuck in limbo for so long. I needed to work, and I needed to do my job, and then I needed to be done and get out of here. With each coping mechanism this situation took away, I was dying a little more.

I could feel my shark gills gasping.

I needed to make my world bigger, not smaller. I needed to go far away, not get further trapped in this same spot. I needed to resuscitate my real life, not double down on a fake one.

Time to shut this conversation down.

"We can talk to Glenn," I said, "but it's still a no."

"IT'S A YES," Glenn said, even after I vociferously, passionately, and very articulately objected to Connie Stapleton's wishes.

We met in the security HQ in Jack's garage. The whole team showed up—including Robby now—except for Taylor.

Who I hadn't seen since I'd watched her smooching my ex-boyfriend. And who I would happily never see again, if I could swing it.

But that was something to obsess over later.

Right now I was busy fighting a losing battle.

It wasn't that my opinion didn't matter. It just didn't matter more than anybody else's.

"Think of it like a paid vacation," Glenn said.

"You say that like it's a good thing."

"I don't see that there's a decision to be made here," Amadi said. "She took the job. The situation has evolved. But that doesn't change our responsibility toward the principal."

"I didn't take the job on purpose," I said.

"That's a lot of negativity right there," Doghouse said.

"I signed up to protect him, not live with him," I said.

Kelly was positively offended by my hesitation. "Do you know how many people would sell their souls to live in that gorgeous ranch house for a month with Jack Stapleton? It was featured in *House Beautiful*."

"What am I supposed to do for four weeks if I have to stay in character twenty-four seven?"

"Umm . . ." Kelly said. "Enjoy it?"

I argued and argued, but I couldn't convince them how suffocating this would be for me. Everybody, without exception, thought it sounded *fun*.

The consensus really did solidify pretty fast: I was being ridiculous. I needed to appreciate my good fortune. And suck it up. And stop whining.

In the face of all that unanimousness, there really wasn't much I could say.

Glenn was loving it, too. "This is your chance to show me your stuff for London," he said.

But it wasn't funny. This was my life. "What stuff?" I demanded. "Nothing about this will show anybody any stuff! It's just forced seclusion with—"

"The Sexiest Man Alive," Kelly finished.

Glenn thought it was all endlessly funny. "Strategy, flexibility, innovation," he said then, to answer my question. "Plus, maybe most crucial: that all-important leadership quality of being willing to take one for the team."

"Fine," I said. But I let myself pout a little.

"Be nice to poor Jack," Glenn finally said. "He can't help it that he's handsome."

AFTER FINALLY LOSING the argument spectacularly in a vote of everybody-else-to-one, I decided to step out for some air.

I needed a minute.

And that's when, out in the circular drive, I ran into Taylor—arriving late.

She slowed to a stop when she saw me. Now that I knew the situation, her body language was unmistakable: The downcast eyes of guilt. The tight shoulders of shame. The shallow breaths of betrayal.

How had I missed it before?

I'd been blinded by warmth and trust and affection. By the idea of what a friend should be.

It's so easy to see what you expect to see.

I narrowed my eyes into a glare, but it was too dark for her to notice.

"What are you doing here?" I asked.

"Uh. Coming to work?"

"You're late."

"Yeah. Traffic."

"Is that a lie?"

"A lie? No. There was traffic."

I could hear it in her voice now. She knew something was up.

"Everybody's inside," I said, tipping my head toward the garage. "In the surveillance room. The room where we monitor all the surveillance footage."

She frowned. She could tell I was trying to say something more than I'd said. "Except you," she said, like that might be a clue.

Dead end. "I'm taking a break." I gave her another shot. "But I have spent a lot of time in that surveillance room. Surveilling things."

"Well, yeah. You're the primary, so—"

"It's amazing what those cameras can catch. Things you would never—in a million years, if you lived your whole life over and over again—expect to see."

And then she knew.

I saw it the second the comprehension hit her. The little zap of shock in her eyes.

"Do you mean . . ." she said.

"You." I confirmed with a nod. "And Robby."

"Oh."

"Yeah."

"That . . . that—"

"That's what happened in Madrid?"

She hesitated. Which was fascinating. Because there was no weaseling out of anything now. Finally, she said, "Yeah." Then, as if she could redeem herself, "But by accident!"

I knew it already, of course. And I thought seeing it would be the worst of it.

But I was wrong.

The confirmation was the worst of it.

"So, all those times I called you and cried over my broken heart . . . you were dating the person who broke it?"

Taylor looked down. "At first, we weren't really dating."

"Just sleeping together."

"But not on purpose. Not entirely."

There wasn't a point in even talking about it. I just wanted her to know that I knew. Then we could all be in agreement that she was a terrible person.

But then she said, "Technically, you were broken up."

I frowned. "What?"

"We didn't cheat on you, is what I'm saying. Technically."

I refused to dignify that with a response.

"I'm sorry. I really am sorry. It just happened. We didn't know how to tell you."

"It just happened?"

"You know how it is on assignment."

"Yes, I definitely do. Specifically with Robby."

"We weren't trying to hurt you."

Again with the "we." *We, we, we.* "Do you not understand the . . . the . . ." I couldn't think of words that captured it. Finally, I went with, "the *emotional atrocity* you just committed?"

"We're not talking about war crimes."

"You looted our friendship. You firebombed the trust I had in you. You nuked my faith in humanity. You're the Enola Gay of best friends."

Maybe I was overstating it a bit. But I didn't back down, even after it occurred to me that this conversation was not that different from how we talked when we were laughing. The one big difference, now, of course, being the white-hot hatred.

I had a real question, though. "Do you not understand what you did," I asked, "or are you pretending not to?" I stared her down, waiting. "I'll hate you forever, either way," I went on. "But in one case, I'll hate you for being stupid, and in the other, I'll hate you for being selfish."

Taylor looked down.

"Never mind. I know the answer. It's 'selfish.' Nobody's that stupid. Not even you." I thought it might feel good to say something mean. But it didn't.

"Look—"

"I hope he's worth it," I said. "You just forfeited our entire friendship. You just gave up every movie night, every margarita Friday, every goofy GIF exchange, every sleepover, every Galentine's Day, every fantasy road trip, every hug, and every atom of admiration, warmth, and affection you could ever have had with me. Right? You gave up borrowing my jeans with the rainbow pockets. You gave up book recommendations, and homemade birthday cards, and late-night tacos. And you gave up the best next-door neighbor ever, too, because I'm definitely moving out."

I could feel my voice shaking.

I was trying to make her feel bad, listing everything she'd just lost. But of course, I had lost it all, too.

"And you *knew*," I went on. "You knew he was terrible. You knew what he did to me—how he abandoned me right after I lost my mom."

I took a long, trembling breath. "That's what kills me. You gave it all up—every nourishing thing we had . . . not just for a man, but for a *bad* man."

"I'm sorry," Taylor said.

"I don't care."

"I don't want to lose you," Taylor said, her voice trembling now, too.

"He's going to leave you," I said. "He's left every woman he's ever been with. Did you know that? He's always the dumper—never the dumpee. And then you'll come to me and beg me to forgive you, but I won't. You want to know why? Because I can't. Because certain broken things can never be repaired."

I was ready for that to be my exit line. I was ready to abandon her there in the driveway with only the echo of those words remaining. I started to walk away.

But she called after me, "You're wrong."

I turned back.

"He's not going to leave me. He dumped all those other women because he hadn't found the right one."

Wow. The hubris. "You think you're the one?"

"I know for sure that you weren't."

Oof.

And here, right here, is the trouble with being close to other people. The better they know you, the better they can hurt you.

"He never loved you," she said then, "because you wouldn't let him."

How dare she side with him? "You have no idea what you're talking about."

"Ask him sometime. He tried."

It didn't surprise me that Robby tried to make himself out to be the victim. But it did surprise me that Taylor would believe him.

She must have really needed to see me as the problem.

Then she shrugged and fixed her eyes on mine. "You're so sure it's all Robby's fault."

"Yeah! And you should be, too!"

"But you won't see your part in it."

How was this happening? She was supposed to stand up for me. She was supposed to feel outraged and wronged on my behalf. That's what best friends were *for*.

"How can you do this?" I asked, my voice sinking. "You were my best friend."

But Taylor shook her head. "I was never your best friend. I was your work friend. And the fact that you don't know the difference? That's your whole problem right there."

Twelve

ANYHOO.

That's how I wound up moving to Jack Stapleton's parents' five-hundred-acre cattle ranch—against all my better judgment.

Not that I had a choice.

But compared to living next door to Taylor, it suddenly didn't seem so bad.

Compared to staying in our fourplex with its papier-mâché walls, eating cereal in my kitchen, and listening to Robby and The Worst Person Ever making waffles on the other side, compared to overhearing the two of them watching horror movies on her sofa, or ordering takeout, or going at it all night in her bedroom . . . compared to all that, moving in with The Destroyer was definitely an upgrade.

I called my landlord *from the car* after that fight with Taylor to cancel my lease.

I'd find a new place online and rent it sight unseen. I'd hire movers to pack up my entire apartment, dirty laundry and all, and haul it away.

I'd leave on assignment, and then I'd never set foot in that apartment again.

And I'd make sure my next rental had a working fireplace so I could unpack, find all the things Taylor had given me over the years—the Wonder Woman T-shirt, the journal with the YOU ARE MAGIC glitter cover, the picture book of the world's cutest hedgehogs—and throw them in the fire one by one to burn them all to ashes.

A purge. A cleansing. A new frigging start.

THE MORNING JACK and I moved out to the Stapletons' ranch, it was Jack who was in a bad mood.

Like *he* was the one who'd earned one.

Gone was that aggressively nonchalant vibe he wore most of the time like a cologne. His shoulders were tense as he drove, his jaw was tight, and his blood pressure—I swear, I could read it from across the car—was elevated.

He barely even spoke to me the entire drive.

It was the loudest quiet I'd ever heard.

It was only then, on the interstate, in Jack's passenger seat, that I realized Taylor had done me a favor, in a way: She had turned going to Jack's ranch into a kind of escape.

It wasn't the escape I'd been wanting.

But it would do for now.

That realization brightened my mood quite a bit.

By the time we got to the Brazos bridge, and Jack got out to walk across, he looked almost nauseated. And by the time we pulled up to the house itself, the air around him was positively brittle with misery.

An escape for me. But maybe the opposite for him.

Though Kelly hadn't been kidding about *House Beautiful*. It was a 1920's Spanish-style hacienda with a red-tiled roof and pink bougainvillea blossoming everywhere. We parked on the gravel drive, and as I stepped out of the car a breeze brushed past us and fluttered the sundress around my bare knees.

It felt nice, actually.

I guess girlfriend clothes had their perks.

"It's so idyllic," I said, of the house.

Jack didn't comment.

But that whole "think of it like a paid vacation" thing?

I could suddenly see it.

This wasn't where Jack had grown up. He later told me that his grandparents lived here when he was little, but after they were gone, it became a weekend place. His parents had only moved out full time after they'd retired, and that's when his mom started the garden, and his dad had converted half of the old barn into a woodworking shop.

I'm pretty sure Jack didn't speak even one unnecessary word as he walked me around and gave me the tour.

I was totally charmed by the stucco walls, exposed ceiling beams, rounded doorways, red ceramic-tile floor, and his mom's collection of chicken figurines on the breakfront. Plus, the decorative painted tiles in the bathrooms and in the kitchen. Windows everywhere, and sunlight, and bougainvillea blossoms in every view. There was a garden that seemed to go on forever near a side porch draped with honeysuckle, and a screened porch bigger than a living room off the other side. It was like an enchanted place from another time.

It was a late October day, and all the windows were open. The kitchen had cotton gingham café curtains, and a bread box, and an old-timey radio on the counter. There were salt and pepper shakers in the shapes of ears of corn at the table. Jack's dad kept a record player on the counter at the far end of the kitchen, and Jack opened up the cabinets above it to show me—instead of dishes, like you might expect—his massive record collection, arranged by decade.

I mean, the whole situation was charming.

Except, maybe, for Jack.

I followed him through a long living room, with three sofas arranged around a giant stucco fireplace, and then into a hallway that led to the bedrooms.

The hallway was covered—absolutely wallpapered—with framed family photos. And half of them, at least, were of three boys, smiling big and goofy into camera after camera.

Jack and I both stopped at the sight.

Like neither of us had ever seen it before.

I touched a photo of a young Jack up on a young Hank's shoulders—while Hank held their youngest brother upside down by his ankles. "This is you and your brothers?" I asked.

Jack nodded, his eyes traveling around the wall.

"Looks like you had a lot of fun."

Jack nodded again.

Then he said, so quiet I could barely hear, "I haven't been here since the funeral."

Jack kept his eyes on the photos, so I did, too.

Most of them were snapshots. The boys as toddlers running in a field of bluebonnets. Down at the beach in the waves. Eating puffs of cotton candy bigger than their heads. Then, older: Tall and skinny in football uniforms. Doing matching handstands. Dangling fish at the ends of poles. On horseback. At the top of a ski slope. Playing cards. Shooting baskets. Dressed up for prom. Hamming it up.

Totally ordinary.

And so heartbreaking.

Just as I found myself thinking I could admire those photos all afternoon, Jack pulled in a sharp breath, opened the door to his bedroom, and charged away, like he couldn't take it one more second.

I followed him inside.

Jack's room was the same as the rest of the house—same ceramic-tile floor and stucco walls, same French doors overlooking bright pink flowers, same arched doorways. But his room felt more manly, somehow. *Leatherier.* It smelled like iron, and had an old saddle in the corner, and an Eames chair by the window.

"This is your room?" I asked, to be sure.

"*Our* room," Jack said.

Of course. We'd be sharing a room. We were adults, after all. Adults in a fake relationship.

"You can have the dresser," Jack said, dropping his suitcase on the floor beside the saddle.

"We can share," I said.

But Jack shrugged. "Doesn't matter."

Next, I looked at the bed. "Is that a double bed?"

Jack frowned, and it was clear he'd never thought about it. "Maybe."

"Do you fit in that bed?"

The tiniest flicker of a smile. "I have to hang my feet off the end."

It had occurred to me that there was a good chance this room would have only one bed.

But here we were.

"I'll take the floor," I said.

Jack tilted his head like it hadn't occurred to him that *anyone* might take the floor. "You can sleep in the bed," he said, and, at first, I thought he was letting me have it—before he added, "I'll share."

I gave him a look. "It's fine."

"You realize that's a ceramic-tile floor?"

"I'll make it work." It was certainly better than my closet.

"I get it if you're uncomfortable, but I promise I won't touch you."

I didn't want to admit I was uncomfortable. That was need-to-know information.

I gestured at him, like *Look at yourself.* "We wouldn't both even *fit* in that bed, dude."

Now an actual, wry smile, and I felt glad to have led us to a less painful topic. "I've squeezed girls into it before," Jack said.

"I prefer the floor," I said, to settle it.

"There's no way I'm making you sleep on the floor."

"There's no way I'm sleeping in your bed."

"Let's not be fussy."

"I think I'm being remarkably *unfussy*, actually."

He thought about that. "Yes. You are. Thank you."

I hadn't expected to be thanked.

"But," he went on, "you still get the bed."

"I really don't want it," I said.

"Neither do I."

"Fine. We'll both sleep on the floor."

Jack studied me like I was odd. "Are you saying that even if I sleep on the floor, you'll *also* sleep on the floor?"

This might be my only area of autonomy for a month. "Yes," I said. "I'll be on the floor no matter what."

"You'd rather sleep on cold, hard, ceramic tile than sleep next to me?"

"I bet you don't get that a lot."

Jack smiled like he was impressed. "Absolutely never."

"It's probably good for you," I said.

Jack shrugged, like *Maybe so*. Then—and it's possible a gentleman would have fought me a little harder—Jack said, "Suit yourself."

That settled, I looked around.

I honestly had no idea what this assignment was going to mean for me. Almost all my normal responsibilities had been shifted over to the remote team, which had secured an off-site rental house just across the farm road as an operations base. They were handling video surveillance, monitoring the perimeter of the property, watching social media, and doing all the things I'd normally do.

Plus we were at threat level yellow.

And we were in the middle of nowhere.

In a house surrounded by five hundred acres of pastures. So there wasn't even that much *to* do. Besides possibly track the positioning of the cattle.

I mean, it might as well be threat level white.

A *paid vacation*, everyone said. But there was a reason I never took vacations. What, exactly, was I supposed to do with myself all day?

I'd be technically working. I just wouldn't have . . . any duties.

But before I could panic, there was a rap on the door as loud as a shotgun.

We both jumped.

Through the door, we heard Hank. "Jack, I need to talk to you."

It wasn't until all of Jack's tension snapped back into place that I realized how much joking around about our sleeping arrangements had relaxed him.

Even his posture shifted. He straightened up and left the room.

Should I follow him?

I hadn't been invited.

In a normal job, whenever I was on shift, I always kept the principal in my sights. But this was anything but a normal job.

Still uncertain, I made my way back to the kitchen, but I stopped when I neared the back door. Jack and Hank were just past it, on the screen porch. I couldn't see them, but I could hear their voices through the open kitchen window.

And they were talking about me.

"You actually did it," Hank said. "You actually showed up here with that girl in tow."

"You seemed fine with it at the hospital."

"Yeah. I seemed fine with a lot of things at the hospital."

"What am I supposed to do? Mom invited her."

"Only because she thought you wouldn't come without her."

"Mom was right. I *wouldn't* come without her."

"You're making things harder on Mom. And you don't even care."

"*You're* making things harder on her. And I care about that very much."

"Doesn't she have enough to deal with right now?"

"I'm only here because she asked me to be."

"She wants to see *you*. Not some stranger."

"Hannah's not a stranger. She's my girlfriend."

I winced a little at the lie.

"She's a stranger to us."

"Not for long."

"Tell her to leave."

"I can't. I won't."

"Tell her to leave, or I'll kick you both out."

"I dare you. I dare you to do that and then tell Mom what you did."

"This is a private, family matter. The last thing Mom needs right now is to be entertaining some Hollywood bimbo."

Then I heard a scuffle. Then a clunk. I stepped closer to peek through the screen, and I saw that Jack had shoved Hank up against a wall.

"Does *anything* about that girl seem like Hollywood to you?" Jack demanded.

It's a heck of a thing to see two grown men fighting over you. Even if you know it's not a real fight. And even if you know the fight is really about something else.

Still. I held my breath.

For a second, I thought Jack was going to defend me.

"She's as un-Hollywood as it gets," Jack said then, his voice low and menacing. "Have you seen my other girlfriends? Have you seen Kennedy Monroe? She's nothing like any of them. She's short. Her teeth are crooked. She barely wears any makeup. She doesn't self-tan, wear extensions, or dye her hair. She's a totally plain, unremarkable person. She's the epitome of ordinary."

Wow. Okay.

"But she's mine," Jack said then. "And she's staying."

I was still coping with "epitome of ordinary."

Another scuffle, as Hank pushed Jack off of him.

I stepped way back so they wouldn't see me. Of course, that meant I couldn't see them anymore, either.

"Fine," Hank said. "I guess I'll just have to make her so miserable that she leaves on her own."

"If you make my Hannah miserable—"

My Hannah!

"—I will make you miserable right back."

"You already do."

"That's more about you than about me, buddy," Jack said.

But Hank was still trying to win the fight. "I'm telling you I don't want her here. But I can't even remember the last time you cared about what anybody else wanted."

"You don't want her here, but I need her here. And so do you, even though you don't know it. So back the hell off."

I guess, at that, one of them decided to storm off, because next I heard the screen door *whap* closed. Then, on the heels of that, I heard it again.

Out the kitchen window, I could see Hank stomping off toward his truck—and Jack charging in the opposite direction, along the gravel road toward a thicket of trees.

What I wanted to do . . . was go hide my plain, unremarkable, epitome-of-ordinary face.

For, like, *ever.*

But Jack was my principal. And this was my job.

So I followed him.

Thirteen

WHEN I CAUGHT up, he stopped walking, but he didn't turn. "Don't follow me."

"I have to follow you."

"I'm taking a walk."

"I can tell."

"I need a moment. To myself."

"That's not really relevant."

"Do you really think you're my girlfriend or something? Don't follow me."

"Do *you* really think I'm your girlfriend? I'm not following you because I want to. You are my *job*."

At that, Jack started down the gravel road again—heading very purposely toward nowhere, as far as I could tell.

I let him get about a hundred feet ahead, and then I took a deep breath and followed.

When Jack said he was taking a walk, he wasn't kidding. We followed the tire ruts in the road through a cow pasture, over a cattle guard, past a rusty metal barn, and down a long, slow hill into a wooded lowland overgrown with vines.

Was I dressed for an excursion like that—in my embroidered sundress with bare ankles?

I was not.

Every hundred feet or so, I had to shake the rocks out of my sandals.

Really wishing I'd changed into those boots now.

Did Jack know I was following him?

He did.

Whenever we came to a gate, he'd unlatch the chain and wait for me. Then, wordlessly, once I was through, he'd relatch it, and take off walking, and I'd wait politely until he'd reestablished our distance.

I even walked in the opposite rut from the one he was using, out of courtesy.

The road descended deeper into the woods, and the grass got taller, and the path got more overgrown, and just as I was trying to remember what poison ivy looked like, we came to a tumbledown, rusty, barbed-wire gate.

Past it, the forest opened up clear to a wide, blue sky, and I realized we'd made it to the riverbank.

As I got closer, Jack was looking me up and down. "Are you kidding me with that outfit?"

I looked down at my bare legs. "I have boots back at the house."

"You should be wearing them."

"Noted."

Jack shook his head. "Never come down to the river with naked ankles."

"To be fair," I said, "I didn't know that rule. I also didn't know we were coming to the river."

Jack turned and looked at the distance ahead. The road stopped at the gate. From here to the riverbank was just tall grass—and weeds and brambles and thistle bushes. And let's not forget poison ivy.

Jack squatted down and turned his back toward me. "Climb on. I'll give you a ride."

"I'm fine, thanks."

Staying crouched down, Jack started counting off all the things in that grass that could come after me: "Sticker burrs, armadillos, stinging nettles, red ants, black ants, fire ants, poison ivy, blackberry brambles, black widows, brown recluses, copperheads, rattlesnakes, water moccasins . . ."

He waited for me to revise my answer.

I hesitated.

So he added, "Not to mention feral hogs, bobcats, and coyotes."

Honestly, he'd had me at "armadillos."

"Fine," I said, and climbed on.

Jack hooked his arms under my legs and stood up fast enough to make me dizzy—so I clutched him tight. Then he launched back into that patented Jack Stapleton walking pace I now suddenly knew so well.

Riding was nicer. Maybe he'd carry me back.

At the riverbank, the forest dropped away, and so did the earth. Jack stood at the crest of the bank for a minute as we both took in the sight of the river down below and its endless sandy beach.

"That's the Brazos River?" I asked.

"Yep."

"It's wider than I thought. And . . . browner."

But Jack didn't respond. Just launched us down the bank until we made it to the shore.

There, he dropped me pretty fast, and walked off toward the water.

He was heading vaguely north, so I decided to head vaguely south and give us both some space.

It was probably two hundred feet to the water itself, and I let my head tilt down as I walked and marveled at all the different kinds of rocks peppering the sand: brown ones, black ones, stripy ones, bits of animal bones, petrified wood, even fossils. Not to mention driftwood, an occasional tangle of rusty barbed wire, and a notable number of old beer cans. I could see why Jack wanted to come here. Across from us was a high bank with nothing but grass and sky, and all around us was the endless breeze that flowing water makes, making it feel like we were miles and miles from anywhere.

Which, of course, we were.

At the river's edge, I kicked off my sandals. It was a warm day, and all that jogging to keep up had left me a little hot. The water was clearer up close—and, as I dipped my feet, it felt great. Cool and swirly with refreshing eddies. It felt so good around my ankles that soon I was sloshing out a little further.

I lifted the hem of my sundress. I really wasn't planning to go past my knees. I was just going to cool off for a minute and enjoy it, honestly. Another few steps, and I was going to turn around. But then, a few things happened all at once.

As I took my next step, I heard a sound like maybe Jack was calling my name, but it was so muffled by the wind, I couldn't be sure. I turned to look, but as I did . . . the floor of the river disappeared.

There was just . . . nothing for my foot to land on. And so I lost my balance and splashed down into the water.

It's always shocking to land in cold water when you're not expecting it, but there was something more shocking about the water in that river.

It had a current.

A really strong current.

A current strong enough that when I hit the water, I didn't bob back up to the surface with a kick or two . . . because the water tugged me downward.

It all happened so fast.

I was sloshing through the water—and then, within seconds, my head was going under.

It actually gives me shivers to think about it now. How close I came to drowning.

But just as it happened, before I had time to panic, I felt something hard as metal clamp around my arm and haul me back up.

Jack.

He yanked me out and toward him like some kind of machine, grabbing me around the waist and clamping me with an *oof* to his chest, then dragged me back to the bank so fast, we both stumbled and fell onto the sandy shore.

Did he land on top of me like we were in *From Here to Eternity*?

Yes, that happened.

Was it in any way romantic like that?

Um. No.

As soon as he could, Jack scrambled up and stomped away, leaving me drenched, and stunned, and coughing on the sand.

When I caught my breath, I said, "What was that? A riptide?"

"Are you *kidding* me?" he demanded, his jeans soaking wet from the thighs down. "Did you just wade out into the Brazos? Did that just happen?"

I stood up and tried unsuccessfully to brush the wet sand off my legs. "Was I . . . not supposed to do that?"

"Nobody's supposed to do that! Don't you know how many people drown in that river every year?"

"Why would I know that?"

"Everybody knows that! *Never swim in the Brazos.*"

"First of all, I wasn't swimming. And second—no. That's not a thing everybody knows."

But Jack was ranting now. "And why? Why can't you swim in the Brazos? Because it's sandy at the bottom, and so the current makes eddies, and the eddies carve caverns in that sandy floor of the river, and the current swirls around in there like liquid tornadoes—and if you're unlucky or stupid enough to get sucked into one, you're done for."

"That's some pretty specialized knowledge, there—" I started, coughing some more.

"So," Jack went on, like I wasn't even talking, "when idiots decide to go swimming or fishing or *wading* in that water, the next thing they know, they're pulled into the undertow. Whole families die trying to save each other, one by one!"

Did he just call me an idiot? I tried to decide if it was worse than being the epitome of ordinary. "So. Not a riptide then."

I eyed the water, so tranquil looking from here. I could still feel the pull of it, like some liquid death magnet. Suddenly there were shivers prickling my arms and legs. "Scary," I said, almost to myself.

My calmness just seemed to make him madder.

"Scary?" Jack yelled. "You're damn right! What the hell were you thinking?"

"I don't know," I said, turning to him now. "I was hot? The water felt nice?"

"You were *hot*?" he said, in a tone like he'd asked me why I was drinking gasoline and I told him I was thirsty.

He went on. "Do you have a death wish? Do you? Because here's why it's called 'the Brazos.' From 'los brazos de Dios,' which means 'the arms of God'—and people think it's from thirsty travelers who were so grateful to find water, but it's actually because it drowned so many people that it's where *God collects their souls.*"

Yikes. Okay. That took a dark turn.

I will grant that Jack was conveying an important safety tip. But, I mean, *really*? I was obviously half-drowned and super-shaken. Did he have to *yell*?

I don't know about you, but I can only get yelled at for so long before I start yelling back. Jack wanted to yell? Fine. I could yell, too. I could yell all day.

"Why are you yelling at me?!" I yelled.

Another first for me—yelling at a client.

"Because!" Jack yelled back. "You're going to get yourself killed!"

"Not on purpose!" I yelled back.

"That doesn't matter once you're dead!" Jack yelled.

"People wade into water all the time!" I yelled. "It's a totally normal thing to do!"

"Not in the Brazos!"

"But I didn't know that!"

"And if you go under, then I go under—because then I have to go in after you!"

"So don't go in after me!"

"That's not how this works! If you die in the river, I die in the river! And I really don't want to fucking die in the fucking river!"

For a second, I had no response. I didn't know what to say to that. And in that second, I realized something else: I was shaking. A lot. Hard. From someplace deep in my core.

Most likely, it was fear.

Though it didn't feel like fear.

But maybe I'd just forgotten what fear felt like.

Usually, the antidote to fear was preparation—but I hadn't been prepared for anything about this week, from watching my job mutate into something I didn't even recognize, to moving in with a bunch of strangers, to losing my best friend, to winding up in the middle of some hatefest between Jack and his brother, to being called "ordinary," to almost drowning, and—now—to getting yelled at like I hadn't been yelled at in years.

It was a lot.

Suddenly, it was too much.

"What am I?" I demanded then. "Some kind of historian of the Texas waterways? How exactly am I supposed to know that this is a *river of death*? I'm just living my life in the city, trying to get to London, or Korea, or anywhere at all that's literally *not Texas*, and suddenly I'm having to move to a cattle ranch and act in this crazy reality show with you and your family? I didn't want this job, I didn't ask for it, and now I'm trapped in it with no escape for weeks on end! So maybe you could give me a heads-up if I'm about to accidentally kill myself or anyone else—"

And right here is where my voice broke.

Right here is where I lost hold of "angry" and my emotions just kind of crumbled. By the time I finished with "instead of just yelling at me out of nowhere like an asshole," my voice sounded broken, even to me.

I froze, and so did Jack, as we both registered that I'd just called my employer an asshole.

I would have liked to march off right then in a gesture of self-respect, but everything was trembling, including my legs.

Without even really thinking, I reached up to touch my beaded safety pin. I just wanted a quick hit of that tiny sparkle of comfort I always got when I felt the beads.

But it wasn't there.

My neck was bare. The necklace was gone, too.

"Hey," I said, looking down. "Where's my safety pin?"

"Your what?"

I pawed at my collarbones, like I might find it if I kept trying. "My safety pin. With the beads. It's gone."

Had it come off in the water? Was it somewhere on the beach?

I started searching the sand.

"That colored safety pin you always wear?" he asked, forgetting we were fighting and starting to look, too.

"It must have fallen off," I said.

I paced the beach, retracing all my steps. I'd been warm on the walk down, but now, after the shock of the river, I felt the opposite. I was drenched, and cold, and I couldn't stop shivering. But I didn't care.

As we looked, Jack's entire demeanor softened.

"We'll find it," he said. "Don't worry." Then he added, "I'm really good at finding things."

I looked up, and when I did, I realized just how vast that beach was—compared to a safety pin. This beach was like *infinity*. We were never going to find it.

And then I did what anybody might do, I guess, in that situation.

I started to cry.

Jack didn't even hesitate. He closed the distance between us and wrapped his arms around damp, trembling, uncharacteristically shaky me and kept them there a minute. Then he stepped back and took off his flannel overshirt, put it on me and buttoned the buttons, and then pulled me back into his arms.

"I'm sorry," he said, and now I was hearing his voice muffled through his chest. "I'm sorry you lost your safety pin, and I'm sorry you almost drowned, and I'm sorry I yelled at you. I should have warned you. It's completely my fault. You just scared me, is all."

Was he stroking my hair? Was *Jack Stapleton* stroking my hair?

Or was it just the wind?

He held me for a long time like that, there on that beach. He held me until my tears had dried up and I'd stopped shaking. Another first: The first time a client had ever hugged me—and the first time I'd ever allowed it.

And as mad at him as I still was, I also really didn't mind.

He seemed to have a knack for it.

JACK WOUND UP carrying me piggyback all the way to the house.

At first, he was just going to take me up the riverbank and through the overgrown grass—just back to the gravel road.

But once we got there, he just kept on walking.

"I'm good now," I said, my legs dangling. "You can let me down."

"This is my workout for the day."

"I can walk. I'm fine."

"I like carrying you. I might start doing it all the time."

"I know how to walk."

"I'm sure you do."

"So put me down."

"Don't think so."

"Why not?"

"Mostly 'cause it's getting dark, and lots of things that bite come out at dusk. You won't be able to see where you're stepping. And you're barelegged, like an amateur."

"We've already established that's not my fault."

"So what I'm doing right now is chivalrously protecting you from danger."

"Ah."

"Also, I feel bad for making you cry."

"You did *not* make me cry."

Jack gave a little *have it your way* pause. Then he said, "Also, it's fun."

"So you're really not going to put me down?"

"I'm really not."

Of course, as we went, I couldn't help but assess safety aspects of the property. That was my brain's default activity. I made mental maps of the layout, including potential hiding spots for bad actors, potential escape routes in emergencies, and areas to monitor.

All, of course, before Jack told me that his parents never locked their doors at night.

"Oh my God, you have to make them do that!"

"I've been trying to for years."

Not good. I'd be highlighting that in tonight's log.

And yet, a lot of my usual anxieties felt unusually muted, there on Jack Stapleton's back. Maybe it was the rhythm of his walking. Or the velvetiness of his flannel shirt enrobing me. Or the solidness of his shoulder under my chin. Or that cinnamon scent that seemed to follow him everywhere.

Or maybe it's just objectively hard to worry about anything when you're getting a piggyback ride.

I could feel the muscles in his back shifting and tightening with each step, especially as we made our way uphill. I could feel him breathing through his ribcage. I could feel the warmth of his body where we were pressed together.

I won't lie. It was nice.

Too nice, maybe.

"You really can set me down," I said.

But nothing doing. "We're almost there," Jack said.

So I guess I had no choice but to stay there and enjoy it.

Fourteen

HELL OF A first day.

That night, as promised, I slept on the floor.

Jack found a yoga mat in the hall closet, and I folded a couple of blankets on top of it.

It was fine. I was fine. I was comfortable being uncomfortable.

At least I wasn't sleeping in a closet.

I'd slept in a million crazy places—hallways, rooftops, even a broken elevator once. What I hadn't done, though, was sleep *in a room with Jack Stapleton.*

A little off-putting. Not gonna lie.

Would you like to know what Jack Stapleton does with his pillow when he sleeps? He doesn't rest his head on it like regular people do. He shoves it under his body, vertically, like a surfboard, and then drapes himself over it.

And wanna know what he wears for pj's?

Loose sweatpants and an aggressively clingy undershirt.

But what does he do with his dirty clothes when he changes into those pj's?

He leaves them all over the bathroom floor.

I walked in when it was my turn to change and found his muddy boots, his wadded socks, the T-shirt he'd worn all day, and his still-damp jeans—with the belt still in the loops and the underwear still inside—just lying there on the floor, splayed out in an almost-human shape, like a bearskin rug made of Jack Stapleton's dirty laundry.

I mean, I had to step over them to get to the sink to brush my teeth.

When I came out of the bathroom, Jack was sitting on the edge of his bed. He looked up.

I stared at him, like *What the hell?*

And he frowned back, like *What?*

So I pointed back at the bathroom floor and said, "Can you come deal with this?"

But Jack just tilted his head.

"Hey," I said. "This is a shared space. You can't leave your crap all over the floor."

But Jack was looking me up and down.

"Hello?" I said.

"Is that what you're sleeping in?"

I looked down. "Um. Yes?"

"Is that what you always sleep in?"

I looked up, like *What?* "Sometimes."

"I didn't even know they still made those."

I looked down again. "Nightgowns?"

"I mean," Jack said, and now he was looking at me like I was funny. "You look like a Victorian child."

"It's a nightgown," I said. "It's a normal piece of human sleepwear."

"Nope."

"People wear nightgowns, Jack."

"Not like that one, they don't."

"Hey," I said. "I'm not making fun of what you're wearing."

"What I'm wearing is normal."

I shuffled over to his mirror and looked at myself. White cotton. Short sleeves. A little ruffle below the knees. "I do *not* look like a Victorian child. A Victorian child would have lace and ribbons. And a little cap on its head."

"Pretty close, though."

"I was just trying to bring girlfriend-like sleepwear."

"I've never seen a girlfriend in anything even close."

"Your girlfriends probably only sleep in thongs."

"At the maximum." Jack gave an exaggerated sigh and gazed up at the ceiling as if remembering it fondly.

I checked my reflection again. "This seemed," I said, in my own defense, "like the most professional of all my sleepwear options."

"But—I mean, is it yours?"

"Of course it's mine. You think I stole it?"

"Yeah. From a ninety-year-old grandma."

Now I was annoyed. He'd called me a lot of insulting things today, from "plain," to "an idiot," to "the epitome of ordinary." Now he was saying "grandma"? To my face?

Somehow, this was the best retort I could manage: "You're not in a position to throw shade, Mister Clothes-All-Over-The-Floor."

It was supposed to be a burn, but Jack just started laughing.

Like really laughing—his shoulders shaking and everything. "That's a terrible burn," he said. "I think that's the worst burn I've ever heard."

"It's not funny," I said.

"I'm sorry," he said, tumping over and pressing his face against the bedspread. "But it absolutely is funny."

"Hey!" I said. "Nobody wants to see your underwear."

"Actually," he said, sitting back up and sobering his face. "People pay very good money to see my underwear."

"Not your *dirty* underwear. On the bathroom floor!"

But he just gave a little *trust me on this* nod. "You'd be surprised."

"Well," I said, feeling like I needed to make this point. "I am not one of those people."

"I know. It's a thing I like about you."

Was he trying to weasel out of picking up his mess by flattering me? I tried again. "Let me ask you this. Am I your maid?"

The more he tried to keep a straight face, the more his face seemed to fight with him. "We established that on day one."

"Then let's just agree that I won't make you interact with my dirty underwear, and you won't make me interact with yours. Okay?"

"Okay," he said, trying to make his face serious. "Agreed."

But now he had the giggles.

Jack Stapleton had the giggles.

He fell back down on the bed.

"Go," I said, walking over to him and shoving at his shoulder to push him off the bed. "Go pick up your dirty clothes."

He resisted for a second, so I pushed harder, and then, on purpose, he gave way fast and I fell onto the floor—landing on my sleeping nest.

Fine with me. It was time for bed, anyway.

"And don't leave your toothpaste cap off, either," I said. "What are you, five years old?"

"It's my bathroom," he said.

"It's our bathroom now."

BY THE TIME Jack came out, I'd already turned off all the lights, and he tripped over me making his way back to his bed.

"Watch it!"

"Sorry."

He climbed under his covers and hung his head over the side to talk to me like we were having a sleepover.

"You really can sleep in the bed, you know."

"No, thank you."

"It's bothering me that you're on the ceramic tile."

"Get over it."

"We could build, like, a wall of pillows down the middle as a barrier."

"I'm good."

"What if my mom walks in and sees you sleeping on the floor?"

I hadn't seen his mom since we'd been here. "Does your mom just walk into the bedroom of her adult son without knocking?"

"Probably not. Good point."

"And even if she did, we could just say we were fighting. Which is true."

"We're not fighting," Jack said. "We're playing."

"Is that what this is?"

The moon came out from behind the clouds and the room lightened a bit. I could see Jack's face above me. He was still looking down.

"Thank you," he said then.

"For what?"

"For coming here and doing this, even though you didn't want to. And for not drowning today. And for wearing that ridiculous nightgown."

I turned on my side to ignore him, but I could still feel him watching me.

After a while he said, "I really do have nightmares, you know. Apologies in advance if I wake you."

"What should I do if you have one?" I asked.

"Just ignore me," Jack said.

So much easier said than done. "I will absolutely try my best."

Fifteen

JACK WAS GONE when I woke up the next morning—his empty bed a tangle of sheets and blankets, as if he'd spent the whole night scuba diving in there.

Where was he? It clearly stated in the handout that he was supposed to stay with or near me at all times. He wasn't supposed to just sneak out while I was sleeping.

I got dressed—jeans and boots this time—and went to look for him.

In the kitchen, instead of Jack, I found his mom and dad.

Being adorable.

His mom was sitting at the table in a chenille robe, and his dad was across the room, wearing his wife's floral apron, standing at the stove, burning bacon. Smoke everywhere. The stove fan running in a too-little-too-late way, and this big man flapping his ruffled hem helplessly at the whole situation.

Should Connie Stapleton be laughing like that? It was the first time I'd seen her since the surgery. Was that safe for her stitches?

Granted, she was more subdued than he was.

I mean, now Doc Stapleton was doubling over at the waist.

He took a minute to collect himself. Then he lifted the charcoal-black strips out of the skillet and brought them to his wife, well aware that bacon was supposed to be a whole different color.

"I blame the stove," Doc said.

"Me too," Connie said, patting the back of his hand.

Then, with remarkable generosity, she broke off a blackened piece, put it in her mouth, and said, "Not bad."

As if burnt bacon really got a bad rap.

I felt so shy, standing in the doorway, as something totally astonishing hit me: These people were *happily married*. Everything about their body language—their faces, the way they were laughing—confirmed it.

Happily married.

I mean, you hear about people like that. In theory, they exist. But I'd sure as hell never seen anything like it before.

It felt like glimpsing a unicorn.

I started to back away. I definitely didn't belong here.

But that's when Doc looked up and noticed me.

Connie followed his gaze. "Oh!" she said, all warm and welcoming. "You're awake!"

No escape now.

Knowing everything Connie had just been through, and knowing, too, how much of an interloper I truly was, I suddenly wished like crazy that Jack were there to cushion the moment.

And then, as if he heard me somehow, the kitchen door swung open, and Jack himself stepped in—looking windblown and manly in a plaid shirt and jeans—with his glasses a little bit crooked.

He also had a golf bag over his shoulder.

"You're up," he said to me, like there was no one else in the room.

Doc took in the sight of Jack. "Hitting golf balls into the river?"

"Every morning," Jack said with a little nod.

"Golf balls?" I asked. "Into the river? Isn't that, like, environmentally unsound?"

Jack shook his head. "It's fine." Then he walked over and kissed his mother on the top of the head. "Hey, Mom. How are you feeling?"

"On the mend," she said, lifting her coffee at him in toast.

Jack seemed to register my discomfort. He strode right toward me, pulled me by the hand to the breakfast table, sat me down, sat himself right next to me, and wrapped his arm around my shoulders.

I think they call that owning the room.

I held very still—astonished at how ordering myself to *relax and act casual* had the opposite effect.

Jack responded to my stiffness with the opposite. Knees apart. Arm languid and heavy. Voice as smooth as chocolate milk.

"You look amazing today," he said. And I'd barely realized he was talking to me before he pressed his face into the crook of my neck and breathed in a full gulp of my scent. "Why do you always smell so good?"

"It's lemon soap," I said, a little dazed. "It's aromatherapeutic."

"I'll say," Jack said.

I knew what he was doing, of course. He was compensating for my bad acting. I clearly had some kind of stage fright, and so he was acting twice as hard make up for it.

He really was good.

The warmth in his voice, the intimacy of his body language, the way he stared at me like he was drinking me up . . .

No wonder I'd seen *You Wish* so many times.

I'd seen so many downsides to coming here. I'd worried about the boredom of being on duty with nothing to do. I'd worried about the difficulty of trying to do my job while pretending not to—and what that might mean for my performance. I'd worried that I might be an unconvincing actor.

It just hadn't occurred to me to worry about Jack.

In those short minutes right after he walked in, though, as he worked to establish us as a genuine, loving couple in front of his folks . . . that's exactly what it felt like we were.

I bought it, too, is what I'm saying.

I felt like he was glad to see me. I felt like he was savoring being near me. I felt like he liked me.

He seemed exactly, convincingly, heartbreakingly like a man in love.

Uh oh.

How would I make it four weeks without getting traumatically con-fused? I couldn't even make it four *minutes*.

Just then, Hank showed up in the kitchen, the screen door slapping behind him. Instead of sitting at the table, he leaned against the counter and glared at the lovey-doveyness.

That was helpful. I could focus on that.

Jack's mom didn't even notice Hank. She leaned toward us and said, "Tell us about how you two met."

We'd planned for this.

Jack eyed Hank for a second before giving his mom his full attention. Then, he poured a cup of coffee from the carafe and said, in a friendly voice, "She's a photographer. She came to my place in the mountains to shoot our infamous albino moose."

I gave Jack a look. The albino moose ad-lib was pushing it.

Hank wasn't buying it, either. He crossed his arms over his chest.

"You have an albino moose?" Doc asked.

Jack nodded. "Very elusive." He gestured at me. "She was trying do a photo essay on it, but she never could find it."

"Too bad," Connie said.

"But I helped her look for a long time," Jack said then, giving his mom a wink.

"You were kind to help her out," Doc said.

"It wasn't kindness," Jack said. "It was pure selfishness."

Hank snorted a laugh.

Jack ignored it. "Because it was love at first sight."

Jack turned then and gave me the dreamiest, most lovestruck look I'd ever seen. Then he tucked a wisp of hair behind my ear. "I just wanted any excuse to be around her." Then he leaned back and put his hands behind his head, like he was reminiscing. "I saw that feisty, stumpy little lady climb out of her Land Rover with five hundred cameras, and I just knew."

I frowned. "Did you just call me 'stumpy'?"

"In a good way, Stumps," Jack said.

I narrowed my eyes at him.

"In a lovable way," Jack insisted. "In an adorable, irresistible, how-can-I-get-this-little-lady-trapped-in-my-mountain-cabin way." Then he turned to his parents, grabbed me in a headlock that messed up my already messy bun, and said, "Look how cute she is."

"I am not stumpy," I said helplessly.

But Jack's mother was totally on board. She leaned forward. "What do you like best about her?"

Jack released me and let me sit back. "I like these little wispy things that never quite make it into her bun. And how she looks like a wet cat when you make her mad. And actually"—he said, like this was just occurring to him—"I like how she *gets* mad. She gets mad a lot."

"You like how she gets mad?" Doc Stapleton asked, like his son might have a few screws loose.

"Yeah," Jack said. "People don't really get mad at you when you're famous. At first, it's great—but after a while it starts to feel like you're living on a planet with no gravity." He thought about that for a second. Then he turned back to me. "But not Stumps! One sock on the floor, and I get the mad cat face. I love it."

I glared at him from under my messed-up hair.

He pointed at my face with admiration. "There it is right now."

Connie was loving this. She turned to me. "And what do you like best about Jack?"

I hadn't prepared for this question. But an answer just popped right into my head. "I like that he thanks me all the time. For all kinds of things. Things I would never have expected anyone to thank me for."

I glanced at Jack, and I could tell he knew that I'd said something true.

He studied me for a second, seeming to fall out of character. Then he picked up a wadded paper towel off the table and threw it at the kitchen trash can like he was making a free throw—and missed.

We stared at it where it landed.

Then Hank said to me, "What do you like least about him?"

"Least?" I asked. I hadn't prepared for this one, either. But another answer popped up like magic. "That's easy. He leaves his dirty clothes all over the floor." Then I added, "It's like the Rapture happened, and they took Jack first."

A half second of silence, and then they all—even Hank—burst out laughing.

As they settled, Connie said to Jack, "Sweetheart, you're not still doing that, are you?"

But as she was saying it, Hank was starting to leave, his face serious again as if he hadn't meant to laugh, and now he regretted it. He moved toward the kitchen door and put his hand on the knob.

"You're leaving?" Connie said with a tone, like *We were all just starting to have fun.*

"I've got work to do," Hank said.

Connie gave him a look, like *Really?* and Hank explained: "I'm starting on the boat today."

From Connie's reaction, that was serious.

It caught Jack's attention, too. "*The* boat?" he asked.

Connie nodded. "I told Dad the other week that if they didn't get busy building it, I was going to sell it on eBay."

Jack nodded. Then he turned to face Doc. "Do you want some help?"

But Hank spun around, like he couldn't believe Jack had just said that. "What?"

The whole mood in the room went rigid, but Jack still kept his friendly, relaxed vibe.

"I'm offering to help you build the boat," Jack said.

"You're offering," Hank said, like he could not have heard correctly, "to help build Drew's boat?"

Jack kept a steady gaze on Hank. "It's better than Mom selling it on eBay, right?"

"Nope," Hank said.

"Sweetheart," Connie said to Jack, "we know you mean well . . ."

Doc let out a shaky sigh. "That's probably not a good idea, son."

At the consensus, Jack put up his hands. "I was just offering," Jack said.

That's when Hank took a step closer. "Well, don't."

Jack was holding still now, all pretense of affability frozen.

"Don't talk about the boat," Hank said now, glaring at Jack. "Don't go near the boat. Don't touch the boat. And for God's sake don't ever offer to help build it again."

At that, Jack was on his feet and moving toward him. "When are you going to let it go, man?"

They were staring at each other like they were in a game of chicken when Hank noticed the leather necklace at the base of Jack's throat. His eyes locked on the sight.

"What are you wearing?"

"I think you know what it is."

"Take it off."

But Jack shook his head. "Never."

At that, Hank reached for it, like he might try to rip it off. But Jack blocked him. "Don't touch me, man."

"Take it off," Hank demanded again—and then they were fighting. Not landing punches, exactly, but grabbing at each other, scuffling, shifting off balance, slamming into the kitchen cabinets. Pretty standard fighting for people who don't fight much.

Doc Stapleton and I were on it right away to separate them. Doc steered Hank away, and I twisted Jack's arms behind him like a pro before worrying that might give me away—and then shifting into an awkward hug.

When we'd broken their momentum, the two guys stood back, breathing, glaring at each other.

That's when Connie said, "Enough!"

They lowered their eyes.

Hank said, "Do you see what he's wearing?"

"I don't care what he's wearing," Connie said. "I care what you're doing."

"He's never touching that boat."

"All he did was offer to help," Connie said. Then, like Hank might not've grasped the words: "To *help*."

"I don't want his help."

"Yes, you do. Much more than you realize."

A pause.

Connie went on, "When I first found out I was sick, can I tell you how I felt? I felt happy. I thought, *Good.* I thought, *Maybe cancer is bad enough.* Maybe this, at last, would force us all to realize that we can't keep wasting our time. And when I saw you all after the surgery, and everybody was getting along, I thought maybe, just maybe, we were going to find a way to be okay. But I guess I was wrong."

The boys didn't lift their eyes.

Connie studied Hank for a second, like she was thinking. Then she said to him, "I want you to move home, too."

Hank looked up. "What?"

"I want you to move back into your room. Here at the house. Stay until Thanksgiving."

"Mom, I've got my own—"

"I know," Connie said.

"It's not gonna be—"

"I agree," Connie said. "But I don't know what else to do, and there's no time to figure it out."

Hank looked down at the floor, toeing a spot with his boot.

"Bring your things by dinnertime," Connie said then. "You boys are going to find a way to get along—or kill each other trying."

Sixteen

A LOT TO process there.

After the brothers stomped off in opposite directions, and Doc helped Connie back to her bed to rest, I found myself sitting in the hammock chair under the oak tree, realizing one very simple thing.

I had to quit.

It wasn't Connie's health troubles. I'd dealt with sick people before. And it wasn't the mysterious beef between the brothers. All families had secrets.

It was Jack.

I'd hoped that being around him in real life would be disappointing— that without a stylist and a writer to feed him his lines, he'd lose his appeal. As much as I didn't want to let the fantasy go, I also knew it was the only way to do this assignment right.

I'd been counting on the reality being worse than the fantasy.

But the reality . . . was *better*.

This was the problem. As mesmerizing as the celluloid version of Jack was, the real guy—the guy who left his clothes on the floor, and made fun of my nightgown, and gave me piggyback rides, and was terrified of bridges—this guy was better.

And whether it was because of those smiley eyes of his, or because I had none of my usual relentless busyness to keep me distracted, or because I'd already let myself swoon over him when I had no idea I'd ever meet him in real life—it didn't matter.

The fact was, none of my usual defenses worked.

When he looked at me like he was in love, my insides melted. Everything I read for pretend on his face . . . I was feeling for real.

He was faking all those feelings—but I was feeling them. Genuinely.

And no matter what your skill level is, or how much you might care about your professional reputation, or what your boss has ordered you to do, or what other rules you might be able to break and get away with it . . . you can't—absolutely cannot—have a thing for your principal.

That's just Executive Protection 101.

And if I had to confess it to Glenn, I would. He'd respect my decision to do the right thing and put the principal first.

Or, at least—I really, really hoped so.

QUITTING.

The end of the job. The end of my career, too, most likely. But there was no way around it.

Love makes you muddled. Love clouds your judgment. Love derails you with longing.

Or so they say.

That hadn't happened to me with Robby . . . but—and this was only occurring to me now—maybe that hadn't been love? Because whatever was going on with Jack Stapleton was far more destabilizing.

I didn't understand it, but one thing was clear. It was complex enough to make things pretty simple.

I needed to get out of here.

I climbed out of the hammock swing, stood up, and started walking along the gravel road toward the surveillance house. I'd walk over, call Glenn, and quit. Easy. But I'd only made it halfway to the gate when I heard an unmistakable sound. The crack of a rifle firing.

I stopped in my tracks.

Turned.

Another shot.

It was coming from past the barn.

I took off sprinting that way, and vaulted the fence, and, as I did, I heard another shot.

What was going on? Who was shooting? Had the corgi-breeding stalker found us? Gone ballistic? Tracked Jack down in a random ravine in the middle of five hundred acres of nowhere? As I charged across the field, stumbling over anthills and thistle bushes, I made mental lists of possibilities for what I was about to find—and a whole set of contingency plans for how to handle each one.

Why, oh, why hadn't Glenn authorized a firearm for me?

"You won't need it," he'd promised.

Too late now.

Whatever I'd find in that ravine, I'd just have to think fast and figure something out.

God willing.

But what I found there wasn't a mad corgi breeder. Or a blood-soaked Jack Stapleton.

It was sweet, kindly, Doc Stapleton, resident patriarch. With a lever-action rifle. Shooting at bottles.

By the time I crested the ravine and saw him, I was close enough for him to hear me. He turned as I descended. I slowed from a sprint to a stop, and then bent over, hands on my knees, panting like crazy and waiting for my lungs to stop burning.

When I finally looked up, Doc was staring at me like he couldn't fathom what I was doing there.

"I heard the shots," I said, gasping. "I thought—" Then I shifted. "You scared me."

Doc made a *pffft* noise and then said, "City slicker."

Fine. We could go with that.

I stood up, still panting, and walked closer. Lined up on rocks against a bend in the ravine were glass bottles—maybe twenty. Green ones, brown ones, clear ones. Below the rocks, on the ground underneath, was a veritable lake of shattered glass.

"Gunshots," Doc went on, as I took in the sight, "mean a whole different thing in the country."

As far as he knew. But I nodded. "Target practice."

Doc held out his gun to me. "Care to take a shot?"

I looked at it. The answer was no, of course. No, I wasn't going to stand around shooting bottles when I was just on my way to quit my job. No, I wasn't going to spend one more minute on this loony-bin ranch than I had to. Or blow my cover at the last minute by putting my skills on display.

No. Just, no.

And yet, I did need a minute to catch my breath.

And it might actually feel good to shoot something right now.

And that's when Doc said, "You don't have to hit anything," in a tone like I was hesitating because I didn't know how to shoot.

I was still resisting that little challenge when he added:

"This rifle's a little tough for ladies to handle, anyway."

I mean, *Come on.*

I could spare five minutes. Right?

I held my hands out for the rifle, and I let him hand it to me. Then I let him give me a lesson.

I didn't lie to him, exactly. I just stayed pleasantly mute while he walked me through the most basic of basic introductions to the gun in my hands: "This is the stock," he said, "and this is the barrel. This is the trigger. You pull this lever to reload between shots." Then he pointed at the muzzle. "This is where the bullets come out. Be sure to point that at the ground until you're ready to make some trouble."

This is where the bullets come out? The urge to show him up rose in my body like water filling a glass.

"Take that little group over there," Doc said, gesturing at row of old beer bottles. "If you can hit one, I'll give you a quarter."

Wow. There was something so inspiring about being so underestimated.

Right then I decided to do more than just hit the bottles. I was going to hit them with some style.

Fast and easy. Like a badass. And also: from the hip.

"Okay, little lady," Doc said then. "Just try your best."

My *best*?

Okay.

I flipped off the safety, stepped into a comfortable stance, pressed the rifle butt to my hip bone, and pulled the trigger with a *BOOM!*

The rifle had a hell of a kick, but the first bottle disappeared in a puff of sand.

But I didn't even stop to enjoy it. As soon as I'd pulled the trigger, I was popping the lever out and back with a satisfying *ka-chunk* and then pulling the trigger again.

Another *BOOM!* And another bottle turned to dust.

Then another, then another, then another. *BOOM—ka-chunk, BOOM—ka-chunk, BOOM!* Right across the row, as the bottles exploded one after the other.

It was over almost as soon as it started.

Then I turned back to Doc with one final shift of the lever—*ka-chunk*. Nice and ladylike.

I flipped the safety, took the rifle off my hip, and said to Doc's gaping face, "That was fun."

I'd just revealed way too much about myself, and I should've been halfway back to Houston by now. But it was worth it.

That's when I noticed something up the ravine.

It was Jack. Watching us. And from the admiring look behind those slightly crooked glasses, he'd seen the whole thing.

He gave me a little salute of respect.

And I gave him a little nod.

And now it was time to get the hell out.

Seventeen

THE FIRST THING I saw when I stepped into surveillance headquarters was Robby and Taylor—with their hands in each other's back pockets.

Before that image could burn itself too deep into my memory, I coughed.

They sprung apart at the sound, but—

Too late. Couldn't blink away the afterimage.

"Where's Glenn?" I asked.

"In town," Taylor answered, just as Robby asked, "Where's the principal?"

"I need to talk to Glenn," I said.

Doghouse, sitting at a desk across the room, lifted the receiver of a landline and held it out to me.

I walked over, took it, dialed Glenn's number, and mentally prepared myself to quit—right here, in front of both of my nemeses—and ignoring all the questions in my head. Would Glenn yell at me? Would Robby and Taylor gloat to see me fail? Was I forfeiting any chance at London?

My body felt as tight as a wire as I waited.

But Glenn's phone went to voicemail.

"It's good you're here, anyway," Robby said, as I hung up. "We've had some activity on the Stapleton property."

I shook my head. "The shots? That was just his dad hitting bottles in the ravine."

"No," Robby said then. "At his place in the city." Then Robby glanced toward the monitors. "Taylor, pull it up," he said. All business. Like a liar.

But what she pulled up on the monitors made me take a step closer. Then another.

"What the hell?" I said.

"Yeah."

They were images from the cameras around Jack's Houston house. All the first-floor windows had been spray-painted with pink hearts and the name "Jack" over and over.

I studied different footage from different angles. "Every downstairs window, huh?"

Robby nodded.

"Was it the Corgi Lady? Do we know?"

"We're ninety-nine percent sure it was," Robby said.

Taylor switched to footage from earlier of a woman in the act.

"That's her? Did we get a face ID?"

Robby shook his head. "No, but she left gifts."

"Gifts?"

"Yep. On the front porch," Robby said. Then he added, "In gift bags."

"What were they?"

Robby checked the texts on his phone. "According to Kelly, it was a handknitted sweater with a remarkably photorealistic image of Stapleton's face on the front, an album of snapshots of her new litter of puppies, and a batch of nudes."

"A batch of nudes?" I asked. "Nudes of who? Nudes of the principal?"

"Nudes of the corgi breeder."

Jesus.

"She also left a handwritten note welcoming Jack home to Houston—

and reminding him that her biological clock is ticking, and she'd really prefer him to impregnate her sometime this spring, if that works for his schedule."

Robby handed me a tablet so I could scroll through the photos Kelly had sent.

"So," I said, thinking out loud. "Does this mean we're we at threat level orange?"

"I think, given the puppies and hearts, we're still at yellow."

"The nudes are a little menacing."

"Point taken."

Taylor piped up. "No threats, though. Not from her, anyway."

"Other than . . ." I thought about what on earth the term for it would be. "Coerced impregnation?"

"That part's worrisome," Robby agreed.

"And the fact that she now knows he's in Houston," Taylor said.

"And knows his address," I added.

We psychoanalyzed the Corgi Lady for a little while, trying to assess the danger she posed, and then we adjusted protocols at the Houston house. Kelly had already filed the police report and begun proceedings for a restraining order. We'd need to switch out the Range Rover for a different color and make, as well.

By the time I left HQ, it was getting dark.

I hadn't even made it to the Stapletons' gate when Robby shouted after me. "Hey!" he called. "Glenn's on the phone."

I'd forgotten about Glenn. But it was pretty late now. Connie would be up from her nap, and she'd need something in her stomach before her next round of meds.

"You know what?" I said. "I'll call him later."

And that's how, without even realizing it, I decided to stay.

I WAS HALFWAY down the gravel road to the house, sweeping my eyes back and forth for any signs of cattle, when I saw Jack running—actually running—out to meet me.

He reached me without even breaking stride and enclosed me in his arms.

"Where were you?" he asked, squeezing tight. "I was worried."

"I had to go to headquarters."

I could feel his heart beating. It did seem a little fast.

For a second, I thought it was real.

I relaxed into it the way you do in a real moment.

But then I thought I should confirm before I enjoyed it too much. "What are you doing?" I asked, my face pressed into his shoulder and my voice muffled against his shirt.

"My parents are watching," Jack said.

Ah.

Got it.

I hugged him back. But now only for pretend.

When he let me go at last, we walked back toward the house arm in arm—also for pretend.

"By the way, you can't be sneaking out to the river without me in the mornings."

"Why not?"

"If you'd read the handout, you'd know that I'm supposed to stay with you at all times."

"I will never read the handout."

"And what are you doing hitting golf balls into a river, anyway? You're going to choke a dolphin."

"They dissolve in water."

"That's a scam."

"Is it too much to want an hour or two to myself?"

"Yes. It is."

"Just sleep in and don't worry about it."

"I have to worry about it. It's my job to worry about it."

"Tell you what," Jack said then. "I'll stop sneaking off to the river when you tell me what that song is you're always humming."

"What do you mean?"

"That song you hum all the time. What's the name of it?"

"I don't hum a song."

"You do."

"I think I'd know if I were humming a song."

"Apparently not."

I frowned. "Do I hum a song?" I tried to remember humming a song.

"When you're in the shower," Jack said, like it might jog my memory. "Also, when you're pouring your coffee, or walking. Sometimes when you brush your teeth."

"Huh," I said. "I'm not sure I believe you."

Jack frowned. "You think I'm making it up?"

"I'm just saying, I think I'd notice."

We fell quiet as we approached the house, and I thought about sticking my hand in his back pocket as a little homage to heartbreak, and my two exes, and how mean life always is.

But maybe that was crossing the line.

AFTER DINNER, I walked Jack out toward the far end of the yard, where I could brief him in private about the corgi situation.

There was a horse pen off the side of the barn with a bench where we could sit. We climbed the fence and sat side by side near the water trough as I filled Jack in on the details, out of earshot from the house.

There's an art to telling clients about threats. A delicate balance that *informs* them without *alarming* them. Or, more accurately—alarms them just enough to get their attention, and their cooperation, and their compliance, without freaking them out.

But Jack wasn't alarmed at all.

In fact, I had barely said the word "nudes" before he started laughing.

"Hey," I said. "This isn't funny."

But Jack just leaned back and tilted his face to the stars, his shoulders shaking.

And then he leaned forward and put his face in his hands.

"I'm sorry," he said, after a little while, wiping at his eyes. "It's the nudes. And the notes. And the phrase . . ."

But he was overtaken by laughter and couldn't finish.

"And the phrase . . ." he tried again.

But nope. More laughing.

"And the phrase," he said again, louder now, as if commanding himself to get it out. "The phrase, 'if it's convenient for your schedule.'"

Now he collapsed forward, his whole torso shaking.

It's surprisingly hard not to laugh when someone's cracking up right in front of you. *This is serious*, I reminded myself. *Stay focused.* Then I said, all business, "You should probably take a look at everything."

"Not the nudes," he said, laughing harder. "Don't make me look at the nudes."

"You need to take this seriously," I said, trying to settle him with my tone of voice.

"I'll take the sweater," he said, wiping his eyes. "My mom loves them."

I shook my head. "It's all being impounded as evidence."

That set him off again. He doubled over, gasping for breath.

"I've never met anybody who laughs as much as you do," I said after a while.

He was still laughing. "I never laugh. I haven't laughed in years."

"You're laughing right now."

Jack sat up at that, as if he hadn't noticed.

The irony. Telling him he was laughing finally got him to stop laughing.

"I guess I am," he said, seeming to marvel at the idea. "Huh."

"You laugh constantly," I said, amazed that he didn't know this about himself. "You laugh at everything."

"Mostly at you, though," he said.

I gave him a look, like *Thanks.*

He studied me, like he was just realizing what he'd said was true.

"You can't ignore these threats," I said, fully ready to launch into a fiery lecture about how small threats could snowball into big ones.

But just then, something unexpected made me lose my train of thought.

A horse walked into the pen where we were sitting.

A *horse*.

A white and brown horse just walked through the open gate of the pen and strode toward us. Out of nowhere, I swear. A naked horse.

I tensed up, and Jack noticed. "Don't tell me you're afraid of horses, too."

"No," I said, on principle. "Just—what's it doing here?"

"*Doing* here? He lives here."

I watched as it came at us.

More accurately, it came at *Jack*—parking itself right in front of him and lowering its velvety muzzle right down to him, nose to nose. And let me assure you: What's true of cows is also true of horses. They look a lot smaller on TV.

This thing's face was the size of a suitcase.

I'd seen the horses of course—from a distance. In the corral. Looking . . . less large.

Jack had explained to me the first day how his folks had adopted a half a dozen homeless older horses who needed a pleasant place to live out their lives.

"Kind of a horse retirement home," he'd explained.

Which was great, in theory.

It's all fun and games until you have a giant pair of nostrils in your face.

"Hey, friend," Jack said to the horse, lifting his hands to stroke its nose. "This is Hannah. Don't bite her."

Then Jack walked away, and came back with a bag of oats.

He sat back down beside me, reached in, and pulled out a handful.

He flattened his palm, and the horse brought his fuzzy lips right down onto it and hoovered up every last grain.

"Your turn," Jack said next, offering me the bag.

"No, thank you."

Jack tilted his head. "You've got the scariest job of anybody I know, but you're afraid of horse lips."

"It's not the lips, it's the teeth."

Jack started laughing again.

"See?" I said. "You're laughing again."

"See?" Jack said, like it was my fault. "You're hilarious."

Jack did the next handful himself—but then he *bwok*-ed like a chicken at me until I finally said, "Fine."

I reached into the bag, closed my palm around a clump of oats, and held it out toward the horse.

"Keep your hand flat," Jack said, "so he doesn't eat your fingers."

"Not helping," I said, as the horse whispered his lips over my palm until he'd cleaned his plate.

"Tickles, huh?" Jack said.

"In a manner of speaking."

"This is Clipper," Jack said then. "He's a retired circus horse."

I looked up at Clipper with new respect.

"We got him when I was in high school," Jack said. "He was only eight then. He got an injury that was just bad enough to retire . . . but he was really fine. I spent my senior year doing tricks on him." Jack patted his neck. "He's an old man now."

"What kind of tricks?" I asked.

In response, without a word, Jack got a halter from the tack room and slipped it over Clipper's head. Then he motioned for me to follow him as he led the horse through the open gate to the paddock.

I stopped at the gate and watched as Jack hoisted and swung himself up onto Clipper's bare back, and the horse, seeming to know just what to do, shifted from a walk, to a trot, to a gentle canter.

The fence around the paddock was oval-shaped, and they followed the perimeter. Jack held the lead rope in one hand, but he didn't even have to steer.

"How have you never done a western?" I demanded.

"I know, right? I have 'horseback riding' on my résumé."

"Do you even need a résumé?"

"Nah. But still."

"You should do a western! This is a total waste of talent."

"Okay," Jack said. "If I ever make another movie, I will."

I was just about to ask him if he *would* ever make another movie, but then he said, "Get ready."

Then Jack leaned forward and grabbed two fat fistfuls of hair at the base of Clipper's mane . . . and I don't even know how to describe what he did next: Without the loping horse ever breaking stride, Jack swung off the left side, landed with both feet, bounced back up, slid across the horse's back, then swung off to the right side, and did the same bounce over there. And then he just kept doing it, back and forth, right and left, bouncing from one side to the other like he was slaloming.

I was so astonished, I couldn't even make a sound.

I just stood there, gaping.

After a full lap, Jack settled again on Clipper's back and turned to me to check my reaction.

Clipper was still loping at that steady pace.

"Cool, huh?" Jack said.

All I could muster was, "Be careful!"

"That wasn't scary," Jack said then, looking pleased at my concern. Then he said, "*This* is scary."

And then, before I could stop him, still holding the lead rope, Jack pressed his hands against Clipper's withers, leaned forward, and brought his sneakers up to the horse's back. Then slowly, carefully, as Clipper continued to canter along beneath him, Jack stood up.

He *stood up*!

Knees bent and arms out, like a surfer.

And Clipper just kept loping around the paddock.

"Amazing, right?" Jack said, when my mute astonishment had gone on too long. "It's all Clipper. His gait is so smooth, and nothing spooks him. You can do anything. You can hang from his neck. You can do a handstand."

"Do *not* do a handstand!" I said.

"Nah," Jack said. "I'm going to do something better."

And then, before I could respond, Jack squatted down low—all without the horse ever breaking stride—pushed himself back, and rolled a backward somersault off the horse's rump, dropping the lead rope as he went, and landing on his feet.

"Jesus Christ!" I shouted, and not in a good way.

Jack bowed deep and low, then turned to me, enjoying my horror, and said, "Been a long time since I did that. I'm gonna be sore tomorrow."

"No more somersaults!" I said, like I was making a rule.

Jack just looked really pleased with himself. "You've got me showing off for you."

"Don't show off for me," I said. "I don't want you to show off for me."

But Jack was walking over toward Clipper—who had slowed to a stop as soon as Jack landed and was now looking at us with his long, somber eyelashes.

Jack collected the lead rope and started walking the horse toward me. "Now it's your turn," Jack said.

"No, thank you."

"God, you're a scaredy cat. How is that possible in your line of work?"

"I don't know how to ride," I said.

"That's the great thing about Clipper," Jack said. "He does it all for you."

"I can't ride a horse," I said, as Jack kept coming closer. "I can do other things. I can drive a car backward on the freeway. I can rappel off a roof. I can pilot a helicopter."

Did I normally like a new challenge?

Of course.

But maybe I had enough skills. Or maybe I just didn't want to embarrass myself any further in front of Jack.

"This should be easy, then," Jack said.

I shook my head. "I'm good."

But Jack and the horse were right next to me now. "Just walking," Jack cajoled. "No tricks. Easy. You'll love it. All you have to do is sit. And I'll hold the lead rope."

I considered the horse, then I considered Jack.

Jack laced his fingers together and bent down to hold his hands like a stirrup. "Grab a big handful of mane, and give me your foot," he said.

I hesitated.

In a whisper, Jack started going, *"Bwok, bwok, bwok."*

I pushed out a sigh and lifted my foot into his hands. "Why is you *bwok*-ing like a chicken working on me? Why does *everything you do* work on me?"

I didn't even have time to worry that I'd confessed too much before Jack was hoisting me up the side of the horse.

"Atta girl," Jack said, moving his hands to my hips and then pushing my butt as I worked my leg around and got situated. "Not so hard, right?"

I was really glad I'd worn jeans that day.

I tried to sit up straight, like Jack had, but that's when I realized how ridiculously high up I was. It was like standing on a high dive.

I let myself lie on my belly and hold on around Clipper's neck.

"You can fly a helicopter," Jack said, "but you can't sit up on a horse?"

"Helicopters have seat belts," I said.

"This is not rocket science," Jack said.

"Settle down, horse boy," I said. "Just because you're the Simone Biles of horse gymnastics doesn't mean the rest of us have to be."

I looked over at Jack, and he'd started laughing. Again.

"Stop laughing," I said.

"Stop making me laugh," Jack said.

Then, with that, we started to walk.

And it wasn't so bad.

Clipper's gait really was very smooth.

I did not let go of Clipper's neck. And Jack did not let go of the lead rope.

"How have you never been on a horse before?" Jack called back over his shoulder after a quiet minute.

"I have," I said. "Once. On vacation, as a kid."

Maybe it was the comforting rhythm of the walking. Or the salty, horsey smell. Or the airy clop of hooves on the paddock dirt. Or the motion of Clipper's neck as he swung his head side to side. Or the solid, rocking weight of him underneath me. Or his bluster as he let out a noisy breath. Or even, if I'm honest, the occasional sight—whenever I peeked—of Jack up ahead, holding the lead rope in such an easy, almost tender manner, and walking ahead of us in such a trustworthy rhythm.

But I said, "It was the last vacation we took before my father moved out. Actually, he left halfway through the vacation. They fought, he left, and I never saw him again."

"You never saw him again? Not once?"

I shook my head. "Nope. Of course, I didn't go looking, either."

"Do you think you ever will?"

"Nope."

I could tell that Jack was hesitating to ask why.

"We were better off without him," I said. It wasn't true, of course. We were far worse without him. And that, right there, was the reason I would never meet him for coffee and make pleasantries. He'd forfeited all rights to the future when he ruined our lives.

"Wow," Jack said.

"Yeah," I said, and that's when Clipper slowed to a stop. When I looked up, Jack's face was all sympathy—like he hadn't just heard what I'd said but had *felt* it.

I'd never told anyone that story.

I'd almost forgotten about it, actually.

But Jack's face, as he listened, was so open, and so sympathetic, and so *on my side* that in that moment, despite all my rules, that memory just shared itself. I wasn't a sharer. I didn't even share things with non-clients. Especially not painful things. But I suddenly understood why people did it. It felt like relief. It felt like dipping your feet in cool water on a hot day.

This really was a revelation to me.

I suddenly felt like I could share things with Jack all night. Looking back, I might've.

But then I got saved by a disaster.

Because, next, we heard urgent yelling from back near the house.

Jack was unclipping the halter and helping me down before we could even make out the words. We took off running toward the sound and both vaulted the fence to cross the yard.

It was Hank, shouting into the darkness: "Jack! Jack!" And then: "Where are you? Jack!"

As we reached him, Hank turned toward the sound of us, his eyes wide and a little unfocused.

"What is it?" Jack said, out of breath.

"It's Mom," Hank answered. "She collapsed."

Eighteen

YOU DON'T CALL an ambulance in the country.

You just get yourself to the hospital.

As we sprinted across the yard, Jack called "get the keys" to me, and I was able to pull the Range Rover around to the side porch just as Jack was coming out with his mother in his arms. He and Hank worked Connie into the back seat, while Doc climbed in the other side to hold her head on his lap.

As Hank ran off to his truck and Jack climbed into the passenger seat, Doc asked, "Aren't you driving?"

Jack said, "Trust me. We want Hannah."

The hospital was twenty minutes away, and I had no idea how to get there. The guys had to direct me with: *Left past the tractor! Right at the longhorns! Don't run the stop sign!*

Even still, we made it in fifteen.

At the emergency bay, I dropped them off, and it was only as I took in the sight of The Destroyer carrying his unconscious mother through the sliding doors that I realized he didn't have a hat.

I mean, how exactly was he supposed to hide that world-famous face without a hat? The crooked glasses would never be enough.

I called Robby at HQ from the parking lot, briefed him, told him to get on the horn with intake to find us a private waiting room, and asked him to bring us "any other incognito items" ASAP.

"What does that mean?"

"I don't know! A fedora? A big newspaper? Get creative!"

I checked the gift shop on the way in, but it was closed.

By the time I got to Jack, it was too late. Jack and Hank were fighting in the hallway just off the waiting room—and every single person there was staring-but-not-staring at them.

"I'll take it from here," Hank was saying.

"We don't even know what's wrong yet."

"Just go home and I'll call you when there's news."

"That's not how this works."

"It works how I say it works."

"I'm staying."

"You're going."

"It's not your decision."

"It's sure as hell not yours."

"If you think I'm just going to carry my unconscious mother into the ER, drop her off, and go on home to watch TV, you're crazy."

"And *you're* crazy if you think I'm going to spend one more second with you than I have to."

Jack was trying to keep his voice low. But that just gave it more pressure. "I didn't ask to come home!"

"But you came, anyway."

"What choice did I have?"

"There's always a choice."

"Not always."

Hank was advancing on Jack now. Their voices were low and tight, but their body language was loud as hell.

"Don't stand there and act like you deserve to be here. You know who you are, and you know what you did. You gave up the right to be part of this family. I'm here, every day, picking up the pieces of everything you shattered. This is my family, not yours—and when I tell you to get the hell out, you go."

Hank had been building like a wave ready to crash.

I rooted for Jack to lift his hands, take a step back, and defuse the situation.

But he went the other way.

"Fuck you," Jack said.

And it was just the permission Hank had been waiting for. He drew his fist up like an archer, ready to let fly—

But I stepped in and caught it.

Caught his wrist, more specifically, and twisted it down by his side. Hank let out a grunt of pain.

Safe to say Hank did not see that coming. And neither did Jack.

The surprise broke the moment.

"We're not doing this here," I said.

In the silence that followed, the murmuring of the waiting room got loud.

I grabbed both of their elbows, clamped tight, and steered them around the corner toward the vending machines.

Whatever they were fighting about was bigger than this moment. But this moment was the only thing I could solve.

"Jack, you're coming with me," I said. And before he could protest, I added, "The entire waiting room is staring at you."

"You think I care about that right now? People stare at me all the time." His face was tense.

"I get it, but there's a bigger picture."

"This is my mom we're talking about."

I turned to Hank. "Go be with your folks. We'll meet you in a few minutes."

But Hank didn't need my instructions—or my permission. After blinking at me, like *What the hell?* for a second, he turned and left without a word.

"We need to find you a room to hide in," I said to Jack.

"That's what I was trying to do," Jack said, his voice tight like a wire. "He won't tell me the room number."

I frowned. "Why not?"

"Because he's an asshole."

Just then, a gaggle of teenage girls rounded the far end of the hallway.

On instinct, I reached to the back of his head to pull his face down toward my shoulder. "Keep your head down," I whispered into his ear, keeping an eye on them. "Pretend I'm comforting you."

Jack didn't fight me. He leaned down and buried his face in the crook of my neck, as I pulled him closer with both arms to cover as much of him as possible.

Just as the girls went past, I felt his arms come around me and tighten.

"Hey!" I whispered, once the girls had passed us.

"You said pretend." His breath tickled my neck.

"Not that much."

"I don't actually have to pretend much. You are genuinely comforting."

I broke away to scan the hallway. Clear now—both directions.

"It would be better if you just left right now," I said.

"Are you taking Hank's side?"

"You're going to be all over the internet if you stay. You don't even have a hat."

I wasn't wrong, but Jack shook his head. "I'm not leaving till we find out about my mom."

Fair enough.

I led him to the stairwell. "Can you wait here? I'll figure out where she is and then assess the route to get you there."

"You're really not kidding."

"Just stay here. Don't make trouble."

But as I started to step back out of the stairwell door, I saw that same roving band of teenage girls. They'd circled around and were coming back our way. What were they even doing here? As they made eye contact with me, I realized they had their phones out.

I ducked back into the stairwell and grabbed Jack's hand, pulling him behind me as I started up the stairs.

"What?" Jack said.

"We've got teenagers after us," I said, noting how silly it sounded.

But seriously—there was nothing worse for spreading the word of a celebrity sighting than a pack of teenage girls with phones. "Come on," I said. "Move."

At the top floor, I pulled him into the hallway, and we made for the elevators. We were halfway there when I saw a closet labeled SUPPLIES.

I pulled us both in, pushed the door closed, and leaned against it.

Taking my lead, Jack did the same—and wedged his sneaker heel against the door, too.

We stood there like that, side by side, breathing, for a minute before I noticed there were towels and sets of scrubs folded on the shelves. "I know how we're getting you out of here," I whispered.

"How?"

"Scrubs."

Jack looked to where I was pointing, but just as he did, we could hear the girls through the door as they passed by.

"It was so totally him."

"It was *absolutely* totally him."

"But that was *not* Kennedy Monroe."

"Yeah. Not even close."

We held our breath, waiting, any second, for the girls to try the handle. But they didn't.

Once all was quiet, I darted over to the scrubs supply. "What size are you?" I whispered, looking him up and down.

"I'm not leaving," he said. "We don't even know what's happening with my mom."

But just as he said it, his phone dinged.

A message from Hank. Guess he had his number now.

Can't find you. Mom's OK. They think she's dehydrated. Possible vertigo. Getting fluids now. Much better. Staying the night for observation. Go home.

Jack held it out for me to read.

"Ah."

He let out a deep sigh and closed his eyes for a minute. "Guess we're going home after all."

"You know," I said, expecting the usual brick wall. "It really might help me to know what's going on with you two."

But this time Jack met my eyes. "Hank hates me because I'm not Drew. Because Drew died and I lived."

"That's it?" I asked.

"That's enough of it."

I felt like an anthropologist. Was this how sharing worked? Had I earned some sharing from him by offering sharing of my own? Anyway, I nodded, like *Go on.*

To my surprise, he did. "I was the dumb one in the family, by the way. Drew and Hank were the smart ones, so they'd hang out and be smart together. I was the one with ADD and dyslexia and dysgraphia, too. The whole package."

"None of that makes you dumb."

"To me, it did. And my teachers, too. So I did the class clown thing. Hank and Drew were total Eagle Scouts with straight As. And I . . . was not."

"That's the deal with you and Hank?"

Jack sighed. "I was always kind of on the outs. Hank stayed here and became the ranch manager. Drew went to vet school here and went into practice with my dad. I was the only one who left. I was closest to Drew, for sure, because I always made him laugh. And he could always see that I was good at different things. He was kind of my buffer zone for the family. But after he died . . . there was no one to be that anymore."

I nodded. "He was important to you."

"I don't know how to be in this family without him."

That did not feel like the whole story.

But it was a start.

And then, realizing something positive, I said, "Hey! You drove over a bridge tonight! Without stopping to throw up."

This was not news to Jack. "Yes."

"That's progress, right?"

Jack tilted his head. "Without stopping to throw up *right away*. I threw up later. In the ER bathroom."

Ah. I took in the sight of him, just standing there being handsome. It's so easy to think that other people have it easy. "Still though," I lifted my fist, like *Yay*. "A time delay. That's progress."

I tossed him the scrubs and a little surgical hat, and then—while he was changing and I was deliberately, specifically not looking—I scanned the shelves for anything else that might help obscure his identity. I found a box of those disposable dark glasses they give you after they dilate your eyes and turned to hold a pair out, like *These?*

But my timing couldn't have been worse. He was just peeling off his T-shirt and I got an accidental eyeful of his naked torso.

I clamped my eyes closed.

"You really don't like the sight of me shirtless," he said, as he wriggled into the top.

"It's like looking at the sun," I said.

"Maybe *you* should wear those glasses."

"Maybe I should."

Then Jack asked, "Like looking at the sun in a good way? Or a bad way?"

"Both," I said, now rummaging the shelves.

"That's not an answer."

"Here's an idea," I said, after a minute. "I've got eyeliner in my purse. Maybe we could draw a mustache on you."

In the wake of that suggestion, the room went quiet. And it stayed quiet for so long, I had to turn back around.

And there was Jack, in a scrub top and his boxer briefs, one leg partway in the pants, and bent over laughing so hard, he wasn't making a sound.

No sound at all. Laughing too hard to even make noise.

Finally, he lifted his head up to the ceiling to take a big breath. "You want," he said, "to *draw* a mustache on me?"

"Look," I said. "This is creative problem solving."

But he was still laughing. "Can I get a monocle, too? And a puppy nose and some whiskers?"

"Put your pants on," I said, lacing my voice with irritation.

But he was pretty irresistible.

I felt an urge to laugh, too. But I tamped it down.

Nineteen

I EXPECTED EVERYTHING to blow up pretty fast after the scene at the hospital.

For days, we waited for photos of Jack and Hank in the waiting room to surface online.

But they didn't.

Every day that passed I breathed a little easier—though, even the possibility of the photos turning up meant we were more trapped on the ranch than ever—because now we really had to lie low.

Here was the problem: It was fun to be on the ranch.

In theory, I knew to be on alert. But, in practice, it really was a forced vacation.

And there's a reason people take vacations, I guess.

They *work*.

Slowly, unintentionally, and fully against my will . . . I relaxed.

A bit.

We fell into a rhythm. Connie returned with an official diagnosis of dehydration-induced vertigo, and she made a new commitment to hydrating. Doc clucked and fussed over her, bringing blankets and fixing cups of herbal tea. Hank and Jack kept a wary truce—not wanting to upset either of their parents. And I made myself useful by cooking all the meals, watering Connie's garden, and collecting bouquets of flowers to place around the house. It was a pleasant, sunny, rural way of life that made the real world feel like a different universe entirely. In a really good way.

Hank redeemed himself a little bit by bringing in broccoli, brussels sprouts, and squash from the garden—and washing it for me in the sink. As mean as he was to Jack, he was never mean to me—and I couldn't shake the feeling that he had to work to hold onto that anger.

Like it maybe wasn't natural to him.

Both of the boys, for example, went out of their way to look after Connie—checking on her in a way that felt almost competitive, like some unspoken Best Son competition.

She was definitely not neglected.

As time went by, she got better.

After a checkup in town, she got the news that the site was healing well.

She still wore her robe every day—saying she might never go back to real clothes—but she spent less and less time in her room, and less and less time napping.

The less sick she felt, the more of her personality came out. I learned, for example, that she liked to hook rag rugs out of old clothing. She was a lightning-fast reader and could finish an entire book in a day. And apparently, last summer, she'd ripped something in her knee when she'd gotten overenthusiastic listening to music while doing housework and had started doing the cancan. She now referred to it as her "cancan injury," and it still acted up sometimes.

Connie also had four hundred pairs of reading glasses. They were everywhere. In the cupboards, between sofa pillows, in bowls on the screen porch, on the kitchen table. She kept one pair on a chain around her neck and had at least two on her head at any given time.

"This is who I am now," she explained. "There are worse fates."

She also had an astonishing hobby. She refurbished old dolls and gave them to the local women's shelter. She had a whole collection of creepy ones she'd rescued from thrift shops—dolls that looked almost like Barbie had undergone extreme plastic surgery: overly made-up cat eyes, and giant, swollen lips. They were supposed to be "teenagers," and they were marketed toward little girls, but they really looked more like mutant porn stars.

But guess what Connie did with them? She took their faces off.

She wiped the faces with acetone until they were completely blank and then started from scratch repainting them to look, this time, like normal kids. Big eyes. Sweet smiles. Freckles. She braided their hair and sewed little play clothes for them. She gave them a second chance at a new life.

How could I not love her?

Doc was utterly lovable, too, by the way.

He took to sitting at the far end of the kitchen, deejaying songs for me from the Stapleton family record collection while I made dinner, and singing along to oldies with Doc Stapleton became my favorite time of day.

Add to that: Jack Stapleton knew how to dance. You saw *American Rhythm*, right? Where he played a ballroom dancer? That was no body double. He learned all the dances himself. So when he'd hear Sam Cooke on the turntable, or Rosemary Clooney, or Harry Belafonte, he'd show up in the kitchen, and pull me out into a spin.

Jack insisted it was essential for the fake relationship. "That's totally what I'd do with a real girlfriend," he promised.

The point is, I didn't resist.

If Jack Stapleton just *had* to make me jitterbug with him every time he heard "Shake, Rattle, and Roll"—and spin me around and dip me and put his hands all over me?

Fine.

It was fake. It was fake. It was all fake.

But it felt so real.

It wasn't just Jack. Hank gruffly helped me turn the compost. Doc nicknamed me Desperado and let me help him groom the horses. And Connie took to hugging me . . . and I didn't stop her.

It made me miss my mom in a way I never expected. Or maybe not her, exactly—but the person she could have been. The relationship we could have had.

I'd always wondered if other people's mothers were as good as they seemed.

In Connie's case, I had my answer.

Yes.

It didn't take long for me to feel a part of that family.

And, despite all its tensions and sorrows, I'd forgotten how good it felt to be surrounded by all those overlapping bonds—of affection, of memory, even of frustration. Sometimes I'd watch Connie swat at Doc for some snarky remark to Jack, and I'd positively ache with longing for more of whatever that was.

I tried really hard not to fall in love with them all, I swear.

But I failed most of the time.

With Jack most of all.

With unexpected things: The way he took every opportunity to shoot free throws at the kitchen garbage can—and missed every time. The way he was trying to make friends with a crow by setting popcorn out on the fence. The way he'd decided that the most sanitary way for everyone to sneeze was to put their face inside their shirt at the moment of impact.

"See?" he said one night, after sneezing into his shirt at dinner. "It totally contains the spray."

We all stared at him. "But you just sneezed on yourself," Hank pointed out.

Jack shrugged. "The shirt dries it off."

"But now you're walking around with snot on your stomach."

"You're missing the point. It reins in the germs."

"But it's gross."

"I'd rather sneeze on myself than sneeze on someone else."

"Are those the only options?"

Then Jack would look at me like we were the only sane people in the room. "Yeah. Actually. They are."

The point is, the deck was stacked against me.

On a normal job, you were with the principals all day, too—but not like this. You were in the background. You were unnoticed—off at the side of the room. You were near them, but not *with* them. You weren't chatting with them. Or getting teased by them. Or letting them *give you noogies.*

This was the opposite of a normal job.

Jack and I spent all day every day together. We fished in the pond stocked with bass. We explored the wilderness area around the oxbow lake. We walked the river beach almost every day. We played croquet in the yard. We threw horseshoes. We spun each other on the tire swing. We harvested pears, figs, and satsumas from the orchard.

My favorite thing was swinging in the hammock chairs outside the kitchen window. We'd swing side by side with our shoes off, feeling the grass blades brushing the soles of our feet, and I'd pass the time by asking him inane questions like, "What's it like being famous?"

He liked that kind of question, though. "People are nice to you for no reason," he answered. Then he turned to meet my eyes. "Not *you*, of course. You're not nice."

I pumped my legs to swing higher. "Not me," I confirmed.

"But the weird thing is," he went on, pumping to catch up, "it's not *you* they're being nice to. It's the fame. They think they already know you, but you've literally never seen them before. So it's very one-sided. You have to be careful not to disappoint them or offend them, so you wind up spending a lot of time being the most generic version of yourself. And smiling. Smiling just constantly. I've come home from doing meet and greets, and had to wait hours for the muscles in my face to stop twitching."

"Huh," I said.

"I'm not complaining," Jack said then.

"I know."

"It's a great job. There's freedom. And money. And clout. But it's complicated."

I nodded in agreement. "Like everything."

"People who want to be famous think it's the same thing as being loved, but it's not. Strangers can only ever love a version of you. People loving you for your best qualities is not the same as people loving you despite your worst."

"So," I said, "until the whole nation has seen your boxer briefs on the bathroom floor . . ."

Jack gave a decisive nod. "Then it's not true love."

I relaxed for a minute and let my swing slow down.

Jack went on. "It skews your perspective, too. Everybody wants to be around you all the time, and they hang on your every word and laugh at everything even if it's not funny, and you're kind of the center of every situation you're in."

"That doesn't sound too bad, though."

"But then you get used to it. You start forgetting to notice other people or ask them about themselves. You start believing your own hype. Everybody treats you like you're the only person that matters . . . and you just start thinking that's true. And then you become a narcissistic asshole."

"You didn't do that."

"I did, though. For a while. But I'm trying not to be like that anymore."

"Is that why you took a break from acting?"

"Yeah," Jack said. "That. And my brother died."

LOOK, I KNEW I was letting myself get confused.

I just didn't know how to stop it.

And then one day, near the end of a late-morning jog we took to the river and back, Jack said—no joke: *while jogging*—"I found your song."

"What song?" I asked.

"The one you're always humming." He took out his phone—still jogging—and pulled up a song on it.

"How did you find it?" I asked.

"I secretly recorded you," Jack said.

"*That's* not creepy," I said.

"The point is, I solved the mystery," Jack said. "You're welcome."

We were on a straightaway, in our last quarter mile, heading back to the house on the gravel road. Jack held the phone vaguely in my direction as he jogged along by my side.

But as soon as the song started playing, I slowed to a stop.

That song? *That* was the song I was always humming? I knew that song.

Jack stopped beside me, letting it play.

"Recognize it?" he asked after a bit, a little out of breath.

"Yes," I said, not offering more.

It was an oldie by Mama Cass called "Dream a Little Dream of Me." When the song started over, I sang along with the first line: "Stars shining bright above you . . ." When I was little, my mom used to sing it all the time—while doing dishes, while driving carpool, while tucking me into bed.

"So what's the deal?" Jack asked.

"It's just a song I know," I said.

"How do you know it?"

"My mom used to sing it all the time when I was a kid. But I haven't heard it in years and years."

"Except for, like, every day, when you're humming it."

I didn't argue.

When the song ended, Jack put his phone away. It suddenly seemed awfully quiet.

"I think she only sang that song when she was happy," I said.

Jack just nodded.

"If I'm honest, I can't remember her singing it—not even once—after my dad left.'"

Jack nodded again, and as I felt the tenderness in the way he was watching me, I also felt a rising pain in my chest—penetrating, like when your hands have gotten too cold and then you put them in hot water. A thawing pain that stung behind my ribcage and then climbed up into my throat.

And I guess the only way that pain could get itself out was to melt into tears.

I felt them sting my eyes.

I stayed very still, like if I didn't move, Jack might not notice.

But of course he noticed. He was six inches away and staring right at me.

"Tell me," he said, his voice soft.

I kept still.

"You can tell me," he said again. "It's okay."

It's okay. I don't know what kind of magic he infused into those two words, but somehow, when he said them, I believed him. Everything I had ever told myself about being professional and staying on guard and maintaining boundaries just . . . fluttered off in the wind.

I blame the sunshine. And the long grass. And that endless, gentle breeze over the pasture. I gave in.

"My dad left when I was seven," I said then, my voice shaking, "and my mom started dating a guy named Travis pretty soon after that, and he . . ." How to phrase it? "He wasn't the nicest guy in the world." I took a shaky breath. "He yelled at her a lot. He picked on her and told her she was ugly. He drank every night—and she started drinking, too."

Quietly, without even shifting his gaze, Jack took one of my hands and wrapped it in his.

"On the night of my eighth birthday," I said, taking a big, shaky breath, "he hit her."

Jack kept his gaze steady.

"Those words are so tiny, when you say them. Three quick syllables, and it's over. But I think, in a way, for me, it's never been over." I looked down, and more tears spilled over. "She was protecting me that night. We'd been supposed to go out for pizza and cake, but Travis decided at the last minute that we weren't going. I was so outraged at the injustice that I slammed my bedroom door. He started to come after me. I'll never forget the sound of his footsteps knocking the floor. But my mom blocked him. She stood in front of the door and wouldn't move until he went after her instead. I hid in my closet, clamped down tight into a ball, but I could hear it. The scariest thing about the punches was how quiet they were. But her crying was loud. When she slammed back against the door, it was loud. When she hit the floor, it was loud.

"I stayed awake all night, curled as small as I could get in the closet, listening, at attention, trying to decide if my mother had lived. I never fell asleep. When the sun was up, she came to find me—and she had a split lip and a cracked tooth. As soon as I saw her face, I wanted to get us both out of there. Every atom in my body wanted to escape.

"But as I started to stand, she shook her head. She climbed into the closet with me and put her arms around me.

"'We're leaving, right?' I asked.

"But she shook her head.

"'Why?' I asked. 'Why aren't we?'

"'Because he doesn't want us to,' she said.

"Then she put her arms around me and rocked me back and forth, in a way that always, before then, had made me feel safe. But I didn't feel safe anymore. I don't think I ever felt safe again after that, to be honest—not really. But guess what I still do even now when I feel scared?"

"What?" Jack asked.

"I sleep in the closet."

Jack kept his eyes on mine.

"Remember my little safety pin with the beads on it? I'd made that pin for her that very same day. I never got a chance to give it to her. By the time that night was over, I'd lost it—or, I thought I had. After my mom died—not that long ago—I found it in her jewelry box. She'd kept it all those years. Finding it again felt like finding some little lost part of myself. I was going to wear it every day forever before I lost it on the beach that day. As a talisman for being okay."

"But you're okay, anyway."

I looked down. "Am I? I don't know. Up until I came out here, I'd been sleeping on the floor of my closet every night since my mom died."

Jack lifted a nonsweaty part of his T-shirt to wipe my face. Had I just cried? Again? What was with me? Then Jack said, in a tender voice, "So sleeping on my floor is an improvement."

I gave him a little shove and started walking again.

He fell into step beside me.

"Anyway," I said, regrouping. "That's the story of that song. I never heard my mom sing it again after that night. I forgot about it entirely."

"Not entirely, though," Jack said.

And then—even though there was nobody around to see—he pulled me into a hug.

Twenty

WE WERE JUST starting to think we'd dodged getting caught at the hospital when a photo of Jack showed up on a gossip site.

And then ten minutes later? It was everywhere.

Sure enough, it was taken in the waiting room of the ER. And though it was from a distance, and it was more the side of his face than the front, it did look a lot like him.

The internet wasn't sure, though. Articles started popping up like, "What's World Famous Jack Stapleton Doing in Katy, Texas?" and "Stapleton Sighted in Nowheresville" and "Reclusive Superstar Takes Obscurity to a New Level."

Enthusiastic internet sleuths found pictures of Jack taken at similar angles and posted them side by side, parsing each detail with Oliver Stone–like precision. Was this the true shape of Jack Stapleton's earlobe? Was the dot on his neck a shadow or a freckle? Was this the same T-shirt he'd worn in a paparazzi shot two New Year's Eves ago?

It was impressive work, actually. Glenn should recruit some of those people.

In the end, the internet broadly agreed: Yes, The Destroyer had been spotted in a random little hospital in a tiny Texas town. The question nobody seemed to have an answer to was *why*.

All to say: Jack being sort-of exposed bumped us up to threat level orange at last.

Maybe a light orange—more like a sherbet—but orange all the same.

The team had to evaluate more internet chatter and track a new explosion of "fans" who looked like they could cause trouble. I started putting on leggings and sneakers every day for "an afternoon run" to jog off the property for surveillance updates at headquarters.

It was just down the road, but it might as well have been a whole other world.

I didn't love going.

And I loved it even less the day I found Glenn there, mid rant.

Doghouse was there, too, as were Taylor and Robby.

"I don't care what your feelings are. Feelings have no place in this room!" Glenn was shouting. He banged his hand on the desk at those words.

"What's going on?" I asked, closing the door behind me.

Glenn, looking pissed, pointed at me. "This is your fault, too."

"My fault!" I said. "I just got here."

"Twenty-five years I went without any of my agents sleeping with each other. Twenty-five years! Then you and Romeo over here break that rule, and now it's a free-for-all."

I looked over at Robby, who was staring at the floor. Then, Taylor. Who was staring straight ahead, her eyes red and her face puffy.

"What happened?" I asked.

"Did you know these two were sleeping together?" Glenn demanded.

I flared my nostrils. "Yes."

"Well, now he's dumped her," Glenn announced, like it was somehow my fault. "And she can't get any work done—and neither can anybody else—because she *cannot stop crying.*"

Did I feel a tiny flicker of triumph?

No comment.

"Does this mean I get London?" I asked. "Since he's such a trouble-maker?"

But Glenn was in no mood. "You've got your downsides, too."

He wasn't wrong. I turned to Robby. "You dumped her, huh?"

"Do you even need to ask?" Glenn demanded. "Look at her!"

Now there were fresh tears on Taylor's face.

"You want a lesson on how to get dumped?" Glenn demanded of Taylor. "*That,*" he said, pointing right at me, "is how you get dumped! She's the gold standard! This guy ripped her heart out on the night after her mother's funeral, but she was back at work the next day like a god-damned superhero."

Taylor was actively crying now.

"Ugh," Glenn said, turning away in disgust. "Get out of here and pull yourself together. Go get some fresh air. Amadi, take her some water."

Taylor scuttled out, and Amadi followed.

Glenn rounded on Robby then. "Just what are you and that horn-dog personality of yours trying to accomplish? Are you trying to drive me into bankruptcy? Is there one woman in this company you haven't screwed?"

Kelly raised her hand cheerfully in the back corner. "He hasn't screwed me!"

"Keep it that way," Glenn growled.

"Yeah," Doghouse added. "Keep it that way."

"Yes, sirs," Kelly said, saluting them both.

"Hey, Kelly," I said with a wave.

"Hey."

But Glenn wanted answers. "What are you doing?" he demanded of Robby. "What are you thinking?"

"I made a mistake," Robby said.

"You sure as hell did."

"No," Robby said. "I made a mistake when I broke up with Hannah."

"Oh God," I said, smacking my hand on my forehead and walking toward the door. "Seriously?"

But Robby stopped me. "You can't go."

I gave Glenn a look. "Are you really gonna make me stay for this?"

Glenn tilted his head. "I believe we still have work to do. You re-member work?"

"What am I supposed to do?" Robby demanded of Glenn, in a voice like there was no bigger victim in this room than him. "All day long, I have to watch these monitors." Robby turned to me. "You know we put cameras everywhere, right? Whatever you two do outside, I'm watching it. If he gives you a piggyback ride. If he helps you in the garden. If he shows you tricks on the horse, or he teaches you how to do a handstand, or he stares at you when you aren't looking. I see it all."

Wait. *Jack stared at me when I wasn't looking?*

Robby kept going. Back to Glenn: "You did this to torture me."

Glenn didn't even lift his eyebrows. "Absolutely."

"Well, it's working. It's driving me insane."

"Good. You deserve it."

"Is this personal?"

"It's life," Glenn said. "And if you're smart, you'll use it to get stronger."

I squinted at Robby. "Is this a caveman thing? Is this a chemical, knee-jerk, nobody-can-have-my-former-woman thing? Are you peeing on me to mark your territory?"

Kelly was still listening. "Please don't let him pee on you."

I gave her a look. *"Metaphorically."*

But Robby shook his head. "I'm sorry, okay? I should never have let you go."

"Let me go?" I said. "You didn't let me go. You *abandoned* me."

"I take it back."

"There's no taking it back."

"Why not?"

"Because now I know who you really are."

Robby pouted at that. Then he narrowed his eyes. "I know what this is. You think he likes you."

I held very still.

"I see you with him," Robby went on. "He's got you convinced. But that can't be right. You're too smart for that. You can't really think that a world-famous actor who could have any woman in the world picked *you*. Tell me you didn't fall for that. Have you *seen* Kennedy Monroe? He's playing with you! He's bored! He's not even that great an actor! Wake up. You're choosing a fake relationship over me."

I didn't know what to say to most of that. But that last point was easy. "Wrong," I said. "I'm choosing *anything at all* over you."

"He doesn't actually like you," Robby said.

"I never said he did."

"But you thought it."

I had to hand it to Robby. A rare moment of insight.

Glenn was done here. "Get Taylor back," he said, flinging his arm at Kelly. "Let's have this stalker meeting and call it a day."

Robby kept his eyes on me. "You asked me the other week why I was being such an ass."

Wow, that was a hundred years ago. "You mean when you said I was not *pretty enough* for this assignment?" I said. "I guess I did."

"Don't you want to know the answer?"

I stopped and turned to look at him. "I know the answer already," I said. "You were being an ass because you *are* an ass. Simple."

But Robby grabbed my arm. "It's because I wanted to get back together."

That got my attention. "You wanted to—?"

"Even then, even that day."

I tried to put it together. "You wanted to get back together . . . so you said I was ugly?"

"I panicked."

"Is that what it's called?"

"I missed you in Madrid."

"You missed me in Madrid—while you were sleeping with my best friend?"

"I've wanted you back ever since we got home. But I felt guilty about Taylor."

"Wait! Are you trying to seem like a good person?"

"I'm saying it's complicated."

"No. It's very simple."

Robby seemed to hold his breath for a second. "Because of *Taylor*?" he demanded, like I was being petty. "That was just an on-assignment thing."

"Not because of Taylor," I said. "Because you dumped me." Then, for good measure, I added, "On the night after my mother's funeral."

Robby made a strangled noise as if we'd had this argument a million times. "When are you going to stop fixating on that?"

"Never," I said. "That's why we're never getting back together. The Taylor thing was just another nail in a well-nailed coffin."

"We were just *bored*," Robby pleaded, like I was being unreasonable.

"Is that what Taylor would say?"

"I'm telling you, the person I wanted then—and want now—is you."

"I'm pretty sure we never really liked each other all that much, any way."

I couldn't believe I was being forced to have this conversation.

Yes, I was lonely. Yes, witnessing Robby and Taylor kissing had shredded me in ways I never knew were possible. But I wasn't *pathetic*. "We're not getting back together, Robby."

"Why not?"

"Because you disqualified yourself."

"You'd rather be alone forever than let me make it up to you?"

"Not sure those are my only options."

"I just want a chance to make things right."

"But there is no way to make things right. And even if there were, you wouldn't know how."

AFTER THE MEETING—AFTER Taylor was dragged back in to sit, catatonic, staring at the floor while Robby snuck resentful looks at me like I was the bad guy, and after Glenn went on another rant about how nobody in this company was allowed to have any sex at all for any reason ever again, and after we talked through all the details and ramifications and policy changes that the viral photo of Jack was going to mean for this assignment, I jogged back to the ranch in a daze, turning one simple, shocking thought over and over in my head.

Robby was right.

Leave it to Robby to suck the fun out of everything.

But he was right.

Liking Jack was a catastrophically bad idea.

I couldn't believe I'd let it happen.

He was *Jack Stapleton.*

Letting myself fall for him was emotional suicide.

That's exactly what I was thinking when I saw the god himself up ahead on the gravel road, walking in my direction.

When he saw me, he shifted into a jog, which gave the distinct impression that he was happy to see me.

So Method.

I didn't slow down—just kept walking, even as he reached me—and so Jack had to U-turn to follow me.

"Hey!" he said, still jogging. "Welcome back."

I didn't answer.

He fell into pace beside me. "You okay?" he asked, trying to study my face. "You look tired."

"Long meeting," I said.

Jack wrinkled his nose. "About the stalker?"

"Yes. Apparently, she TP'd your house with pink toilet paper. And left a painting for you."

"A painting?"

"A self-portrait. On canvas," I said, as we arrived back in the yard. I pulled the photo up on my phone. We paused in Connie's garden to take a look. "A nude," I said, to prepare him. Then I added, "Self-Portrait with Corgis."

Jack let out a low whistle. "It's actually pretty good."

I nodded. "She's talented."

"Maybe I *should* impregnate her."

"Hey!" I said. "You're not impregnating anybody on my watch!" Then, in case that was too strident, I added, "Unless you want to."

There he was, again—laughing. "I missed you," he said then.

"What?"

"Just now," Jack said, gesturing back at HQ. "You were gone a long time."

"We had a lot to discuss."

"What do you think about that?"

"About what?"

"About me missing you."

Maybe it was because Robby had just weaponized this whole setup against me, but now I couldn't see anything Jack did as real. There he was, with a shy half smile, looking down at my sneakers and leaning in toward me—just *textbook* bashfully . . . and I could only see it as calculated, and constructed, and hollow, and fake. And the fact that he was faking it so well—that I hadn't even been able to tell the frigging difference—was just humiliating.

He was acting. He'd been acting all along.

But I wasn't.

Was I supposed to play along? I couldn't. I wouldn't. What did I think of him telling me he missed me? "I think you're a much better actor than anybody gives you credit for," I said. Not even trying to disguise the bitterness in my voice.

Jack winced at that—microscopically, but I felt it.

Fine. Good. Better that way.

Because something was hitting me then, surrounded by Connie's fall garden, out in the middle of nowhere. I was not all that different from the Corgi Lady. I was living in a fantasy world, too.

My chances of winding up with Jack Stapleton were just as bad as hers.

Worse, maybe, even.

At least the Corgi Lady knew how to paint.

Twenty-One

I WAS ALL set to keep my distance after that.

But then, that night, Jack had a nightmare.

A bad one.

I woke to the sound of him thrashing and choking. He had said not to be alarmed, but I'm not gonna lie: It was alarming. He's not a small guy, and whatever was going on in that nightmare . . . he was fighting it with everything he had.

I stood up fast, heart thumping, and clambered over to him.

"Jack," I said, trying to steady his shoulders. "Wake up."

But he was thrashing like a wild boar. His arm came up and smacked me across the collarbones like a wood plank. I took a step back, found my breath, and regrouped.

I stepped closer again. "Jack! Wake up!"

This time, he heard me, and opened his eyes. He grabbed my nightgown to pull himself up—gasping, coughing, sobbing, and looking around like he had no idea where he was.

"You're good!" I said. "You're safe!" I said, as he tried to focus. "Just a dream. Just a really bad dream."

And then what did I do? I hugged him.

I sat close to him, and squeezed my arms around him tight, and said every soothing thing I could think of.

As soon as it all registered—where he was, who I was, what was happening—he clamped his arms around me and wouldn't let go.

So I stayed right there.

I stroked his back and patted it. I waited for his breathing to settle. I comforted him. Like real people do with people they really care about.

Even after he'd gotten quiet, when I thought maybe he was feeling better and might want to be left alone to sleep, it was—let's say— challenging to leave him. When I tried to unfold myself from his arms, he tightened his grip.

"You're okay now," I said.

But then he said, "Stay with me a little longer, okay?" His voice was so shaky, there was no other answer but, *Of course.*

And when he decided to lie back on the pillow and kept his arms around me, clamping me close like I was his teddy bear, I let him do that, too.

"Just another minute," he said.

I could manufacture a hundred reasons why I stayed. But the only one that matters is this: I *wanted* to. I liked it there. I liked holding him—and being held. I liked feeling like I mattered to someone. There's nothing like the mutuality of a hug—the way you're giving comfort but you're getting it, too.

I didn't know what was real or fake anymore, but right then, it just didn't matter.

We faced each other on our sides. He kept his arms wrapped around me. I rested my head on his bicep.

I gave myself five more minutes. Then another five. I decided to wait until he fell asleep. But he didn't fall asleep.

I'd close my eyes, but every time I opened them, I saw his, right there, open, gazing at me, pupils dark and wide.

After a while, I asked, "It's the same dream every time?"

"Yep."

Then I asked, "Can you tell me what it is?"

But he didn't answer.

Finally, I said, "Because I read up on 'how to cure nightmares.'"

"You did?"

"Yeah. I read up on a lot of things."

"Were you going to tell me about it?"

"I'm telling you right now."

"Let's hear it."

"There are lots of methods, but one big one is to talk about the dream."

"I don't want to talk about the dream."

"I get it. But apparently it helps. You tell the story of the dream—while you're awake . . . but then you rewrite the ending."

"How can you rewrite the ending if it's already ended?"

"You rewrite it for next time."

"I always hope there won't be a next time."

"But there always is."

Jack nodded.

"So let's try it, then."

Jack smiled then and let his eyes roam around my face. "I can see why my mom likes you."

I didn't want to enjoy that too much.

"Rewriting the ending," I said, "is like offering your brain a different script. So when it goes to tell that story again, it has a choice to tell it a different way."

"There is no different way."

"Not yet. Because you haven't written one."

Jack sighed like we were talking in circles.

"Like one example," I went on, "is a guy who had a recurrent night-mare about a monster chasing him. For years and years. And then one day, he turned and asked the monster why it was chasing him—and then he never had that dream again."

"Nice solution," Jack said. "One problem for me, though."

"What?"

"In my nightmare, *I'm* the monster."

"Oh."

A minute went by. Then Jack said, "It's the same every time."

I waited while he took a breath.

Then he went on, "I'm in a sports car with my little brother Drew. It's a Ferrari. I bought it to show off. It's so new, it still has paper tags. Drew thinks it's awesome. And we're going so fast, it's like we're flying. The faster we go, the faster we go—until a bridge appears up ahead. It's late afternoon in winter—and even though it's not that cold out, there's black ice on the bridge—the kind that's the color of pavement, the kind you never see until it's too late. As soon as we hit it, we just go sliding. We're spinning and everything's a blur and then we crash through the railing. I can't believe it's happening, even as it's happening. Everything's in slow motion and at hyper speed exactly at the same time. We go over the edge and then we're in this free fall where gravity is turned inside out. It all happens in seconds—and hours—and years . . . and then we hit the water's surface—the chassis flat, like a belly flop. *This is good*, I think. *This gives us time.* The car bobs at the surface—and time goes sideways. I roll down my window and shout at Drew to do the same. I hold the button with one hand, and I fumble with my seatbelt with the other—and then I look over at Drew, and he hasn't done anything. His window's up. He's buckled. He's staring at me in shock. *Put your window down!* I lean over and pop his seatbelt. I press against his chest to hold his window button—and it's halfway down when the car fills up a rush of water and it's so cold and so angry. *Swim up!* I shout before the water overtakes us, and as I push him out his window and follow him. The water's so gray, it's *black*, but I pump my arms and legs with everything I've got—but I can't find the surface. I've lost the surface, and there's no time to find it. The water tangles around me, pulling me deeper, and when I wake up, I'm drowning."

Wow. Okay.

No wonder he got mad at me at the Brazos.

I was in over my head for sure. An hour of internet research was not going to equal enough expertise to cure this.

But I'd gotten this started. I'd told him to tell the story. No quitting now.

So I asked the first question that came to my mind. "Why do you think it's the exact same dream every time?"

A long pause. Then Jack said, very slowly, "Because—except for the part where it's me drowning—that's pretty much the way it happened."

I pulled back a little to check Jack's expression. "That's what happened? In real life?"

Jack nodded.

"You went off a bridge into a river?"

Jack nodded again.

"I'd heard it was a car accident."

"Technically, it was."

Jack pulled his arms away from me and rolled onto his back, crooking one arm over his eyes, covering half his face. "He died in the river. The police think he got turned around in the darkness and swam down instead of up."

So this was the version of the story that got buried.

Was it Jack's fault? Was there alcohol involved, like the rumor said? Had Jack killed his little brother?

I couldn't bring myself to ask.

"I'm so sorry," I said at last, hoping my voice could make up for the inadequacy of those words. "I didn't know."

Jack nodded. "The PR folks covered it up. Nobody knows. Except me. And my family. And a few local officials in North Dakota. And, of course, Drew."

I thought for a second. "Is this why the studio insisted on you hiring protection?"

Jack nodded. "I've caused them enough trouble."

Next, I said, "And this is the war between you and Hank?"

Jack nodded. "The troublemaker is my mom. She keeps wanting to see me. She keeps asking me to come visit. She just keeps on loving me and forgiving me."

"And when she got sick, Hank didn't want you to come here?"

"That's right."

"But you came, anyway."

"I couldn't exactly tell her no."

"And now you're just waiting until you can disappear again?"

"That's basically it."

"I think it sounds like you're being awfully hard on yourself."

"Next time you let someone drown in a river, call me and we'll compare notes."

"So you can't forgive yourself?"

"Can't," Jack shrugged. "Won't."

"Seems a little harsh."

"I just wake up every day thinking about how a person—a really great person, a much better person than me— isn't here, and I am. The only way to make my existence bearable is to try to do something every day that justifies my life."

"What do you do?"

"Oh, you know, start foundations. Fund scholarships. Make celebrity appearances at children's hospitals. Help old ladies with their groceries. Donate blood."

Wow. Some lucky person got The Destroyer's blood and didn't even know it.

"Big things," Jack went on, "and little things, too. Just—*something*. One good thing every day."

"That's a lot of repentance."

Jack nodded. "You'd think the nightmare would have faded by now, but it's still going strong."

"Okay," I said. "What if the nightmare isn't a punishment? What if it's a *chance*?"

Jack met my eyes. "A chance to do what?"

"See your brother again."

"Pretty slim, as chances go. Since he's dead."

I kept going. "I have an idea, but you'll probably hate it."

"That sounds like a challenge."

"You've heard of lucid dreaming, right? Where you're aware that you're dreaming in the dream?"

"Sort of."

"What if you taught yourself how to do that and then . . . talked to Drew?"

"Just taught myself to dream on purpose?"

"I mean, yeah."

"And then had a conversation with my dead brother?"

I nodded.

"How? When? As the car is filling with water?"

"What if you just . . . steered the dream in a different direction?"

"That's not how dreams work. They're not screenplays."

"But you are technically writing them. We all are."

"It's a terrible idea. And even if it worked, it wouldn't be the real Drew."

"But maybe talking to Drew could be a way of talking to yourself."

Jack looked at me for a minute. "You're right. I hate it."

"Fine," I said, moving to crawl away. "Hate it. Whatever."

But as I shifted, he caught me and yanked me back, pulling me against his chest. It was solid, and warm, and smelled as ever like cinnamon. "Stay."

My head landed on the pillow beside him. "I'm tired."

"Two minutes."

"Sixty seconds," I said. "Take it or leave it."

"Sold," Jack said.

"Sixty seconds it is," I said. "Just don't let me fall asleep."

Twenty-Two

OF COURSE, I fell asleep.

When I woke up the next morning, I was in Jack Stapleton's bed, under that maelstrom of whatever it was he did to his sheets every night, and I was pinned to the mattress by one of Jack's enormous arms, slung across my shoulders, and also one of his legs—tangled around one of my own.

All of which felt pretty nice, actually.

I gave myself a moment to savor it.

I mean . . . *right*? That kind of thing doesn't happen every day. I was tempted to snap a selfie so I'd believe it later.

But then my phone—which was set to never ding before 8:00 A.M.—started dinging at 8:01.

A lot.

And by the time I'd wriggled out from under Jack to check it, I found a thousand texts from every single person I worked with, and plenty of people I didn't.

Apparently, I'd accidentally gotten famous overnight.

Because while we'd been sleeping in here—out there on the internet, things were wide awake.

In less than twenty-four hours, three major Jack-related things occurred.

One: The Corgi Lady decided to update her Jack Stapleton fan page
with photos and videos of all her stalking shenanigans—spreading the
word far and wide that Jack was in Houston and that she'd managed
to find his house. Countless posts showed up with captions like, "Love
is in the air at my one and only's luxury rental estate in Houston! He
can run, but he cannot hide! #JackStapleton #JackAttack #JackHammer
#TrueLove #CorgiAddict #CheckOutMyNudes #LetsMakeABaby."

Two: A photo of Jack and me from the hospital—that night, when
I told him to hide by leaning into me—showed up and then exploded
online. We definitely looked like we were embracing, possibly even making out like crazy, even to me. And this photo was everywhere under
headlines like "Who's Jack Stapleton's New Girlfriend?" and, "Mystery
Woman Sucks Face with Jack Stapleton," and just plain old, "Get It, Jack!"

And three: The Corgi Lady apparently saw the photo, lost what was
left of her mind, and delivered a basket of stuffed-animal corgi puppies
to the doorstep of Jack's rental house in Houston . . . with a note tucked
inside letting Jack know that she was definitely, without question, going
to murder me. In graphic detail.

Glenn, needless to say, was not pleased.

Take a jog to HQ! ASAP! his final text said. Let's figure this the hell
out.

This definitely bumped Jack up to threat level tangerine. Or maybe
even persimmon.

It wasn't a death threat against the principal, but it was a threat
against his "girlfriend," which was close enough. Also, the photos she'd
posted included all sorts of revealing clues about Jack's house that en-
terprising fans could study. Also, the world now knew that he was back
in civilization—which made him fair game.

Before I left Jack's room, I gave myself a minute to pause at the door
and look at him—still fast asleep in the bed where *I had also been* just
minutes before. The guy in that bed was so different from the person all
over the internet. From his crooked glasses, to his death-defying tricks

on circus horses, to the way he could not land a piece of trash in the can to save his life.

It's so funny to look back at that moment now: Jack sleeping so peacefully, and me, watching him, still blissed-out from a night in his arms and feeling—without even realizing it—closer to him than I'd maybe ever felt to anyone at all.

I was so confident that we'd handle this new complication like we'd handled everything else.

But sometimes confidence just isn't quite enough.

Because my fake-yet-somehow-impossibly-true relationship with Jack Stapleton?

It was pretty much already over.

BACK AT HQ, everything was moving double-time.

Glenn was howling orders, Kelly was collating printouts, Amadi was correcting somebody on the phone. Taylor had called in sick, but Robby was there—and the idea of a death threat against his former woman had thrown him into macho mode.

"You have to take her off the assignment," he badgered Glenn, as I walked in. "It's not safe now. She's a target."

"Simmer down, Romeo," Glenn said. "You don't get to tell me what to do."

"Damn straight," I said, closing the door behind me.

Glenn didn't even glance my way. "You don't get to tell me what to do, either."

"I can stay on the case," I said. "It's fine."

"I'm not sure it is fine," Glenn said, shuffling through a stack of printouts. "These are very specific. This lady has really thought it through."

"There's more than one?" I asked. "I thought she just wanted to run me over with her car."

"She also wants to push you off a roof," Glenn said. "And electrocute you. And poison you with rat bait."

"Thorough," I said, stepping close to Glenn to look over his shoulder.

"Rat bait is no joke," Robby said, but I ignored him.

"How did she come up with all this in twenty-four hours?" I said. "That photo of me just surfaced."

"Maybe she had a contingency plan at the ready," Glenn said, "for any girlfriend that might come along."

"We're fine as long as we stay on the ranch," I said, surprised at how badly I wanted that to be true.

But Glenn was shaking his head. "You're compromised now. You're a risk to the client and to yourself."

"We can minimize those risks if we—"

Glenn cut me off. "If we take you off the gig."

Robby looked infuriatingly triumphant.

"Look," I said to Glenn. "I can handle it."

"But there's no reason to," Glenn said. "We have plenty of available agents who can take over."

"I'll take over!" Kelly volunteered from her back corner.

"But . . ." I wasn't sure what to say. "What will we say to Jack's parents?"

"Simple," Glenn said. "It's time to come clean."

"About me?" I asked.

"About all of it."

"You mean"—I said, feeling sparks of panic in my chest but trying so hard to sound like I was just clarifying for my mental file—"I'm going to have to tell them it was all a lie and then just . . . leave forever?"

"Pretty much," Robby said with glee.

"Shut up, Robby," Kelly and I said, in unison.

"I was okay with the deception when the threat level was yellow," Glenn said. "But now it's orange for the client, and it's red for you. If you stay, you're *luring* danger—toward yourself and toward them. They need to know what's going on. Everyone's safer if you come clean and go."

I thought about that.

"You don't want to put the Stapleton family at risk, do you?"

"Of course not."

"Then it's settled. You leave tonight."

Wait! What? "Tonight?"

Glenn looked at me, like *This isn't hard.* "Tell them today, then leave tonight. I'll send Amadi with the car after dinner. And we'll put an agent at your apartment to keep an eye on you for the next few days." Glenn turned to check his roster.

I crossed my fingers for Amadi. Or Doghouse. Or Kelly.

"Taylor's free," Glenn said.

"Seriously?" I said. "She's my nemesis!"

"Get over it," Glenn said.

Then, with dread, I realized that if he was putting Taylor on my detail, that left Robby free for it. I said, "Who's taking my place?"

Glenn knew what I was asking. But he played it like he didn't. "Once everything's out in the open, we'll move a team in at the ranch and also place a team at the house in town. And I'll put Robby on the principal."

I saw it coming. "Come on!"

"Hey," Glenn said. "It's exactly like the op Robby ran in Jakarta. You want the best for your boyfriend, don't you?"

"Don't call Jack my boyfriend," I said.

"Yeah," Glenn said. "I guess that's all over now."

Robby nodded with a smirk that made me want to punch him in the face.

"But here's the great news," Glenn said. "You're still in the running for London. And now you are free to go to Korea." Then he tapped his watch, like *Eyes on the prize*—thinking I was getting exactly what I wanted. "Two short weeks."

Twenty-Three

I COULDN'T EVEN muster the energy to pretend to jog back to the house. I just walked, all slouchy—protesting every disappointment in my life with bad posture.

Jack met me on the gravel road in his newly switched-out Range Rover.

"Saw the news," he said. "Let's go to the river."

"Okay," I said with a limp shrug, and climbed up to the passenger seat.

We didn't talk on the drive down. I just watched the scenery with that slowed-down awareness that comes when you'll never see something again. The barbed-wire fences. The rutted gravel lane. The grass fluttering in the fields. The tall pecan trees brushing the sky. The buzzards circling lazily overhead.

It was like no place I'd ever been—or would be again.

I was never emotional to end a job. That was part of not getting attached. You were just working. When you left, you'd be working somewhere else.

I didn't know what to do with the sadness that was soaking into my heart. It felt so full, I could wring it out like a sponge. What did people do with sadness like this? How did they dry it out?

When we got to the end of the road—to the same place where Jack had given me that piggyback ride back at the start—Jack cut the engine, but neither of us got out.

I explained everything to him, and what it all meant, and why we had to do all the things we now had to do.

He tried to argue with me. "I don't want Bobby to replace you."

"He's not replacing me. He's not going to, like, sleep on your floor in a white nightgown."

"Thank God."

"It'll be a whole different deal because there's no more pretending. He'll just stand around, secret-service style."

"That might be worse."

"It will be," I said.

"I get why we have to tell my parents, and I get why we need to step everything up. But I think you should stay."

"I should stay?"

"Stay with me and be protected."

"By my own company?"

"You're in danger now."

"That's not how it works. I'm only in danger because I'm near you. Once I leave, the threat level's totally different."

Jack thought about it, then argued some more, then finally gave in. Our whole meticulous setup felled by a homicidal part-time corgi breeder.

"So this is our last day together," Jack said, when he'd run out of ways to argue.

"Yep. I'm leaving after dinner."

"After dinner? That feels fast."

"The faster, the better."

"And then—I won't see you after that?"

"Nope."

Then Jack asked me the strangest question. "Does this mean," he asked, "you're not coming to Thanksgiving?"

Thanksgiving? What a weird thought. "Of course I'm not coming to Thanksgiving," I said. And then, because he didn't seem to understand, I said, "I'm not coming to anything at all—ever again."

Jack turned to read my eyes.

"When jobs end, they just end," I said. "You don't, like, become friends on Facebook or anything. Robby will finish out the job—and then you'll go back to your albino moose, and I'll go to Korea and eat black bean noodles, and it'll be like we never met."

"But we did meet, though," Jack said.

"That doesn't really matter. This is how this works."

Jack looked very serious. "So what you're telling me is this is the last day we'll ever see each other?"

I mean, yes. That was what I was telling him. "Pretty much," I said.

"Okay, then," Jack said, nodding. "Then let's make it a good one."

JACK INSISTED THAT he carry me to the beach, for old times' sake, even though I would've been fine in my sneakers—and I just let him.

We walked along the shore for a while, picking up pieces of petrified wood as well as rocks and pebbles and driftwood. The wind was as constant as the river current, and I couldn't help but feel soothed by its fluttering.

After a while, we came to a washed-up tree trunk, and Jack decided to sit on it.

I sat next to him.

Usually, when you see people for the last time, you don't know it's the last time. I wasn't sure if this was better or worse. But I didn't want to talk about it. I wanted to talk about something ordinary. Something we'd be talking about if it were just any old day.

"Can I ask you something about being an actor?" I asked then.

"Sure. Shoot."

"How do you make yourself cry?"

Jack tilted his head at me like that was a pretty good question. "Okay. The best way is to get so into your character that you feel what he's feeling—and then if he's feeling the things that make people cry . . . suddenly you're crying, too."

"How often does that happen?" I asked.

"Five percent of the time. But I'm working on it."

"That's not much."

Jack nodded, watching the river. "Yeah. Especially on a movie set. Because there are so many distractions—so many cranes and booms and crew members and extras everywhere. And it's too cold or too hot or they put a weird gel in your hair that's kind of itchy. When it's like that, you have to work a lot harder."

"Like how?"

"You have to actively think about something real from your own life—something true—that makes you feel sad. You have to go there mentally and feel those feelings until the tears come."

"That sounds hard."

"It is. But the alternative is messing up the shot, so you're motivated."

"What if you just can't cry?"

Jack looked at me like he was assessing if I could handle the answer. "If you just can't cry, there's a stick."

"A stick?"

"Yeah. The makeup folks rub it under your eyes, and it makes your eyes water. Like onions."

"That sounds like cheating."

"It's totally cheating. And everybody knows you're cheating because they just watched it happen. And they're judging you. And that makes it all even harder."

"Vicious cycle," I said, like *Been there.*

"Exactly. But I have another trick."

"What's that?"

"Don't blink."

I blinked.

"That's the trick," Jack said. "Just don't blink."

"You mean just hold your eyelids open in a stare?"

"Be subtle about it—but, yeah. If your eyes start to dry out, they'll water. Then, presto. Tears."

"How do you do that without looking weird?"

"How do you do anything without looking weird?"

"Wait," I said. "Tell me you did not do that for *The Destroyers*."

Jack clamped his mouth shut.

I leaned closer. "Tell me that when The Destroyer is weeping for an entire lost universe and it's one of the most moving moments in the history of cinema that he did not just have . . . dry eyeballs."

"No comment."

"Oh my God! You're a monster!"

"You *asked*," Jack said.

I stared at him.

Then he squinted at me. "You know I'm not really The Destroyer, right?"

"Of course." Mostly.

"That was a movie."

"I know that."

"I was paid to act in it. It wasn't real."

But I was still processing. "Should I be mad at you right now?"

But Jack was moving on. "No," he said, rotating toward me on the log. "You should be admiring me." He swung his leg over the tree trunk, so he was astride it, swatting at my knee for me to do the same, until we were facing each other, knees touching. "Okay," he said, leaning in. "First one to cry wins."

"What are you doing?"

"I'm teaching you how to cry."

"I don't need help with that."

"How to *fake* cry. It comes in surprisingly handy. Just think of it as a staring contest."

"I don't want to have a staring contest."

"Too late."

I gave him a short sigh of capitulation.

"Come on, come on," Jack said, waving me closer.

Fine. I leaned forward a little.

Jack leaned forward, too.

And then we were staring at each other, noses a few inches apart—not blinking. The air between us felt strangely silky.

And when it got too intense, I said, "I've heard there's a scientific thing that if you look into someone's eyes for too long, you'll fall in love."

Jack looked away.

Noted.

Then he looked back. "Don't mess me up. Starting over."

After a little longer, I said, "My eyes are starting to sting."

"That's good. Lean into that. In sixty seconds, you'll be a professional actress."

"It's not . . . comfortable."

"Excellence never is."

I should appreciate this moment, I thought. I was here, in person, with Jack Stapleton—*the* Jack Stapleton—in the midmorning light, drinking in the contours of his in-real-life face. The crinkles at his eyes. The stubble of his not-yet-shaven jaw. By tomorrow, I'd only ever see him again on screens. *Remember this*, I told myself. *Pay attention.*

"No cheating," Jack said then.

"How would I even cheat?"

"If you don't know, I'm not telling you."

"You're trying to *win* this, aren't you?"

"Of course."

"I thought you were just teaching me."

"Have to keep it interesting."

It was already interesting, but okay.

"And don't make me laugh," Jack said, all stern.

"You never laugh," I said.

"I'm serious," he said. "Stop it."

"Stop what?"

"Stop doing that with your face."

"I'm not doing anything with my face."

"It's making me laugh."

"That's your problem, not mine."

But next, Jack broke. His whole face just shifted into a full-territory smile. Then he dropped his head and his shoulders shook.

"You're terrible at this," I said.

"It's not me, it's you." He still hadn't lifted his head.

"So it's not that the first person to cry wins—it's the first person to dissolve into giggles loses."

"Men don't dissolve into giggles."

"You do."

Jack lifted his head, eyes still bright, still smiling. "I guess it's easier if you dislike your scene partner."

That got my attention. "Do you dislike your scene partners?"

"Sometimes."

"Not in the rom-coms, though. Not Katie Palmer."

Jack made a face. "Katie Palmer is the worst."

I gasped in protest. "That can't be true."

But Jack nodded, like *Sorry.* "She's rude, she's narcissistic, she's sucks up to the bigshots. She's the kind of person who humiliates waiters."

I put my hands over my face. "Do not speak ill of Katie Palmer! She's a national treasure."

"Well, she's a mean-ass person. And she's a terrible actress."

I covered my mouth with my hand. "Stop! You're ruining her!"

"She was already ruined."

"But that movie! You guys were so in love."

"Guess what? We were acting."

"But that kiss. That epic kiss!"

"You wanna know why that kiss was so good? Because the sooner we got the take, the sooner the shooting day was over."

"But! But . . ." This was how today was going to go? Jack was going to ruin my favorite kiss of all time?

Then he added, "And she has terrible breath, too."

Dammit! "That can't be true."

"It's true. She's famous for it. Her breath smells like elephants."

"Like *elephants*?"

"Like when you go to the zoo and stand near the elephants. *That* smell. But warm. And moist."

I just squeezed my eyes closed and shook my head.

Jack went on, "That's why people call her 'Peanuts.'"

Now I opened my eyes and blinked at him.

"I have great breath, by the way," Jack said then.

I blinked again.

"Like cinnamon rolls," he said, giving me an actual wink.

What was happening here? "But . . . what about the thing you said about crying—when it's really working, you're feeling the feelings as the character?"

"That's a good question," Jack said, all professorial, pointing at me. "When you're working with someone really good, that can happen. I could totally do that with Meryl Streep."

"Wait—have you kissed Meryl Streep?"

"Not yet. Give me time."

I punched him in the shoulder, like *Rooting for ya, buddy.*

"All to say," Jack concluded, "yes. You can kiss each other as the characters."

"Thank you," I said, like he'd just put the world back in its proper order.

Then he added, "But not when you're kissing Katie Palmer."

"Dammit!"

He kept going. "It's all choreographed. You're thinking about your blocking, and the angles, and hitting your mark, and not having a double chin, and making sure your lips don't get folded up in a weird way. It's very technical. You talk about everything beforehand. You know, 'Will there be tongue?' That kind of stuff."

"*Will* there be tongue?"

"Almost never."

Was that disappointing? I couldn't decide.

"You have to block it out in advance," Jack went on. "That's true for all on-screen kissing, really. It's the opposite of real kissing. Screen kissing is all about how you look. Real kissing, of course"—he glanced away for a second—"is about how you feel."

"Huh," I said.

"Yeah," Jack said.

"So you hated kissing Katie Palmer . . ." I said.

"Affirmative. I hated kissing Peanuts Palmer."

"My favorite kiss of all time," I said, trying to absorb the news, "was a hate kiss."

Jack shook his head. "Your favorite kiss of all time was a let's-get-this-done-and-get-out-of-here kiss."

I sighed. I looked at the river, just over there flowing along like nothing had happened. Then I said, "I miss the time when I didn't know that."

"So do I."

"You just ruined my favorite kiss."

Jack gave me a little shrug, like *Them's the breaks*. Then he said, "Maybe someday I'll make it up to you."

Twenty-Four

AT DINNER, I kept waiting for Jack to confess the fake relationship to his parents—and Jack kept putting it off.

I'd made us fish tacos for dinner. Maybe he didn't want to spoil the meal?

I didn't want to spoil the meal, either.

I found myself looking furtively around the table. I didn't figure Hank would care too much, but I dreaded the moment when Doc and Connie would realize we'd been lying to them all this time.

When Doc was starting to clear plates and Jack still hadn't said anything, I got it started. "Doc? Connie? There's something Jack and I need to tell you."

Connie lifted her hand to her collarbone in delight. "I knew it."

"You did?" I asked, glancing at Jack.

"I called it like a week ago. Didn't I call it, honey?" Connie said to Doc.

"You called it," Doc confirmed.

I looked at Jack.

"I don't think this is—" Jack started.

"Let's do it here," Connie said. "We'll handle everything."

"Do what?" Jack asked.

His mother frowned, like *Duh*. "The wedding."

Jack looked over at me.

I sighed.

"Mom," Jack said, "we're not getting married."

But Connie just waved that notion off, like *Nonsense*. "Of course you are."

"Mom—"

"I'm telling you. I already called it. You're perfect for each other."

Jack looked a little green. This was going to be worse than he thought. "Mom, we're not getting married. In fact," he glanced over at me for courage, "Hannah's not even really my girlfriend."

Jack's dad had returned to his seat—and now they both stared at us, uncomprehending.

"Not your girlfriend?" Connie asked. "Why not?"

"She's actually . . ." Jack said. "You see . . ." he tried again. "The truth is . . ."

"I'm a bodyguard," I said.

Both Jack's parents blinked at me, but Hank fixed his eyes on Jack.

"I'm *his* bodyguard," I clarified, pointing at Jack.

We gave it a second to sink in.

Then Doc said, "Aren't you a little short to be a bodyguard?"

"I'm taller than I look," I said, just as Jack said, "She has a tall personality."

Jack elbowed me and said, "Take him out in the yard and flip him."

Doc frowned and shifted his eyes to Jack. "Can she?"

"Like you wouldn't believe."

"We were pretending to be a couple," I went on, staying focused, "so I could stay near Jack and protect him."

I don't know what kind of reaction I was expecting . . . but what I got—from Connie at least—was not it.

"Well, that's ridiculous," Connie said. "You should be dating. You're clearly in love with each other."

"It was all pretend," I said very gently.

But Connie turned to Jack like she didn't believe that for a second. "Jack," she said, "was it all pretend?"

Jack held her gaze for a second, and then, with a decisive nod, said, "It was all pretend."

"*Please*," Connie pooh-poohed, shaking her head.

"I'm so sorry," I said. "He was acting."

But that just made her laugh. "He's not that good an actor."

"It was a fake relationship," I said again.

"You've been sleeping together this whole time. Were you faking *that*?"

Jack looked down. "Hannah slept on the floor."

This got her attention. "On the *ceramic-tile* floor?"

"I offered her the bed," Jack said. "She wouldn't take it."

Now *this*, Connie was pissed about. She stood up and reached across the table to bat at Jack's shoulder. "You let our Hannah sleep on that cold, hard floor? I raised you better than that! Be a gentleman!"

My heart fluttered a little at the words "our Hannah."

"I was fine," I said. "I'm tough."

"You shouldn't have to be," Connie said, and for some reason the tenderness in her voice made my eyes sting.

I coughed. "The point is, we were trying to keep Jack—everyone—safe. Without worrying you."

Now Hank, who had been menacingly quiet, had a question. "Safe from what?"

I looked over at Jack.

Jack took the reins. "A minor—almost nonexistent—stalker situation."

"We didn't want to take chances," I said, "but we also didn't want to create stress for anyone."

"You had a stalker?" Hank asked.

"Have," Jack said with a nod. "Just a minor one."

"But rather than just tell anyone about it . . . you lied?" Hank said

"Well . . ." I said, trying to think of a way to spin it better. "Yes. But with . . . honorable intentions."

"I don't care if you lied," Connie said. "I just want you to get married."

Jack shook his head. "Mom, we're not getting married. We're not even together."

"Bullshit," Connie said, shocking the whole table. Then she offered Jack a deal. "Propose right now, and all is forgiven."

But before Jack could respond to that, Hank had another question for us. "Why now?"

"Huh?"

"Why are you telling us now? Why not just wait until after Thanksgiving and go on your way, no questions asked?"

"Ah," Jack said. "So . . . you see . . . the minor stalking situation recently became a little less minor."

Hank tensed. "What does that mean?"

"It means the stalker—who's always been very harmless, writing me love letters and knitting me sweaters—"

"That's where the sweaters came from?" Connie asked.

Jack nodded.

"She's very talented," Connie said, with a nod of respect.

I decided to help out. "She's recently ramped things up a bit."

"How?" Hank asked, still bracing for the full news.

"Turns out," I said, trying to make it fun, "someone snapped a photo of Jack and me when we were all at the hospital the other week, and, from the angle, it really kind of looked like we were kissing—which we most definitely were not—and now the whole internet thinks I'm Jack's girlfriend."

"I told you they were in love," Connie said to Doc.

Doc patted her hand.

"Which wouldn't matter too much," I went on, "except that the Corgi Lady seems to have kind of—"

"Snapped," Jack said.

I nodded. "And now she's become a smidge more aggressive."

"How?" Hank asked.

Jack and I looked at each other for a second, and then Jack took a breath and said, "She wants to murder Hannah."

I nodded. "In a lot of creative ways."

I was trying to make it at least a little funny—but Hank wasn't going there.

"Jesus!" he said, standing so fast he knocked over his chair. He started pacing the kitchen. "You've got a murderous stalker on your tail?"

"We only found out this morning," Jack said.

"She really has been very benign until now—" I started.

"Does she know where we are?" Hank said, stepping to peer out the window.

"No," Jack said.

"Hank," I said, trying to sound as professional as possible now. "You're not in any danger at present."

"That we know of," Hank said.

"No threats have been made against you," I said, "or any member of the family. The only person in danger here is me—and I can handle myself just fine."

"What if she shoots at you and misses?"

"That's why we're removing me from this assignment and replacing me with a full team—both here and at Jack's place in town. The agency I work for is the best there is. Once I'm gone, the danger will be minimal. There's a car coming tonight to take me back to town."

I hoped my tone was reassuring.

"I'm still struggling with the basics, here," Hank said to Jack, the anger building in his voice. "You were worried enough to hire a bodyguard, but you didn't see fit to tell us what was going on?"

"I didn't want Mom to worry."

But Hank's voice just kept getting tighter. "Did it occur to you that it might've been useful for us to have this information?"

"The threat level was very low," I said.

"It was an abundance of caution," Jack said.

"You knew you were in danger," Hank said, much louder now, "but you came here, anyway."

"I wasn't really in danger."

"But now you are."

"Even now—" I started.

But Hank wasn't really interested in what I had to say right then. He turned to Jack with his eyes as dark and hard as obsidian. "Your selfishness really knows no limits."

Jack stood up fast, so they were facing off. "Don't call me selfish. You have no idea."

Doc, Connie, and I stayed seated at our end of the table—out of the line of fire—as Jack and Hank faced off.

"There were a million reasons I didn't want you coming down here," Hank said then, his voice shifting up toward yelling, "starting with the fact that I'd be perfectly happy to never see you again. But I confess that you getting us all killed did not cross my mind."

"I didn't get anyone killed!" Jack shouted—so loud that the silence afterward felt as brittle as crystal.

"Well," Hank said next, downshifting to a low tone that was somehow a hundred times more menacing. "I think there's one dead person in this family who might disagree with that."

At those words, Jack grabbed his dinner plate and smashed it to the floor so hard I half expected it to leave a crater. Then he shouted, "I didn't kill Drew!"

"Really?" Hank shouted back, his voice saturated with bitterness. "You're giving yourself a pass?" He held up fingers as he counted off: "You got in the car—drove too fast—hit the bridge going eighty-five—spun out on the black ice—crashed through the railing and plunged yourself and our baby brother into an icy cold river! Which part of that didn't kill him?"

"The part"—Jack shouted—"where *I wasn't driving*!"

The room fell quiet.

Jack blinked at the floor, like he couldn't believe he'd actually said it.

Hank took a step back and shook his head, like he was trying to clear it out.

"Honey, you . . ." Connie said, looking up at Jack utterly bewildered.

"I wasn't driving the car that night," Jack said again, quieter. "Drew was driving."

Hank's voice was quiet now, too. "You're saying . . ."

"I'm saying I didn't realize Drew had been drinking until we were already on the road. And when I told him to pull over, he went faster. I'm saying that the whiskey bottle they found in the car was Drew's."

"But Drew didn't drink anymore," Doc said, squinting up like he couldn't make it all fit. "Not since high school. He was in AA. It had been years."

Jack let his eyes rest on the floor. "I guess he was having an off night."

Connie's face was now bright with tears. "Why didn't you tell us, sweetheart?"

"Because," Jack said, "Drew asked me not to."

Everybody waited.

"When we crashed through the railing," Jack said, "and hit the water, we floated at the surface for a minute. I was rolling down the windows and popping our seatbelts, but all Drew could do was shake his head and say, 'Don't tell Mom and Dad. Don't tell Hank.' He said it ten times—maybe twenty? Over and over. And I was just trying to get him focused and get him out, so I just kept saying, 'I won't, buddy. Just roll your window down.' In the end, when the water came in, I pushed him out of the window. And when they found him drowned, all I could think was, *That was his last request. That was the last thing he wanted. To not let them down.*

"And so I honored it. It seemed like the least I could do for him— for all of us. To not make things worse. Even after the rumors started that I was the one who'd been drinking, I didn't feel like I could break that promise. I was going to take it all to my grave, whatever it took. But I guess I couldn't even do that much."

He pushed out a sigh like he was disappointed in himself.

For a minute, we all just stared.

I thought about how, in his dream, it was always Jack who had to drown and not Drew. Maybe Jack was still trying to save him. Or, maybe he wanted to take his place.

He seemed like the kind of guy who would do that, if he could.

Then, in decisive steps, his ropers crunching over broken bits of Jack's dinner plate, Hank walked straight over to his brother.

"That's why you're wearing his necklace?" Hank asked.

It was Drew's necklace.

Jack nodded, and then he leaned in and pressed his forehead against Hank's shoulder. Hank brought his arms up and crooked them into a hug.

And then I could see from Jack's shoulders he was crying.

That's when Doc helped Connie stand so they could go to the boys and put their arms around them.

And just as I was thinking I should probably back away quietly and let this little family have a moment to themselves . . . Connie reached out for my hand and pulled me into the group hug, too.

NEXT, HANK TOOK Jack outside to get some air. A long overdue brotherly moment.

It was only after they were gone that the rest of us remembered that I'd been right in the middle of saying goodbye.

After a beat, Connie turned to me and asked, "Does this whole pretend relationship thing mean you won't be coming to Thanksgiving?" She was blotting her teary face with a napkin.

I shook my head. "I won't."

"Will you and Jack still see each other?"

"No. Not after I go."

"Not even for fun?"

"I'm not very big on fun," I said.

At that, Connie burst out with a laugh and said, "You're the most fun Jack's had in years."

I thought of Robby telling me I was no fun, and I felt so grateful to Connie for contradicting him.

"You're always welcome to come visit us," Connie said then.

But I shook my head. "That's not how it works," I said, noting how tight my throat felt. "I really won't see any of you again after today."

Connie shook her head, like she just couldn't make sense of that.

Poor Doc and Connie. They had a lot to take in.

And that's when I decided to go ahead and say something real. "I know the timing's very odd," I said. "But since it's my last chance to say it, I want you to know that this was a highly atypical assignment for me. I never, ever get attached to clients. But I got very attached to you."

"To me?" Connie asked.

"To all of you. In different ways," I said—and then I hadn't planned to say this, but before I knew it, it was happening: "My mom died this year, and being with you has been very . . . meaningful for me."

"Oh, sweetheart," Connie said, reaching for my hand and pressing it between hers.

"She wasn't anything like you," I found myself saying. "She was troubled. And difficult. And she always made things worse instead of better. You don't remind me of her, but . . ." My throat felt thick, but I kept going. "I guess you remind me of the mom I always wished I had."

Connie met my eyes. "I'm glad I could be that for you."

"While I was here," I went on, "I felt like I had a family." I took a breath. "My childhood wasn't . . ." I didn't know what to say. "I guess I never knew what a loving family felt like. And even though . . ." I felt my voice starting to tremble. "Even though I won't be able to be a part of this one in the future, I loved being with you. And I'm just so grateful to know that families like yours even exist."

I took a deep breath and held it, trying to settle myself. But there was one more thing.

"I'll miss you, is what I'm trying to say. Genuinely."

"What about Jack?" Connie asked. "Will you miss him?"

I debated how much to confess. "I will," I said. That seemed like plenty.

"He likes you. I can tell."

But here we were, at the end. I wouldn't even let myself wish that were true. Instead, I shook my head. "I think maybe," I said, "he's a much better actor than you think."

Twenty-Five

AMADI SHOWED UP to take me back to town before Jack and Hank came back.

"You're a little early," I said, checking my phone.

"Yeah," Amadi said. "We've got a sick little one at home, so my wife . . ."

"Got it." I nodded.

It hadn't taken long to pack up my things. There wasn't all that much to do. I even put Jack's toothpaste cap back on for him.

I thought, for a second, about leaving a note or taking a picture. How else would I remember the sight of Jack's unmade bed, or the Jack-shaped piles of his clothes scattered around like bearskin rugs?

But I fell back on professionalism. There was a leave-no-trace protocol for these things. *I was never there.*

Amadi loaded my suitcase into our black, secret-servicey company Tahoe, and then, without breaking stride, he opened the passenger door for me and walked around to the driver's seat.

He was ready to move.

I walked to my door, but I hesitated.

I looked around for signs of either brother, but nothing—just trees rustling, the faint beginnings of stars, a clump of cows by the fence watching us with their sad eyes.

"I'm sorry—" I said. "Can I just have a minute?"

Amadi checked his watch, but he said, "Okay."

There was a light on in the barn. Maybe they were there?

But the barn was empty.

I walked back slowly, scanning the fields. I could see Clipper in the paddock. I blew him a kiss.

The idea of not saying goodbye to Jack made me feel . . . panicky—even though I never said goodbye to clients. Would saying goodbye even matter? It wouldn't change anything. But I felt like I had a hundred urgent messages for Jack—and all I wanted was to convey them all. Whatever they were.

Back at the Tahoe, I stood by the open door for another minute, scanning the yard and waiting.

And then it was time to quit stalling.

I climbed in, swung the door closed, and buckled up.

"Okay," I said. "Let's go."

Amadi pulled onto the gravel drive and steered us out of the yard, over the cattle guard, and down the long road where Jack had fake hugged me so many times.

It was fine. It was better this way. Probably.

I took a breath and held it tight in my chest. I was not going to cry. Not in front of a colleague. Not over a client. That was something to focus on, at least: holding it together. I could do this. *I could do this.*

But then Amadi braked. He slowed, then stopped, in the road.

He was checking the rearview mirror. "Is that the principal?"

I twisted around to look out the back.

Yep. It was Jack. Running after us down the gravel lane.

"Give me a minute," I said, climbing out.

Jack met me, stopping barely two feet away, out of breath. "You left," he panted, "without saying goodbye."

"I waited," I said. "But we had to go."

Jack tried to let his breath catch up. "I thought we had more time."

"Where were you?" I asked.

"Hank had some things to say."

I nodded.

"I'm really sorry," Jack said then, "about the death threats. I'm really sorry that I put your life in danger."

"I'll be okay," I said. "As long as I stay away from you."

It was a half joke, but Jack didn't think it was funny.

"Don't worry," I said then. "The Corgi Lady will move on eventually. That's how these things work."

"Thank you. For everything," he said, taking a step closer. "I wanted to say that to you before you left."

I nodded. "I wanted to say something to you, too."

Jack met my eyes and waited.

But then twenty different things popped into my head. There was no way to say it all. Or even prioritize. I finally went with, "You did the right thing just now."

Jack let out a funny little laugh and looked down.

"I know it was Drew's last wish, and I never even met him, but I don't think he'd want one thing he said in a panic to rip your family apart forever."

"Let's hope not," Jack said. Then, "Too late now."

"Your mom was right," I said.

"My mom's always right."

"Forcing you and Hank together was a good thing."

Jack nodded. "Good thing he's so great at pissing me off."

Back in the car, Amadi flicked the lights on and off.

"Looks like it's time," Jack said.

"Yes," I said. "But I need you to know . . ."

I hesitated. It really was time to go. There was a tiny part of me that thought I should tell Jack something real. That I liked him. That I'd fallen for him. That even though it had been fake—maybe even because it had been fake—it had somehow become the most real thing in my life.

But how humiliating was that?

Once we parted, there'd be no way to get in touch with him. He'd disappear behind that curtain of fame that separates celebrities from everybody else, and I'd disappear into my workaholic, on-the-run life. If this really was the last time I'd ever see him, then this was my only chance to tell the truth, and I didn't want to spend the rest of my life regretting everything I should've said.

He had meant something to me. He had mattered to me. He had taught me things I didn't know I needed to learn. My time with him had changed me, and I was grateful.

I wanted him to know that.

This was my only chance to say it . . .

But I chickened out.

It was too unprofessional. It was too scary. It was too much like the Corgi Lady.

That was me, apparently: scared of cows, and scared of love.

Instead, I held my hand out to shake like we were a corporate event. "I need you to know that it was really great working for you," I said.

And then, just like that, once I'd popped us back into that professional framework, Jack had no choice but to follow.

He frowned, but he took my hand and shook it. "Thank you for your service."

I gave a professional nod, turned in tight formation, and started walking back toward the car—the cap sleeves of my embroidered girlfriend blouse fluttering at my shoulders.

But as I pulled open the door, I heard Jack call, "Hannah!"

I turned.

He had his hands in his pockets, and he looked at me for a good moment before he said, "I need you to know something."

I held my breath.

Then Jack said, "I will really miss you. And I am not acting."

Twenty-Six

I LEFT THAT night, but I didn't go home.

Home was my old apartment, a sweet little old-timey pad in a 1920's fourplex in the funky part of town. Home had an archway into the living room and a little built-in telephone shelf in the hall. Home was where I'd lived for three years before fleeing in a desperate attempt to never have to see Taylor next door again.

The apartment I went back to now was one I'd rented sight unseen on the eighth floor of a brand-new, ultramodern, totally generic complex—also in the funky part of town.

And can I just note the irony of this? When I found my way to the front door for the first time, who was standing guard at it?

Taylor.

Because *of course* she was.

"It had to be you, huh?" I said, as I worked the keypad. Then I said, "Glenn must be an actual sadist."

She didn't turn her head. "I asked for this duty."

Was I supposed to respond to that? Was I supposed to thank her or something? No. No way. She could do a lot of things to me, but she couldn't force me to make chitchat. I stepped inside and closed the door behind me, and that was the only response she got: a loud, hollow *clonk*.

And then I was alone.

Really alone. For the first time in weeks.

The place was stacked high with boxes, and the movers had taken a just-drop-it-anywhere approach to the furniture. The bed, for example, was in the middle of the bedroom, like an island.

But it was fine.

I walked over to the balcony and stepped out to take in the view.

This was good, I told myself. This was personal time. Time to recharge and reflect. Maybe I'd start a gratitude journal. Maybe I'd take up calligraphy. I had some time before I left for Korea. There had to be a way to make the most of it. *Maybe it's not a punishment. Maybe it's a chance.*

But a chance for what?

I ordered Korean takeout for dinner, and when the delivery guy showed up, I said, *"Kamsahamnida"* to him with a little nod in my warmest possible voice—to make utterly clear to Taylor, standing right next to us, that *he* was someone I warmly respected . . . and *she* was most definitely not.

Then I went inside and sat on some boxes with disposable chopsticks and ate by myself.

By the time I was done, I had eaten too much, dripped on the box, and had so much leftover bulgogi and bibimbap that I couldn't stop the thought from entering my mind that I should take some out to Taylor.

But then that felt like letting her win.

Instead, I put the leftovers in the fridge for breakfast, sat cross-legged on the floor, and stared out my curtainless windows.

My mind was a blank. This apartment was a blank. My life was a blank.

I should have felt happy. I should have felt relieved. If I hadn't wanted to go to the ranch in the first place, and if escape was my favorite thing, then I should have driven back to the city in triumph.

But it felt like the opposite of triumph.

I'd gotten what I wanted—it just wasn't what I wanted anymore.

I'd fallen for our fake relationship, like the dumbest of dumb dummies, and I'd done a complete one-eighty. Now all I wanted to do was *stay*.

But of course, I couldn't stay.

I had played my role and done my job. I'd done what Glenn wanted. I'd kept myself in the running for London.

It was time to get back to my real life. And my real life—the way I'd set it up, the way I'd always preferred it—was always about *going*, not staying. I was good at it. I reveled in it. In less than two weeks, I'd leave for Korea and start fresh in Seoul—a new job, new clients, and nothing at all to remind me of Jack Stapleton.

Except he'd probably show up on Korean billboards somehow. Knowing him.

The point is: No, I wasn't going to unpack these boxes. I wasn't going to go to Ikea and buy throw pillows and arrange house plants in colorful Scandinavian pots. I wasn't going to *nest*. I was going to let my life in Houston feel as sad and sterile and unwelcoming as possible, for as long as possible, so I would have nothing at all to make me yearn to stay here.

Nothing else, anyway. Besides the obvious.

That became the plan. I would max out my misery levels so anything at all seemed like an improvement.

It wasn't a great plan, or even a good one. But it was all I had.

And it turned out, I wouldn't have to work that hard to make myself miserable.

The world was going to do it for me.

Because three nights after leaving the ranch, when I was sitting on a packing box, eating takeout Tex-Mex out of the container and scrolling mindlessly through my phone, I happened to come upon a promoted video by none other than Kennedy Monroe.

"Holy shit," I said out loud, dropping my taco.

She was in Texas, apparently—filming some kind of superhero movie located in a desiccated hellscape out near Amarillo.

And she'd just decided to pop down and surprise her boyfriend. Jack Stapleton. In Houston. On camera.

"What prompted the trip to Houston?" the camera guy asked.

"Oh, you know," Kennedy Monroe said. "I was in the neighborhood."

"What neighborhood is that?"

She smiled. "Texas."

In the neighborhood? Please. Amarillo was nine hours from Houston. If you didn't get caught in a dust storm.

But I was mesmerized by her. The perfection. The otherworldly beauty. She didn't have a bump, or a lump, or a nonsymmetrical place on her body. She could have been built in a factory—and, okay, she probably was. I mean, sure, she was a poster child for cosmetic surgery . . . but it was *good* cosmetic surgery. I had to hand it to her. She was a work of art.

I was just admiring my own ability to be so complimentary and emotionally generous with her, rather than, say, rotting inwardly with jealousy, when the camera pulled back a bit and I realized that she was standing in front of a very stylish blue front door.

Next to an unmistakable full-height fiddle-leaf fig plant.

Oh, shit. She was *at Jack's house.*

All generosity of spirit disintegrated.

Apparently, this was some kind of sneaker-upper Web series where she was surprising Jack with her visit. She walked up to the door at the sleek entryway and knocked. Then she turned back to the camera guy, pouted her pouty lips, and made a *Shh* gesture.

I paused the video to text Glenn.

Do you know that Kennedy Monroe took a camera crew to Stapleton's house???

Yes. This is old news. It's being handled.

I sent a few more texts—What the hell? Who let this happen?—but when Glenn didn't reply, I switched back over to finish watching:

Jack's door swung open, and out stepped the man himself.

Barefoot. In his Levi's. And his favorite flannel jacket over a T-shirt I'd last seen wadded up on the bathroom floor.

Just the sight of him—even phone-sized and made of light pixels—sent a buzzy pleasure cascading through my body.

"Whoa! Hey!" Jack said, as Kennedy Monroe arched herself into a hug that somehow made her seem like a Siamese cat. Was it the way she stuck out her ass and pressed her underboobs against his torso? Or the way she rubbed against him like she was marking her territory? Or the way she purred?

Whatever. It would be something I could never unsee.

"I just wanted to say hi," Kennedy Monroe said then, turning back to the camera, "and I brought some friends along."

And then she launched into the most vapid, pointless celebrity interview I'd ever seen in my life—comprised mostly of hair flips, giggles, accidental cleavage shots, and hard-hitting questions for Jack like, "Are you getting hotter?"

I will spare you the insulting details. I watched it so you don't have to.

Actually, I *rubbernecked* it.

I couldn't force myself to look away.

It was mostly Jack, of course—the sight of him was like a feast for my salivating eyes. But it was also Kennedy Monroe. Seeing her there, with him. Trying to imagine the two of them as a couple. Looking for any kind of spark or chemistry between them at all. Anything.

I'd kind of forgotten about her.

Jack was gracious and charming and relentlessly handsome.

But I realized something else as I watched him. He wasn't attracted to her.

After all these weeks of feeling like my radar was off—like all the acting had scrambled all my signals—I suddenly realized I'd been underestimating myself.

I could read Jack just fine.

Kennedy Monroe was posing for the camera, and tossing her hair, and preening—and he was watching her and playing along. But the tilt of his head, the crook of his eyebrow, the squint of his eyes, the angle of his smile, the tension in his spine . . . they all said, *Nope.*

I'm paraphrasing, but still.

The point was, *I could read him.* What's more, I could *see* the acting. All this time, I'd thought I couldn't discern the truth about him. But it turned out I could read him as well as anybody else. Maybe better.

And one thing was clear as day. He was more attracted to that fiddle-leaf fig than he was to Kennedy Monroe.

Could this be a fake relationship, too?

When she flipped her hair, he barely noticed. When he smiled, it was mechanical. When she pulled his shirt to try to bring him in for a kiss, he twisted away like he thought he'd heard someone call his name.

"Jack," Kennedy said then, turning back to the camera and looking straight into it. "I'm going to need your full attention."

Jack turned back around. "Okay," he said. "You've got it."

"Because I've got a big question for you, and you don't want to miss it."

"Okay," Jack said, putting his hands in his pockets. "Shoot."

At last she turned away from the camera to meet Jack's eyes. "My question," she said, now leaning in closer, "is this." She turned back to give the camera one more wink. Then she turned back to Jack and said, "Will you marry me?"

AT THOSE WORDS, I dropped my phone.

And by the time I picked it back up, the video was over.

Did I just see that? Did Kennedy Monroe just propose to Jack?

Suddenly, I felt a lot less sure of myself.

Had I been able to read him? Or had that all just been my own wishful thinking?

I rewound the ending, wanting to see Jack's answer to the proposal. But my second watch was no more useful than the first. Apparently, they'd ended it on a cliff-hanger. Kennedy pops the question, then the camera zooms in on Jack staring at her, and then we're done for the day.

I rewound it one more time. Just in case.

No answer that time, either. But on this third—and, honestly, not even final—viewing, I noticed something more interesting than the shock on Jack's face.

At minute 8:03, just in the wake of her kiss attempt when she'd pulled on his T-shirt, as Jack turned back to the camera, his shirt was askew. Kennedy Monroe had pulled it forward and shifted the collar down.

Which revealed his leather necklace for the first time.

I zoomed in a little on his face, letting my eyes savor him for minute. Why not? A victimless crime.

And that's when I noticed more than just Drew's necklace.

Hanging from Jack's neck, right there—colorful and defiant and unmistakable—was my beaded safety pin.

I DIDN'T EVEN have time to react to the sight of it before there was a knock at my apartment door.

I looked through the peephole, and it was Robby, still wearing his sunglasses inside, like a douchebag.

"Go away, Robby!" I shouted through the door.

"I can't hear you!" Robby shouted. "Soundproofing!"

I cracked the door to shout *Go away!* again, but, as I did, Robby wedged his toe into the crack.

"I need to talk to you," Robby said. "Let me in."

"I'm not letting you in," I said. I looked down at his shoe holding my door open.

Robby stepped back. "I really need to talk to you," he said, taking the sunglasses off and glancing over at Taylor, stoic as hell.

"Talk, then."

"Inside."

"You're not coming inside."

"Look," Robby said, glancing sideways at Taylor again. "I know that when you were out on the ranch you were in Jack Stapleton's clutches, but I'm hoping now that you're free, you can think a little more rationally."

I kept my eyes level. "I was never in anyone's clutches, Robby. Not even yours."

"You know what I mean."

"I'm in the middle of something, so—"

"I knew dumping you was a mistake as soon as the plane landed in Madrid."

I paused. "So you went after Taylor."

"I was sad! I was lonely! I was rejected!"

"*You* dumped *me!*"

Robby glanced over at Taylor, and then decided to keep talking, anyway. "I didn't even like her, okay? She was just . . . there."

I felt a glimmer of empathy for Taylor's ears, hearing that. "You realize that makes it so much worse."

"At a hard time in my life, she was better than nothing, okay? That's all she was."

Did it feel good to win like that in front of Taylor?

Undecided.

I mean, was anybody really winning in this situation? "You realize she's standing right there, right?" I said.

"That's your fault!" Robby said. And then he said something that hit me in just the right way at the right time: "You wouldn't let me in!"

At those words, I paused. Every now and then, something really, genuinely true cuts through all the chaos of life and just gets your full attention. "I wouldn't let you in?" I echoed, more to myself than to him. It was like somebody had flipped the lights on in a shadowy room. "Oh my God, Bobby. You're right."

"Stop calling me Bobby," Robby said.

"You're right, though. You really are."

Robby frowned. "I am?"

It was like I was seeing him for the first time. "I wouldn't let you in. When I was working and missed your birthday party? And when I had to drop out of our getaway weekend at the last minute? And when I lost the bracelet you gave me? When I 'worked all the time'? When I was 'no fun'? That was me not letting you in."

Possibly also when I was a "bad kisser." But I wasn't going to dignify those words by speaking them out loud.

Robby glanced at Taylor, like *What's going on?*

She ignored him.

I went on. "I thought you were blaming me, but you were just telling the truth. I thought if we were sleeping together, that was love. But you were so right. I didn't know what love was."

I thought about Jack. I thought about the piggyback ride he gave me back from the river. I thought about what it felt like to make him laugh. I thought about how I rooted for him every time he tried to shoot something into the kitchen trash and missed. I thought about the buzz of fear that went through my body when he somersaulted off Clipper, as if Jack breaking his neck might break mine, too. I thought about the full-body bliss of waking up in his bed, tangled under his weight. I thought of the crackling agony in my body as I'd looked for him in vain that last night to say goodbye. I thought of the roiling, dark-green jealousy just now at watching Kennedy Monroe slathering her undeserving self all over him.

Now I knew.

I nodded at Robby. "You were right. I didn't let you in."

Robby just stared. How often in life do you accuse an ex-girlfriend of something and just . . . watch her agree with you?

"I mean," I said, looking him up and down, "you didn't *deserve* to be let in. So it's a good thing in the end. But thank you."

Robby was so befuddled, his mouth hung open. "For what?"

"For showing me what love isn't," I said.

And I shoved my door closed and flipped the dead bolt.

Twenty-Seven

THE DAY BEFORE Thanksgiving, my phone rang, and when I checked it, it read: POSSIBLE SPAM.

I answered anyway, if that gives you a sense of how lonely I was.

But it wasn't a telemarketer.

It was Jack Stapleton.

"Hey," he said when I picked up, and I knew him from one syllable. I could also hear he was grinning.

Then suddenly he was FaceTiming me—me, still in my nightgown with hair pointing in ten different directions—and I could *see* he was grinning.

"Did you miss me?" he asked, looking pleased with himself.

I was distracted by the reflection of myself in the phone. "No," I said, pawing at my hair.

"So nice to see my favorite nightgown again."

"Why are you calling me?"

"Important business."

"How do you even have my number?"

"I sweet-talked it out of Kelly."

"I'll bet."

"The point is," Jack said, "I'm calling to tell you about the plan we came up with to catch the stalker."

"You came up with a plan to catch the stalker?"

Jack nodded. "A sting operation. To catch her in the act. And then haul her down to the clink. And then scare, pressure, and cajole her into, you know, *not murdering you*."

"That's the plan you came up with?"

"Yes," Jack said, looking pleased with himself.

"You got Glenn on board with that?"

"Yes," Jack said. "Glenn, Bobby, and a bunch of police."

It was so strange to see his face again, even through the phone. Since leaving, I had tried to avoid anything that might force me to see it—watching television, scanning magazines in the checkout aisle, or even, since that whiskey endorsement, glancing at buses as they drove by.

I hadn't anticipated getting a FaceTime call.

"Look," I said, "I hate to disappoint you, but it's almost impossible to do anything about stalkers."

"Thanks for the negativity."

"I'm not sure if what you just described is even legal."

"Don't worry about it. I've got a whole team of advisors."

"Why would you even care about the stalker? You're leaving after Thanksgiving, anyway. Two more days, and you're out."

"That's the thing, though. I might not be."

I didn't mean to, but I held my breath.

"My mom had this idea that I should maybe stay for a while. Do some fishing. Hang out. Do a little personal healing."

"That's a great plan," I said.

"You still don't like my stalker plan, though, huh?"

"I don't even know the details. But I can tell you already that it'll never work."

Jack smiled. "But guess what?"

"What?"

"It already did."

I leaned closer to the phone. "You did it already?"

"We did it already."

How did I not know about this? "And it worked?"

"It worked. I'm a genius. I'm also very lucky."

"Nobody tells me anything."

"I put some posts on social media as a lure saying I couldn't wait to spend a lazy weekend at my house in Houston."

"That was enough to lure her to your house?"

"The Kennedy Monroe video didn't hurt, either."

"I need to talk to you about that."

But Jack was celebrating his triumph. "And then, when the Corgi Lady showed up, we arrested her for trespassing."

"That's not going to stick."

"No. We were going try to scare her with lawyers and threats and doomsday scenarios, but then something better happened."

"What?"

"She used her one phone call when they booked her to call her sister—who wasted no time hopping on a plane to Texas, packing up her conversion van, and moving her, corgis and all, home to Florida."

The sister had apologized profusely to Jack and promised to keep her on her meds. "She's always been mostly harmless," she'd said. "She was fine until the divorce last year. We should have made her come home sooner. We're on it now."

"That was easy," I said to Jack. Then I frowned. "Was it too easy?"

"There's no such thing as too easy."

"But I mean, how reliable is this sister?"

"I don't know, but a stalker with her sister in Florida has got to be better than a stalker all alone right here in town."

"Agreed," I said.

"Anyway," Jack said. "That's why I'm calling."

"To say I'm less likely to get murdered now?"

"To invite you to Thanksgiving."

I paused. Then I said, "I can't come to Thanksgiving, Jack."

"Why not? Your would-be assassin is halfway to Orlando by now."

"It's not a good idea."

"That's not a real reason."

An image of Kennedy Monroe *spreading* herself over Jack like he was a cake and she was his icing appeared in my head. "I think it's best," I said, "to make a clean break."

"Just one day. One meal. To say a proper goodbye."

"We already said goodbye." I didn't want to do it again.

"I have something to give you, though."

And then he lowered his phone down past his famous mouth and his legendary Adam's apple, angling the camera down and down until he stopped on his necklace. And there, just leaning against his collarbone, in remarkably sharp focus, was my safety pin.

"You found it," I said, touching my finger to the phone screen. I'd known it, of course—but I hadn't entirely believed it.

"I did."

"Where was it?"

"On the beach by the river."

"How could you find it there? That's impossible."

"I'm pretty good at impossible things."

"But—how?"

"A lot of looking. And some delusional optimism."

I'd have to revise my opinion of delusional optimism.

Jack went on. "Remember all those mornings I told you I was hitting golf balls?"

"Yeah."

"I wasn't hitting golf balls."

"You were looking for the safety pin?"

Jack nodded. "With my dad's metal detector. The one my mom told him was a total waste of money."

"That's what was in the golf bag?"

"It sure as heck wasn't nine irons. I can't hit a golf ball to save my life."

"You went down there every morning?"

"I did."

"That's what you were doing?"

Jack looked into my eyes and nodded.

"I just thought you were being a pain in the ass."

"That was a side benefit."

"You should have told me."

His expression shifted one step more serious. "I didn't want you to get your hopes up."

"But, Jack . . ." I studied his face. I was so bewildered. "Why?"

He frowned like he wasn't quite sure how to explain it. Then he said, "Because of the look on your face when you realized it was lost."

I felt tears in my eyes. "I don't know how to even start to thank you."

Now he was smiling. "In other news, I've started a bottle cap collection."

I laughed a little, but when I did, the tears spilled over. It seemed like I'd cried more in four weeks of knowing Jack Stapleton than in my entire life before that. This guy just kept cracking me open. But maybe that wasn't entirely a bad thing.

When he spoke again, his voice was softer. "I'm guessing you'd like it back."

"Yes, please."

"Easy," he said then. "No problem. We can make that happen. All you have to do"—and here he paused to look straight through the phone like he really meant business—"is come to Thanksgiving."

Well played, Jack Stapleton. Well played.

I sighed. "Fine, dammit. I'll be there."

Twenty-Eight

I GUESS I expected Thanksgiving to be the five of us. Just like old times.

But it turned out to be the whole darned county.

I arrived to find the yard glowing with string lights, haphazardly zigging and zagging from tree to tree, and a long table running the length of the garden, covered in different colored gingham tablecloths.

Neighbors, and relatives, and, actually—to my surprise—the whole Glenn Schultz Executive Protection team were milling around the yard. Hank was chatting with Amadi. Kelly was admiring Connie's pashmina. Doc and Glenn were checking out something on Glenn's phone. Guess they'd all really bonded.

"Looks like we've relaxed a bit since sending the Corgi Lady to Florida," I said to Doghouse.

"Threat level white, baby!" Doghouse said, lifting his hand for a high five.

There were thirty people there, at least.

Doc wore a bow tie with little turkeys on it. Connie, looking hearty and well-recovered, was rocking a popped collar and a linen tunic. And Jack just wore jeans and a simple red flannel shirt.

He looked so good, I almost forgot to breathe.

I'd worn a girlfriend sundress, for nostalgia. But with a sweater, tights, a pom-pom scarf . . . and my red cowboy boots.

The Stapletons did Thanksgiving potluck style. Because, as Connie put it, cooking an entire Thanksgiving meal was "backbreaking and ridiculous," everybody brought a couple of favorite dishes and set them out in the kitchen to share. Folks served themselves, then wandered outside to find a seat. Candles lined the table, along with cut flowers in antique glass Ball jars and bottles of homemade schnapps made with Fredericksburg peach syrup and Doc's own homemade moonshine.

I wasn't a big drinker—my mom had definitely drained the glamour out of that—but every now and then I had a sip or two. Today felt like a good day for it. How often do you get to sit in a country garden drinking moonshine?

As I approached the table, there was an open seat next to Jack. Should I sit there? I felt a tickle of shy hesitation behind my ribs, but I made myself start walking toward him. He was talking to someone down the table, his profile lit up by the candles, and my eyes slurped in the sight of him. I kept him in my sights as I moved closer, but then, just as I was rounding the corner, the seat got taken.

Really taken.

By Kennedy Monroe.

At the sight of her, I spun around to face away from them. *She was here?* Had Jack invited her? Were they together after all? Wait—were they engaged? From a reality-TV proposal of hers? Why on earth was I even here?

I took a deep breath to steady myself.

She was better looking in real life. Her hair was shinier. Her lips were plumper. Her boobs were . . . boobier. She radiated sexy-farmgirl perfection in jean short-shorts and a gingham blouse tied just below her cleavage. She looked like a poster of herself—and, needless to say, also wildly out of place among all these lumpy, misshapen normal people.

She was like a living Barbie doll. And as badly as I wanted that to be an insult . . . it just wasn't.

He must've said yes, right? Why else would she be here?

And who could blame him?

Faced with all that extreme, textbook, irreproachable beauty, no one could possibly say no.

At the sting in my chest, I had my answer.

Why was I here? For the same reason Doghouse and Glenn and Amadi were here. The same reason all the other ordinary people were here. I thought of Connie slapping Jack on the shoulder that time and saying, *Be a gentleman!*

I looked around.

It was Thanksgiving. I was here just like all the other people that Jack Stapleton *did not have a thing for* were here. To give thanks.

I fought the urge to set my plate down in the grass, walk straight to my car, and drive back to the city going a hundred.

But that would be worse, of course.

Feeling humiliated was one thing. *Admitting* to feeling humiliated was another.

I did a three-point turn and found a seat at the farthest end of the table, next to Doghouse, who could at least partially block my view.

I squeezed my eyes closed. Of course this was how things were. It had been an act of self-jinxing to imagine anything different.

I took some breaths, but my lungs felt trembly.

So I did what I always did: I made a plan to escape. I would tolerate this moment in my life as long as I could, and then I'd graciously stand up with a smile like I had another event to go to, and then I'd elegantly sneak off into the shadows and disappear.

Easy.

How long *could* I tolerate this moment?

I decided on fifteen minutes—which was far too many—and then I kept my eyes on my plate so I wouldn't accidentally look at Jack and Kennedy.

Holy cow. What a preposterous couple name.

But Doghouse was looking at them enough for the both of us. "Can you believe she's here?" he kept saying, elbowing me. "That's Kennedy Monroe. She's Marilyn Monroe's granddaughter."

"That was debunked," I said.

"She's better looking in real life," Doghouse said then. "*That* wasn't debunked."

"Anyway," I prodded. "Don't you like Kelly?"

"What?" Doghouse said, his voice going up like on octave.

But I was done with pretense. "It's so obvious, dude. Just kiss her already. Be a man and make it happen."

Doghouse looked down at his plate and thought about that for a second.

And then he did.

Not kidding. He stood, walked over to where Kelly was sitting, tapped her on the shoulder, and said, "Hey, can I kiss you?"

Kelly blinked up at him for a second, and then she just said, "Yes."

It was that easy.

I watched him take her hand and lead her off toward the barn.

"Holy shit," I said out loud. Was that all it took?

He left me with no alternative but to take a big swig from my jar of moonshine.

The schnapps was sweet at first. But then the moonshine hit.

I guess there's a reason moonshine's mostly illegal. It was like drinking straight antifreeze. My throat burned like I'd swallowed acid, and, for a second, I wondered if I might die. To try to get some of the fumes out, I leaned over and hissed down at the ground like a cat.

Just then, Jack's sneakers—I'd know them anywhere—showed up in my field of vision. "Burns, doesn't it?"

I looked up. He was nodding, like *Been there.*

In response, I made a hacking noise.

He sat down in Doghouse's empty chair. "It'll take the paint off your car, for sure."

I sat up and stared at him, like *You drink this?*

"It's also good for cleaning jewelry. My mom soaks her wedding ring in it."

I put my hand to my throat to massage it a little.

Jack nodded, all sympathy. "You have to build up an immunity."

What were we doing? Why was he even here? Were we hanging out like friends? Who needed friends when they had Kennedy Monroe?

Next, Jack offered me Doghouse's half-drunk water glass with one hand, then he took a forkful of something that did not resemble food off Doghouse's abandoned plate. "You should chase that with some yam and marshmallow salad."

I shook my head. That was insult to injury. Then, making words at last, I said, "You should go back to your seat."

But Jack just frowned at me. "This is my seat now."

That's when Doc stood up at the far end and clinked his moonshine jar with his fork until we all gave him our attention.

"Please join hands," Doc said, all formal.

Jack took my hand—and the warm, smooth feel of his skin against mine sent tingles through my body.

Or maybe that was just toxins from the moonshine.

"On this beautiful evening," Doc said, "here with so many friends, I offer thanks to whatever gods and goddesses we all pray to: for our blessings, for our big, beautiful, imperfect country, and even for our hardships. May we look after each other, tolerate each other, and forgive each other. Amen."

Then Doc looked at Connie and said, "Does our hostess want to add anything?"

Connie stood up and raised her glass. "You all know I've been sick this year. I'd never have chosen to get sick, of course. But I've been thinking a lot about the upsides of it. How it forces you to slow down. How it makes you take stock of your life. How it lets you guilt-trip your family into spending time together. I'm grateful my lymph system was clear. I'm grateful they got clean margins. I'm grateful to be on the mend. And: More than anything, I'm grateful to have learned how to be grateful." Then she nodded. "Thanks for coming tonight. Be careful of the moonshine. Amen."

Folks took their hands back and turned to their plates.

Then Doc added, "If you've joined us before, you know the missus always likes us to go around the table and say something we're thankful for—large or small. Starting tonight with"—he pointed—"our son, Jack."

Jack didn't miss a beat. He lifted the fork he was still holding as if making a toast and said, "I'm thankful for this yam and marshmallow salad."

I thought I'd be next, but the man on Jack's other side took the baton. "I'm thankful that the rain forecast was wrong."

The lady next to him went then. "I'm thankful for my new grandbaby."

The next guy was thankful for Doc Stapleton's moonshine.

And we went on down the line. Amadi was thankful for his wife and kids. Doc Stapleton was thankful for Connie Stapleton, and Connie was thankful for him right back. Glenn was thankful to have found an empty seat next to Kennedy Monroe, Kennedy Monroe was thankful to have reached twenty-four million followers on Instagram, and Doghouse and Kelly were nowhere to be seen—and I'll bet they were both very thankful for that.

I always feel a little shy in situations like these. Every time I heard a new answer, I changed mine in my head.

At my turn, I just . . . hesitated.

Everybody watched me, and waited, while I tried to decide what to say.

Finally, Connie leaned forward. "Can't you think of something you're thankful for, Hannah?"

I met her eyes. "I can think of too much."

The whole table laughed in relief at that.

"Just do them all, sweetheart," Connie said.

So I did. I blame the moonshine. "I'm thankful to be here," I said. "I'm thankful for the tire swing. I'm thankful for the Brazos River. I'm thankful for that turkey bow tie Doc's wearing. I'm thankful for the time I've spent in this garden. I'm thankful for the honeybees. For the Stapleton record collection. For Clipper. I'm thankful for all the bougainvillea everywhere. I'm thankful to have seen what a real, loving family actually looks like. And I think . . ." I suddenly realized my voice was trembling a bit. I tried to cover by making it louder. "I think just because you can't keep something doesn't mean it wasn't worth it. Nothing lasts forever. What matters is what we take with us. I've spent a lot of my life trying to escape. I've spent too much time on the run from hard things. But now I wonder if escape is overrated. I think, now, I'm going to try thinking about what I can carry forward. What I can hold onto. Not just only always what I have to leave behind."

The table was quiet for a few seconds after I stopped talking, and I felt a little squeeze of panic that maybe I had overshot "thoughtful" and landed, instead, on "crazytown."

But just as I started to give up on myself, the whole table broke into applause.

And then Doc lifted his jar of moonshine and said, "To everything we've lost. And to what we hold onto."

And the whole table raised their glasses, too.

AFTER DINNER, JACK and Hank built a fire in the firepit.

I was watching the flames when I noticed Jack, on the other side, sitting on one of the garden chairs, looking straight at me through the firelight.

I looked away. But when I looked back, he was patting the seat next to him, like an invitation.

And so I made my way around the fire, unsure what anything meant anymore, and I was just about to sit down beside him, when Kennedy Monroe slid in and took the seat first.

I stopped short.

"Is this the girl?" she asked Jack, as if I weren't right there. "The one you made out with in the hospital?"

"We didn't make out," Jack said.

"Sure."

"For real," Jack said. "It was the angle. You know how that works."

"I do," Kennedy said, looking me over. "And, anyway," she added, "now that I get a good look at her, I can see she's very . . ." Kennedy Monroe drew the pause out so long that other people started to listen. She finally settled on, "Ordinary."

I got it. No girlfriend would want to see suspicious photos like that all over the internet. No girlfriend would want another woman cradling her boyfriend's head to her shoulder the way I had that night—even if it was for a good reason. Of course she would be none too pleased to see me here.

The same way I was not particularly thrilled to see her.

All to say, I jumped in to reassure her. "We definitely weren't kissing in those photos."

She honked out a really loud laugh—loud enough to get the attention of the whole crowd. Then she stood up—kind of unfurled herself—took a step closer to me, and said, "Yeah. Duh."

"I was just on his security team," I said. "We were just trying to keep him from being photographed."

"Oh my God," Kennedy said, her voice falsely friendly. "You're hilarious. You really don't need to tell me the two of you weren't kissing." At first her voice had a high, sweet tone that conveyed a vibe, like *I trust my boyfriend*. But then she dropped it like an octave and added, "That's a given."

Jack stood up. "Kennedy—"

"I mean . . ." She leaned toward Jack. "Just look at her."

With that, she looked me over, from head to toe and back again—at a glacial pace that invited everybody else in the crowd to do the same.

I went positively stiff under the scrutiny. I found myself wondering if this was what rigor mortis felt like.

"I mean, come on," she said. "Right?"

"Don't get competitive, Kennedy," Jack said, in a voice like *We've talked about this.*

"I'm not getting competitive," Kennedy said. "*The internet* got competitive. Have you seen all the posts? All the comments?"

"I thought we talked about reading the comments."

"People are texting me! DMing me! Even my mom wants to know!"

"You know nothing's real," Jack said, trying to cajole.

"Nothing's real, but it's still insulting." She steered her eyes back toward me. "I mean," she went on. "The whole world thinks you chose *this*"—she gestured at me—"over *this*"—she put a hand on her hip and lifted her boobs like she was going to set them on a shelf.

Even I had to admit she had a point.

What was the upside of looking like her if somebody who looked like me could—in semblance if not in fact—convince Jack Stapleton to cheat on you? I got it. It violated the natural order of things.

"It was all a misunderstanding," I said.

"But that's my point!" Kennedy said, her voice louder now. "How could that misunderstanding even happen? Right? I mean, *come on*. That's the rude part. That anybody could think Jack would choose a"— and here she studied me, trying to find the words—"plain, ordinary, totally average person over me!" Her eyes looked a little wild, if I'm honest. "Right?" She looked around the crowd. "Right? It's preposterous!" She turned her eyes in my direction for a second, like she was looking at a bug. "Because what is the point of being *me* if the whole world can so easily believe Jack Stapleton would pick *you*?" She turned back to the crowd. "Seriously! Show of hands. Who in this crowd would pick this girl over me? Who? For real! Is there anybody? This is a serious question! I really need to know. Let's see! Anybody? Would *even one person* here do that?"

And then she fell quiet.

And so did the crowd.

And as much as I did get that she'd felt humiliated by the photos online and so now she wanted to humiliate me back—I was also so horrified by the scene that was unfurling around me that I froze. The obvious way to shut it all down would've been for me to leave. Just walk away. Right? I didn't have to just stand there and endure a beauty contest I'd never entered against someone I'd just seen on the cover of *Vogue*.

Time to walk away.

And yet: I couldn't move. I was immobilized by horror.

And so was the rest of the crowd, from what I could tell.

Everybody just stared—gaped—at Kennedy Monroe as she stood there, aflame with righteous indignation. She waited. She gave it plenty of time. An epoch went by—or maybe it was just a few seconds. But she made sure, in slo-mo, that no one could deny the results.

Then, in what should have been the kill shot, she said, "Last call! We're doing this! Who in this crowd picks her over me?"

And that's when Jack raised his hand. "I do," he said. Then he added, "In a heartbeat."

I was frozen too tight to feel any relief.

Then he turned and met my eyes, his expression soft. "I absolutely do."

And as soon as he'd broken the surface tension, another hand went up: Hank's. "So do I."

And then, in a beautiful cascade, everybody else joined in—stepping forward and raising their hands: Amadi, then Glenn, then Kelly, then—after an elbow to the ribs from her—Doghouse. A chorus of "I do," "So do I," "Me, too," and "Team Hannah" rose up. Even Doc and Connie jumped in, waving their arms to make sure their votes counted.

Folks put their hands up and kept them there—until, at last, Jack looked around and made the call: "Unanimous."

Kennedy's expression sank into a simmering pout.

And in response to that, Jack leveled his gaze at her. "You know what that means, right?"

She frowned at him.

Jack gave a little shrug. "Time to leave this party to the folks who were actually invited. And time for you to get the hell out."

I HAVE TO hand it to homemade moonshine.

It's a very relaxing drink.

Poisonous, but relaxing.

Connie was delighted to find out that I'd accidentally gotten a little tipsy and would have to stay the night. "Jack can lend you a T-shirt to sleep in. And we'll put Jack on the sofa and put you in his room," she said, patting me on the knee. Then she added, "Unless you prefer the tile floor for old times' sake."

"No, thank you," I said.

"You were happy there before," Jack said.

"It was my job to be happy there before."

One by one, the friends and neighbors left, and the elder Stapletons went on to bed.

Jack and I wound up out under the night sky watching the fire burn down. The two of us together. Just like old times.

"I saved you a seat at dinner," he said. "Why didn't you sit there?"

I swilled my moonshine jar. "That seat was taken."

"Not really, though."

"What was I supposed to do? Sit on Kennedy Monroe's lap?"

"I'm making a bigger point."

Was he? What were we talking about? Thank God for the moonshine. I decided to ask, at last. "So. That interview you did with her ended on kind of a cliff-hanger."

"Did it?"

"Yeah. She asked you to marry her."

"Did she?"

"You don't remember that?"

"It's possible I wasn't listening. It's hard not to zone out with Kennedy."

"But what did you say?"

"When?"

I kicked at him. "When she proposed to you?"

Jack shrugged. "I have no idea."

Now I leaned closer. "A woman *proposed marriage to you*, and you have no idea what you said in response?"

Jack frowned at me like he couldn't imagine why that was weird. Then something occurred to him. "It wasn't real. Of course. It was all for the cameras. I thought you knew that."

I felt my body relax, like it was starting to melt. "Why would I know that?"

He frowned. "How could you not know that?"

"So . . . it was just for show?"

Jack looked at me like I was an adorable dummy. "Of course."

"Kennedy Monroe is not . . . your fiancée?"

"Please."

"Is she your girlfriend?"

"Absolutely not."

"Does *she* know she's not your girlfriend?"

"Of course."

"So what was she doing here?"

Jack shrugged. "Boredom? Photo op? Her publicist called my publicist and asked if she could crash."

"But what was all that at the bonfire?"

"Competition. And pathological insecurity."

I shook my head. "How can a woman who is the prototype for physical human perfection be insecure?"

"That's a really good question."

"So. Just to sum up: You and Kennedy Monroe are not together?"

"We were never together."

"Your matching-sweater *People* cover tells a different story."

"That was all made up."

It was so hard to comprehend. "But why?"

"To give people something to talk about."

"But don't you care that it wasn't true?"

Jack leaned back. "I'd rather have people gossiping about fake things than real ones."

I tried to take it all in. "So. One more time. Just to clarify: You never dated Kennedy Monroe?"

Jack gave a nod, like *Affirmative*. Then he said, "Never."

My whole body melted with relief. Then I smacked him on the shoulder. "Why didn't you tell me that sooner? I've been thinking she was your girlfriend this whole time."

Jack shrugged. "I'm not really supposed to talk about it."

"But I specifically asked you about it back when we first met."

"It was need-to-know information. And you didn't need to know." He added: "Back then."

Fair enough.

"And what about you?" Jack asked next.

"What *about* me?"

"I heard Bobby went by your place the other night."

"How did you even hear that?"

"You didn't get back together or anything, did you?"

I looked at Jack's impossibly handsome face, highlighted by the fire. Fine. Were we doing this? "Um. He dumped me on the night after my mother's funeral, and then he slept with my best friend, and then he dumped her, too, so . . . no. We did not get back together."

"Whoa," Jack said.

"But that's not the worst of it."

"What's the worst of it?"

"He said something really, really terrible to me. Something I'll never forget."

Jack leaned closer. "What did he say?"

"I can't tell you."

"Why not?"

"Because I'm terrified it might be true."

"It's definitely not true. Whatever it is. He's dead wrong."

"You don't even know what he said."

"That's why you have to tell me."

"I can't!" I said, jumping to my feet and pacing around the fire pit.

Jack got up and paced with me. "Just tell me. I'm way too drunk to remember."

I looked him over. I was good at judging these things. "You're not even close," I said.

But Jack was ready to make this happen.

He walked right up to face me and stood inches away. "You haven't asked me for your safety pin back yet."

I narrowed my eyes. "I got distracted by your mean-ass girlfriend."

Jack lifted his hands to his leather necklace, unfastened the clasp, and lifted it off his neck, my safety pin still attached. "I never could find the necklace part," Jack said, "so take the necklace, too."

"That's Drew's necklace."

"He wouldn't mind."

Jack was giving me Drew's necklace? Something about that seemed like a very big deal.

Jack held the necklace and the pin out, like I was supposed to take them.

But as I reached out, Jack just gave me a mischievous smile, closed them both in his hand, and, instead, lifted his fist high above our heads.

My mouth fell open at the unfairness of it all.

"Give it!" I said, jumping for his hand.

"Maybe it's a finders-keepers situation."

"This is not cool." I jumped some more.

"You're hilarious. You're like a Chihuahua."

"Give it back!" I said, still jumping, using his shoulder for a boost.

"On one condition," Jack said.

And when I stopped to find out what that was, he said, "Tell me what Bobby said to you."

I started jumping again. "Never."

"Okay, then, Stumpy. Kiss this fun little rattly thing goodbye." He drew his fist back behind his head, like he was about to pitch my safety pin off into the pasture.

He wouldn't. Of course he wouldn't. But the threat of it was enough.

I sighed. I stopped jumping. I looked into Jack's eyes. "Fine. But don't call me Stumpy."

"'Fine' what?"

"Fine, I'll tell you."

"Really?"

"Really."

"Are you lying?"

"No."

"Are you going to make something else up so you can take the pain of whatever that jackass actually said to your lonely grave?"

That got my attention. "No. But that's a great idea."

Jack brought his fist down, with an expression on his face like *Okay, I'm trusting you.*

Then he leaned down so close I could feel his breath against my skin, lifted the necklace around my neck, and fastened the clasp.

When he let go and stepped back, I reached up and touched the beads, awestruck that they were really there. He'd found them. He'd looked and looked until he'd found them. And now he was giving them back to me—something so precious of mine, along with something so precious of his own.

What was he doing?

He stepped back. I could have run off right then so I'd never have to tell him what Robby had said.

But I didn't.

I blame the moonshine. Or maybe it was Jack Stapleton's irresistible gaze. Or maybe it was the way he had chosen me tonight—in front of his folks, my coworkers, and Kennedy Monroe, herself. But I took a second to appreciate my safety pin, now back safe and sound, and then . . . I told him.

I still can't believe I said the words out loud. Maybe moonshine magically removes inhibitions. Or maybe I knew all too well how unspoken secrets can fester. Or maybe, just maybe, I was daring to hope that Jack might try to prove me wrong.

The point is, I did it.

"Bobby said . . ." I began, taking a long breath. "He said . . . that I . . . was a *bad kisser.*"

The minute the words were out, I regretted them.

Because what did Jack do?

He burst out laughing.

I'd just shared the most humiliating thing I knew about myself—and he laughed.

"Forget it," I said, turning away.

"Wait—" Jack said.

But I didn't wait. I might be too tipsy to drive home, but I was more than sober enough to go inside and lock myself in the bathroom until I could escape in the morning.

Jack followed me. "I'm sorry I laughed. I'm sorry!"

"It's not funny," I said, my voice wobbly.

At the side porch, just as I reached the door to the house, he caught up with me and spun me around by the shoulder. "It *is* funny. It's hilarious. But only because it's so wrong."

"Don't make fun of me," I said. And now I could feel tears in my eyes. How humiliating.

"I'm not making fun of you. He's a liar."

"Of course he is. But he's gotten more than a few things right."

"Well, he's not right about the kissing."

"You can't know that."

"I definitely can."

"How? When he's kissed me for real tons of times and you've only ever kissed me for pretend?"

"Just trust me."

"*Trust you?*"

"I can tell, okay?"

"How? How can you tell?"

"I just know. I've kissed a lot of people, all right?"

"Look, you're sweet—"

"I am hardly sweet."

"—But I can't take your word over somebody *who has actually kissed me.*"

"A thousand dollars," Jack said.

"What?"

"I'll bet you a thousand dollars. *He's* the bad kisser, but he's blaming you."

"That's ridiculous, Jack. You think I have a thousand dollars just lying around?"

"I'll lend it to you."

"Jesus, man. Just let it go."

"No."

"We can't all be great kissers, Jack. It's fine. I'm good at other things."

"He doesn't get to lie you. And you don't get to just . . . *believe him.*"

Great. Self-esteem tips from the Sexiest Man Alive. "Thanks for the advice. I'm going to bed."

I turned to open the screen door, but that's when he put his arm out to smack it back closed.

"I'm not wrong," he said then, staring straight into my eyes with intensity.

"Okay," I said. "You're not wrong. I'm amazing. I'm heartbreaking. I'm life-shattering. Happy now?"

But Jack just shook his head.

And then he leaned in, and he pressed his mouth to mine.

And when I say "leaned," I mean his whole body. He pressed me up against that door with everything he had.

And I guess I'd been waiting for it all along.

My arms reached up around his neck, and my hands found their way into his hair, and my legs wrapped themselves around his waist. Did he lift me, or did I jump? We'll never know. But he was kissing me, and I was kissing him, and it was happening.

I remember it in snapshots of feeling. Tenderness, and tension, and warmth, and connection. The stubble on his neck, and the tightness of his arms, the smell of cinnamon, and that incomparable feeling of being held.

Of being *cherished*.

I'd been longing for that kiss for so many weeks, so many days, so many endless hours—and I'd thought all along that it would never happen, that it was impossible. . . . So when it did happen, out of nowhere, no matter what it was, or what it meant . . . there were no decisions to make. There was nothing to do but go all in.

It was as easy as flipping him on his ass.

I didn't think about the thousand dollars. I didn't think about Robby. I wasn't trying to prove anybody wrong.

I just wanted that kiss.

And this was my chance.

And I wasn't going to waste it.

Before I knew it, we were working our way through the door, lips still touching, him still holding me, me still wrapped around him, and stumbling our way through the living room—off balance, colliding with a sofa and then almost toppling a ceramic rooster on the breakfront—toward Jack's bedroom.

Then we stopped beside his doorway—him pressing me against the wall as he searched for his bedroom doorknob with one hand.

A good kiss eclipses everything else.

Everything except touch and longing and each other.

And this was one hell of a good kiss.

When Jack didn't find the doorknob right away, he let it go and just fell back into the moment. His hand behind my neck, his body pressing up to mine, his mouth on my mouth. It was like no one and nothing in the world existed besides the two of us.

That is—until we heard Doc's voice from the master bedroom down the hall.

"Jack? Is that you?"

That broke the spell.

We froze, opened our eyes, and stared at each other, still breathing.

"That's my dad," Jack whispered.

"I know," I whispered back.

Jack shook his head as if to clear it. Then he lifted his head and tried to sound coherent. "Yes, sir?"

"Go spray the hose on the fire pit to put out the embers, will you? It hasn't rained in weeks."

"Yes, sir," Jack called back.

"And Jack?"

"Yes, sir?"

"While you're out there, can you take a look around to make sure all the food came back in and there's nothing to draw the coyotes into the yard?"

"Yes, sir."

"And Jack?"

Jack sighed at me, like *Really?* "Yes, sir?"

"Go find that girl something to sleep in and send her off to bed." Then Doc added, "Alone."

Jack sighed.

After another few seconds: "You got that, Jack?"

"Yes, sir."

"Attaboy."

Mood broken, Jack relaxed his arms and loosened his hold on me. I slid down to my own feet.

It was good that we got interrupted.

Never go to bed with a famous actor after a jelly jar of moonshine just before you're moving to Korea.

Isn't that a saying?

We faced each other like that for a minute, catching our breath and shifting gears, as Jack pulled at my shirt to straighten it, brushing me off and neatening me up.

I leaned back against the wall and looked up at him, like *What just happened?*

Then Jack said, "Hannah?"

I met his eyes. "What?"

"Go on a date with me."

"What?"

Jack nodded. "A date. Tomorrow. Back in town. With no parents anywhere."

"You want to go on a *date?*" I asked, like that word might not mean the same thing to both of us.

"Yes. I want to order takeout and sit up on the roof of my house and eat it with you."

But I still wasn't quite sure what we were talking about. "Why?"

He frowned like it was obvious. "Because I have a thing for you."

"I don't understand."

"What's to understand? I like you."

"But . . . aren't we pretending?" I asked.

"Are *you* pretending?" Jack asked.

I didn't know how to answer that. "I thought we both were. Wasn't that the whole concept?"

"I'm not pretending," Jack said. "Not anymore."

I know I've already confessed my insecurities about whether or not I was lovable.

But those were deep, subtle issues.

I need to point out here that most of the time, in my life, I walked around feeling reasonably confident. I was good at my job. I was a nice person. I had good hair. If this had been a *regular* man saying he liked me, I'm pretty sure I would have thought that sounded plausible.

Why not, right?

But this wasn't—I think we can all agree—a regular man.

Come on. This was *Jack Stapleton*. And I was just . . . me. I mean, from any rational perspective, *none of this could possibly be happening*.

That wasn't my opinion.

That wasn't me being hard on myself.

That was just . . . true.

"I think I'm having a stroke or something," I said. "What are we talking about?"

"I'm telling you I have a thing for you."

"And I'm telling you that doesn't make any sense."

"It makes sense to me."

"Maybe *you're* the one having the stroke."

"Is it so hard to believe that I like you?"

"Um. Kinda, yeah. You called me 'plain,' and 'non-Hollywood,' and 'the epitome of ordinary.'"

"Okay. But those are *good* things."

"And stumpy!" I added.

"Well. You're not tall."

"I've seen your girlfriends, Jack. I've got a whole file on them. I am nothing at all like any of those people."

"That's exactly what I'm saying."

"What? What are you saying?"

"I'm saying you're *better.*"

I gave him a look. "Now you're just insulting everybody."

"You're a real person."

"Real people are a dime a dozen."

Jack thought for a second. "Okay. You know the dolls my mom rescues?"

"Yeah?"

"What I'm saying is, the women in your file—those women from my past—they're the 'befores.' And you . . ." He looked right into my eyes. "You're the 'after.'"

And just like that, I got it.

I got what Jack Stapleton meant by "real."

More than that, I believed him.

Jack kept going. "When you're not around, even for a little while, I feel like I have to go find you. I just feel this pull to be near you. I want to know what you're thinking, and what you're up to, and how you feel. I want to take you places and show you things. I want to *memorize* you—to learn you like a song. And that nightgown, and the way you get so cranky when I leave my stuff all over the place, and the way you tie your hair back in that crazy bun. You make me laugh every single day— and nobody makes me laugh. I feel like I've been lost all my life until now—and somehow with you I'm just . . . found."

Jack paused and waited for me to argue with him.

But I just said, "Okay."

"'Okay,' what?"

"'Okay,' I believe you."

"You do?"

I nodded.

"So is that a yes, then?"

"To what?"

"To the date."

"Yes," I said, more determined with each word. "Yes."

That's when we heard, "Jack?" again from Doc in the back bedroom.

"Yes, sir?"

"The fire pit? Sometime before the sun's up?"

"Yes, sir."

I expected Jack to walk off then, but instead, he leaned closer, catching himself on the wall behind me. He brought his face very close, still a little breathless, he lingered there for a second, and then he put his mouth on mine again—this time softer, and sweeter, all lips and warmth and silkiness.

And I just melted into it.

His hand was against the wall, and we weren't touching anywhere else . . . but there was absolutely nowhere I didn't feel it.

And when he pulled back, he looked as lost as I felt.

Then he seemed to remember something, and he gave me a sly smile.

"What?" I asked.

The smile deepened, and he looked down at the beaded pin against my neck and then back up to my eyes. And then, as he took a reluctant, almost woozy step backward, he pointed at me, like *Gotcha*.

"You," he said then, "owe me a thousand dollars."

Twenty-Nine

A DATE. AT Jack Stapleton's house.

What the hell was I thinking?

I was crazy to go. But I'd be crazy *not* to go.

Still, it was going to take some courage. And some prep.

Especially since I hadn't unpacked. So when I suddenly needed to find a great outfit—one that could, in theory, if I chose right, help me feel up to the challenge—I couldn't find one.

I mean, after a while, I just started dumping the boxes out on the floor and pawing through them.

I had some date-wear in there somewhere.

I'd left myself plenty of time, but as box after box turned up wrinkled sweatpants, I started getting tense.

That's when I heard a knock at my door.

I looked through the peephole.

There, in the fish-eye lens, was Taylor.

"I'm not home," I called through the door.

"You clearly are."

"I'm busy, though."

"Can I have sixty seconds? I need to say something."

I cracked the door. "Sixty seconds," I said.

She held out a grocery sack, and as I looked at it, she said, "It's the shoes you lent me for that thing. And it's your heart-shaped baking pan I borrowed. And some books."

"Keep it all," I said. "I don't want it."

"I'm not keeping it," she said.

"Fine. Donate it, then."

"You love these shoes!"

"Not anymore."

Taylor had been holding the sack out to me, but at that, she pulled it back.

"Okay, then," she said.

"What did you need to say?" I asked then, like *Let's get this over with*.

"More like 'ask,' really."

"Fine. Ask."

"Is there . . . anything I can do for you?"

I frowned. "That's why you came here?"

"I just . . . want to do something for you. Anything."

"What could you possibly do for me?"

"That's what I'm asking."

"Are you trying to make amends?"

"We don't have to label it."

Of course my answer was no. No, there was nothing she could do for me. No, I wasn't going to let her make herself feel better by magnanimously doing me favors. No. *Hell no*.

But.

Something about the quietness of her voice got my attention.

"I guess," she said then, "I just want you to know that I'm genuinely sorry."

It's not all that often that people who've wronged you actually apologize. Usually, in my experience, they go on and on maintaining their innocence. Insisting that they weren't so bad, or they had their reasons, or you were somehow partly to blame.

But, in classic Taylor fashion, she was just owning it.

It made me miss her.

She was backing up now, and then turning, and then walking off down the hallway. The collar of her jacket was flipped the wrong way.

My plan was to let her go.

I told myself to let her go.

But then I heard myself say. "You could help me find something to wear."

Taylor froze. Then she turned around. "Something to wear?"

I stood up a little taller. "I have a date."

Taylor had the good manners not to ask who it was with.

I went on, "And I can't find anything to wear. I mean that literally. The movers didn't label the moving boxes. So you could help me find my clothes."

Taylor tried to hold back her smile. "I can totally do that."

"I'm not forgiving you, by the way," I said, pointing at her as she walked back toward me.

"I wouldn't want you to."

"I'm just letting you reduce a small amount of your soul-crushing guilt."

"Thank you." She stopped in front of me. "Do you maybe also need your hair and makeup done for this date?"

I held very still. Now she was pushing it.

"I just offer because sometimes when you do your own eyeshadow you wind up looking like you got punched in both eyes by two different people."

"Thanks for that." She wasn't wrong.

Also, she was very good at hair and makeup.

And I was going on a date with frigging Jack Stapleton.

"Fine," I said. "But just to reiterate—"

"I know. I know," Taylor said. "I'm not forgiven."

TWO HOURS LATER, walking up Jack's driveway, as I battled intrusive thoughts of Jack's many, many past girlfriends, it seemed pretty clear I'd made the right choice.

If you're ever going to let Taylor do something for you, it should be hair and makeup. And she'd talked me into wearing the slinkiest red dress I had.

I'd been tempted to put on a pantsuit.

Did I feel achingly vulnerable with my shoulders bare and the silk hem whispering around my naked thighs? Of course.

Emotionally—and physically—I felt naked as hell. And not in a good way.

"They're the 'befores,'" I repeated, like a mantra, as a veritable cat-walk of ex-girlfriends strutted through my head. "You're the 'after.'"

Everything about me was quivering.

I was fine with caring as long as it was mutual. But was it? It had seemed more than mutual yesterday, when he was pressing me up against the wall in his parents' hallway.

But yesterday was a million years ago.

I wondered if the triple punch of it all—losing my mom, then losing Robby, then losing Taylor—had left a bigger scar than I'd realized.

Was I lovable? I mean, are any of us really lovable if you overthink it?

It was tempting to chicken out.

But then I thought of Jack going *bwok, bwok, bwok*, and then I wondered if having faith in yourself was just deciding you could do it—whatever it was—and then making yourself follow through.

So I decided something right then: Every chance you take is a choice. A choice to decide who you are.

And so that's what that long walk up Jack's driveway was about for me. Not about what Robby and Taylor had done. Or what Jack might or might not say or do or feel. It was about me choosing who to be in the face of all . . . and refusing to give up on hope. Or myself.

Was it totally ridiculous for me to try to date a movie star?

Absolutely.

Was I going to do it anyway?

You bet.

Thirty

BECAUSE JACK'S THREAT level had been downshifted to white, there was no security team at his place—thank God. The last thing I needed in those strappy heels was to make my way through some kind of EP agent obstacle course of judgment and mockery.

The security cameras on the property were still running, of course.

I rang Jack's doorbell, trying not to imagine Glenn surveilling me and saying, "Is that *Brooks*? In a *dress*? What the hell's she got on her feet?"

I just had to hope nobody was monitoring them.

But Jack didn't come to the door right away.

I watched an ant making its way across the concrete.

Then I rang again.

Maybe he was in the shower? I crossed my fingers that he hadn't decided to *cook*, God forbid.

Then, a few minutes after my second ring, Jack opened the door—but only partway.

He'd gotten a haircut—and now it was spiking up in an intimidatingly movie-starish way, like he'd just finished a shoot for *GQ*. He was also freshly shaved. He had a Norwegian sweater on. And another change: He was wearing his contacts instead of his glasses. It was the first time I'd seen him without his glasses in real life.

All together? It made him look a little like a different person.

Less like Jack Stapleton the piggyback-ride giver—and more like Jack Stapleton the movie star.

Holy shit. *Jack Stapleton was a movie star.*

I felt a cramp of anxiety. The impossibility of it all hit me again.

Was this happening? I guess it was.

But that's when Jack said, "Yes?" in a voice that sounded . . . blank.

Just a very slightly clipped tone—anonymous and disinterested, like he didn't know me, and he was pretty sure he didn't want to. Like I was maybe a cable repair guy. Or a political canvasser. Or a census-taker.

It was just that one syllable. But it was enough to register.

"Hey," I said, holding up a wine bottle with a slight air of caution. "I brought wine."

I took a step closer, expecting him to swing the door open.

But he didn't.

Instead, he frowned. "Why?"

"Why what?"

"Why are you here?"

"Okay," I said. "Let's not even joke."

But that's when Jack nodded back toward the interior of the house and said, "I've actually got some guests here right now, so . . ."

"You do?" I said.

"Yeah. So."

"Wait—wasn't it tonight?"

"Wasn't what tonight?"

What was going on? He *had* asked me out, right? I hadn't *dreamed* it, had I? "What's going on?"

He frowned at me like he had no idea what I was talking about. "I've just got friends over, so . . . Kinda busy."

He started to swing the door closed.

On instinct, I tried to use the Robby trick of blocking the door with my foot—forgetting, of course, about my ridiculous footwear—and Jack wound up shoving the door closed on it, the metal weather stripping slicing my toes and breaking the leather sandal straps.

The pain shot up my leg like a rocket. I snatched my foot back, let out a string of curse words, and then hopped around for a minute before I noticed I was bleeding.

"Ouch," Jack said in a sucks-to-be-you voice. He watched me without any detectable sympathy—mostly just looking bored.

When I'd settled, he said, "Anyway," and moved to close the door again.

"Wait!" I said.

Jack gave an irritated sigh.

"What about . . ." I started. But I didn't know how to ask the question. I held up the bottle of wine.

"You can just leave that on the porch," he said, like I was a delivery person. "I'll get it later."

"Jack!" I said then, finally standing straight. "Wasn't tonight our date?"

Jack frowned like he had no idea what I meant. The utter noncomprehension on his face was enough to flood my whole body with humiliation. Then, as if pulling a vague memory from the deep mists of time—and not, you know, *yesterday*—he said, "Ohhh." Nodding. Like that explained everything. "The *date*."

What the hell? He'd asked me out twenty-four hours ago. Was he joking? Sleepwalking? Drunk? And who accidentally injures another person—another living creature, even—to the point of bleeding all over the doorstep and just stands there like a psychopath? What was happening?

I turned the situation around in my head like I had one last puzzle piece, but it just wouldn't fit.

But then Jack slid the piece into place for me.

He tilted his head, and in a voice nothing short of saturated with pity, he frowned in mock sympathy and said, "Did you think that was real?"

Everything in my body just stopped at that moment. My heart stopped beating, my blood stopped flowing, my breath stopped moving in and out.

Maybe time itself stopped, too.

Jack looked at me like I was supposed to answer that question—and waited. His face was all curiosity.

"Was it not . . . real?" I asked, when time started up again. My voice seemed like it was coming out of someone else's body.

Jack's eyes made an expression I can only describe as "incredulous disdain." "Of course not."

Of course not.

Then Jack added, "You really bought it? You believed me? That's so funny."

"Wait—so . . ." I shook my head. "Yesterday? Everything that happened?"

Jack gave a little shrug. "Fake," he said.

I couldn't seem to stop shaking my head. "You were . . . ?" I didn't know what I was asking.

"Bored," he confirmed.

"So you pretended . . . ?"

"I was doing a thing they call acting."

"So . . . the thing where you"—the question stung my mouth with humiliation, even as I asked it—"chose me over Kennedy Monroe . . . ?"

But Jack just nodded big, like I'd made a great point. "I know, right? I got both of you with that one. A twofer."

I felt myself sinking. "You were acting," I said, trying to absorb it.

"Just another day at the office."

"But . . ." I still didn't get it. "But why?"

Jack gave a short sigh, like *Try to catch up*. "Do you remember when my mom said I really wasn't that great of an actor?" Jack asked then. "That felt like a personal challenge."

"You pretended to like me," I paused for a second, putting it together, "to show up your mom's assessment of your acting skills?"

He shrugged. "It was something to do. Right? How else do you keep busy in the middle of nowhere?"

My head just kept shaking itself. "So . . . yesterday? All that . . . kissing?"

"Choreographed," Jack confirmed with a nod.

I felt lightheaded. I put my hand against the doorjamb to steady myself. Somewhere, in another universe, my bleeding foot was throbbing.

"I'll take the wine, though," he said, in a tone like *Moving on.*

Weirdly, I handed it to him.

He checked the label. "Cheap."

The air around us suddenly looked strange, like it was made of fumes. I wondered if I might faint.

"Speaking of bored," Jack said. "I really do have friends waiting."

We hadn't been "speaking of bored," but okay. "Sure," I said.

His eyes looked dull and flat. "They're going to laugh so hard at this story. It's so hilarious when you think about it."

"Is it?" I asked, not sure there was an answer.

"We're done here, right?" Jack said.

And then, without even waiting for me to respond, he just . . . closed the door. Presumably to go recount the story of the dumbest, most gullible security guard in all of history to some vicious group of A-list movie-star friends gathered around a charcuterie board.

This was how the love of my life would end? With me as the butt of Jack Stapleton's joke?

It's so hilarious when you think about it.

I have no idea how long I stood there after that. For all I knew, time had collapsed in on itself in an infinity loop.

My brain felt like white noise. My throat felt like sand. My entire being positively *vibrated* with shame. The humiliation was total. There was no cell in my body that wasn't saturated with it.

He was acting. He was acting. He'd been acting the whole time.

Of course he was acting.

Of course.

In slow motion, I squatted down to take off my sandals, and I noticed for the first time how bad the cut was on my injured foot, and how slippery the blood was making the sole.

Next, barefoot and bleeding, I stood back up.

He'd been acting.

As if going through a checklist, I swallowed, pulled back my shoulders, and lifted my chin. I clutched my dumb little purse with one hand and let the shoes dangle from the fingers of the other.

And then I limped back down the driveway as if the whole world were watching me go.

IT TOOK A thousand years to reach my car.

For one thing, I was walking barefoot on crushed granite, which feels more like broken glass than you might expect.

For another, all my senses were going haywire.

So I had to take it slow.

From the outside, I probably looked like a woman with a foot injury, sensibly taking her time.

The inside, of course, was a different story. My mind was positively *assaulting* itself, replaying every minute of that encounter at Jack's front door over and over so vividly that I could barely see in front of me.

It's a wonder I didn't wander off into traffic.

It's a wonder I didn't die from misery.

It's a wonder I didn't just *cease to exist.*

But . . . in the end . . . I made it to my car.

A car that had been driven here by a very different person than the one returning to it.

I walked up to it, bent over, and pressed my head down against the hood.

What the hell just happened?

The person I should have been hating at that moment was Jack.

Obviously. I knew that. I should have hated him for being the most callous, soulless jackass in the history of the world. I should have burned with incandescent and purifying rage.

But Jack wasn't the person I hated right then.

The person I hated was myself.

I hated myself for being taken in. For being fooled. For wanting to be loved so badly that I'd so easily become somebody's mark.

I should have known better.

I should have protected myself better.

The part of me that was always supposed to be on guard, and on alert, and on duty—the part that was tasked with the job of protecting the rest of me—had failed. Massively.

Again.

I was supposed to anticipate these things. I was supposed to keep a watchful eye. I was supposed to keep all my flaws and shortcomings forever at the front of my awareness so I'd never foolishly—ridiculously— hope for more.

I knew that. I'd known it since the night of my eighth birthday.

Later, I decided, I'd get angry at Jack. I'd summon my self-righteous rage, and salvage my dignity, and find the strength to carry on.

I was *not* the asshole here. I hadn't done anything wrong.

I'd stand up for myself, eventually. I would.

But right now, in this surreal moment of aftershock, the only thing I could manage to feel was just apocalyptically disappointed in myself.

Leaning against the hood of my car, I was astonished at how physical my reaction was.

My head was spinning. I couldn't catch my breath. I felt dizzy.

Flashes of what had just happened kept appearing on the screen of my mind without my permission. Jack opening his door in full movie-star mode—his face totally blank, like I was a stranger. Jack tilting his head in mockery as he said, "Did you think that was *real*?" Jack slicing the hell out of my toes, and then watching, emotionless, as I bled in front of him. Jack's posture as rigid as a mannequin as he waited for me to catch up, grasp my own contemptible stupidity, accept my fate, and move on.

Hey—

Wait a minute . . .

Jack's posture as rigid as a mannequin?

Jack Stapleton—famous sloucher and world-champion manspreader—with posture as rigid as a mannequin?

That didn't seem right.

With that, my thinking started to shift. I know that he'd just told me it had all been a joke and that he'd never really liked me. But the longer I stood there, the more I started to wonder if I one hundred percent believed him.

It was hard to know what to believe.

But the more I thought it over, the more I wondered if the besotted version of Jack I'd seen so much of last night was more convincing than the psychopath I'd just met.

Now my brain shifted gears, and I started flipping back through the pages of my memory with purpose to reread that moment.

Some things about it were off, for sure.

Jack had only opened the door partway, for example—but he was much more of a fling-the-door-wide-open kind of guy. I'd assumed he was trying to keep me separate from his friends, but if he was really enjoying the joke he'd just played, wouldn't he let them see me? And if he was really a sociopath, would he have cared if I'd seen them?

I kept scanning for abnormalities. There had been an unfamiliar tension in his face—like he was trying to look relaxed without actually being relaxed.

And had the expression in his eyes been coldness—or intensity?

Had the tightness of his voice been irritation—or anxiety?

I kept flipping through the interaction, scanning everything with different eyes—until one moment stopped me still.

Right after he said he'd been acting, just after he gave me a nod of confirmation, Jack had glanced to his left. Almost like there was somebody standing right next to him. And the emotion that had flashed across his face right then, in the second of that glance, was pretty unmistakable if you've been in this business long enough. . . .

It was fear.

SOMETHING WAS WRONG.

There was something in that house Jack was afraid of.

Someone.

I grabbed my keys, hit unlock, and dived into the back seat for my iPad.

I logged in to check the security footage on Jack's camera, scrolling back and forth at time-lapse speed.

Nothing on the driveway cam. Nothing on the backyard cam. Nothing on the pool cam. But then, suddenly, on the motion-activated interior camera in Jack's front hall, I saw Jack talking to a tall man in jeans. Slowing down to get a better look, I wondered if this might be one of the "friends" Jack claimed were there.

Until the man pulled out a 9 mm pistol and pointed it at Jack's head.

Holy shit.

I scrolled through the footage fast, trying to get the basics. I saw Jack put up his hands, but then lower them again. I saw them both turn toward the door, and then I saw Jack open it, just a few inches, and the other man take a step back and settle into a stance a few feet away with his gun pointed straight out.

That was enough.

That was all I needed to see.

I called 911 to get the police on the way.

Next, I called Glenn.

"Code Silver at Jack Stapleton's in-town residence," I said to Glenn, as I started back toward the house, not even feeling the gravel under my bare feet now. Then I added, for good measure, "Hostage situation."

Glenn wasn't following. "Brooks, what are you talking about? He's threat level white."

"Check the video footage," I said. "There's a man with a gun inside Jack's house."

"Right now?" Glenn asked.

"Right now."

"Where are you?"

"I'm in the driveway. Approaching."

"Are you alone?"

"Yes. But so is Jack."

"Jack's not alone. He's with an armed intruder."

"Right. Worse than alone."

"Are the cops on the way?"

"Yes."

"Wait for the cops," Glenn said. "I'm alerting the team."

"I'm not leaving Jack in there by himself."

"Brooks! Wait for the cops!"

"Get the team on it," I said. "Check the video. Call me if you get anything I can use." At that, I put my phone on silent.

"Brooks! Do not enter the scene! It isn't secure."

I knew he was right. Of course. I didn't have a weapon. I didn't have a plan. I didn't even have shoes. Remember when I said footwear really is crucial? That was back when I thought there was nothing worse than high heels.

As I moved toward the house, I rated my survival chances at a solid fifty-fifty.

I mean: I was good at my job. But I wasn't a superhero.

Part of being good at this job was making smart choices.

Was this a smart choice?

Not a chance. But I didn't care.

Only one thing really mattered to me right then: Two people on Jack's side were better than one. Even if I was barefoot, weaponless, backup-less, and injured, I wasn't leaving him in there alone.

"Brooks!" Glenn yelled through my phone. "Listen and listen hard. I'm telling you to stand back. If you go in against my orders, you can kiss London goodbye."

Of course he would say that. Of course he would use the one thing I wanted the most to try to keep me from getting myself killed. It was his best leverage.

Except for one thing. The thing I wanted most wasn't London anymore.

The thing I wanted most was Jack.

I hung up the phone.

Screw London.

I was already running.

I KNEW THE door code. I let myself in.

The ground floor was empty. There's a stillness you recognize in an empty room once you've been doing this for a while. But I checked everything anyway—every closet and nook. Even the pantry.

Nothing.

Passing the dining table, I saw a charcuterie board with a bottle of cabernet, open and breathing, next to it. And next to the wine bottle? A corkscrew.

At last. A weapon. I grabbed it as I went by, without missing a step, and—because women in this world somehow don't deserve pockets— shoved it into the side of my bra.

The second floor was empty, too.

They'd either left the house, or—

They were on the roof.

I took the stairs to the third-floor game room two at a time.

I edged my way past the pool table to the door that led to the rooftop patio.

I cracked the door to peek out and evaluate the scene—and, there, I beheld the most surreal sight: The bulb lights strung up around the roof's edge were glowing, the downtown skyline was lit up by the setting sun, the sky was deepening purple as it gave itself over to night . . . and there stood Jack Stapleton, his wrists and ankles bound by zip ties, and facing, maybe six feet away, a man exactly his same height, dressed in a ripped T-shirt and dirty jeans, aiming a gun at him, finger on the trigger.

Any other agent would've waited for the police.

But there wasn't any time. A finger on a trigger was one impulse—or one itch, or cough, or sneeze—away from doing irreversible things.

Time to intervene. However I could.

I was just slipping out, ready to gently announce my presence with my hands up so I didn't startle the gunman, when three things happened at once.

One: As I slid through the doorway, a burst of wind flashed across the rooftop from nowhere, yanked the door handle from my fingers, and slammed the door closed with an almost sonic *boom* that startled even me.

Two: At the sound, the gunman jerked in my direction and apparently pulled the trigger as he did, because . . .

Three: He shot me.

Thirty-One

AT FIRST, I thought he missed.

At first, it was just a sound so loud I felt it in my chest and a blast of wind past my face.

Then: I felt it before I understood it.

When I think about it now, I see it in slow motion. The bullet hissing past my head, shaving off a thin line of hair as it went. A sharp sting taking over my consciousness, and then a warm wetness rolling down my neck like someone was squeezing a bottle of chocolate syrup.

It wasn't syrup, of course.

But here's the thing—at the feel of it, I decided I was okay.

The blood on my neck convinced me: It was only a graze.

I don't know how I knew it, exactly—I just did. It just felt exactly the way you'd imagine it would feel to get grazed by a bullet—tight, small, stinging. Almost like a cut crossed with a burn.

I just didn't feel like a person whose brains were splattered all over the wall behind her.

Did I know that for sure?

No.

But I decided to run with it until I had evidence to the contrary.

I must have looked ghoulish, though.

The gunman stared in horror. "Jesus!" he shouted. "You scared me!"

The irony.

I put my hands out. "I'm sorry," I said.

"Don't slam the door at somebody when they're holding a gun, okay?"

"I didn't mean to," I said. "It was the wind."

His voice was all frustration. "Now you made me shoot you."

My neck was warm and wet with blood, running down to soak into the fabric of my dress. So much for being Jack's personal blood bank. "You didn't shoot me."

"Um. All that blood says otherwise."

"Just a scratch," I said. "Just a graze. I'm completely fine."

"Well, you look like hell," the gunman said.

"Head wounds bleed a lot," I said, like *No big deal*. "It barely even stings."

Beyond him, Jack looked utterly appalled to see me. He was crouched for action now, as if he'd forgotten that his wrists and ankles were bound, and he might—*what?* Hop over to save me? As soon as he realized he couldn't really move, he did the next best thing. "What are you doing here?" he demanded.

"Um. Helping you?"

"Didn't I just tell you to leave?" he said. "Didn't I just say there's nothing between us that's real?"

"Yeah. I didn't believe you."

Jack stared at me, like that made no sense.

So I added, "You aren't that great of an actor."

Not even a courtesy chuckle. "I sent you away," Jack said. "In no uncertain terms."

I nodded. "Yeah. But then I checked the security footage."

"Go home," Jack said, moving his eyes back to the stalker. "This is not about you."

"Well. It kind of is now."

The gunman was looking panicked now. Never good.

His hands were shaking so bad, I could see the gun vibrating. He'd lowered his aim—forgetting about the pistol for a minute, it seemed—and he was looking back and forth between me and Jack. "This wasn't how this was supposed to go."

He sounded disappointed.

I tried to think back over my hostage negotiations protocols. I was a little rusty. *Establish a relationship* came to mind, and so I said, "Hey, friend, can you tell me your name?"

No resistance at all. "Wilbur," he said.

"Wilbur?" I asked. "*The* Wilbur?"

Wilbur wasn't sure what to say.

"WilburHatesYou321?"

That made him smile—a little flattered to be recognized. "You know my handle?"

"You're very memorable. Mostly because of the book."

"What book?"

What else could we be talking about? "*Charlotte's Web.*"

Wilbur just looked at me like I was bananas.

Okay. Enough bonding.

"Hey, Wilbur?" I said then, like I'd had a fun idea. "Can you give me the gun?"

"I wasn't trying to shoot you," Wilbur said.

"I know," I said, making my voice like velvet. "It was an accident. I'm really fine."

"Somebody's gonna die up here," he said next, "but it's not supposed to be you." Then he gestured between himself and Jack. "Jack and I already decided. When you rang the bell, I said, 'Who's going to die tonight? You or the lady?' And he didn't even hesitate. He volunteered to die *in a heartbeat.*" Wilbur gave a little shrug. "Isn't that sweet?"

I nodded, like *Very.*

Time to get that gun.

Slowly, I took a took a step forward.

But as Wilbur saw what I was doing, he shook his head. "You can't have it," he said. "I need it."

That's when he took several steps backward—and as he did, I could see that he was limping. He angled himself toward the ledge of the roof, and he used his good leg to step up onto it.

"What are you doing?" I asked.

"I bet you think that guy's pretty great," Wilbur said to me then. "Everybody thinks he's so great."

"He's okay," I said with a shrug.

"Everybody loves him. The Destroyer. They think he saved the universe. Right? They all thought that was really him." Wilbur shook his head at Jack and pointed the pistol back at him. "But he's no hero."

"That's right," I said, all gentle. "He's just a person. Just a regular person." Emphasizing Jack's humanity seemed like a good idea.

"But not *regular*," Wilbur said. "Not like you and me. Because he has everything he wants." He turned to Jack and lifted the gun, holding it straight out toward him. "Don't ya, Destroyer? Don't you have everything you want?"

Jack shook his head slowly. "Nobody gets everything they want."

"But enough. Too much, even. And I don't have anything anymore. So if you get to be The Destroyer, then I get to be The Punisher."

You could feel the energy shift just then. Jack and I glanced at each other. Something was about to happen. It was almost like a click. We'd shifted to the next gear.

Was I going to have to push this guy off the roof to save Jack? I could make a running dive and send us both over the side.

A three-story fall won't kill you.

Probably.

But that's when Wilbur turned to me and said, "My wife left me for him." Then, to Jack, "Are you with her now? Are you two together?"

Jack just frowned.

"Lacey?" Wilbur went on, almost like they were playing the name game for old college friends. "Lacey Bayless? Mrs. Wilbur Bayless? Did she find you?"

"I don't know anybody named Lacey," Jack said.

Wilbur turned toward me. "After I got hurt at work"—he gestured at the leg he'd been limping on—"she got obsessed with him. Started a fan club, then another. Started sending emails to his agent. Spending all her time online making GIFs. And I was like, 'It's okay. It's healthy to have a hobby.' Right? I supported her! I wasn't jealous! I was like, 'Live your best life, honey'! But then one night I came home and there were suitcases by the front door. And she'd left a lasagna in the fridge. And she told me she was leaving." He looked over at Jack. "She told me my mangled leg turned her stomach. That she'd fallen in love with Jack, instead. I'd never be able to compare. Why couldn't I kiss her the way Jack Stapleton kissed Katie Palmer?"

I looked at Jack, like *Should we tell him?*

I flipped through all my de-escalation training in my head. I remember you were supposed to use people's names as much as possible. The sound—in theory, at least—was comforting.

"Wilbur," I said. "That's hard. I get it."

But Wilbur didn't want my sympathy. "What do *you* think?" he asked me.

"About what?"

"About if I'm handsome."

Was Wilbur handsome?

Um. Was this binding?

I scanned his pear-shaped physique, his receding hairline, his yellow teeth, his oily skin, his dirty jeans, and his limp Darth Vader T-shirt that read: COME TO THE DARK SIDE. WE HAVE COOKIES.

And then I said, "I think you're very handsome, Wilbur." I added, "*Very.*" Then, when he didn't look convinced: "Dashing, even."

"So," he gestured with the gun between himself and Jack. "If you had to choose between the two of us, who would you pick?"

Jack had rescued me last night by picking me, and I was going to save him tonight by picking . . . Wilbur.

"You, Wilbur!" I declared in a flash. "A hundred percent you! In a heartbeat!"

"Right?" Wilbur said. "That's what I kept telling her! 'Jack Stapleton is a famous dipshit.'"

"A legendary dipshit," I agreed.

Jack gave me a look.

Wilbur continued. "'He could never love you the way I love you,' I said."

"He doesn't know the first thing about love."

Jack coughed.

"'He's not going to build you a birdhouse from scratch with little working shutters and hand-painted camelia flowers!' No contest, right?"

"No contest," I confirmed. "Jack Stapleton's never built a birdhouse in his life."

Jack flared his nostrils at me, like *Settle down.*

Wilbur fell silent for a minute.

Should I try to get his weapon?

Then Wilbur went on. "But she left. She left anyway. She took the birdhouse with her. She won't take my calls. She won't answer my texts."

"How long has it been, Wilbur?"

"A month."

A month was a long time. Long enough to totally upend your life. I could attest.

"Things are going to get better, Wilbur," I said then. "Things get better, and then things get worse, and then things get better again. That's the rhythm of life. That's how it is for everyone."

But Wilbur was into telling his story now. "Then I saw he was right here in town," Wilbur went on. "And I thought I'd come find him. See if she might be here, too."

"She's not," Jack said, just to confirm.

"But then I saw the picture of Jack smooching his new girlfriend. I mean, really going at it. Like, 'Get a room!' You saw that picture— *amirite?*"

"We saw it," Jack and I said, in unison.

"And I thought," Wilbur went on, "'I've gotta put a stop to that.'"

"Why was that again, Wilbur?" I asked.

Wilbur frowned at me, like it was so obvious. "So it wouldn't hurt Lacey's feelings."

"You threatened to kill Jack's new girlfriend to free him up so your wife could have him?"

Wilbur nodded, looking proud. "The things we do for love, right?"

"Nope. That's not—" I started.

"The death threats were you?" Jack asked then. "We thought it was a middle-aged corgi breeder."

Wilbur tapped his head with the gun to gesture at his brains. "I copied her style. To throw everybody off."

"It worked," Jack said.

But Wilbur kept going. "Only I didn't want to *kill* the girlfriend. Just scare her so bad she'd leave him."

"Just terrorize her into ending the relationship," I offered.

"Exactly," Wilbur said. "But it didn't work. And now I'm a mess. I can't sleep. I can't eat. I'm so alone all the time. And I just . . . can't take it anymore."

Then, just as I was trying to figure out how to make it to Wilbur before Wilbur shot Jack, Wilbur said, "So that's The Destroyer's punishment. He has to watch me die."

At that, Wilbur lifted his arm and brought the muzzle of the gun to his own head.

He wasn't here to kill Jack. Or me.

He was here to kill himself.

I had some experience with hostage negotiations, but this was not, suddenly, a hostage situation anymore. Not like I'd been expecting, anyway. I didn't have a manual, or a playbook, or any idea what would work.

I just had to go on instinct.

"Wilbur," I said. "I need you to put down the gun."

Wilbur shifted his gaze from me to Jack to see if he agreed. Jack nodded and said, "She's right."

I took a step closer. "I know you feel alone right now, Wilbur," I said. "But you're not alone. Jack and I are with you. We want you to be okay."

I kept going, thinking my best shot was to say something true, and so I grabbed for the first thing I thought of—even though it had nothing to do with his story.

Though later I'd wonder if maybe it did.

"On my eighth birthday," I said then, "my mother's boyfriend beat her up so badly, I thought she was dead. I hid in a closet all night."

Wilbur looked at me.

"It was a bad night. It was the worst night of my life. As it was happening, it felt like it would never end. But it did end. And now it's a distant memory. Do you see what I'm saying?"

Wilbur shook his head.

"Terrible things happen. But we can get through them, Wilbur. And more than that . . . we can be better on the other side."

Wilbur considered that.

Then he used the muzzle of the pistol to scratch an itch on his head.

I kept pushing. "You can't control the world—or other people. You can't make them love you, either. They will or they won't, and that's the truth. But what you can do is decide who you want to be in the face of it all. Do you want to be a person who helps—or hurts? Do you want to be a person who burns with anger—or shines with compassion? Do you want to be hopeful or hopeless? Give up or keep going? Live or die?"

Then Wilbur said something that pierced all the adrenaline of the moment and kind of broke my heart. "I just want my Lacey back," Wilbur said.

"I know," I said. "That could happen. That could still happen. But it can't happen if you're not here."

Wilbur frowned, like he hadn't thought of that.

"Your life is important, Wilbur," I said. "The world needs more painted birdhouses."

"But who am I making them for without her?"

"Make them for the birds! Make them for all the people who'll be delighted to see them. Make them for yourself."

There were tears on Wilbur's face. And then he said something I still think about to this day. He said, in a voice that sounded genuinely weary, "I just hate myself so much for not being loved."

Oof.

I absolutely got it.

I made my voice soft. "You can't make people love you. But you can give the love you long for out to the world. You can be the love you wish you had. That's the way to be okay. Because giving love to other people is a way of giving it to yourself."

Wilbur chewed his lip as he thought about that.

"That's all we can do," I said. "All we can do is put away our anger, and our blame, and our guns"—*see what I did there?*—"and try to make things better instead of worse. That's the only answer there is."

Wilbur wiped at his tears with the back of his gun-holding hand.

I took a step closer. "Give yourself some time—and give me the gun."

Wilbur lowered the gun and looked down at it in his hand.

"You can change your life," I said then. "You can make good things happen. You can fill up your yard with painted birdhouses. Hundreds of them. Thousands." My voice felt a little shaky. But I kept going: "I'd really, really love to see that. How magical would that be?"

Wilbur didn't look away. He knew I was telling the truth. He felt how much I meant it.

"Come down and give me the gun, okay?" I said.

Wilbur looked down then, peering over his feet. Then, with surrender, he stepped back toward us, down off the ledge. As he landed, his injured leg crumpled under him, and he collapsed.

In that second, Jack and I both tackled him—Jack, still bound, throwing his whole body down to keep Wilbur pinned, and me going for the gun—though Wilbur had gone limp at that point and didn't need much restraining.

As I landed, the wine opener in my bra flew out and went skittering across the rooftop.

I twisted Wilbur's arm behind him and wrested the gun out of his grip, and then I looked up to see Jack staring at the corkscrew. "What, exactly, were you planning to do with that?"

But I just said, "You don't want to know."

Pretty easy, right there at the end.

"I was never going to kill you, you know," Wilbur said to me then, his cheek against the roof. "Or Jack, either. The only person I wanted to murder here was me."

"That's gotta change, Wilbur," I said, my knee on his back. "You need to learn how to be kind to yourself. And then you need to share that kindness with the world."

"With birdhouses," Wilbur said, clearly liking my idea.

"That's one way," I said.

We could hear the sirens now. And voices down below. And boots on the gravel drive.

Shouldn't be long. They'd follow my bloody footprints up to us pretty fast.

While we waited, Wilbur said, "I just have one question for Jack."

Jack, stretched across his legs to keep them pinned, said, "What is it?"

That's when Wilbur lifted his head, angled back to give Jack his best smile, and said, "Any chance of a selfie?"

Thirty-Two

THE DOC AT the ER called the scrape on my head a "million-dollar wound."

Bad enough, in theory, to earn me some time off work, but not bad enough to need stitches.

Or, you know, *to have killed me.*

"One millimeter closer," the doc said, after letting out a long whistle, "and it would be a whole different story."

Once they cleaned me up and got a good look, it was like a two-inch-long, pencil-lead-wide trench above my ear—with the sides built up a tiny bit, like a berm.

Jack took a bunch of photos with my phone so I could see.

They didn't have to shave too much of my hair, which was nice. Just pulled the bulk off into a surprisingly perky side ponytail. Then they irrigated and disinfected it, packed it with an antibacterial ointment, and covered it with a dressing—encircling my head with gauze like the sweatband of a 1970s tennis player.

"This is actually a good look for you," Jack said.

I just kept thinking it could've been so much worse.

They didn't even keep me overnight. Once the MRI came back fine, they discharged me with some antibiotics, industrial-strength Tylenol, and strict instructions to "treat it like a concussion." No driving, no sports, no roller coasters.

Check.

Jack and I had arrived at the ER in an ambulance, and so Glenn sent a car later to pick us up. And in a classic, Glenn Schultz–style sadistic flourish, he made Robby drive it.

Do we need to review all the times Robby said there was no way I could ever pass for Jack Stapleton's girlfriend? Do we need to reflect on Robby's astonishing callousness from the breakup and beyond? Do we need to have a moment of realization here that Robby's strategy for keeping me in a bad relationship was to convince me that I didn't deserve a better one?

All true.

But maybe we can just savor this particular, exquisite moment from that night, right as Jack and I reached the car, when Robby, trying to manifest some big secret-service energy, opened the back door of the Tahoe and started to help me in.

Robby might have passed for a cool guy in that moment.

If he weren't standing two feet from Jack Stapleton.

And if I hadn't just come to a whole new understanding of what, exactly, a cool guy was.

Anyway, Jack stopped him as he reached for me.

"I got it, man," Jack said.

"It's my job," Robby said, trying to continue.

But Jack stopped him again, stepping between us to block Robby's access, moving in with such purpose that Robby just lost his momentum.

Next, Jack put his arms around me, all tenderness, and lifted me up. He set me in the back seat, clicked the buckle like I was something precious, gave me a brief but suggestive kiss on the mouth, and then turned to Robby. "That may be your job," Jack said, gesturing at the Tahoe, "but this"—he placed his hand on my thigh like it belonged to him—"is my girlfriend."

So.

Not the worst night of my life.

In the end.

JACK WOUND UP sleeping over.

At my place. In my bed.

No wall of pillows necessary.

Nothing physical happened, of course. Roller coasters aren't the only no-nos with concussions. Plus, I had surgical gauze wrapped around my head like Björn Borg. Which pretty much put the kibosh on anything, ya know, nonspiritual.

But *emotional* things happened.

Like, we held hands. And we thanked each other for everything we could think of. And we felt grateful to be alive.

There may or may not have been snuggling involved.

And I guess there really is something profoundly healing about letting somebody love you.

Because the next morning, when I woke and found Jack sitting on the side of the bed with his head in his hands, I could tell something was different.

Before I could ask, Jack turned and took in the sight of me—head bandaged, hair making its own rules. He stood up, came around to my side, and said, "How's your gunshot wound?"

I waved him off. "Totally fine."

"There's blood on the bandage."

"It's like a paper cut."

But he fussed over me anyway. He made me change the bandage on my head—and also around my toes. Which hurt much worse. He also made me brush my teeth, and put on a soft chenille robe, and drink some warm tea, and take my antibiotics.

And then he thanked me, again, for not dying.

And only once we'd taken care of all those things did Jack confess to me, "I had my nightmare again last night."

"The same nightmare?" I asked.

He nodded. "Yes. But it was different."

Different was good, I hoped. "What happened?"

"I got in the car with Drew, like I always do. We headed straight for the bridge, like we always do. But then, as we got close, I saw something in the road."

"What?"

"A person. Waving us down to stop."

"And did you stop?"

"Barely. Drew slammed on the brakes, and we skidded like a hundred feet." Jack shook his head. "It was so real, I could smell the burning rubber."

"But you stopped," I said. "That's different."

He nodded. "Just in time. I mean—just inches from hitting her."

Her? "Was it your mom?"

Jack shook his head. "It was you."

I leaned in to get a good look at his face. "Me?"

Jack nodded. "You came to my window and gestured to roll it down. And then you said the bridge was closed. 'You have to turn around,' you said.

"But that's when I saw that Drew wasn't in the car anymore. I got out to look around for him and saw him walking away—off toward the bridge, like he was going to cross it. 'It's closed!' I yelled. 'We have to go back!'

"He stopped. And turned. But he didn't come back.

"'Hey,' I called, all determined, like if I convinced him hard enough, we could change things. 'Hey. We have to go back.'

"But Drew shook his head.

"So I got out and ran over to him and stopped just a few feet away. 'There's ice on the bridge,' I said. 'We have to turn around. Come on.'

"But Drew just looked into my eyes. He needed a shave. And his cowlick was making that one little sprig of hair stick up in the back. And he wouldn't say anything. Just stood there until I knew for sure that he wasn't coming back with me. And then I could feel tears on my face. I tried one more time. 'Just come back with me, okay? Let's just go back together.'

"But Drew just shook his head. And I knew he wasn't coming. That there was nothing I could do.

"And then my voice was so shaky I almost thought I wouldn't get the words out. But I said to him, 'I am so sorry that I couldn't protect you.'

"And then Drew nodded, like *I know. It's okay.*

"And he turned and walked off toward the bridge. I watched him until I couldn't see him anymore. And I think—at least it felt this way—like you stood beside me and watched him go, too. When I woke up, I was crying. But I felt better, in a way."

For some reason, hearing about it gave me shivers.

"I know it wasn't real," Jack said. "But it felt real."

"Maybe it was real enough," I said.

"Thank you for being there," Jack said.

I could have pointed out that he put me there. But I just said, "You're welcome."

"Anyway," Jack said, "I think you were right about the dream."

"I was?"

Jack nodded. "That it was a chance."

"To say goodbye?" I asked.

But Jack shook his head. "To say I'm sorry."

THAT DREAM WAS the last one Jack ever had about the icy bridge.

He still dreamed about his brother from time to time—almost always about looking up in a crowd to see Drew smiling at him, or winking, or giving him a nod, like *You got this.*

Jack didn't believe those dreams, exactly. He didn't think they were literal windows into the afterlife. He figured it was just his imagination telling stories.

But they were good stories. Comforting stories. And he was grateful for them.

They were stories he needed to hear.

Did they cure his fear of bridges?

That depends on how you define "cure."

He's still not a fan of them. But he can cross them now.

He gets a little concentration dimple in his cheek, and he tightens his hands on the wheel, but he makes it across every time. Without throwing up afterward.

And we go ahead and count that as a win.

Thirty-Three

AFTER THE NIGHT I got, um, *shot in the head*, Glenn made Taylor cover the first two weeks of my Korea assignment so my million-dollar injury could heal completely. He offered to have Taylor take the whole thing, but I declined. "No more giving Taylor my assignments," I said.

"Good point," Glenn said.

Jack waited a respectful length of time for my emotionally-alarming-but-not-all-that-lethal-or-even-painful injury to heal . . . and then he talked me into trying our date again.

He said, "Can we just have a do-over?"

"On what?"

"The date."

"*The* date?" I asked. "The one that almost got me killed?"

Jack nodded, like *Yup.*

"No thanks," I said. "I'm good."

"I just need a do-over," Jack said. "And so do you." Then he leaned in closer, marshaled all his handsomeness, and said, "I promise you won't regret it."

Did I want to walk up Jack's driveway in ridiculous footwear and nervously ring his doorbell again, even knowing for certain that Wil-burHatesYou321 was in custody?

Not a chance.

"Let's just do something else," I said. "Mini golf. Bowling. Kara-oke."

But Jack shook his head. "I had some very specific intentions for what I was going to do to you in that moment, and I really need to see them through."

"You mean the moment when I showed up at your door all nervous and you flat-out rejected me?"

"Let's note for the record that I was saving your life."

"But I got shot anyway."

"Grazed," Jack corrected.

I thought about it. Could I bear to try again? I studied him. "You're trying to re-create the date?"

"Yes."

"Why?"

"Because," Jack said. "I need a version of that story that does not have Wilbur in it."

I could see the value of that. "Fine," I said.

"Tonight," Jack said.

"Fine."

"And wear that red dress."

I sighed. "The one I bled all over?"

"You washed it, right?"

"I mean . . . yes."

"So it's all good."

"The shoes are in the trash, though," I said.

"I don't care about the shoes. Come barefoot if you want."

I shook my head. Then I pointed at Jack and said, "I'll wear my cow-boy boots." And as he nodded, like *Cool*, I said, "I'm never wearing stu-pid shoes again."

*　*　*

THIS TIME, WHEN I rang the bell, Jack swung the door wide open right away.

He was dressed, he was clean-shaven, he was blindingly good-looking . . . and as soon as he saw me, he let his eyes sweep down to my boots and back up in a slow nod of appreciation. Then he reached out, hooked his fingers into the fabric tie around my waist, and pulled me into his entranceway—swinging the door closed behind us.

He had a look on his face like he was about to kiss me into oblivion.

But that's when I lifted a finger and said, "Can I just check something with you?"

Jack had a certain momentum. But he paused. "Sure."

"The last time we did this," I said. "You stopped me at the door and told me that you never liked me. That you'd been faking everything the entire time."

"I remember."

"So, as long as we're having a do-over," I said. "Can I just get you to confirm that you were lying about faking?"

Jack frowned. "Don't you know that already?"

"I mean, yes. I do. But that moment really kind of firebombed the quadrant of my brain that we'll just call 'my worst fears about myself.' So. As long as we're rewriting the story . . . can we fix that part?"

Jack nodded, like *Of course.*

He met my eyes. "I was really nervous about the date. Did I tell you that? We'd been living together for weeks, so I shouldn't have been. But I was. I'd ordered takeout for delivery, so when the doorbell rang, I just answered it. But it wasn't the food. It was Wilbur. With a gun. And he was a lot more terrifying than anybody named Wilbur should ever be."

Agreed.

"He was wild-eyed," Jack went on. "Breathing fast and manic-seeming, like anything could happen at any second. I thought he might well be on drugs. I knew for sure he was pointing a pistol at my chest. I remember having a hard time letting the idea of the date go. I remember thinking, *Now's really not a good time.* I tried to talk him into giving me the gun. He asked me a thousand questions without ever explaining anything. And just as I was thinking, *What would Hannah do right now?* and trying to remember exactly how you'd flipped me that time, you rang the bell."

Jack sighed.

He went on. "Wilbur went on high alert. He wanted to know who it was, and then he looked through the peephole and saw you, and he said, 'It's a woman in a slinky dress.' Then he turned to me and said, 'Okay. Who's it gonna be?'

"I asked what that meant, and he said, 'Who should I kill? You? Or her?'

"So I said, 'Me. Of course. Obviously.'

"'You didn't even think about it,' Wilbur said, like he was disappointed.

"So I said, 'There's nothing to think about.'

"'You want to die?' Wilbur asked.

"'No,' I said. 'But between the two of us, it's no contest.'

"'I can't believe you're picking yourself,' Wilbur said.

"'Well I'm sure as shit not picking *her*.'

"'Okay, then,' Wilbur said. 'Get her out of here.'

"I reached for the door, but then Wilbur added: 'And do it right. If she figures out something's up and calls the cops, I guarantee you I'll kill us all.'

"'I believe you,' I said. And I did. So I opened the door and I did the only thing I could think of to make you leave and not come back."

I looked into Jack's eyes. "You acted like you didn't like me."

Jack nodded. "Didn't take all those improv classes for nothing."

"Why didn't you use the code word?"

Jack gave me a look. "Um. Because I didn't want my last words to be 'ladybug'?"

"Seriously, though."

"Seriously? Why would I have done that?"

"So I'd know something was up."

"The point was for you *not* to know."

"You realize I do this for a living? I was way more qualified than you to handle Wilbur321. There were ten different ways I could have disarmed him."

"I didn't think about that."

"Obviously."

"I just wanted you not to die. I really, really," Jack said, stepping closer, "didn't want you to die."

I appreciated that. I did. "Thank you."

"So I acted my heart out."

"You really got me," I said.

"Well," Jack said, "I do *this* for a living."

I peered into his eyes. "Just to confirm: You didn't not like me."

"I didn't not like you," Jack said.

"You liked me," I said again. "For real. Actively."

"For real. Actively," Jack confirmed. "More than anyone else ever in my whole, dumb life."

I studied him.

"I didn't care if he shot me," Jack went on. "The only thing I cared about was tricking you into leaving—and doing it so well that you didn't come back."

"Well. You crushed it."

"But then you came back. Like a dummy."

"I think you mean *like a heroically courageous badass*."

"You weren't supposed to save me. *I* was saving *you*."

"I guess we saved each other."

"That's one way of spinning it."

"Aren't you a little bit glad that I saved your life?"

"Wilbur says he was never going to kill me, after all."

"All evidence to the contrary."

"As soon as I picked you to save, he decided I was a good guy. It was a test. And I passed."

"But why test you if he wasn't going to kill you, anyway?"

"It was a *friendship* test."

I studied Jack's face. "So it wasn't that heroic when you saved me, after all."

But Jack just gave me a look. "It was pretty damn heroic."

Jack sighed. "I am honored that you came back," he said. And even as he was talking, he was stepping closer, cupping both hands behind my head, looking into my eyes like they were a place he wanted to go. "But," he said then, "don't ever fucking do it again."

Then he brought his mouth to mine, and pressed us back up against the door, and kissed me like he might never get another chance.

Yep.

Heck of a do-over.

Apologies to everyone in the world who is not me . . . but the truth is—as good as Jack is at screen kissing, he's a thousand times better at the real thing.

I mean, he makes it easy.

You don't overthink it.

You don't think at all, in fact.

You just let yourself get lost, and your body takes over, and before you know it, your arms crook up around his neck, and you're pressed against that washboard stomach, and you're melting against him and dissolving into a moment that's so mind-numbing it's as if he hijacked every single one of your senses.

In the best possible way.

He kisses you like it's destiny. Like that's what always happened. Like there's no other conceivable version of the story.

And you kiss him back the same way.

And your whole body feels like fireworks.

And so does your soul.

And it's like you're in your life and flying above it at the same time. Like you are both on earth and in the heavens. Like you are all heartbeat and rushing pulse and warmth and softness—but you are also the wind and the clouds. You're just everything, all at once.

It's as if loving somebody—really, bravely, just all-in loving somebody—is a doorway to something divine.

And later—many hours later—after he's taken you to bed, and your red boots are forgotten on the floor, and you're both exhausted and tangled and half asleep, and you have helped him do whatever crazy thing he always does to his sheets, Jack, all casual, yawns and stretches out that famous torso, and says: "I wonder if anybody's monitoring the surveillance footage."

"What surveillance footage?" you ask.

"In the front hallway."

Of course, Robby is. Since he's still the primary agent on Jack's detail.

You lift up on your elbows to read Jack's face. "Did you kiss me in the front hall like that to show up Robby?"

"I kissed you in the front hall because I've been desperate to do that exact thing for weeks and weeks," Jack says, clamping his arm around you and pulling you to him tight.

Then he adds: "Showing up our old pal Bobby was just a bonus."

AND, IN THE end, do you ever truly know for sure if you're lovable?

What a question.

You don't. You can't. Of course not.

Life never hands out the answers like that.

But maybe that's not even the right question.

Maybe love isn't a judgment you render—but a chance you take. Maybe it's something you choose to do—over and over.

For yourself. And everyone else.

Because love isn't like fame. It's not something other people bestow on you. It's not something that comes from outside.

Love is something you do.

Love is something you *generate*.

And loving other people really does turn out, in the end, to be a genuine way of loving yourself.

Epilogue

"*HOW'S WILBUR DOING* these days?" might not be your most pressing question right now.

But can I just tell you? The man is thriving.

He's living his best life, times ten.

All to say: The birdhouses really took off.

After he got out of prison, he started a birdhouse-building company, and he filled up his entire front yard with them. Hundreds. In all different colors, on poles of all different heights, in all different shapes: barns with sliding doors, Dutch windmills that spin, and even a little modern replica of Fallingwater. It's become the most photographed birdhouse-themed location on the internet. Not only for its whimsy, but also because it's a perfect selfie background.

He named his company Make It Better Birdhouses.

Nowadays, he'll tell you that night on Jack's roof was the darkest moment of his life. In fact, it's in the mission statement on his website, under the heading, "Why Birdhouses?" He encountered a powerful dose of kindness at exactly the moment he needed it most—and it was a revelation. He got some professional help, and some medication, and now he tries every day to pay it forward.

To reject rage—and to choose kindness, instead.

And birdhouses.

He even did a TED Talk about it.

Last time I checked, it had four million views.

Dammit if Wilbur didn't turn out to be the wisest one of us all.

I mean, sort of.

He's also very aware that he almost killed both me and himself that night long ago, and not only did he send a sternly worded letter to the man at the gun store who sold him that pistol *even after Wilbur hinted at what he planned to do with it*—he now uses his platform to advocate for stronger gun laws every chance he gets.

It's not theoretical for him, he says. It's personal.

Also, every year on my birthday, he sends me a birdhouse.

Does it freak me out that he knows where I live?

Absolutely.

But not that much more than everything else.

The motto for Wilbur's company is, after all: "Make the birdhouse you wish to see in the world."

He seems to have found a healing vocation for himself. And to be making a pretty good living. And he's definitely become a folk-art hero of the birdhouse community.

He says getting lost in darkness forced him to look for the light.

He also mentions Jack Stapleton as his "biggest fan and best friend" pretty frequently.

Which is fine. Jack hasn't seen Wilbur once since the night he shot me—but it's fine.

Jack has actually featured a couple of Wilbur's birdhouses on his Instagram. And I follow his TikTok. As fans of both birdhouses and people who courageously change their thinking, we're very glad he's doing well.

In theory.

From a distance.

The question of the hour, of course is: *Did Lacey ever come back to Wilbur?*

She did not.

She filed for divorce.

But, as luck would have it, on the day he got served the papers, Wilbur decided to eat an entire sheet cake as a method of self-care, and when he called the order in to the bakery and asked to personalize it with YOUR LOSS, LACEY! KISS MY ASS, the cake decorator thought it was so funny that she slipped her phone number into the cake box with a note that read: "You're hilarious. Call me! Love, Charlotte."

A year later, on Valentine's Day, Wilbur and Charlotte eloped.

So I sent them a copy of *Charlotte's Web* as a wedding gift.

DID JACK WIND up making the sequel to *The Destroyers*?

He did.

Turns out it's harder to give up being a world-famous movie star than you'd think.

Especially when you don't hate yourself like crazy every day anymore.

Though he also made a One Movie a Year rule.

In the five years since filming *Destroyer II: The Redemption*, he's made five movies. A space adventure, a political thriller, a war movie where everybody—even Jack—gets eaten by sharks (I will never watch that one), a rom-com (you're welcome), and a western.

He did his own stunts for the western.

But nobody believes it.

It seems to be just the right work-life balance. A little filming, a little promoting, and a lot of walking the banks of the Brazos looking for fossils. And I do a similar thing, too, now—one assignment a year. And we time them just right so we're gone at the same time.

We go off on our separate adventures, and we do our work. And then we go home to Texas.

If Glenn has an assignment for me, and I hesitate, Jack'll gesture at his own ribcage and say, "Don't forget your gills."

But the truth is, I think about escape a lot less than I used to.

Because Jack did move back to his parents' ranch, and he did build a place a few pastures away—just at the perfect spot on the Venn diagram between "too close" and "too far."

He and Hank and Doc did wind up building Drew's boat—and naming it "Sally," after Drew's favorite childhood hamster. One of these days, they're going to sail it down the Texas coast. Just as soon as they learn how to sail.

Jack also turned the oxbow lake into a nature preserve. The Drew Stapleton Texas-in-the-Wild Brazos River Bottom Nature Preserve & Wildlife Center. But everybody just calls it Drew's Place for short. They cleared hiking and mountain biking trails. They set up classes on butterfly gardening, birding, and waterway conservation. They started summer camps to teach kids how to fish, and build fires, and look after nature.

So that—as Doc says—keeps him out of trouble.

Jack still does something good every single day in honor of Drew. Whether it's weeding the garden for his mom, or donating a library building to a school, or surprising a group of ICU nurses by showing up to serenade them in a snug-fitting T-shirt, Jack—faithfully, devotedly, and daily—works to honor the memory of his little brother and to justify his own remaining time on this earth.

And he marks it every time by saying, quietly to himself: "This is for you, Drew. Miss you, buddy."

That's enough, it turns out.

That's enough to go on.

WHO WON THE competition for the London job?

Robby did. Glenn was not bluffing when he told me to wait for the cops or kiss London goodbye.

No surprise there.

So Robby got the London job and left the country.

Fine with me. And Taylor, too.

It bugged Kelly that I didn't get it, though. "You saved a person's life that night!" she insisted one night over margaritas. "Why should Robby get to win?"

But I guess it depends on how you define winning.

I mean, Robby has to spend the rest of his life *being Robby*.

That's losing by definition.

Did I really go on assignment to Korea and leave Jack behind in Texas as soon as my sick leave was up?

Of course. I had a job to do.

But did Jack follow me there a few weeks later, showing up unannounced outside my hotel in a softer-than-velvet cashmere scarf for one magical, snowy night in Seoul?

Officially? Absolutely not. I was working.

More importantly, did Jack finally give me a taker for that Valentine's vacation to Toledo?

He did. Though he bought my nonrefundable bargain tickets from me and we somehow wound up on a private plane. And he made me let him pick the hotel.

All to say, we went—but don't ask me what we thought of the botanical gardens. Or the art museum. Or their world-famous chili dogs.

We didn't get out much.

Am I saying we spent the entire week in a fancy hotel room without leaving even once?

I'll leave that to your imagination.

Let's just say that Toledo is now my favorite city of all time.

THOUGH I SHOULD mention that Jack and I aren't dating anymore. You can't date a guy like Jack forever.

Not with Connie Stapleton after you twenty-four seven to "hurry up and get married" and "make some grandkids" before her "corpse is in the flower garden."

She continued reminding us of her possible imminent death long—
long—after she was fully recovered in every possible way.

Unrepentantly.

"I've earned it," she said. "Now get busy."

To this day, Connie swears that death—the threat of it, the promise
of it, the looming guarantee of it, even if you're well—has its upsides.

It helps you remember to be alive, if nothing else.

It helps you stop wasting time.

JACK AND I got married at the ranch, of course.

I had a bouquet of fresh-cut honeysuckle and bougainvillea. Jack's
boutonniere had a speckled feather he'd found by the river. We made
beaded safety pins and gave them out as keepsakes. And we got Clipper
the horse to officiate.

Just kidding.

We got Glenn to officiate. Turns out, he was also a justice of the
peace. Who knew?

By then, he was on Wife Number Four, so he declared that pretty
much made him an expert. And nobody dared to argue.

We kept the guest list pretty small. Mostly family. And a handful of
world-famous movie stars. Of course. But only the ones Jack actually
liked.

Kennedy Monroe, for example, did not make the cut.

But guess who did?

Meryl Streep.

She couldn't make it, but she sent us a set of French steak knives—
which would henceforth be known as "Meryl Streep's steak knives"
even to our future kids. As in, "Babe, can you grab me one of Meryl
Streep's steak knives from the drawer?" Or, "Do not try to pry that
open with one of Meryl Streep's steak knives!" Or, "How did a four-
year-old manage to bend one of Meryl Streep's steak knives so badly we
can't bend it back?"

So she really wound up quite a guest of honor.

And did I let Taylor be a bridesmaid, even after she begged?

Um. Not exactly.

I did let her pass out programs, though.

And Kelly? Long-suffering Kelly? Who had tried so hard for so long to find a place on Team Jack but never caught a break from anybody?

We sat her in between Ryan Reynolds and Ryan Gosling—and we sat Doghouse across from them and let him burn with jealousy all night. Then she accidentally spilled a jar of moonshine on one of them—I can never remember which—and she wound up having to help him take off that slim-fit dress shirt and change into one of Jack's spares.

So in the end she had a pretty okay time.

Sometimes enthusiasm is its own reward.

WHAT'S IT LIKE to be with Jack Stapleton, you want to know?

I imagine it's like being with any kindhearted, comically good looking, world-famous guy who laughs all the time.

It's pretty great.

Is Jack's handsomeness still exhausting?

Absolutely.

Poor guy. He really can't help it.

And it's tempered by reality. When he goes for a run and leaves his sweaty T-shirt in a clump on the bathroom floor. When his glasses get bent and he doesn't notice. When he sneezes into his shirt and then takes a bow like he's the world's biggest genius. When he laughs so hard at dinner that he spits water all over the table. When he tries to throw an expired tub of yogurt across the kitchen into the trash can for a three-pointer, misses completely, and then darts out the door before you can make him clean it up.

I mean, he's not perfect.

But you don't have to be perfect to be lovable.

One thing that's changed is that I know for sure I can read him now. I know the *acting* Jack from the *real* Jack at a glance. I know his fake laugh from his genuine laugh. I know his irritated smile from his delighted smile. I know his actual passionate kisses from his pretend passionate kisses.

Another thing that's changed is that I can read *myself* now.

And by "read," I mean: appreciate.

I mean, sure, we should all just know our own inherent worth, and see our own particular beauty, and root for ourselves wherever we go.

But does anybody really do that?

It doesn't hurt to have a little help, right?

It doesn't hurt to spend your life with people who see what's great about you—in a way that you maybe never would have on your own.

The people we love help teach us who we are.

The best versions of who we are, if we're lucky.

That turns out to be my favorite thing about Jack Stapleton. It's not the handsomeness. Or the way he wears those Levi's. It's not the money, or the philanthropy, either. And it's certainly not the fame.

The fame's a little bit of a pain, actually.

The best thing about Jack Stapleton is a particular ability he has— and now I know he got it straight from his mom—to see the best in people.

Whoever you are, and whatever you have to offer, he sees it.

He sees it, and he admires it, and then he calls your attention to it. He mirrors back to you a version of yourself that's infused with admiration. A version that is absolutely, always, undeniably . . . lovable.

All to say: Peanuts Palmer will never fool me again.

Remember when I called that on-screen kiss Jack had with her "my favorite kiss of all time"?

Yeah. Jack Stapleton took that as a personal challenge.

A personal challenge that he won.

Well . . . to be fair: We both did.

Acknowledgments

IT'S ALWAYS HARD to write acknowledgments. I just want to thank everyone who's ever read, loved, recommended, reviewed, or posted about my books. Because every little butterfly-wing flap of love for a novel helps it find its readers: the folks who will love it, and feel changed by it, and help other people find it, too. Writers absolutely cannot write books without readers who want to read them. I'm so beyond grateful to get to spend my life obsessing over, getting lost in, and writing stories. So . . . to readers, and bookstagrammers, and bloggers, and podcasters, and all the beautiful other authors out there lifting each other up . . . *thank you*. And a special thanks to novelists Jodi Picoult and Christina Lauren for letting Jack Stapleton star in fictional movies of their real-life books.

This book involved a fair bit of research, especially into what the world of acting is really like, and I'm beyond grateful to the beloved actresses Sharon Lawrence and Patti Murin for graciously taking time to talk with me about fame, the acting craft, and life in the entertainment world. I so appreciate their time, insights, and honesty. I also learned a lot from Justine Bateman's compelling book, *Fame*, and I'm grateful to teacher David Nathan for sharing some insights from his Almost Famous course with me. Two very detailed books about life in the world of executive protection were helpful for my research: *Finding Work as a Close Protection Specialist* by Robin Barratt, and *Executive Protection Specialist Handbook* by Jerry Glazebrook and Nick Nicholson, Ph.D. Much of what Hannah tells Jack about his protection detail is taken from those sources. I also truly enjoyed taking a deep dive into the YouTube channel of executive protection specialist Byron Rodgers—a rich and engaging resource for not only the details of that career but also the psychology of it. His interview with legendary agent Jacquie Davis was particularly inspiring and helpful. I'd also like to thank Dr. Natalie Colocci for medical consulting, as well as my dear friend Sue Sim.

Books never happen—or find their way out to the world—without profound encouragement and support, and I owe so much to the folks who keep cheering me on and supporting my writing. My editor, Jennifer Enderlin, and my agent, Helen Breitwieser, are two of my favorite people and really make it possible for me, every day, to keep bringing my A-game. I'm beyond grateful for the fantastic people I get to work with at St. Martin's Press: Sally Richardson, Olga Grlic, Katie Bassel, Erica Martirano, Brant Janeway, Lisa Senz, Sallie Lotz, Christina Lopez, Anne Marie Tallberg, Elizabeth Catalano, Sara LaCotti, Kejana Ayala, Erik Platt, Tom Thompson, Rivka Holler, Emily Dyer, Katy Robitzki, Matt DeMazza, Samantha Edelson, Meaghan Leahy, Lauren Germano, and many others. I also need to thank writer/director Vicky Wight for being my hero and adapting not one, but *two* of my books into gorgeous Hollywood movies—including, most recently, *Happiness for Beginners*—and for introducing me in real life to the very inspiring actual movie star Josh Duhamel. Much gratitude also to Lucy Stille Literary for her representation.

Big hugs and many thanks as always to my family: my sisters, Shelley and Lizzie, and their families; my dad, Bill Pannill, and his wife; and my two astoundingly fantastic kids, Anna and Thomas. And the dream team: my legendary mom, Deborah Detering, and my equally legendary husband, Gordon Center, who are, in their different ways, absolute *fountains* of support, encouragement, tolerance, and inspiration. If there's one thing I know in this life, it's that I lucked out like crazy.

Author's Note

THIS IS MY pandemic book.

I started this story in the summer of 2020 and finished it in the spring of 2021.

It's a story I wrote when my real life, like most people's, was full of worry, and stress, and uncertainty, and fear, and isolation. I always try to find a balance between darkness and light in my stories. For this book? The balance was *as much light as possible.*

I remember talking with my editor, Jen, about the big plot elements of the story very early on. I wasn't liking the career I'd given to one of my main characters, Jack. The job he had back then was so dull, I couldn't even focus when I tried to research it. So Jen said, "Why can't he be a movie star?" And my first response was, "Isn't that too fun?"

We talked about it a while and decided: *There's no such thing as too fun.*

Especially not that year.

All to say, writing this book got me through 2020.

It was the thing I held on to, the thing I looked forward to, and the thing that helped me make my own sunshine during some very gray times.

It could easily have been a thousand pages long. I loved being with my main characters so much, I would've happily added scene after scene of them teasing each other, accidentally snuggling, and giving each other piggyback rides.

The setting of this story is my own beloved grandparents' Texas cattle ranch. The Stapletons' house *is* my grandparents' place—a rambling farmhouse with a bright kitchen, screen doors that slap closed, and the smell of leather and honeysuckle everywhere. My grandparents are both gone now. The house is still there, but we rent it out, and I haven't been inside in years. But writing this book let me go back and visit, at least in my head. It let me travel to a place I loved, that I can still see every inch of—and it was such a bittersweet joy to be there.

It really left me thinking about what stories are for.

Because writing this book was more than just fun. It was like a tonic for my weary soul.

There's a quote I love about writing by Dwight V. Swain: "A story is something you *do* to a reader." I'm so grateful for what this particular story did to me. It *nourished* me in profound ways that I'm not even sure I could've asked for.

I always want my stories to be about love, and light, and making sense of hard times, and getting back up after life has knocked us down. I always want them to make us all (me included) laugh and swoon . . . and give us something wise to hold on to.

That's never been more true than with *The Bodyguard*. I thought about it so often during 2020: How much laughter matters. How much hope matters. How much joy matters.

How the right story at just the right time can lift you up in ways that feel like a rescue.

That's all writers can really ever hope to do for readers: invent stories full of all the magic we're longing for ourselves. I hope your time on the ranch with *The Bodyguard* did all the soul-nourishing things for you that it absolutely did for me.

Katherine Center